Forgetting Betrayal

Brook Lynn Dorcent

Forgetting Betrayal
Copyright © 2014
Taylor Made Publishing

Unless otherwise indicated, all Scripture quotations are taken from the King James Version of the Bible.

FOR INFORMATION CONTACT
Taylor Made Publishing
www.taylormadenc.com
OR
Brook Lynn Dorcent
brooklynndorcent@gmail.com
www.brooklynndorcent.com

For Nicole, You <u>Are</u> Your Sister's Keeper

Brethren, I count not myself to have apprehended: but this one thing I do, **forgetting those things** which are behind and reaching forth unto those things which are before, I press toward the mark for the prize of the high calling in God in Christ Jesus. (Philippians 3: 13-14 KJV)

Acknowledgments

To My Lord and Savior Jesus Christ, I am so humbled that you chose me to write life-changing novels. Thank you for my gift, my abundant life, my eternal life, and the lives of those connected to me. I love you, Lord!

To my **Pastor Bishop Rosie S. O' neal**, without your teachings, guidance, prayers, and encouragement, I would not have embarked upon this journey. I love you!

Husband Jacques, once again, we did it. We made another baby! Thank you for supporting and covering me. I love you!

Children, you are my heart! Thank you for putting up with the writer in me. Mommy loves and adores you.

Parents Lula, James, and Gwen, thank you for all you've done and your love and support. I love you!

Sisters and Brother Nikki, Tiffany, Kia, and Malcolm, I am so proud of you all. Nikki and Tiffany, thank you for sitting with me at the book signings when I only sold one book. I love you all!

Friend Carrol, because of your honest responses, you helped me write a better novel. Thank you for your voice and your ears. I love you!

Friend Donna, you are remarkably diligent. I could not have done this without you. Thank you. I love you!

Diane Taylor and Taylor Made Publishing, thank you for believing in me. Words cannot express my heartfelt gratitude. Your confidence and guidance infuses me to believe; possibilities do become realities!

Editor Jorge Hernandez, thank you for doing such an amazing job!

Book Clubs: Daughter of Glory, Expressions, and Blessings Book Club, you ladies are the best! Thank you for embracing me. I love our book discussions. I learn so much from you all.

Women's Power Networking, Ladies, OMG! I love you! You are my support system. Thank you!

Readers, You ladies and gentlemen are so gracious. Thank you for every word of encouragement, support, and prayers. I appreciate every e-mail. Thank you for bringing my books to life with your responses. I love you!

Books by Brook Lynn Dorcent

The Mark Series
Missing the Mark – Novel One
Pressing Toward the Mark – Novel Two
Forgetting Betrayal… – Novel Three

Devotionals
Spirit over Will – Devotional

What happens when the offender is you?

The Bible speaks of no greater love than laying down one's life for a friend. Is the greatest betrayal against a friend?

What happens when you and I become the offender, hurting those we hold dear?

Let me tell you a story; take you on a journey of lies, betrayal, and deceit.

Let me show you that the offender is never unloved.

The offender must forgive thy own self.

And one day...forget

Chapter 1 – Old News – New Friends

Ollie,

Can you understand a man's longing and desire for an insatiable woman? Do you understand what she did to me…for me? It wasn't supposed to be her in the ground. The bullet was for you. I carved your name onto it. She fought for your life, struggled, and received the death you should have.

I loved her. I don't care if you believe that. But I did. More than you ever could. I don't think you loved her at all. When you found her dancing as a stripper you exploited her, used her body, and took her money. She left that world, but since she never completely trusted you, she went back to it. All she ever wanted was a secure future; going back almost cost her life.

She recovered and I found her. I gave her everything her heart desired and she loved me. Where do you think she got the money to start the dance studio? I was the bank she went to. I made her dreams come true.

We were happy, until one day, you confused her and took her away from me. I never fully understood it, because she never shared why she left me. She used to share all her dreams with me. Did you know that she dreamed of one day being a professional dancer in Paris? I was going to take her there but, like I said, something changed in her. I think it happened when she went to Florida to visit your family. After that, I could no longer reach her, and for that I hate you. It is all your fault she's dead.

Today, I sit in this jail cell wondering why. Asking God for answers and doubting Him all at the same time. If there is a real God, why is she dead, and you are not? I am separated from my family. They are living without me while you raise your daughter.

I see you have another woman. So soon, Ollie? See, you never loved your wife. I can't even think about another woman. It's only been 27 months since her death.

This is not how it was supposed to end. You should be dead!

You're opening an arts foundation in her name. I see you smiling all over the television proclaiming your love for her. Do you really think you can justify your actions by naming the foundation after her?

You're such a liar. You may have fooled your family and the world, but not me.

And what of your daughter? You think she will forgive you for what you did to her mother. One day Ollie, I am going to find your baby girl and tell her what you've done. The gun was in my hand, but it was you who pulled the trigger.

It was you....

Ollie closed the letter and then his eyes. It had been a little over two years since his wife Sapphire "Sassy" Sparrow's death and his daughter's birth. Her murderer, Marcel Reid, taunted him with blaming letters.

His family advised him to stop reading them, explaining they would only plant seeds of hate and doubt, creating emotions able to take on life and shape -- something Ollie couldn't afford to carry in his heart. Truthfully, he loathed the man. Marcel showed no remorse during the trial, no regret. Yet he wrote cruel and disturbing letters as if he truly had a conscience.

Unable to understand the depth of such evil, Ollie opened his eyes and checked his watch. His plane would land in an hour and he would be back from touring Europe. Oliver "Ollie" Sparrow was a successful artist and art gallery owner in New York whose business had gone international.

After his wife's death the dealers approached him with the option for international exposure. At first he declined, too much to take on as a single father. Respectfully, they backed off for a while. A year later they resurfaced, proposing once again that he take his work international. He had his doubts, but when he learned the interested parties were Christians and a good portion of the proceeds supported world missions, he stepped on board.

Ollie hadn't looked for love. He was searching for a way to honor his late wife. She had been a woman with incredible talent and strength. Sadly, she became trapped in a world of lust and money.

Part of Marcel's letter was true. There had been a time when Ollie separated from his family and savior and he found the exotic dancer. Sapphire supported him in more ways than one. Her last act was most unselfish. She fought for Ollie's life. Marcel aimed the gun at him, she wrestled with it. Why? Why didn't she think of her safety...the baby she carried?

He had to honor her. Ollie began researching how he could open an arts foundation that would provide underprivileged children the opportunity of a free education, studying dance and the arts. During his search, an angel of aide, Desiree Davenport, walked into his life. As a principal of an inner city school in Brooklyn, she connected him with other educators and students for the foundation. Desiree helped him with the research and wrote the business plan. They dedicated countless hours planning. It helped them both with their grieving.

Desiree grieved the sudden loss of her own mother. Out of their grief developed a desire for their community and to love each other. She fit into his world like the missing piece of the puzzle. His daughter, Olivia, developed a bond. Ollie loved watching them interact. And when she called Desiree "Mama," he cried. They both did.

Still, he corrected his baby girl and said, no Rae-Rae. Admirably, to Olivia, Rae-Rae meant Mama.

He was thankful he had found love. Yet in his dreams, visions of his wife dying from a fatal gunshot wound still plagued him. He heard her screaming for him, felt her clutching his shirt, saw her eyes bulging from the searing pain where the bullet had ripped through her flesh.

In the horrific tragedy, a miracle occurred. Sapphire gave birth to their daughter. Minutes before she took her last breath, she told them she loved them, named their child, closed her eyes, and her spirit floated away.

Feeling a wave of grief overshadow him, he left his seat and went into the restroom. He looked at his reflection, thinking he'd never fully recover from the events of that night. He wished Sapphire had redirected the gun. Maybe Marcel was right. Should he be the one in the ground?

Ollie pulled it together and walked back to his aisle seat. His plane partner smiled at him and asked, "Bad news?"

Ollie opened his mouth, not sure what the man referred to. He explained. "The letter you were reading, was it bad news?"

"Old news."

"Yeah, that old news likes to linger."

His seatmate sighed. Ollie gathered the man had some unpleasant old news he was dealing with. Extending his hand, he introduced himself, "Oliver Sparrow. I prefer Ollie."

He shook hands with him.

"Deacon Stephens. Call me Deacon. I really don't like being called Deke. Sounds too much like Zeke, and I feel like I should be wearing overalls and a straw hat."

Both men let out an easy deep laugh. Ollie couldn't picture Deacon in overalls. Although he was thin, he wasn't skinny. Deacon had a comfortable style about him dressed in jeans and a navy t-shirt.

Deacon looked out the window, letting out another deep sigh, he said, "We're almost there."

"You from New York?" Ollie asked.

"Brooklyn, born and raised."

"You?"

Deacon tore his gaze away from the clouds, looked at Ollie.

"I was born in Florida. I moved to Queens when I was five. Now I live in Brooklyn."

"Florida." Deacon nodded. "I've spent some time there. Actually, I spend time in a lot of places."

Before Ollie, could ask, Deacon explained, "I'm a missionary."

Impressed, Ollie lifted his brow and asked, "A real life missionary? Like Paul in the Bible?"

Deacon let out a shaky laugh. "I wish. Please, don't compare me to Paul. But yeah, I travel, care for the sick, help the lost, and share the good news."

"Hmm, that's interesting."

Ollie didn't ask why Deacon chose that profession. He understood if the man was doing what God had designed him to, that was the answer. As an artist, when he created a piece, he used the colors to bring it to life – to make it portray a message. He had a feeling Deacon did God's work, portrayed God's message. He did have one question. "How do you handle the traveling…moving from place to place?"

"I enjoy it. I get to meet all kinds of people, see the world, and try different foods."

Deacon saw Ollie's face harden a little. "You travel, but you don't like it. Does it interfere with your family?"

Ollie had a great support system. He just felt guilty about being away. "I'm a single father. I hardly lack for babysitters, but I just feel wrong leaving Olivia – she's two. My wife passed away. I already feel like Olivia's starting out with a strike against her, and since my work has taken me international, I wonder if she'll suffer without me."

Deacon didn't have a wife or children. In his travels, he met many single parents and some children raising their siblings. However, the families that were most successful were those that made the most of their time when they were together.

He asked, "Do you spend time with your daughter when you're in the states?"

"As much time as I can. I take her to the gallery with me some days."

Deacon lifted his brows and his voice.

"You're an artist!"

Ollie smirked at the excitement in his voice.

"Yeah, my gallery is in Brooklyn." He passed Deacon a business card.

"I'll have to stop by. Maybe bring my brother and…," he paused, not ready to say her name. And really, after all these years and what he did to her, would she be interested in even seeing him – spending time together? "Old news," he pondered. Deacon was returning home to deal with his old news.

Ollie picked up where Deacon trailed off. "And who?"

"I'm not sure what she is to me. I know what she used to be. I haven't been home in fourteen years."

"Wow."

Ollie patted his leg – an old habit he used to do when feeling for his cigarette pack. Since Olivia was born, he gave it up. He told Deacon, "I stayed away from my family for seven years and it wasn't because I was doing the Lord's work. It was quite the opposite. I'm sure whoever she is, she'll understand."

That's what Deacon had hoped and prayed for -- Desiree Davenport's understanding.

Chapter 2 – Why Wait?

After they landed the men parted with a promise from Deacon that he'd stop by the gallery one day. Ollie looked forward to the promise. With everything in his life, he had little time to build new friendships.

Kyle Carraway, his brother-in-law, picked him up at the airport. As they weaved through the traffic and onto the highway, he said, "Welcome back."

Ollie looked out the window. It was just as cloudy on the ground as it was in the air. He thought about the wedding he had to attend that evening. Desiree's youngest sister was getting married. He shook his head. He loved Desiree and her family but, really, all he wanted to do was take his little girl home, share a bowl of ice cream, and watch Elmo. Man, he had changed.

Kyle wondered about Ollie's shaking head.

"Jet lagged?"

"Rayne's wedding is tonight. I promised Desiree I'd be there."

"You are taking Olivia, aren't you? If she sees you and you leave again, she's going to pitch a fit."

Ollie knew that and answered, "I'm taking her. Desiree even had a little blue dress made for her. I gave it to Vaughn," he mentioned, referring to his sister.

Kyle looked over, said slowly, "Oh, yeah...that's why Vaughn gave Olivia a facial, manicure, and a pedicure."

Ollie bolted straight up in the luxury SUV.

"She did what?"

His brother-in-law let out a hearty laugh.

"Joking, man. She wouldn't do that. But she enjoys having a little girl around. The twins are rough tumblers."

Kyle and Vaughn had twin rambunctious boys that were only two weeks younger than Olivia. Ollie worried that taking care of three small children under the age of 3 might be overwhelming. Not for his sister. She loved it, said it wasn't any different than having triplets.

"I'm trying to convince Vaughn to have a little girl," Kyle put out.

"I can't believe she's agreed to that."

"You're right. She'd rather wait a couple more years."

Kyle looked over and then back at the road.

"But, I figure...if we're going to have more children, we should just go on and be done with it. Plus, we'd enjoy the baby making."

Ollie made an O with his mouth.

"Not getting much candy?"

"I'm on a once a week diet."

Landing a slap on Kyle's shoulder, he said, "At least it's on the menu. A brotha ain't gettin' nada."

"That's by your choosing. I understand the toil the children and the business take on my wife. That does not stop me from wanting her fine self. I just wanna take her and...."

"Hey, that's my sister!" Ollie put in.

"Yeah, and she's holding out."

Kyle went on and on about how he thought of taking his wife away for a couple weeks and maybe put an end to their dry spell.

As Kyle talked about his restrictive diet, Ollie thought about his non-existent one. He and Desiree didn't want to complicate their relationship. They agreed not to have sex outside of marriage. They really desired God to bless them. And to be strategic, they put rules into practice, helping them not to cross the line.

The challenge seemed nearly impossible. Desiree, truly a desirable woman, made him want to marry quickly. He reached down into his bag and presented a ring.

Kyle stopped talking about his wife and shouted, "Good googly moogly...that's crazy!"

"I got it in Europe. You think Desiree will like it?" Ollie asked doubtfully.

"Heck yeah, she's going to love it. I didn't know you and her were on the fast track."

Were they? "I don't think it was fast. I think it's simple. I love her, she loves me and Olivia loves us both. Why wait?"

Ollie had a point. But Kyle reminded him of something.

"Before you left for Europe a couple weeks ago you told me Desiree seemed distracted. That she wasn't talking about what was bothering her. Before you pop the question, you should get some answers."

He nodded at the sound advice. Maybe he was rushing things. He decided after the wedding, they'd have a nice long talk.

Chapter 3 – Be Anxious for Nothing

The sisters fussed over the blushing bride-to-be. Rayne Davenport was the youngest of the five Davenport girls, but not the last to marry. Ironically, the oldest and the first to become engaged hadn't actually married. Not yet. But three had, and now Rayne was the fourth.

She peered over her shoulder away from the fussing sisters who were ooing and ahhing over her wedding gown. In the distance, her eldest sister, Desiree, stood in a trance – not part of the fuss at all. Her distraction did not offend Rayne – it saddened her. She could see Desiree traveling back into time, 14 years ago when she was engaged and planning to be Mrs. Sterling Pipman.

Then, Desiree had just turned 21, preparing for finals, graduation, and planning a monstrous size wedding. Both families, his and hers, went gaga over the upcoming nuptials. Their parents had been friends for years. Naturally it seemed appropriate for their first-born children to tie the knot.

Sterling had been an only child. To his parents, it was like raising a house full of growing boys. Sterling had a rambunctious character. Very much like his best friend, Deacon. The boys were inseparable and always getting into more trouble than a little bit.

Yet something happened in their last year of high school. Sterling mellowed and took notice of the little girl who played at his house all the time.

Desiree had been a late bloomer. She blossomed in 12th grade. The braces on her teeth had shed and the wavy thick hair straightened. She had it parted on the right and wore it in a nice sassy flip. The style enhanced her mocha with a gentle blend of cream skin tone.

Sterling approached her on the first day of school with a star-struck look in his gold-flecked eyes, and Deacon by his side.

Desiree remembered how he dragged out her name, "Des-sa-rayyy?"

"Hi, Sterling, Deacon."

She smiled, thinking, "So the little obnoxious boy likes my new look." And since all he did was look, she turned away with a butt-swinging switch. As she swayed away, she flipped her head around and saw he enjoyed the eye candy.

His cheeks turned beet red, but he didn't turn away.

Sterling did not look for long. He formulated a plan…get the girl and marry her! By the end of their senior year of college they were engaged and joined at the hip -- she, Sterling and Deacon.

Sterling and Desiree scheduled the wedding seven days after graduation.

She was majoring in education and Sterling, criminal justice, and Deacon still had no desire to be anything. He decided to get a degree in liberal arts.

One day desire did strike Deacon. Desiree remembered she had been the one in the room when it awakened him.

If she remembered correctly, she had been in the room first. Then, here he came. She had tucked herself away in a study room of the library at school and studied until her head hit the book on the table, to be later interrupted by Deacon.

Disruptive as he normally behaved, he dropped his knapsack onto the table. She lifted her head.

Sulking, he remarked, "Oh, it's you," falling into a chair across from her.

She wiped the drool off the side of her lip.

"What time is it?"

He checked his cell.

"1:37"

Looking at her child psychology textbook, she opted not to ask him his troubles.

Oh, well. He told her anyway.

"You know, I've been in school four years – I'm barely making it. Still don't know what I'm gonna do with my life. And still can't learn this stupid math."

Observing him, she wondered, "Why in the world is this Sterling's best friend?"

Deacon literally rolled out of bed, wearing the same thing he had on the day before. At least he washed his face and brushed his teeth.

She already put him on notice. As the best man at her wedding, he had to go with her father to the barber and get properly groomed.

Most days he looked terrible, never shaved, or got a decent haircut. Even now the coarse mane had a violent appearance.

But he was Sterling's friend. Moreover, like a brother. Okay. She could not help him decide what he should be in life. She could, however, help him with the math. She loved to teach and, besides, this would be good practice for her.

Desiree took the seat next to him – looked at the page he stared at.

"Give me some paper," she demanded.

He did.

Basic Algebra, she mused.

"Deacon, think of Algebra as a scale. You gotta keep it balanced. Whatever you do to one side, do to the other."

He watched, listened, and learned. Her simple way of running through the steps and neat handwriting captivated him.

"Did you get that?"

He nodded.

"Alright, I'll do another one and then you can try the next on your own."

And…to his surprise, he did. He got it right!

"Man, you should be a teacher – my teacher!" he said, in awe of himself.

"Well, I'm glad you got it. Keep working at it. That's the thing with math – the more you practice, the better you'll be at it."

She got up, started down toward the end of the table and packed up her books.

"I've got to get to class."

He was staring at her.

"What?"

"I can see it now, why Sterling chose you. You know he's all about streets, cops, and robbers. I thought you were uptight…stuck up."

"Thanks," she mumbled, zipping up her bag.

"You're amazing."

She knitted her brows together.

"Please."

She draped her bag over her back.

"I just helped you with a couple math problems."

They weren't even that hard, but she didn't want to insult him.

"No," he told her, "you showed me I can do the problems."

She started for the door, but had to pass him to get out. He stood up, blocking her exit.

"Wait. Do you think I'm smart?"

"Deacon, you have to think you're smart. It does not matter what I think."

"It does. I know you know that Sterling is smart. He's going to be a cop, a good one. You probably wonder why he hangs with me."

Again, she thought not to confirm her thoughts.

"Desiree, I just want to know. No teacher that I can ever remember thought I could do anything. I got ADD, you know?"

She knew, kept that to herself, too.

"Anyway, just tell me…do you think I'm smart?"

Something softened in her. She lifted his chin with her fingertips.

"Deacon, I know you're smart. And I know God made you to do something great in this world. You are graduating with me and Sterling – maybe not with honors, but you'll graduate. And that's with ADD. Be proud of that."

Simultaneously, their eyes locked, but focused beyond into a strong magnetic force. He leaned in and she did not turn away. She received his kiss, and he received hers.

The gentle contact triggered a shock. What source of power was it? Fire? Electricity? She didn't know.

"Oh, God! Oh, no!"

She stumbled backward, knocking over one of the chairs and pushed him aside.

He stuttered, "I'm…I'm…Desiree…please."

Desiree ran out of the study room.

Oh, yes, desire had awakened, but not only Deacon but Desiree as well.

The snapping fingers of the bride-to-be pulled Desiree out of her trance.

"Hey, can you get the glue? The flower on my headpiece broke."

Desiree had missed it all -- the commotion over the broken headpiece, and just 30 minutes before the wedding her sisters were in a tizzy.

She looked up, awakening from the memories -- all the eyes of her sisters staring.

"Yeah, be right out. I mean back."

Desiree rushed out of the room and tripped. She got up, and heard someone yell, "And check on Dad."

She found her dad before she found the glue. He was mumbling under his breath and struggling with his bow tie. She eased into his bedroom.

William Davenport glanced over and was calmed by her stunning appearance. Rayne had chosen the right color for the bridesmaid's dresses – a cool slate blue. The elegant lace dresses, not gowns, curved around the shoulders exposing them. And the length of them, cut right at the knees showed off their fine legs.

"Beautiful," he said, holding his tie in his hands.

She smiled. "Dad, I'm Desiree, not Beautiful."

"I know you're not 'Beautiful.' Nor, am I senile, yet. I am telling you Desiree, you look beautiful."

"Oh, Dad."

She stepped to him, took the tie, and began tying the perfect bow.

"How'd you know that I needed you?" he asked.

"I didn't," she said, still fixing his tie. "I'm looking for glue. Rayne's headpiece broke."

"You tried the junk drawer downstairs in the kitchen?"

"No luck. I'll run out and get some."

He checked the bow in the mirror. She lifted her arched brow, awaiting his approval.

"Perfect," he told her. "And I'll make the run for the glue. I can't have my beautiful little girl running out looking like that. You might get kidnapped," he joked.

Actually, she would not mind the distraction. It would be better than going back into Rayne's room without the glue so her sisters could badger her about when she might get married.

"Dad, I don't mind. Really."

"Scared," he teased.

"Dad, they're all marriage experts. I can't take it."

He kissed her forehead.

"You can. You've always been the strongest. And whether you believe it or not, Rayne needs you. You two have been so close since your mother died. So, suck it up and go help her."

Father knows best. This was the first wedding their mother would not see. Desiree took a deep breath and turned on the five-inch heels. She realized her feet were going to be killing her before the night ended.

She returned to Rayne's room and heard her sister Beautiful, speaking into her cell phone.

"Hold on handsome. She's back."

She waved the phone at her.

"It's Ollie."

Desiree took the phone. Before she pressed it to her ear, Beautiful asked, "Where's the glue?"

"Dad's going out to get some. We don't have any."

Another sister, Sparkle, certain that they did, commented, "I just got some glue. I used it for the flowers on our shoes. It's downstairs, in...."

"It's not in the junk drawer," Desiree cut her off.

Sparkle picked up the headpiece, barked, "I know it is."

Desiree sharply retorted, "Find it then."

Rayne tapped Desiree's shoulder.

"Ollie, phone."

"Oh."

She pressed it to her ear, turned, and walked to the window away from the others.

"Is it a war or a wedding?" Ollie asked.

"Depends on how you look at it. I'm glad you're back. " She pulled back the curtain and saw the white stretch limo waiting.

"I may need back up," she cautioned.

"I'd love to provide it. Got a bit of a problem."

She didn't like the tone of his voice.

"Oh?"

"Olivia threw up her spaghetti as a welcome home present for me. We thought it was a one-time thing, but she's still throwing up. My nephews didn't want to feel left out, they have joined in."

Desiree thought about his precious little girl and her curious cousins.

"I'm so sorry the children are sick."

"Me, too. I don't want to leave her with Vaughn and Kyle."

Desiree understood, and at the same time, dreaded it. She needed Ollie, badly. Deacon was going to be at this wedding. She had not seen him in 14 years, and she didn't want to see him without her man at her side.

He took her silence to be grand disappointment.

"Desiree, baby, I'm really sorry. I know this is a hard day for you, without your mother being there. I just don't know if Olivia is contagious. I...."

She could not be selfish. Not when it came to his child.

"It's Okay. I'll make it."

"Forgive me?"

"Ollie, there's nothing to forgive. You're a wonderful father. I'll come by after the wedding. It'll be late though."

"You sure? Olivia might be contagious," he repeated.

"Hey, I'm a principal of an elementary school. I think I'm immune. I'll bring you cake."

She heard him smile.

"That sounds nice. I'll make coffee."

"I like mine light and sweet, like you."

"Oooooo..."she heard.

Desiree turned around at her ogling sisters, ending her call.

"Coffee and dessert at midnight? You are not married, Desiree," Beautiful reminded her.

For some strange reason, it gave her pleasure having her sisters think she'd be having dessert at midnight. If that's what they wanted to believe, then so be it. There had been only one man, other than her gynecologist, that knew what was under her skirts. She considered herself to be a 35-year-old reborn virgin. Her first and only intimate experience never settled with her. Desiree never wanted to feel that way again.

Sparkle bolted back into the room.

"The photographer's waiting Rayne, she wants some shots."

Beautiful whirled on her.

"You fix the headpiece?"

"I can't find the glue."

Desiree twisted her lips.

"Told you."

"Shut-up," Sparkle snapped.

Rayne looked as if she'd faint.

The peacemaker and second youngest sister, Melody, had a plan.

"We're all ready. The photographer can get shots of us until Dad gets back. Come on."

She tugged Beautiful's arm.

Rayne held a hand to her forehead. "Sounds good, but y'all go on down. I want to speak with Desiree a minute."

The room cleared out and Rayne shut the door, took the little vanity stool and sat on it.

"You going to make it?"

"Of course. Today's your day. I'm sorry I zoned out earlier. I'm here. Can I do anything for you?"

Rayne smiled and Desiree could see their mother in the room. She was the baby, but she inherited their mother's spitting image – the tall slender body, the soft face, and the sweetest smile.

Rayne had been the only daughter who could wear their mother's traditional ecru lace wedding gown. And just with a tad of alterations, it fit to a T.

"I have everything that I need. I'm marrying my best friend today. That is why I hate to see you so sad. And now Ollie's not coming."

"I'm not sad. Not really."

She shook her head. She could be honest with Rayne. She was the only one in the family who knew her true history with Deacon and Sterling.

"I'm anxious. It upsets me. Why am I this way?"

"Don't beat yourself up for feeling what you feel. You loved him."

"He didn't love me back. I was a fool to think he did. He left me."

Rayne reached out, held Desiree's hand as she looked into her eyes.

"Do you…love him, still?"

She felt tears starting to fill her eyes and willed them away.

"I love Ollie and I know he loves me."

"Okay."

Her sister, the therapist, advised, "Then it's good that Deacon is in town. Resolve whatever feelings you have concerning him, then move on for you, Ollie, and his little girl."

Rayne stood, and the sisters shared a long embrace. Desiree thanked her and said, "I better get downstairs and into those pictures. Oh, I forgot to tell you. You look beautiful, Mrs. Evan Ross."

Chapter 4 – Welcome, Brother!

Mr. Evan Ross paced the small office of the cold dreary church basement. Rayne had wanted to marry on Valentine's Day. He checked his watch. At the rate she was moving, it was going to be Valentine's Night before they married.

Mitch, his first cousin and best man, asked, "You break in those shoes good yet?"

"Not funny. You don't know what this is like. You forty-year-old bachelor."

"Hey, cops don't marry. It's against the law," He smirked.

"Yeah, I know that law. Leave the door open for all that free booty."

Mitch thought nothing in life was free. Everything had a price. His father's double life proved that. By day, his father was an upstanding law-abiding citizen – ran his own law firm – kept the books clean. By night, he played the gangster. He lived the charade for 20 years – until he took his own life.

Mitch remembered his brother was a junior in college when he had started the force. That's how he stumbled across his father's dealings. And the guilt forced his father to swallow a bullet. His death sent Mitch and his brother, Deacon, into a dark place. There was just enough light for them to see their way out. His brother graduated college and left for 14 years.

Thanks to their cousin Evan's wedding, Mitch would get to see Deacon. At long last, his brother was on his way home. Mitch checked his watch, thinking he should have been at the church by now.

Chapter 5 – No Place Like Home

Deacon Stephens never did like driving cars. He preferred bikes and he had many in his collection. He left one motorcycle in Florida. In his line of work he had several locations across the country where he laid his head. He never stayed in one place too long.

He had to admit, the sleek midnight blue Mercedes was pretty cool to drive. He zipped it all the way from the airport. Because of his travels and his friendly personality he had good friends. One friend made sure he had transportation when he landed in New York. He had no idea it would be the beast of cars. He had to thank him when he got the chance.

Finally in Park Slope in Brooklyn, he parallel parked the little monster, got his garment bag, and hopped out of the car.

Deacon took a good whiff, smelling the electrifying city of New York. He loved the aroma and regretted he had not been home sooner.

The locks of the home had never been changed. His brother left everything as it had been before he left. He hit a light switch, checked his smart-phone – 5 o' clock.

He dropped his bag on the sofa and started stripping on his way to the bathroom for a cool shower. Not that he was hot. It was February. He just didn't enjoy hot showers.

The water washed away the fatigue of his travels. "What a trip." He thought of where he came from. He left Jerusalem three days prior and ended up in Europe helping with a crusade.

Stepping out of the shower, he wrapped a towel around his six-pack. He found Mitch's shaving supplies and went to work on a nice thin trim of his beard and mustache. He had gotten a hair cut in Jerusalem, so that was Okay.

He remembered he left his cologne there. After smelling the potent scents of his brother's, he decided he didn't need any.

Not in the wedding, he didn't have to wear the black tux. He unzipped the garment bag, took out the navy suit, silk navy shirt, but no tie.

He dressed in five minutes flat. Keys in hand, he jogged to the car, roared the engine, and got to the church in 20 minutes.

Deacon's feet crossed the threshold of All Praise Church 11 minutes before 6. The first person he saw in the vestibule was Natalie Jones - the pastor's one and only child. She recognized him.

Nat's mouth fell open. Deacon had grown into a male model. His thin chiseled features and rich complexion put her in the mind of a fine mixture of Taye Diggs and Morris Chestnut. He walked over and hugged her.

"Hey."

Almost speechless, she stumbled out the words, "You? They said you were coming. Wow, Deacon."

He figured he would get surprised eyes from most of the members who remembered him. And from what he remembered of All Praise Church, it still struggled. The carpet had ripped years ago. Actually, he and Sterling played in that vestibule so much they had ripped it.

Pastor Jones' way of fixing it had been duct tape. The rip remained but the tape had been replaced--maybe a form of improvement.

"Why would Rayne want to marry in this rickety ole building?" he thought. It was home for them, he knew. And so many memories came flooding back. He was ready to see his family.

"Can I get in to see the groom and best man?" he asked.

"Of course, they're downstairs."

She led him. When she turned the knob, she said, "Deacon, welcome back."

"Thanks, Nat."

He walked in. Evan stopped pacing and Mitch jumped up. Both brothers were pretty firmly built, but Mitch was thicker, taller, and buffer. They put their strong arms around one another.

"I started thinking you'd miss the ceremony."

Deacon joked, "Hey, I heard a Davenport woman never gets married on time."

He then looked at his first cousin.

Evan grabbed Deacon. At 6 feet 8 inches tall, he towered.

"Man, glad you made it."

When Evan let him out of the bear hug, Deacon folded his arms over his chest, studied the groom, and asked Mitch, "Is this the boy that used to eat dirt?"

Mitch laughed.

"That's him - got him a fine Davenport woman."

Deacon cleared his throat and turned when someone knocked.

Mitch opened it.

"Show time."

Evan let out a deep breath. Before he stepped forward, Deacon handed him a check.

"Congratulations."

He looked at it, frowned.

"A thousand dollars, Deacon?"

"I was saving it for Mitch's wedding, but since he'll never marry, it's yours."

Deacon shot his brother a glance.

"Hey, you're not married either," Mitch remarked.

Evan folded the check, put it in his pocket. "Thank you." He looked between the brothers. "I'm ready."

They smiled. Deacon told them, "I'll find a seat in the sanctuary."

The groom and best man took their places.

Chapter 6 – Hold My Heart Forever

Deacon found a seat against the wall on the groom's side of the church. He saw the surprised looks, smiling faces, and frowns of those who remembered him, and recognized the man who stood on the edge of the altar singing Rayne and Evan's favorite love song. It was Edward Davenport, the girl's youngest uncle. He remembered Brother Davenport had one of the strongest baritone voices in all of All Praise Church. He taught Deacon and Desiree a thing or two about music.

And all of the Davenport girls could sing. However, only Melody, Sparkle, and Desiree enjoyed singing in the choir. Deacon wondered if they still sang, or if they'd share a little of their divine gift at the wedding.

The first sister to grace the aisle was Melody. He took a breath, expected it to be Desiree, thinking they'd come down from oldest to youngest.

The next was Sparkle. He smiled remembering why her mother named her Sparkle. Simone Davenport had named all the girls. She said Sparkle, having the brightest eyes, lit up any room.

It hurt him that Simone Davenport had passed on. She was a pleasant and affectionate woman – always generous and always smiling. He got the call of her passing while in Haiti on a mission trip. He wanted to fly home. Something held him in place, kept him working in a medical center.

The next sister to grace the aisle was Beautiful. Oh, yes, she most certainly was. All the young boys at church talked of dating or wanting to date that one particular Davenport sister, including his brother Mitch. Not Deacon, though. Beautiful on the outside, but on the inside, she knit-picked every little detail. He thought her name should have been Bothersome.

Deacon had not met the sisters' husbands, but from what he gathered, they were the groomsmen. They waited in the center of the long aisle, and when each sister approached, they took their arm and escorted them the rest of the walk. Each man shared a possessive gleam in their eye for their bride that simply said, "Mine."

The maid-of-honor was the last one. He held his breath and let it out when he saw her. She looked straight ahead, smiling like an angel.

Desiree Davenport had blossomed into a beautiful woman, and his heart ached. She still wore the layered sassy flipped hairstyle. Her hair was fuller, thick, black, and shiny. She also had gained weight -- no longer a size 2. Studying her, he tilted his head as she passed his aisle, gauged she might be a size 6. From where he stood, he considered her blessed in all physical areas.

She reached her place with her sisters and he chastised himself for checking her out, way too much.

The music signaled as everyone stood. Rayne took the long sweet walk with her father and accepted the hand of the man she loved.

Deacon lowered his head as Pastor Jones prayed, hoping for the day when Desiree Davenport would accept his hand and he would be the man she loved.

Chapter 7 – You Hold My Feet in Your Hands

The church may have been rickety, however, the dining hall at the Regal Hotel had been exquisite.

The reception felt like a reunion for Deacon. He had the opportunity to meet new friends, fellowship with old ones – but not Desiree. She avoided him.

Just as she suspected, her feet were killing her. She sat at the table with her aunt, slipped her feet out of her shoes, pulled a foot onto her lap and rubbed.

"You doing Okay, Aunt Brenda?"

Her senior aunt tugged on the silvery blue wig. "I'm fine, sweetie." She looked over two tables.

"Hey, I know that young man. I just can't place him. He's different, mature, but his eyes are the same. He's got dreamy, playful eyes," said the 70 year old.

"Aunt Brenda!" Desiree exclaimed, looking on her left and at Deacon. He was clearly talking to someone while giving her the occasional gaze.

Not beckoned by her niece's disdain, her aunt continued.

"A man with eyes like that keeps things interesting. I know. I'm married to your uncle. Don't you see me always smiling?"

She gave Desiree a grand smile, showing off her oversized dentures.

"Oh, Aunt Brenda." Desiree shook her head.

Aunt Brenda lifted her hand and waved at Deacon.

"Yoo-hoo! Come here, son."

Desiree's heart rate sped up. She whispered, "What are you doing?"

"I want to know the young man's name. I know; I know *him*."

"Oh, boy," Desiree thought.

She did know him, and so *did* Desiree. Excusing himself, Deacon got up and weaved through the tables and chairs and stood over the ladies.

"Good evening, Aunt Brenda, Desiree."

"Oh, so I do know you, son. I know your pretty eyes. So, tell me your name."

Desiree saw his dreamy eyes twinkle at her Aunt.

"I'm Deacon Stephens – the groom's cousin."

She clapped her hands together.

"Oh yes. You grew up here. You and what was the little boy's name you used to run around with, tearing up the church?"

She looked up at him, waiting for his answer.

" Sterling Pipman."

"Oh, yes, that was his name. So...." She pursed her lips before her next question. "Are you married, son?"

"No, ma'am, still single."

Aunt Brenda leaned over and placed a hand on Desiree's hand – she was still rubbing her aching feet. She gave her niece a consoling look. Desiree was the first to become engaged and the last to marry. Aunt Brenda looked at Deacon again.

"So, where's Sterling, your partner in crime?"

He cleared his throat.

"He didn't come." Deacon looked for Desiree for confirmation.

She confirmed, "No. His parents said he and his wife are away for Valentine's Day."

Aunt Brenda might have been 70, but she knew a vibe when she felt one. Looking at Deacon, she asked, "You got a problem with feet?"

He put a hand on his chest, let out an awkward cough. "Feet...are...good...."

He looked at Desiree.

"Well, good. My niece here has been walking her pretty little legs all day in those stilts. She could use a foot massage."

Desiree choked on the air in her lungs. Coughing, wheezing, and blinking, she grabbed the water glass and tried to sip.

Aunt Brenda slapped her on the back, hard. That made it worse. She hacked out a cough. Deacon sat next to her.

"You alright?"

It took a few seconds to clear her throat.

"I'm good. I'm good," she huffed.

Aunt Brenda angled her head and then looked down at Desiree's feet. Deacon turned his chair and keeping his eyes on Desiree, he took her size 7 foot in his hands.

She trembled at the strength and softness of his hands.

"Uh, please. Don't...."

"Girl, let the man rub your feet. It's not like he's a stranger," Aunt Brenda encouraged her; then seemed to get a burst of energy. She whipped her head from left to right.

"Is that Sister Pinetree?"

Deacon and Desiree turned their heads.

"Aunt Brenda, who is Sister Pinetree?"

She jumped on her little feet.

"Oh, you don't know her. Excuse me."

She waved her hand, then bobbed and weaved through the room.

Deacon let out a laugh.

"She's not changed."

Desiree attempted to tug her foot out of his hands. He tugged it back.

"I don't mind."

She *did* mind. "Fourteen years later, he shows up and gives me a foot massage – a very good one," she thought. She wanted to close her eyes and drift away – forget she was in a room full of wedding guests.

He looked down at her fine legs.

"I thought often what I'd say to you when I saw you again. I never imagined this."

He smiled a smile that melted her heart and upset her all at once.

"And what would you say to me, Deacon?"

He shook his head.

"I could never come up with the words. Is it true? Sterling's away with his wife?"

"Yes."

He grunted.

"Did you ever…tell him…everything?"

"I couldn't."

"Did you?"

"I haven't spoken to him since I left. I hurt him and you, I'm sorry."

With her foot in his hands, she closed her eyes. Was that all she wanted to hear? An apology – had that resolved things as Rayne prescribed?

Before she answered, Beautiful walked up, looked down at their intimate scene.

"Oh!"

Desiree tugged her foot again and Deacon tugged it back.

"Uh, Rayne's ready to change. You wanna help? I see you're…occupied. I thought you were having dessert with Ollie tonight," Beautiful threw out.

Desiree looked at Deacon. "Please. I have to go."

"Could her dessert date be the same Ollie he had met on the plane earlier? Oh, God!" Deacon thought. Concerned, he released her foot, stood and planted a kiss on Beautiful's cheek.

"You look beautiful. Take care, Desiree."

He eased away and her sister gave her a disciplined look. Not saying a word, Desiree picked up her shoes and started for the bridal suite of the hotel.

Chapter 8 – Beautiful Beginnings

Desiree and Beautiful were the last to enter the suite. Sparkle worked on the seemingly hundreds of buttons on the back of Rayne's wedding gown.

Melody had laid out a white dress and shoes for the bride. Beautiful looked at the cute dress on the bed and commented, "I don't know why you're putting that on. You're going to go downstairs, say goodbye to your guests, and then come back to this room for Evan to rip it off."

Rayne looked at Desiree, who had taken a seat near the balcony and said, "I hope my husband doesn't rip anything off."

Sparkle chuckled behind her.

"You say that now."

Beautiful concurred.

"If you two have been holding out, like you've told us, then trust me, he is going to rip that little number off you."

She walked over to the closet and pulled out a little Intimate Secrets box.

"Got you something for tonight's festivities."

Sparkle had finished with the buttons and helped Rayne step out of the gown. Melody handed her the dress. Rayne slipped into it, afraid to touch the little box that Beautiful was shoving at her.

"Here, you can thank me later."

Rayne pulled in a deep breath, opened the box, and let out the air in her lungs. She lifted the item.

"They're little red panties."

"Eaty Kinies, edible underwear," Beautiful schooled. "Wear these tonight, and nothing else."

Rayne looked at her sisters.

"This is our wedding night. Not freak night."

Beautiful realized they needed to have "the talk" with their baby sister. Granted, she was 27 years old, and an excellent therapist, she still needed some guidance from those with experience.

She motioned for them all to sit, but pulled Rayne over to the bed and they sat together. Beautiful looked at Melody and Sparkle, since they were married, and disregarded Desiree.

"Baby girl, this is your wedding night and you want it to be special. Knowing Evan, he'll be patient and give you what you've been dreaming of. But don't be selfish. When he's done being sweet with you, you've got to be his freak."

Melody and Sparkle said, "Hmm, hmm. That's right."

She looked at Desiree for help.

"Don't look at her. She's not married," Beautiful advised.

Desiree just shook her head. She wasn't going to bite into the conversation. Or else, they'd start in on her.

Rayne turned to Melody, the quiet one.

"You can't be serious. Not you, Mel."

Melody told her what she'd learned after five years of marriage.

"Every now and then, your man is gonna want some variety. It's your job to provide it. Wear the panties."

Rayne pushed herself up off the bed.

"I've got guests to greet with my husband."

She took a long look at her sisters and scoffed, "I know my husband. He'd never enjoy anything like edible panties."

The sisters cackled, even Desiree.

"All right, if you say so," Beautiful said and told them she'd be right down. As soon as the room cleared out, she found Evan's bag and stuffed the red underwear into it.

She laughed on the way out, thinking, "Rayne, you've got a lot to learn."

******

As the guests cleared out, Rayne and Desiree were left talking, while Evan said his goodbyes to the best man and Deacon.

Desiree smiled at her sister.

"This is it. I'm sorry that I didn't help you upstairs," she said, referring to the edible underwear ambush.

"Coward," Rayne teased.

"Look who's talking? You're not going to wear them?"

Rayne shuddered. "No. Can you believe..."

Desiree lifted Rayne's long dainty fingers, admired the rock on her hand.

"As crazy as Beautiful is, she's only trying to help. And to be honest, I think it's a good idea."

She saw Rayne getting heated under the collar. Desiree looked her in the eyes.

"You don't have to rush your inner freak. Just know marriage is a long time. Spice it up from time-to-time. I love you."

She hugged her sister.

Rayne appreciated Desiree.

"I love you, too."

They let one another go. Rayne had to ask. "Did you speak with Deacon?"

Desiree shook her head.

"Briefly. He said he was sorry."

Rayne lifted her brow.

"That's good, yes?"

It wasn't enough.

31

"For now, it's a start." She looked over and saw Deacon and Mitch walking out of the hotel. Desiree smiled.

"You're on."

Evan started in their direction. Rayne let out a deep breath.

"Nervous?" Desiree asked.

"No, anxious. And I'm anxious, because I'm anxious."

"Be anxious, for nothing. Enjoy your husband."

Evan approached the ladies. Desiree kissed his cheek with a short order, "Take care of my sister."

She left the lovebirds.

Evan turned Rayne toward him and stared into her eyes.

"Mrs. Evan Ross, have I told you how much I love you?"

"Only a million times."

She kissed his lips. He scooped her up, carried her onto the elevator. Intense desire reflected in his eyes.

"I love you, too, Mr. Ross."

His gentle smile melted away the anxiety and replaced it with anticipation.

Chapter 9 – When Sleep Escapes

Odd to him, Deacon couldn't sleep. As a traveling missionary he had trained himself to *SOD* -- sleep on demand.

He made the demand, but something in him failed to obey. He threw his legs over the side of the bed with hopes that something to eat might do the trick.

He stepped out of his old room, eased into the darkness. Mitch hadn't left one light on. His foot kicked the foot of the sofa. He stifled a curse, limped to the kitchen, and found the light over the stove was left on. He opened the door of the refrigerator and considered his choices -- cheese or pickles. "Mitch lives pretty badly," he thought.

Grabbing up the morsels, he straddled a chair, and dug his fingers into the pickle jar. On his way to popping one into his mouth, his hands went flying into the air, along with his pickle.

Mitch came charging into the kitchen, his weapon drawn.

"It's me! It's me. Mitch!"

"I'm Mitch."

It took a second for the sleep to leave his eyes and focus on his brother. He lowered the weapon and apologized, "Sorry, man, I don't have many houseguests."

Deacon shook his head, dug in for another pickle.

"I'm not a houseguest. You could have *shot* me. You couldn't even see straight."

True, he acted on a cop's impulse.

"I said, sorry."

He laid his gun on the table, sat, and reached for the cheese.

"What are you doing up at one in the morning."

"Can't sleep."

There were many reasons why Deacon may not have been able to sleep. But Mitch knew the very one that held the key.

"What do you want to know about her?"

"Who's Ollie?"

He ran it down, clear-cut, dry, fast – cop style.

"Oliver Sparrow. Goes by Ollie. Widower, single father, has a baby girl, Olivia. He's thirty-three. Five-eight, one eighty-five, fair skinned, hazel eyes, owns his own art gallery. He and Desiree have been seeing each other about a year."

Deacon didn't eat anything as he listened to the details. "Could this really be the man I met on the plane?" he thought. He needed to know.

"What happened to his wife?"

Mitch provided, "Murdered by her ex-lover. She cheated on Ollie. Got pregnant. Ollie was the father. She left the lover. The lover didn't leave her. He shot her while she was in labor. She died right after she delivered."

"Tragic," Deacon rolled it all over in his mind. He asked one pertinent question, "Is it serious between 'em?"

"Define serious?"

Deacon knew what Mitch meant. Desiree had been engaged to his best friend and that didn't stop the feelings he had developed for her.

"Are they in love?"

Mitch grabbed the pickle jar.

"You have to ask her."

After a minute, he said, "Deacon, whatever you do, do it right. I consider him a friend. He's been through a lot."

"You don't have many friends."

Mitch provided, "When we heard about Ollie's case, all of us at the station got angry. We see too much insanity. And this was at the top of the list. I wanted to kill the guy myself. But you know the system…justice, due process, and all…. The guy's behind bars, but Ollie's the one living the nightmare. I think when Dez and Ollie hit it off, it was good for him. I know he loves her."

Deacon nodded, listened, and wondered, "How'd they meet?"

Mitch answered, but even he couldn't understand.

"I stayed in touch with Ollie after the case closed. I don't do that with my cases -- connect -- but I'd stop in to see him from time to time. I don't know why. I guess I just felt sorry for him. The man has a little girl to raise….His wife is dead. Ollie started working on his arts foundation and I thought about Desiree. She was grieving over losing her mother. You know how the Davenport women were about their mother."

Deacon nodded.

"She was a great woman, like a mother to us."

He remembered how they grew up without a mother.

Mitch agreed and continued, "Ollie was grieving over his wife. So I hooked them up. It seemed to work out."

"*You* hooked them up?"

Mitch heard the disapproval in his brother's voice.

"I know you can't be mad. You left!"

A sigh, followed by a confession, and he said, "You're right. You're right. He's an Okay guy, Ollie?" He didn't even know Ollie, but Deacon had a good feeling about the man.

"Too good, if you ask me. After what his wife had done to him, he still took her back."

Why wasn't it ever easy for him? As his head fell into his hands, Deacon confessed, "I love her, Mitch. There hasn't been a day since I left that I haven't thought about her."

"Are you going to tell her that?"

"That's the plan."

Chapter 10 - Love Is Fair

Desiree gazed at Ollie, feeling slightly out of her element. One of their strict rules...no late nights alone together or, in this case, early morning talks. But since he had just gotten back from Europe and missed the wedding, they made an exception.

The crumbs from the wedding cake they shared an hour ago held her gaze.

"I know you had a long day. Ready to go?" Ollie asked.

She had a lot running through her mind – Deacon's incredible foot rub, her sister Rayne, her deceased mother, and the fact that not one of her sisters mentioned their mother at all. She decided to go with the last thought.

"We didn't talk about her. I feel like we dishonored my mother today."

Ollie understood. On the anniversary of his wife's death he refused to speak her name. He somehow felt it helped him through it.

"Can I ask you something, Desiree?"

"Yeah," she hesitated a little.

"Do you think Rayne had a beautiful wedding?"

She shook her head in awe of it.

"Perfect, as Davenport weddings go. We all had a moment when we cried. I think Rayne made the most beautiful bride of all my sisters. She looks so much like my mother."

She thought a little more, and concluded, "Rayne was happy."

Ollie got up. The kitchen chair, no longer comfortable, and he reached for her hand, led her to the living room and onto the sofa. Intertwining his fingers with hers, he said, "You honored your mother by making sure you and your sisters did all you could to give Rayne a perfect day. You honor her every day by being the wonderful women she raised you to be."

He leaned in, whispered in her ear, "I'd like to tell your mother thank you."

"You say the most perfect things."

"It's easy, I'm talking to you," he said, tilting her head into position for a gentle kiss. The kiss melted her soul, stirring hunger, sending a rumbling through them. Desiree repositioned herself somehow, found her bottom sinking onto his lap. Ollie knew they could easily cross the line. It surprised him. She usually stayed very guarded with him.

"Desiree," he murmured as she caressed his neck with warm eager lips.

A minute more of the intense affection, he wouldn't be able to stop.

"Desiree," he repeated. "Baby, I think...." He eased her off his lap. "I think...."

She lifted her long lashes, realized how excited she'd gotten. Self-conscious now, she apologized, "I don't know what came over me."

"It's late. Olivia is sleeping. You're tired. It's a natural way to end the day," he reasoned.

She took a breath, laid her head back against the sofa. She didn't look forward to the short drive home. She'd have to drive pass Deacon's house, and he was there, she knew.

She needed Ollie more than ever.

"You're coming to Sunday dinner tomorrow?" she inquired.

Ollie smirked, thinking he'd have the pleasure to be bombarded by her sisters. Regardless, he regretted missing Rayne's wedding.

"Sure, we'll be there."

"My sisters are excited about seeing you and Olivia."

Speaking of Olivia, she stood up. "Can I give her a kiss on my way out?"

Ollie eased up on his feet and led her to his daughter's room. The princess nightlight that Desiree brought her glowed in the darkness. She leaned over and pecked Olivia's warm cheek. She thought she saw a small hint of a smile as the child slept.

They left the room.

"I love her," Desiree admitted on the way to the door.

"And we love you."

Ollie turned her toward him.

Desiree wrapped her arms around him.

"Thanks for being so wonderful."

He held her, flaring up her guilty feelings of loving Deacon's touch, his strong hands caressing her feet.

She absently spoke, "You can easily take advantage of me."

He gave her body a squeeze.

"I could, but when we do this, we're going to do it right. God's way, or no way at all."

Ollie released her body, took her hands in his, thinking about the elegant diamond he'd put on her finger. As he studied her fingers, she pressed, "Tonight I won't say no."

He creased his brow at the look in her eyes. He didn't understand. "She's not hearing anything that I'm saying," he thought.

She wasn't listening, but reasoned that loving Ollie might help her forget about Deacon. His dreamy bedroom eyes, his square regal features against that deep chocolate skin, and those soft lips. Oh, how she never forgot their first electrifying kiss.

Ollie's gaze went to her striking eyes. Passion was holding there, begging for wild release. He liked that sultry look in her eye, too much.

"Dez, baby…," he grinned. "I better walk you to your car, before there's no going back. My self-control is getting shaky."

He meant it. She had a choice. She could seduce him; see if it would lead her mind away from Deacon. Crossing the line wouldn't have been fair to Ollie. She did love him. Being fair, she let him lead her to the car. As she settled into the driver's seat, his smooth artistic hands fastened her in.

"See ya at dinner tomorrow."

He kissed her forehead.

Desiree smiled as she pulled out into the street. Ollie was a *good* man. Thankful for him, she decided and thought, "Deacon, you're my past, my unhappy heartbroken past."

She needed to resolve whatever upset her and move on.

Chapter 11 – It's Not My Hormones

After church the next morning, Desiree entered her father's kitchen. Her sisters Beautiful and Sparkle huddled over the kitchen sink, reading a text message.

Beautiful lifted her hand and Sparkle matched it with a high five.

"What's going on?" Desiree wondered while draping an apron over her brown sweater and tweed slacks.

Beautiful taunted, "For married eyes only."

"Oh, Rayne wore the underwear," Desiree announced casually.

The sisters frowned.

"How'd you know?" Beautiful pouted.

"She texted me first and said, 'Evan enjoyed them for breakfast.' I texted back, told her to forward it to you. They should be on their way to Rome."

Desiree checked her watch and moved over to the sink. She shooed them away, pushed up her sleeves, and began washing the soaking chicken.

Beautiful sulked. She hated being the last to know. Huffing, she found something to complain about with Desiree.

"Why are you washing that chicken in the sink? I was about to start washing the greens."

Desiree didn't bother looking over her shoulder.

"Use the other sink," she referenced the one over in the corner. Their mother had renovated the super large, state of the art kitchen. Desiree loved cooking in it.

Beautiful sucked her teeth and stomped to the other sink. Sparkle just shook her head and started working on the sweet potato biscuits and macaroni and cheese.

Desiree pointed out, "Why are you even in here? Beautiful, you know you can't cook." She smirked.

Sparkle let out a cackle.

"I can cook."

Washing the greens, Beautiful turned on the water.

"Just ask my husband."

The sisters laughed. Beautiful had no culinary skills, none at all. That's why God made her the most beautiful.

The cooks in the family were their late mother, Rayne, Sparkle, and Desiree.

She offered, "Go watch the game with the men and Melody."

"I don't like football," she snapped.

Sparkle lifted her head, slowly recalled, "You married a football player."

"Former, he's retired," Beautiful corrected.

Desiree educated her, "They're watching college basketball."
"Oh."
Beautiful shrugged her shoulders. Clearly not affected by the correction, she pushed Desiree's buttons.
"I invited Deacon and Mitch to dinner."
Desiree's heart leaped, but she kept her voice steady, "And, are they coming?"
"Wouldn't you like to know," Beautiful teased. She speculated about Deacon and Desiree's history for years. After seeing her sister's foot in Deacon's lap last night, she saw she had the hots for the tall, dark, and handsome man. She turned, watched Desiree's body tighten, and finally gave in.
"They had a prior engagement. Pastor Jones invited them over. I'm sure he'd love for his daughter to hook up with a gem like Deacon."
Desiree turned.
"Nat's too young for Deacon."
"How would you know? Deacon may enjoy a tender young thing."
Beautiful smirked, shot Sparkle a sideways glance. They both turned to Desiree as her eyes hardened. Their sister had the sharpest, yet sexiest eyes. They changed with her moods. Beautiful was glad she didn't inherit that trait from their mother. She went on taunting her sister so she could see each reflection in Desiree's eyes.
"I heard Deacon's a traveling missionary, does a lot of work all over the world -- got a nice bank roll, too. Pastor Jones' daughter might appear shy, but I found her in Deacon's face quite a bit last night."
Beautiful relaxed at Desiree hanging onto her every word. She refused to let up.
"Did you see how fine he was yesterday? He looked like a prince in that midnight blue suit -- and his face, so strong and angular. I saw his eyes staring you down, one too many times. Natalie Jones was looking at him and he was looking at you."
Finally Desiree found her voice.
"I have no control over a person's eyes."
"What about your feet? They were in his lap," Beautiful flung out the information like a Frisbee. Sparkle jumped and caught it.
"What?"
Easing up to Sparkle at the island counter, Beautiful explained, "Deacon gave Desiree a foot massage, right in the middle of the reception. I guess it was a good thing Ollie didn't come after all."
She dipped her hip, placed her hands on her curvy waist.
Desiree whirled on her.
"Shut up! You don't know what you're talking about."

That was the button Beautiful wanted to push and she laid on it, telling her confused sister, "And you don't know what you want. You never have. You get a good man and then, bam, you mess it up. You were engaged to Sterling, Deacon's best friend. But...."

Desiree tried to shut her up, raised her voice.

"You don't know the story, Beautiful. Mind your business!"

"I know this!" she shouted, "You're going to be alone, Desiree. You need to control your hormones."

She pointed her greasy chicken fingers at her sister.

"My hormones? What about yours?"

Desiree pulled up some tired old news. It was a weak attempt to get back at Beautiful. But she also knew what buttons to press, and she did.

"I know what you and Mitch did a couple years ago. You repent about that yet?"

It was Beautiful's turn to shout, "Shut up! Nothing happened!"

"That's because Evan walked in and stopped you."

Beautiful looked stunned.

"Yeah, I know," Desiree spouted.

"I know how you almost got busy with Mitch. You've had the hots for the man since he's been promoted to detective. What, you like the fact that he has multiple guns?"

Sparkle, truly on no one's side, interjected, "Did Mitch let you fire his gun, Beautiful? Which one?" She grinned, mixing up her dough for the biscuits.

Beautiful looked at her sisters. They had picked a very soft spot. Her eyes turned misty.

"I thought Big John was cheating on me. I was upset and it didn't happen. We...."

She decided to just let it go. She lowered her voice.

"Stay out of my business, Desiree."

"Oh, you shouldn't dish it, if you can't take it. STAY out of my business!"

Beautiful was on her way out of the kitchen when her husband walked in. The sisters froze.

Big John looked at the bickering women.

"We can't hear the game," he chastised. "Your father told me to tell y'all to keep it down."

They felt like kids, having their father send them a message.

Beautiful hoped her husband hadn't heard what they were shouting about. She said, "We're sorry. Honey, go on."

She patted his massive shoulders. The man was so big he looked like he was in full football padding all the time.

He blinked at his wife in her Sunday best, bedroom shoes, and a ruffled apron.

"What are you doing?"

"I'm helping with dinner."

She sounded surprised at his question.

He laughed.

"You can't cook."

She resented her husband for embarrassing her in front of her sisters.

Desiree and Sparkle went back to their tasks at hand. Beautiful turned her back and worked on the greens.

He realized he hurt her feelings and slid his hands around her waist with an apology.

"I'm sorry," he whispered, kissing her cheek.

"Forget it."

"No, really. I'm sorry, Beautiful. Besides," keeping his voice low, he reminded her, "you know what you're really good at."

She whispered, "We're in my father's house."

He began stepping away, taking his wife with him.

"You can't starve a man because he's in your father's house. We've been here a week. Let Sparkle and Desiree handle this. You know just how to handle me, Beautiful."

Her sisters pretended like they didn't see Big John and Beautiful saunter out of the kitchen.

Desiree took a deep breath, glad her sister was gone. Thinking over Beautiful's comment about controlling her hormones, she took another breath. Hormones had nothing to do with her past with Deacon. It went much deeper than that. Maybe, if that were it, she'd be beyond her feelings.

Chapter 12 – Love Never Fails

Ollie and Olivia had a surprisingly nice dinner. The sisters hadn't attacked. Actually, Beautiful, the one he expected to let him have it, was pretty quiet.

He reached over and helped Olivia with her mac and cheese.

Sparkle smiled at the little girl.

"She's so well behaved."

"Only around strangers," Ollie remarked. "You should see her at home."

Desiree commented, "She's fine at home – typical, busy toddler."

Big John reached for the bowl of fried chicken, added a thigh to his plate.

"So," he said, before taking a healthy bite, "Desiree's the last single Davenport woman."

Desiree loved Big John. All the sisters did, but she really hated when they started on the topic of her being single.

Ollie gave a sly smile and revealed, "I'm hoping to do something about that very soon."

Eyebrows lifted around the table. She thought she heard her father let out a sigh of relief.

The comment should have brought her peace. Instead, it rattled Desiree. They had discussed marriage and not just with each other, but with Ollie's uncle and pastor. She knew Ollie wanted to marry her. And she thought she wanted to marry him, but since receiving news of Deacon's return, she had trouble focusing.

Closing her eyes for a few seconds, Desiree didn't allow her feelings to show.

"Y'all don't start in on Ollie. We're going to do what we want in our own time."

As Ollie suspected, Beautiful spoke up, "You're thirty-five Desiree. If you and Ollie want to have more children, you've got to move it along."

Desiree looked at her sisters, their ages ranged from 33 to 29, and none of them had children.

"Don't start. I don't see any of you reproducing around here."

Melody shifted in her seat and her eyes watered. She got up and left the table. Her husband, Ron, followed.

Their father shook his head, sorrowfully.

"What?" Desiree forced.

"She had her second miscarriage a couple weeks ago."

Disappointed, Desiree shook her head. She didn't know about Melody's first miscarriage. She began to rise and Ollie held her hand.

"Let her go, Ron's with her. You didn't know."

None of them did, but their father knew. Melody didn't share a lot of herself with her sisters, she never had.

"I'm sorry, Dad."

"She'll be alright."

He sighed and looked to his other girls. "I would like to be a grandfather before I die."

Beautiful loved being the princess bride. Big John treated her like royalty. She knew it was selfish, but having children would change things.

Sparkle, on her third career change, announced, "I'm going to law school in the fall." Her husband, James, an English professor, supported her with the hopes this would be it and then they could start a family.

William Davenport looked at his daughters again, offered what he learned.

"I'm proud of you all. You have turned out to be successful positive women. You have Christ in your lives. You've married good men. Desiree, you have a good man. And at the end of the day, what matters most is the people you've loved in this life. Remember, love is never selfish. Love each other."

What did that mean? Desiree looked at Ollie and Olivia. Was she being selfish? She still allowed Deacon to hold a large portion of her heart. Ollie deserved all of her.

"God, help me. I've got to let Deacon go," she thought.

Chapter 13 – Double Minded and Unstable Actions

Ollie opened his eyes, stared at the high ceilings, and wondered where he was. He heard a sweet giggle. His eyes drifted onto the floor where his daughter and Desiree played. The sounds of a cartoon trailed in the background.

He sat up on the sofa, rubbed the sleep out of his eyes, and apologized, "Sorry."

She could see it embarrassed him that he'd fallen asleep on the sofa, in her father's house.

"You haven't gotten much sleep lately."

She smiled.

Still, he thought it to be disrespectful.

"Where's everyone?"

Olivia climbed onto Desiree's lap, started pulling on her hair.

"I comb," she murmured, referring to combing her hair. Desiree let her run her little hands over her hair.

"Sparkle and Melody had flights to catch. Dinner made Dad sleepy. He's napping. Beautiful and Big John's flight doesn't leave until morning. They went into the city for a while."

Ollie listened, feeling a kink in his neck. He rolled it, pulled out his cell phone for the time. At 9 o'clock, Olivia should have been in bed already.

"I'm going to get her home."

He was welcome to stay, but he wouldn't. Besides, she also needed to go home. Desiree stood, picked Olivia up.

"Home? Ready, to go home?"

She put a loud smooch on Olivia's cheek.

"No, home. I comb."

She grabbed a fist full of Desiree's hair.

"Ouch."

She tried to loosen Olivia's grip.

Ollie watched her with his daughter. She had a knack with children, especially his child. She made a sad face.

"Olivia, you hurt Rae Rae."

The little girl mimicked the sad face, pouted little lips.

"Ert?"

"Yes, precious, you hurt my hair."

Olivia let the hair go.

"No home," she declared, still using the sad face.

Desiree looked to Ollie.

"You heard the woman, no home."

Ollie pushed up off the sofa, walked over and kissed Olivia's forehead.

"We have to go, sweetheart. We'll see Rae Rae tomorrow."

He took his toddler in his arms and tears flooded her big dark brown eyes.

"I'll get her things," Desiree offered.

She got the small brown and turquoise baby bag, packed up the toys and cups. She held up the little dungaree jacket that matched Olivia's jumper.

"Can I help you with your jacket, Olivia?"

The child pouted and cried more tears.

"Want Rae Rae. No home!"

Desiree saw Ollie tense up.

"It's alright," she soothed. "Dad's a hard sleeper."

She sat with Olivia on the sofa.

"I love you, sweet pea. I'll come by tomorrow and see you. Promise," she said, tugging on her arms in order to slip the child's jacket on.

Ollie had just remembered something.

"We have a dinner date tomorrow."

Baffled, Desiree looked up at him.

"We do?"

"We're having dinner with Dr. Zoe Landry, the psychiatrist I might hire to work with the Sapphire Arts Foundation. You know her."

Desiree did know Zoe as a colleague and she had totally forgotten.

"I have choir practice tomorrow."

He recalled she had mentioned changing the rehearsal schedule, but he didn't know when it would begin.

Desiree relayed, "We practice every Monday and Friday evening until April. Ollie, I'm really sorry. I can do it any other night this week."

Olivia let out a yawn while the grown-ups went back and forth. Her head leaned and fell onto Desiree's chest.

Ollie thought a minute.

"I'll call Zoe in the morning. See if she can reschedule. The problem is, my sister agreed to watch Olivia for me tomorrow night. I'll also have to arrange for childcare if we reschedule."

She felt horrible.

"I should have checked my calendar before I committed. With Rayne's wedding, and...."

She trailed off, careful not to say, thoughts of Deacon coming home had consumed her, she explained, "I just had a lot on my mind."

He sat next to her.

"Don't worry about it. I'll see what I can do and let you know." He smiled at Olivia sleeping peacefully now.

"You have a way with her," he mentioned.

"She's such a sweetie pie. So much like her daddy."

"Careful, I'll kiss you in *your* daddy's house."

She lifted her head and he melted in her dreamy eyes.

"Go ahead. You haven't kissed me all day."

The kiss, so easy, confused Desiree. She needed her therapist. When Rayne got back from her honeymoon, she would ask, "How can I even think about Deacon, when I have such an incredible amazing man like Ollie?"

Chapter 14 – Where Is There Peace?

In the morning Ollie dropped Olivia off at daycare. He then went to work at his gallery.

He appreciated early mornings, although New York never slept. The crowds hadn't quite shifted into rush hour mode. Pedestrians strode casually to their destinations – including him. With his jacket open, he eased down the block, welcoming February's early morning breeze.

His studio opened at 8, so at 7 he wondered why a woman waited at the door. He wondered if she were a local starving artist interested in having him display her work. That's how artists were half the time. They'd just walk up practically offering their soul and body for a chance for their work to be appreciated. But she looked harmless, petite with large almond shaped eyes and well put together. Her hair was piled into a round ball on the top of her head. She wore a black trench belted around her tiny waist. Still, one could never be too careful. He remained cautious.

"May I help you?"

She looked up and in her eyes he recognized the pain trapped there. She was grieving.

"I don't know."

She let out a watery laugh.

"I walked past your gallery several times and finally decided to stop in over the weekend. They said you were out of town."

Ollie held the keys in his hands.

"That's right."

To her, he seemed cautious and tired.

"Has he been writing you letters, too?" she asked.

He knitted his brow. In addition to her grieving, she was disoriented.

"Miss?"

"I'm sorry. I haven't been sleeping since I got into New York. My name is Lacy Reid. Marcel is my husband."

Instantly, he took a step back. She rushed on, "I've been living in France. My father...." Her voice cracked. "He had a stroke. I've come back to care for him. I found old newspaper articles and clippings in my dad's home. I don't know what to say...."

The teardrops enlarged.

Ollie invited, "Please, come in."

He turned to unlock the gallery doors and shielded her from the onlookers.

He stopped once they were in and punched some numbers into his smart-phone, which turned on the lights.

"I have an office here," he said.

She followed him, observing the gallery's culture. If she had a word to describe it, it would be eclectic. The paintings reflected the city, the life and bustle of it. Others showed character and the struggle of man – from days of slavery to crime. Then there were paintings and sculptures depicting cultures from Asia, Rome, Africa, and the Middle East. Yeah, she would describe it as eclectic with commonality for mankind, family, and love. It was a beautiful peaceful place.

An artificial burning altar shot out violent flames of amber, white, and blue. She stopped, pointed, "What does this represent?"

He turned to her, reported, "Holiness, God's faithfulness to me. It brings me back to His Holiness."

Not a woman of faith, she said, "I see."

She had so many questions. Was his wife a Christian who had had an affair with her husband? Did she believe like Ollie did? Lacy knew God existed, but to know Him as a holy God, she could not comprehend.

Tucked in his office, she apologized, "I'm sorry to come here unannounced. I didn't know if you'd see me."

Ollie sat aside his brown leather knapsack, peeled off his jacket. Lacy noted he wore black dress pants and a white shirt. It had strings at the top that he didn't tie, but left open showing off chest hairs. He extended his hand for her to take a seat.

They both sat. Ollie didn't sit next to her, but behind the odd shaped marble desk.

He knew grief, understood it could make you incoherent. He listened, attempted to follow.

"Marcel would not stay away from your wife. You know the police had been to my house twice because he refused."

Ollie had no prior knowledge. Lacy saw the blank look on his face.

"Years ago your wife had been beaten at a party. Marcel was there too. A witness....I believe her name was Opal."

Remembering, she rolled her eyes around, continued, "Yes, Opal. She told the police that she saw Marcel running away from the bedroom where Sapphire was assaulted."

Confounded, Ollie remained silent. He knew about the beating, yet had no idea Marcel had been on the scene. She asked, "Is it alright that I call her Sapphire?"

"Uh...yeah."

"You didn't know when their affair began."

Lacy shook her head, waving the dark circles under her eyes. "It wasn't only your wife. I learned Marcel slept with his office staff, and other women, on occasion."

Ollie suspected Marcel had other affairs, but apparently no woman was off limits.

"I'm sorry," he said. "You mentioned something about letters?"

She nodded, dragged out a tissue from her coat pocket, and wiped her nose.

"I found a stack of letters written by him. My father never forwarded them to me in France. Since I've discovered them, I've been reading them at night...when the children are in bed. They're painfully written."

She laughed weakly, and said, "The letters sound so sincere, as if Marcel truly loved me."

Ollie wanted to know more about the letters, but first he asked, "Your children, are they alright?"

"They miss their father. They think he's abandoned them. I haven't told them where he is. Frankly, I think they're too young to understand. The oldest is five and the baby is three."

Back to the letters, he asked, "What do the letters say?"

"He loves me and that he had a sex addiction problem that your wife fueled. She used his addiction to her advantage for money to start her business and keep up her expensive lifestyle."

Ollie blinked and placed his elbows on the desk as his face fell into his hands.

"You alright?" Lacy wondered.

"Surprised," he admitted, and wondered if that were really true. Would he ever really know the truth about the affair between his late wife and Marcel?

"Is Marcel writing you?"

"His letters...," he paused, not wanting to bring her anymore hurt. "His letters, blame me for Sapphire's death."

"How?"

"I'm not sure. Lacy, I'm sorry about your father. Sorry you had all of this dumped on you...."

She interrupted, "Mr. Sparrow. I want to know the truth. Was your wife that kind of person? Would she use Marcel?"

He huffed.

"I believe they used each other. They both had addictions to danger, sex and an expensive lifestyle. They also had deep rooted issues. As a teenager, my wife was repeatedly raped by her uncle."

Lacy nodded. "Thank you. I'm sorry for your loss as well. I just don't know how you go on. I feel like I'm going to lose my mind. If my father dies, I don't know what I will do."

Ollie peered into her troubled eyes.

"I have a relationship with God. He's the keeper of my mind. I'll pray for you and your father."

Reaching into the desk, he pulled out a booklet, and offered, "Try this at night. I hope it offers some comfort."

She accepted the sentiment, wondering if anything could really bring peace to her heart.

Chapter 15 – Friendly Prayers

After Ollie saw Lacy out, he sat at his desk dazing. How would he get any work done? First he was getting letters from his wife's murderer, and now the wife showed up. He wanted to help her. He thought if they talked about their pain and the past murder, it might help them move forward. Then again, he wanted to forget the nagging questions of his past.

His cell phone rang. Hannah, his curator, spoke into his headset. "Mitch is here. He's heading your way."

"Thanks, Hannah."

That seemed to put a smile on his face. After losing his wife, he gained a friend. He appreciated the impromptu visits. Especially since his morning got off to a disturbing start.

He stood when Mitch tapped the door with his knuckles.

"It's open."

"Man!" Mitch walked in and slapped Ollie's hand. "You look like you're jetlagged."

For the moment he didn't want to talk about himself.

"You know I don't enjoy traveling."

"Then you should switch jobs with me. I had a crazy homicide to deal with. Drugged up daughter, stabbed her seventy year-old mother."

Mitch sat in the guest seat. Ollie took the one next to him.

"I'd take Europe any day," Ollie realized.

"So, what'd you get?"

"Got some good pieces coming in. Going to ship some out. The artists are going to trip when they find out they're getting the exposure."

"You're doing a good thing." Mitch nodded.

"You do a good thing. That's a shame about that daughter killing her mother. When she gets sober…God help her."

Mitch didn't want to talk about his work either.

"Did you get it?"

Thinking about it, Ollie slid the ring box from his pocket, handed it over to his friend.

"Whoa!" Mitch shouted at the platinum band masked with diamonds and emeralds. "When's the ax gonna drop."

Ollie shook his head. Mitch had a deep fear of the marriage commitment.

"I planned to propose at Rayne's wedding. Olivia got sick – a stomach bug."

Mitch hesitated. It wasn't uncommon for him to drop by the gallery, but he did come with an agenda. Shoot. He hated being in the position of brother and friend. Ollie had been through too much.

"I'm gonna tell ya something. And it ain't my place to say."

Ollie squinted, poked out his lips.

"What is it?"

"It's about Desiree and my brother."

He waited.

A bell rang loud in his head.

"Deacon? Your brother is Deacon. I met him."

Mitch stared as Ollie explained, "On my flight home, we were sitting next to each other. He started up a conversation. Seems like a nice guy."

"I hope you think he's nice when I tell you that he's Desiree's ex."

Frowning, Ollie asked, "Ex what?"

Mitch shook his head.

"Don't know. Look, it's not my place to tell you the history. Desiree should. Then again, it was so long ago; maybe she didn't see the need. He's back…I know I hooked you and Dez up. I didn't think that Deacon would…."

Ollie halted him.

"Mitch, I've never seen you uptight. What you sayin' man?"

"Deacon and Desiree had a thing back in the day. I don't know everything, but I do know they got busy."

Ollie understood that busy translated into Deacon and Desiree had been intimate.

"You're tellin' me this 'cuz Deacon wants to hook up with Desiree again?"

With another shake of his head, Mitch exposed, "It's more than that. Deacon is in love with Desiree."

Ollie closed his eyes for a few seconds and said, "It doesn't matter what Deacon wants. My only concern is Desiree."

Mitch hadn't let out the breath of anxiety, yet he asked, "What are you going to do? Are you still going to ask her to marry you?"

Something or someone was trying to throw Ollie off balance. He saw it clearly, and remembered the prayers and sleepless nights it took to strengthen him. He replied, "I've got work. I need to call the artists, arrange the transfers and finalize things for the arts foundation."

Mitch shifted his head.

"That's it?"

"Yeah," Ollie answered, nodding. "I appreciate you tellin' me this. You know I've got to hold it together for Olivia. Do me a favor, pray for me."

Mitch agreed. He didn't have a close relationship with God like Ollie did. But he could do that. He could pray for his friend.

Chapter 16 – Deal with Your Own Mess

Dr. Zoe Landry, psychiatrist, slammed down the phone, picked up the paperweight and flung it into the door. It would take forever to find every shattered piece of crystal.

Her assistant came barreling into her quaint office. When her shoes met bits of Zoe's fury, she said, "Ohhh, kaaayyy. You didn't have to break that one. It was a gift from me."

Amusing, yet Zoe's lips scowled. She made two tight fists, brought her arms in the air and shook them.

"She makes me so…Ohhh."

She groaned, bit down.

"Pissed," Chelsea said, taking a seat across from Zoe. She continued, "It is alright to say, pissed, teed off, angry, upset, mad, outraged. Admit your feelings and go with it, Zoe."

Now Zoe's lips curved as her assistant crossed her legs, lifted Zoe's reading glasses from the desk, placed them onto her nose, and pretended to take notes.

"I thought I was the doctor?" Zoe asked.

"Oh, you are. That's why I don't know why it's so difficult for you."

Chelsea gave her dear friend a sympathetic stare, used her nickname, "Zee, just say it. Your mother's a witch."

She casually shrugged her shoulders.

"Chelsea, she's just difficult."

Zoe eased up and walked over to a small antique table by the wide uncovered window, poured a cup of lemonade. She took a sip and skewed her face.

"Where's the sugar?"

"You drink too much sugar. I cut back."

Not agreeing with that at all, Zoe walked back to her desk and pulled out a sugar substitute, tore the package, and added the contents to her cup. She found a plastic spoon and stirred.

"You know your father died of diabetes," Chelsea reminded her.

Zoe took another sip, tasting just right, she smiled.

"No, I'm not quite sure about that. I'm convinced mom killed him with her difficultness."

Chelsea looked around the bright Manhattan home office. Zoe did a fantastic job of making it warm and inviting for her clients, but since she could not come to terms with her mother issues, the room never was warm enough. The evidence of her caged behavior reflected in the multi-million pieces of shattered crystal all over the floor.

"I'll get the vacuum cleaner," she offered.

Zoe held up her empty hand, took another sip.

"I got it. My mess, I'll clean it."

Her desk phone rang. She checked the caller ID. Grateful it wasn't her mother, she answered, "Dr. Landry."

"Zoe, hello, Ollie."

"Hi, Ollie."

Chelsea lifted a brow.

"Listen, got a bit of a problem," he said. "Can we reschedule dinner for tomorrow, Wednesday, or Thursday?"

"Hold on, Okay?" Zoe looked at Chelsea.

"He wants to reschedule dinner," she whispered, covering the receiver with her hand.

"You're booked. You have church tomorrow, something with your mother on Wednesday, and a meeting on Thursday. You're free Friday."

"Thanks." She put the receiver to her ear. "How about Friday?"

"Can't Friday."

"Right, you said that."

There was a pause.

Ollie decided, "Let's just keep it as planned for tonight."

She hesitated. "Sure, but, next week, I...."

"Really, not a problem. See you tonight, Zoe."

Zoe returned the receiver and eyed Chelsea.

"He sounded a little frustrated."

Chelsea related, "Single father, business owner and now starting this foundation in honor of his late wife, I'm sure he has a juggling act to deal with."

Zoe, on the verge of agreeing with Chelsea, stopped, closed her mouth. Her assistant realized, "You don't have a date for tonight. We both know Ollie wants this to be a casual interview. He's taking you out of the professional scene and bringing his girlfriend. You should have a date, too."

"This *is* my casual way. I don't date."

Zoe craved another cup of lemonade and stood up to pour one and returned to her desk.

"We both know you do not date to irritate your mother. She desperately wants you to get married, especially now that your sister is engaged."

Zoe drank, kept her back turned away from Chelsea while staring absently out the window. She didn't want to think about her mother. She was happy for her sister, but now her mother would be relentless about her singlehood.

"Hey," Chelsea called her back. Attentive, Zoe turned and listened to a suggestion.

"What about that guy you met a couple months back? He's in town and has left you two messages already."

She snapped her fingers, attempting to remember his name. She jumped in her seat when it came to mind.

"Garrett."

Zoe remembered his messages on her electronic notebook. She hadn't returned his call.

"I'll call him, but not to invite him out with me at the last minute. I'm meeting Ollie as I am -- happily single. And it has nothing to do with my mother."

"If you say so."

Chelsea put out, "You're going to be the skinny white girl."

Zoe's chin snapped up.

"You're white, too!"

Thinking about Chelsea's opinion, she added, "And I'm not skinny."

Chelsea glanced over Zoe at the window. Her wavy dark brown hair fell over her shoulders, matching her deep brown eyes. She was tall, with a firm body, lean legs, thin waist, and solid arms. "Zoe, you'll be working with a diverse group of children in Ollie's program. He wants to see you relaxed, down to earth."

A little insulted Zoe turned her head, shot at Chelsea, "And I will be. What does having a date have to do with me loosening up? It'll make me more nervous, if anything. I don't think he has a problem with me being white."

Beating a dead horse now, Chelsea got up.

"Suit yourself."

Realizing her friend made too much of her singlehood, she watched her carefully cross the office, avoiding the broken crystal.

Chelsea said, "I'll get the vacuum."

"My mess, I'll clean it."

Chelsea paused on her tippy toes, and turned.

"I never said I was going to clean it. I'm getting *you* the vacuum." She laughed, and tiptoed out.

Chapter 17 – My Death Brings Life

Monday evening, Desiree lifted her arms before the choir. It signaled them to ready themselves. They were going over the first song a second time. She chose something upbeat and lively to get them going.

Hyped teens and adults lifted up hands, filling the old church with praise. When the music started, some members pointed behind her. Excitement waved through the church as the members cheered and clapped.

Desiree turned to see a handsome Deacon strolling in with that incredibly sexy grin on his face. She stopped gawking when she heard someone announce, "It's Deacon!"

Webster shouted, "Hey man, welcome back!"

Deacon waved off his fans, took a seat back about five pews from the choir-stand.

Webster held up his finger, asking for permission to be excused. Desiree nodded. She was losing the crowd. The teens didn't know who Deacon Stephens was. However, the adults did. He had a reputation of being the wild guy and a protean musical genius. He sang, and could play several instruments -- guitar, keyboard, piano, organ, and drums.

Why had he shown up at their practice? Whatever the reason, she couldn't let the choir lose focus. She held up her hand, showing Webster that he had five minutes and five only.

Webster jogged over to Deacon. The men hugged, loudly patted each other's backs.

"So, what's up?" Webster asked, "You came to help us out?"

Deacon smiled big, shook his head.

"Just a spectator. Y'all got this. Desiree will make certain of it."

Webster leaned in, covered his mouth, stated, "Slave driver. That's what she is. Oh, we'll be tight no doubt, but she whips us into it."

Deacon lifted a brow; looked at Desiree, who was looking at her watch, and prompted, "Go on. I want to hear what y'all got."

Webster tugged his arm.

"We could use you on piano."

He looked over at the lonely instrument in the corner.

Deacon pointed out, "I don't even know the songs."

Webster twisted his lips.

"Oh please, as if you need the music. You know you can pick up whatever we throw down. It'll be like old times. Come on."

Deacon shrugged.

"Why not?"

As he walked toward the piano, he knew Desiree's pilot light was flickering. She wanted to protest. The applause coming from the choir was all the approval Deacon needed. He took the seat, let his fingers dance across the ivories, and winked at Desiree. She rolled her eyes and let out a deep frustrated breath. Lifting her arms, the song began.

Within seconds Deacon caught onto the tempo.

Desiree ignored him, keyed in on her choir members, and directed like they were in concert. Hands clapping, feet stomping, and some jumping, the place glowed with joy.

A rush of jubilance embraced them. By the time the song ended it had lifted Desiree's feet. They jumped into a dance along with some of the other choir members.

They did another song after the hearts and souls quieted – a slow one. The soloist knew the words and definitely had the voice for it, but not the confidence.

Desiree dismissed the other choir members and told them they could go downstairs into the fellowship hall for dinner. She stayed with Miki and helped her feel the music.

Deacon watched from across the room as he sat at the piano, picked up the tempo, and played along. The way Desiree lead Miki demonstrated her gentle guidance. It reminded him of the day she taught him how to do basic algebra problems in college years ago.

She just had a way about her. The words of the worship song seemed to drift out of him. He sang along with Desiree and Miki. The blended voices made a soothing trio.

Their help boosted Miki's confidence. Desiree stopped singing, held up her hand for Deacon to stop as well. Miki's eyes closed, and she fell into the melody.

Desiree nodded as Miki hit every note with precise pitch. The teen had it. She felt it. When she finished singing, she opened her eyes, asked timidly, "How was that?"

Like a proud parent, Desiree smiled.

"Great, Miki. Really good. Keep practicing like that."

"Thanks, Ms. Desiree."

"Thank *you*. This song is really gonna stir things up. You worked hard, please have dinner with the others."

The 15 year old all but skipped off.

Desiree looked up, saw Deacon heading in her direction and from the corner of her eye saw Webster heading down for dinner.

Desiree started collecting copies of the lyrics left in the seats. Deacon walked up, shoved his hands into his pockets.

"Hey."

"Hey."

She barely looked at him, but noticed he had on a navy t-shirt, jeans and navy tennis shoes. "He must really be into blue," she thought.

"What a rehearsal! I forgot how you dance. It was really nice to see."

"I remember when we were growing up you used to make fun of my dancing."

He did, maybe because it showed her intensity. He didn't understand it then. Now he saw it was one of the most beautiful acts of worship he'd ever witnessed.

"I've grown up, Desiree."

"I see," she said, tucking the papers into a folder.

He smelled the fried chicken and fish floating through the vents.

"Who cooked?"

"Mother Marilyn. She agreed to cook for us on Mondays."

She saw his lips about to drool.

"You're welcome to stay, Deacon."

He slanted his head, hoping.

"You coming down?"

Nothing else to do upstairs, she nodded. They walked down the center aisle of the sanctuary. He gently touched her elbow when they reached the door of the sanctuary. Without exiting, he confessed, "I know I shouldn't have left like that. I couldn't stay here."

He stared into her eyes, praying she'd see how much leaving her had hurt him.

She didn't want to talk about this – not now – not in church. Shaking her head, she said, "Forget it," and took the next step.

He touched her again.

"If you really want to forget, that's fine. I know I'm asking a lot, but will you hear my side of it?"

She said nothing, and he saw in her intense smoky eyes that she needed answers. He realized, "You know we've got to do this. I won't leave until we talk about everything. For now, can we enjoy dinner?" He smiled.

"You know nobody has a fish fry like Mother Marilyn."

He waited for her compliance.

"Sure, for now."

Dinner was pleasant enough. In essence, Desiree did little talking to Deacon. The other church members monopolized his time, asking of his travels. She enjoyed listening about his work in the Middle East and the Christians there.

Someone asked, "Why would you put your neck out like that? You walk into danger."

He answered, "I'm called to. If I lose my life, for the sake of someone's salvation, it's worth it. In the end, we all win."

He said it so causally, and then took a bite of his fish sandwich. Desiree considered his answer and careless attitude for himself. He had no fear. However, the thought of him dying terrified her: "Why him, Lord?"

She remained silent as he talked.

Chapter 18 – Relative Goodness

It was a quarter after nine when the church cleared out. Deacon, still by her side walked Desiree to her car. He didn't want the night to end.

"Take a ride with me?" he invited, peering into her brandy-colored eyes. "Wow," he thought. He could lose himself in those eyes. And he remembered the one time that he did. She said earlier, "Forget it." Looking at her now, he shook his head, wondered if he ever could…simply forget.

She didn't breathe, as he seemed to peer into her soul, connecting to a place that she held in her heart protected. Afraid he'd remove the barriers, hurt her again, she attempted to back out.

"I have school in the morning. Besides, I'm too tired to talk about the past tonight."

So was he.

"I don't want to talk – not tonight."

He wanted to take his hand, and feel the softness of her face, instead, he promised, "I won't keep you long. I'll bring you back to your car. I just need to check something out and I don't want to do it alone."

She looked at his sporty Mercedes parked behind her. Let out a breath.

"No more than an hour, Deacon."

"You got it."

He hit the car remote, the lights twinkled, and the doors unlocked. After letting her in, he glided into the driver's seat.

He passed her the fish sandwich Mother Marilyn wrapped up for him. She held it, wondering how traveling missionaries purchased expensive cars.

"Nice ride."

"I like it. But it's a loan."

"Someone loaned you a Mercedes?" she lifted her voice.

"I know." He laughed. "I've got really good friends. I've learned how to be a better friend."

She knew he was thinking of Sterling and what they had done to him. Pushing it aside, Desiree stared into the night. They headed into the crowded streets of downtown Brooklyn.

He seemed to be looking for someone as he leaned close to the steering wheel, turned his head left and right.

"What?" she inquired.

Continuing to sweep his eyes, he told her, "I met this homeless man today. I was checking to see if he'd want that sandwich."

He referred to the food she held.

She furrowed her brows.
 "You're looking for a homeless man?"
He shrugged.
 "I am."
 Intent on finding him, he turned a corner.
Desiree shook her head.
 "Some homeless people are not mentally stable, Deacon."
 "They didn't start out that way. See how mentally stable you'd be, if you lose your home, your dignity?" he asked, searching.
He had a point – a good one. She turned, looked out the window.
 "What does he look like?"
 "He was wearing a gray coat and hat. Dark skinned, short guy. Told me his name's Nicodemus."
She looked left and ahead, saw someone on the corner. They had a fire going in a trashcan.
 "That him?" She pointed, diagonally.
Deacon squinted.
 "Yeah, yeah!"
 He sounded excited then realized, "We've got to find parking and walk back."
He saw she wore a short black jacket, no hat or gloves.
 "You going to be warm enough?"
 He didn't have all the appropriate winter clothing either.
 "What about you?"
He scanned the streets for parallel parking, declared, "I'm doing a lot better than our friend, Nico. I'll be fine."
A half a block down, they found a parking space. Deacon helped Desiree out of her seat and engaged the alarm. She gave him the fish sandwich and stuffed her hands into her jacket pockets. The wind was howling, pushing directly into their faces. They ducked, forged ahead.
Deacon smiled big at Nicodemus, approached slowly while pushing Desiree behind him.
 "Nico! Remember me?"
The man frowned, holding his tattered gloves over the fire. It took a minute, before he remembered.
 "Yea, Deson."
Close enough, Deacon smiled.
 "I brought you something. You like fried fish?"
 He held out the aluminum foil as Nicodemus stared at it.
 "Where you get it?"
He lifted his chin at Desiree, standing behind Deacon.
 "The pretty lady make it?"
Deacon stepped aside, feeling comfortable introducing Desiree.

"She didn't. This is my friend, Desiree. We got the sandwich from our church. It's still warm, if you want it."

Nicodemus accepted the gift, sniffed it.

"Smells good. You alright Deson. When you said you'd find me again, I ain't believe you."

Deacon looked at him.

"You gonna sleep out here tonight?"

"No."

He shook his head, opened the foil and took a bite.

"I'll be getting on the train soon. I'll ride throughout the night, stay warm. I'm good."

Desiree stood speechless at the man's acceptance of his lot. He said he was good because he'd sleep on a warm train all night. And that was good, compared to the bitter cold streets.

Deacon turned, reviewing the choices of restaurants.

"Can I get you something to drink -- something hot?"

Nicodemus thought a minute and wrapped up the leftovers of his sandwich.

"I'm gonna save the rest for my friend. She meets me in the subway. She used to fry fish like this."

Deacon and Desiree did their best not to cry over what Nicodemus had just said.

"That's thoughtful of you. You like coffee, Nico?" Deacon asked.

"Yeah, black."

"What about your lady friend?"

"She likes the sweet stuff – hot chocolate."

Deacon held up his hands.

"Don't move. We'll get you something."

"Hurry up," Nicodemus warned, "our train's coming soon."

They walked off quickly and found a crowded fast food place. Deacon cringed. He started to say they should try another place. Desiree explained, "They're all going to be busy. Let's just wait."

It took 15 minutes to get their order. They took off, sprinted to the corner where Nicodemus stood. The fire was out and Nicodemus, gone.

Chapter 19 – Tell Me More

Ollie was late for his dinner meeting with Zoe. She sat, analyzing the restaurant's customers and staff. Observing was something she had a gift for and she did it with pleasure.

The couple to her left ate in complete silence and not once did they look up from their plates. "Okay, they thought coming to this fancy restaurant would help with their communication problems. Somebody, say something!" she thought

On her left, a family of five talked all at once – father, mother, and three teenagers. She smiled when their laughter followed. "Hum, strong family," she thought.

She saw a woman across the room get down on one knee, and propose. From the disappointed look on the woman's face, Zoe gathered the man said, "No."

"Uh, oh," she thought. The woman began to cry, alerting the maitre d'.

Zoe, completely engrossed in the conflict across the room, failed to see Ollie approach.

He called her name.

She shook her head and looked up at him.

"Ollie, hello. Sorry," she apologized, and gazed back at the couple. Ollie looked in the same direction and heard the faint cries from the rejected woman.

"What happened over there?"

Before answering him, she asked, "Where's Desiree?"

He pulled out his chair and sat.

"Rehearsals for her church choir began today. She's one of the directors and soloists."

She saw Ollie understood, but also regretted that Desiree could not join him.

"Do you sing?" Zoe asked, cheerfully.

That got a short laugh out of his raspy voice.

"My singing is tragic."

He looked back at the couple leaving the restaurant.

"What happened?"

Zoe eyed the couple as they left.

"She asked him to marry her, he said, 'No.'"

Ollie lifted his brow.

"You heard that from all the way over here?"

She laughed.

"I saw her actually get down on her knee and propose."

"Ouch."

Ollie put a hand on his heart.

"Yeah, I feel for her. I bet they've been dating a long time and she was tired of waiting. So she went for it. Did it in a public place, thought that would force him to comply. She needs to get out, and quick, if she really wants to marry. For whatever reason, he's not ready."

"Impressive," he thought.

"You did get that from all the way over here," he said, referring to her professional skills.

"It's what I do," she said confidently, and sipped her water with lemon.

Since the subject had come up, he asked, "How long do you think a couple should wait before they get married?"

"I'm not a marriage therapist, although…your question is typical. You lost your wife, how long ago?"

"Twenty-seven months."

"You think it's too soon to marry again?"

He looked at her, thinking he was asking the questions. "I don't *know*. Desiree and I have only been dating thirteen months. I know that I want to marry her."

"Ollie, I can't tell you how long a person should grieve before giving their heart to someone else. I can tell you to go over all the reasons you want Desiree in your life. She can't take Sapphire's place. She can create a new place in your heart, however."

Ollie nodded. That Desiree had done. She had created a warm place in his heart and Olivia's. He wouldn't factor Deacon in the equation. He trusted Desiree.

Casting the thought aside, he focused on the reason for this meeting. Who was Dr. Zoe Landry? Would she be the counselor to the children in his arts foundation? Actually, she would assist in selecting the children as well as act as an ear for them, providing guidance for their emotional and spiritual health.

Their server came up as Ollie began to ask if she knew what she'd like to order. She did, and went for steak and he chose the fettuccine.

Once their menus were removed, he said, "My mom referred you. She said you were a big help with my stepsiblings. You worked on their case as a social worker."

Zoe nodded, recalling that awful case involving his stepsisters and stepbrother. The children's mother began drinking and abusing them. Thanks to Zoe, they were placed in the safe care of Ollie's mother and stepfather.

"Your parents are incredible," she mentioned.

"At that time, I was still living in Florida. Your mother was fighting breast cancer and your stepfather was doing all he could to care for her and the children. They had an unwavering faith that I knew nothing about. We had zero faith or religious practices in our home growing up. My mother thought that it was for the weak."

She smiled, remembered when Ollie's stepfather asked if she was a Christian. He might as well have asked if she were a man. She had no point of reference. What was a Christian? Zoe, one to do her homework, and after watching Ollie's parents fight an unbelievable battle, she found out.

"Your parents made me curious. And since my mother said religion was for the weak, it gave me all the motivation I needed to investigate. I started going to your parent's church. I studied the Scriptures and found who Jesus Christ is. I also found a joy and strength that I never knew possible."

Ollie stared at her, mesmerized by her analysis.

She smiled.

"Mom was right. We are weak. We get weak. All of us. When we do, there's someone there. Someone that's perfect. We can rest in knowing He's supporting us. He gives me clarity of mind to make good choices -- the kind of choices that bless my life and the lives of others."

She moved him. She didn't come to Christ because she was broken or had made poor choices that had torn her life to pieces. No, she came because she simply wanted to know God. And she had found him.

Ollie, a naturally sensitive man, picked up his napkin and wiped the tears filling his eyes. He cleared his throat and said, "You have a beautiful testimony. Thanks for sharing it with me."

Their food was placed before them and Ollie did the honors of gracing it. He picked up his fork and spoon and starting twirling his pasta. "Why are you no longer a social worker? Why did you move to New York?"

Holding her fork and knife in place, she said, "I always wanted to be a psychiatrist, as well as work with children. I don't believe in having only one career for all of your life. I worked as a social worker while I continued my studies."

"Ambitious," Ollie remarked,

"I can be."

She included, "I moved here to get away from my mother." She didn't add that her mother had also taken up part-time residence in New York.

He didn't have to be a shrink to determine her mom to be a thorn in her side. He tried to lighten the mood.

"You like New York?"

It worked, she smiled. He noted she was beautiful and even more so when she smiled.

"I love it here -- the energy and the warmth. New Yorkers get a bad wrap. I've learned if you befriend a New Yorker, you've got a friend for life. One in particular is my assistant, Chelsea. She's like my protector."

She laughed sweetly, telling him, "My mom thinks she's my lover."

Ollie frowned.

Zoe quickly clarified, "Mom *thinks* she's my lover. Neither I, nor Chelsea is gay. I met Chelsea when I first moved here. She needed a job and a place to stay. Her roommate at the time was on drugs. They lost their apartment. And I needed an assistant. I immediately snatched up Chelsea after I brought a house here. I work out of my midtown home."

Ollie put some pasta in his mouth. He liked her.

"I think you'll work well with the children. Not only did my mom give you a glowing reference, so did Desiree. She met you through some of the children you counseled at her school. She said you did it for free."

"I enjoy what I do and I'm looking forward to working with you on the foundation. I do have one request."

He looked up; waited, hoped it wasn't weird.

"I don't want you to pay me directly. Change the offer to show my salary as a reinvestment into the foundation. I don't need the money," she said casually.

That was weird, or maybe not.

"You've set up a good client base with your private practice?"

She had, but really, she didn't need the money from that either.

Not one to block a blessing, Ollie agreed, "If you're sure about it?"

"I want to do this for the children, for the cause and for your late wife. Your mother told me how she passed. It wasn't in vain."

Who was Dr. Zoe Landry? He really wanted to know more. They talked until midnight.

Chapter 20 – You Don't Belong to Me

As promised, Deacon took her back to her car but not only that, he also followed her home. Her brownstone was only two blocks away from his. She bought it three years ago, got a great deal on it, and had it renovated to her liking.

She almost talked herself out of purchasing it. Why buy a house so close to the Stephens' house? Then again, why not? Deacon was long gone.

Deep down she wondered if she hoped he'd come back – tell her what a mistake he made for leaving and beg her forgiveness.

Now he was back. When he said, "Take a ride with me," she thought, they'd ride into the city, take a walk or maybe get dessert, get reacquainted. Not hardly. Deacon took his calling and missionary work very seriously. They went hunting for a homeless man.

Desiree took off her jacket, tossed it onto her sofa, and pulled a throw over her. She closed her eyes, let out a soft breath, realizing she admired the man Deacon became, and knew he belonged to no one.

He was like some traveling angel. His shining smile brought comfort, hope and a sharp pain in her heart. She figured that Deacon hadn't returned to New York to confess his undying love for her. He had to face his old ghosts and right his wrongs to be a complete man of God.

For the first time in a month since she heard he was coming to Rayne and Evan's wedding, she exhaled. She would give Deacon a call in the morning to set up a time when they could talk. Then he'd be free and so would she.

God had given her a man, and the opportunity to be a mother to the most adorable little girl she ever laid eyes on. Thinking of Ollie and Olivia, she wondered why he hadn't called after his dinner with Zoe Landry.

Chapter 21 –Waiting Makes It Difficult

Deacon rose early, prayed, meditated, and made breakfast. He was shuffling hash in a frying pan when a tired Mitch stumbled into the ancient kitchen after working 16 hours on a homicide case. He fell into a chair.

"That smells good."

"Just a little somethin', somethin', I whipped up."

Deacon sat a mug in front of Mitch and poured him a cup of coffee. Mitch took a sip.

"Yeah, man, that's good. It ain't what I buy," he commented.

Deacon drank a little of his coffee, rested his mug on the counter, and went back to his hash.

"I went shopping -- got the good stuff and some food for this place. I don't like eating out."

Mitch rested his elbow on the table. He needed the support to hold his coffee mug.

"You travel all over this world and you don't like eating out?" he asked, surprised.

"I guess that's one of my occupational downfalls. I do get invited into people's homes. That allows me to get some decent homemade meals."

The hash was ready. He spooned it onto two plates and carried them over to the table.

Mitch immediately began eating and Deacon chastised him, "Say grace, Man."

Mitch slid the fork out of his mouth, continued to chew. "Grace?"

He lifted his brow.

"Give thanks."

Mitch closed his eyes. Both brothers attended church growing up thanks to a neighbor. After Mitch learned about his father's criminal dealings, he lost faith and Deacon. He stopped giving thanks. He guessed having his brother back and a hot meal was something to say thank you for.

"Lord, thank you for this food and keeping my brother safe and bringing him home. Amen."

Mitch opened his eyes, tilted his head.

"Okay?"

Deacon smiled.

"Okay."

They ate quietly for a couple minutes. Mitch was on his way down. Before he hit the bed, Deacon needed his help.

"Can you run a check on somebody for me? I want to know if they have a criminal record."

Mitch kept his eyes on his plate, asked, "Sure, who?"

"All I have is a first name. Don't even know if that's his real name. You might know him -- homeless man -- hangs downtown."

Mitch looked at his brother.

"What's the name?"

"Nicodemus."

He sat back, snapped his fingers.

"Yeah, Nico," he said with a smile.

Deacon perked up.

"You know him?"

Mitch twisted his lips.

"No, I don't know him," he barked, sarcastically. "Do you know how many homeless people there are in this city?"

"Too many."

Disappointed, Deacon looked at his plate. Mitch noticed his little brother really wanted the information. He explained, "I need more than that. But I'll do what I can – ask around."

Fair enough, Deacon thanked him and finished his meal. Mitch asked, "What are you going to do with the information?"

"I want to make sure he's not a criminal. Although, my heart's telling me he isn't. I wanna help him find some family, a friend, someone to take him off the streets."

"What about a shelter?"

"He won't go."

Deacon thought for a second and told him, "I'm going shopping today to buy him some new clothes."

Mitch understood, but hoped to help Deacon realize, "Where's he gonna keep them, Deacon? He's homeless."

"I know… he can…."

Mitch's cell rang.

"Desiree? Hey, yeah. Hold on. He's right here."

He handed over his cell.

Deacon accepted with caution. "Everything Okay?"

"Fine. I don't have your cell number."

"Oh, sorry. It's…."

"No, that's alright. I just wanted to know if we could talk, soon."

Deacon twirled his fork against the empty plate.

"Whenever you want to."

"Tonight, at six, I can come by."

"I'll come to you."

"Fine. Good bye, Deacon."

Mitch needed to share something with his brother as he received the phone back.

"I told Ollie about you."

Deacon looked over but said nothing.

Mitch sucked his teeth, took a couple gulps of coffee and confessed, "I had to. I told you I like Ollie. He's my friend. They were happy. Desiree and Ollie. They were hurting, but together they were happy. You about to mess that up, Deacon."

Never good at hiding his true feelings, he asked, "What do you want me to do? I love her."

"You sure about that? She was engaged to your best friend. You left her."

Deacon squinted.

"I'm sorry things happened the way that they did. I want to tell her and Sterling I'm sorry."

Mitch's strong jaw line tightened, causing Deacon to yell, "I'm sorry!"

"You think saying sorry will make it right? Then you and Desiree will race off in your new Mercedes?" Mitch stared harshly at his brother.

"It's not new, or my Mercedes. It's a loan."

"Whatever."

"Look, it is Desiree's call. I need to do this. I can't wonder about it anymore."

Mitch rubbed a hand over his face that needed a trim.

"He has a ring for her."

Deacon sat up taller.

"An engagement ring?"

Mitch nodded.

Deacon sat, praying. He had waited a long time for this. And it wasn't going to be easy.

Chapter 22 – Stop, in the Name of the Law!

Desiree stood at the front door, waiting. Anticipating their talk elongated her day. And now he was 30 minutes late.

She didn't let him give her his cell number earlier so she couldn't call him. Then it dawned on her. What if he was out looking for the homeless? What if something had happened to him?

She turned and walked over to the desk on her left and picked up the phone. She'd call Mitch; maybe he would know. On the verge of dialing the last number, her doorbell rang.

A sigh of relief, a drop of the phone, and a race to the door had her face-to-face with him.

He was, well, standing there, looking regal as her sister referred to him on Sunday. But trouble reflected in his eyes. Before he stepped in, she asked, "What's the matter?"

He shook his head.

"May I come in?"

There was disappointment in his voice.

"Sure...." She asked again, as he walked over, sat on her sofa, "What's wrong?"

At first, he said nothing, folding his hands together, and placing his elbows on his knees. He creased his brows, and asked, "Have you eaten?"

Confused, she stuttered, "Uh...no...I." She had been too anxious to eat.

He stood up.

"Mind if I make us something? Cooking helps me relax," he explained.

"The kitchen's this way."

She turned to her right and led the way.

He liked her kitchen. It had an antique feel, but not ancient like his. He could tell it had been renovated. It even held a brick fireplace.

"Restroom," he asked, after observing the space.

"Oh, back through the living room, on the left."

He left her and she stood there. She had waited for this moment. And he wanted to cook for them? He offered no reason for his lateness and apparently, she figured, he had no plans to.

When he walked back in she noticed he had shed the nicely cut wool blazer. Not surprising, he wore a navy t-shirt. It had a V-neck cut that showed chest hairs that rose all the way up to his neck. She took notice of his arms – firm biceps and triceps. Turning her head, she cleared her throat, focused on the stainless steel stove.

He asked, "What would you like?"

"Huh?" She looked up at him.

"What would you like for dinner?"

"Oh, I don't know."

She walked over to the fridge, leaned down.

It seemed she had trouble giving him any choices, so he walked over, hunched down with her.

"May I…take a look?"

She backed away, almost stumbled. The close contact made her nervous. He must have just showered, because he smelled of fresh soap and water.

He came up and out with two bell peppers, one green and one red. He laid them on the counter and checked the freezer.

"Yes!"

He found she had ground beef and Italian sausages. Taking those out, he asked, "You got rice and tomato sauce? Oh, and I need fresh onion and garlic."

She had all the ingredients. He laid everything on the counter and she stood dumbfounded. Finally, she said, "You want an apron or something?"

He smirked.

"No thanks. Would you like to help? I'm making us stuffed peppers."

She turned to the kitchen sink, washed her hands, dried them on a towel and wondered, "What can I do?"

"Make a cup of rice, defrost and start browning the meat."

She did, and he got to work chopping up the onion and garlic.

"I have a food processor," she offered.

"I like doing it this way."

She noticed his voice did relax and he had a professional way of dicing. She turned, kept her eyes on the microwave while it did its thing, and Deacon at the island, doing his.

"All your sisters went home?"

He finished dicing the onion and garlic, went to the sink, washed the peppers, and cut them in half.

"Yes, we're all so spread out. Melody and Ron live in Atlanta. Sparkle and James live in Pennsylvania. Beautiful and Big John in California. You know he retired from pro football and started a car detailing business."

Deacon dried the peppers with a paper towel and rested them on a plate.

"Deep frying pan?" He waited.

She retrieved one from under the cabinets.

"Thanks."

He twirled it in his hands by the handle before laying it on the stove. After turning the flame on low he saw she had olive oil on the counter. He poured a little in the pan, added the onion and garlic.

"Your sisters don't work?"

"Melody works from home, technical support/customer service. Sparkle doesn't know what she wants to do. She was teaching, then selling cosmetics and now she's announced she is going to law school."

Deacon grunted, using a wooden spoon to stir the veggies.

She went on, "Beautiful's the princess. She never worked and never will."

She thought for a moment, then added, "It works for her and Big John – she babies him and he babies her. They're together all the time. I think that's why she lost it when he started spending time out."

He turned around, asked, "What happened?"

She gave a crooked smile.

"Mitch didn't tell you?"

He knew, but since she brought it up, he asked, "What's your take on it?"

The meat was ready, she asked, "You want to add this to your mix?" and started working on the rice.

He turned, reached for the meat and said, "I'm waiting."

She didn't have anything to do since the rice cooked itself. He had it under control. She sat and admired him.

"My take is this…Big John and Beautiful are two spoiled babies. I *thought* Big John was going through a mid-life crisis and Beautiful didn't know how to handle it. She started communicating with your brother. And if I remember correctly, Mitch used to have a thing for Beautiful. So that played just right for her. She was getting the TLC from somewhere. Then things got worse and my sister was convinced Big John was cheating on her.

"We told her to just talk to her man. But no, nobody knows her man like she does. She had all the evidence that she needed. And being the baby that she is, she was going to get him back."

Deacon turned and injected, "Using my brother in the process."

"That's right. They had arranged to sleep together."

Desiree opened her arms wide.

"She flew all the way from California to New York for a booty call."

"My Lord."

Deacon shook his head.

"Yep. That's what we said. And they were going to do this, until…." Desiree held up her hand and laughed. "Until, your cousin Evan comes banging down the door."

Picturing the scene she laughed harder.

"He comes banging on the door screaming bloody murder. Mitch comes running to the door in his underwear. And Evan is pleading with him, 'Don't do this. Don't defile another man's wife.'"

Deacon could speak to that part.

"At that moment, I bet Mitch didn't want to hear that, did he?"

"Nope. So Evan called for my sister. She came out, wrapped in a sheet. He almost passed out, asked if they had…you know. She said, 'No.' Evan told her, 'Get dressed, we're leaving.'"

Desiree rolled her eyes and paused.

"Well, you know Beautiful. She has to get all loud, she yelled, 'I ain't leaving! Two can play this game.' Evan calmly told her, 'Beautiful, your husband is not cheating on you. He's been sick. Thought it was cancer. He didn't know how to tell you. He's on his way to New York, now!'"

Deacon laughed.

"Mitch was left alone. And I bet pretty ticked off."

"I'm sure he was. Evan didn't have much to say about Mitch. He did a good thing stopping those two."

The meat was almost brown and Deacon asked her for cheese. When she put the package in his hands, he asked, "Why didn't anybody stop us?"

Chapter 23 – Love Never Lies

Desiree observed Deacon's graceful hospitality. He served her, took his seat, blessed the food, and let out a sigh. Looking into her eyes, he saw such anticipation and asked the question that nagged at them for so long.

"If Mitch would have found us sooner than later, would we have crossed that line?"

"No one stopped us. I didn't think that you wanted anyone to. I didn't."

She looked at her meal and away from his intense gaze.

"Afterwards, you were so cold to me. That hurt me. You ripped my heart out."

"Desiree," he whispered her name. She lifted her eyes, listened. "You came to me the night before you were going to marry another man, my best friend. And we made love. It was my first time, also. I didn't know it was yours!" He lifted his voice a little higher.

"Sterling and I had decided to wait…We…."

"You didn't," he interrupted. "You came to me and offered yourself to me. I thought it meant you weren't going to marry him. That wasn't your plan. After what we shared, you were still going to marry him."

She saw the pain and the hurt in his eyes. She let him get it out. He went on, "I was devastated. You had to know that I loved you, Desiree. It was killing me when I realized my feelings for you and knew I could never have you. And that night, I did. We both knew it was a sin. But I thought you belonged to me. How could you deceive me like that?"

"Deacon, it wasn't a trick. I felt trapped. I wasn't in love with Sterling. I thought I was. He was my first and only boyfriend. Later, I developed feelings for you. Our futures were already set. Our families were crazy over the wedding. I had no choice, Deacon. I thought I'd never have you either. That night I decided I wouldn't break my marriage vows, but before I pronounced them, I would know what it was like to make love to someone that filled my heart."

Deacon rested his elbows on the table and his face fell into his hands. Without looking up, he declared, "We had choices. We made the wrong ones. I've lived the past fourteen years loving you - thinking about you."

She once again looked at the lovely meal he prepared, but couldn't touch it. After a minute, he lifted his head, let his hands fall.

"Why didn't you marry him?"

Her lips started to tremble.

"You know what happened to Sterling that night. He couldn't get you or me on the phone. He got suspicious and went driving. Someone blindsided him."

Deacon held up his hand to stop her. He didn't want her to say how his best friend was left paralyzed from the waist down.

"Just tell me why you didn't marry him."

"I'm getting to it, Deacon. Sterling never asked about that night. He was remarkably humbled by his accident. There was no way I was leaving him. We planned to marry when he was strong enough. We were going to tell you...."

This time, she put her elbows on the table and her hands together. A sob rose from deep within her.

"You left. You didn't even say goodbye."

"There was a lot going on with me," he admitted, keeping his voice gentle.

"It wasn't just you and Sterling. Mitch and I were also dealing with our father's suicide. I couldn't handle being here. I always blamed myself for Sterling's paralysis."

She did also.

"I didn't marry Sterling because he cheated on me."

Deacon frowned.

"I guess I deserved it. Sterling went home from the hospital. His parents gave me a key. I'd go by everyday and check on him. The last time I did, I came in and found his nurse going for the ride of her life."

"Maybe she was taking advantage of him?"

Desiree gave a weak laugh.

"Yeah, I never went back."

There were so many layers, so much more to uncover. Deacon reached for her hand and held it while years of disappointment seeped quietly from her eyes.

They had talked enough for the night.

Chapter 24 – Only a Test

Two days later after his meeting with Zoe, Ollie hadn't called Desiree. That night, he used the lateness of the hour as an excuse. The following morning, he figured he'd call too early. Truthfully, excuses were sometimes a form of procrastination. And he was holding out, listening to his heart. He felt *something* innocent and pure with Zoe - a connection.

He battled with reason and guilt.

"Focus," he muttered to himself as he walked the stairs of the sanctuary.

He had much to focus on, his daughter, his gallery, his international dealings and travels, his arts foundation. With much to do, Ollie set aside thoughts of Zoe's delightful spirit. For now, he was home.

Home, church was home, literally. His beloved uncle was the senior pastor, and the woman he was on his way to see was his cousin, friend, and attorney.

Her office doors slightly ajar allowed him to hear familiar voices. He clearly recognized Sister Agnes, head of church security. Her voice was as deep and raspy as Ollie's. Then a sweet voice followed; he recognized it as Lily's. Knocking, he stepped in, and saw his cousin offering Sister Agnes and her granddaughter legal advice at a small round table.

He noticed crutches leaning against the wall as Lily greeted him, "We're wrapping up. Come on in."

Ollie smiled at Sister Agnes and Tiffany. The 16 year old and her grandmother shyly smiled back. He had that effect on women.

"What happened to the leg?" he asked the teen.

"I got my permit," she explained, "Grandma let me drive and a bread delivery truck ran into us."

"On her first day," Sister Agnes added. "Now the guy's suing us! Tiffany is afraid to drive. Can you believe it?"

The large woman looked up into Ollie's comforting grin.

"Life can't scare you off, Tiffany," he encouraged her. Squatting, he took a careful look at the cast covering her leg.

"Can I sign this?" he asked, studying the cast.

"Oh, please!"

She bounced then carefully looked at her grandmother who had already forbidden anyone from marking up the device, afraid it would look like graffiti all over the child's leg.

Sister Agnes' jaw clinched, but she didn't oppose. Still looking at the leg, Ollie lifted his hand, and asked his cousin, "Lily, you got a blue marker I can use?"

Getting up, she found one in her cabinet and placed it in his palm. Concentrating quietly, Ollie drew the body of a delivery truck. Then he sketched a girl standing on top of it. Several seconds later Tiffany realized it was her. Her arms held high triumphantly in the air as she stood on top of the truck.

Ollie looked up at the teen with that crooked smile.

"See, you conquer the truck, the fear. You're healed, and in the picture, your leg's not broken."

The girl looked down at his sketch, smiled.

Sister Agnes barked, "Well, you gonna sign it?"

Smirking, Ollie scribbled his signature.

"There," he declared, standing, "an Oliver Sparrow original."

The concept even had Sister Agnes' scowl transforming into a proud smile. She declared to her granddaughter, "This man travels the world buying and selling art. And you got this for free."

"My pleasure."

He returned the marker to Lily then gripped the back of Tiffany's chair.

The large woman stood – taller than Ollie. Her pixie of a grandchild followed.

"We better get going. Tiffany's got a doctor's appointment." She gave Lily and Ollie a curt nod.

"Thanks to the both of ya."

As they cleared out, Lily pressed to her feet and began clearing the table of documents. Ollie commented, "That baby you're carrying is getting big."

His cousin was four months pregnant with her third child. Although her second was only a year old, she beamed at his comment, and admitted, "I know. It is one big happy baby. Michael and I found out yesterday, it's not twins."

"Is it a boy?" he asked, on his way over to the soft leather couch in her office. He pulled out documents from his knapsack for her to work on and sat.

"We don't know. We're going to wait till he or she tells us. We have the pair. So another boy or girl doesn't matter to us." Lily joined Ollie on the couch. Nudging him with her shoulder, she said, "Come on, you know I'm dying to see it."

Reaching into his pocket, he pulled out the ring box, handed it over. She cracked it open and gushed.

"It's beautiful! Desiree is going to flip. It's so unique."

Ollie looked at the antique oval ring Lily wore on her right hand -- a loving gift from her husband and also a family heirloom.

"I wanted it to be unique -- something we can pass down to our children."

Still studying the ring, she believed he made the right selection. Finally she closed the box and returned it to him.

"When will you propose? You know Vaughn and I are throwing the engagement party."

Ollie thought about his sister, Vaughn who absolutely loved Desiree Davenport.

The silence lingered too long, raising Lily's eyebrows.

"You're still reading his letters," she realized, referring to his late wife's murderer.

"I read the last one on the plane."

Lily reached over, her soft hand held his.

"Why? You can't move on with him taunting you. You and Desiree deserve to be free. Love each other. That doesn't mean you have to stop honoring Sapphire."

He said nothing.

"Ollie," she said quietly, "Sapphire wants you to be happy. I know she does."

Taking his hand back, he folded them in his lap. Sometimes the pressure in life pushed too hard. Closing his eyes, his head fell backward onto the sofa.

"I miss her. I want her here. Not just for me, but for Olivia. The people responsible for her death live. It's not right."

"Life isn't fair. It's livable. Desiree is waiting."

Without opening his eyes, he said, "Maybe, but not for me."

"What?" she lifted her voice.

"Dez has been distracted for a few weeks now. I mentioned it to you."

He had. She nodded.

"I thought it was Rayne's wedding stressing her out. The wedding's over. She's not herself. Or maybe I don't know who she is."

"What's going on, Ollie? You're not creating problems to back away."

Opening his eyes, he looked at his cousin.

"Mitch told me. I'm not creating anything. And God put it right in my face," he stressed.

"Speak English."

Ollie rubbed his hand over his mouth, afraid if he expressed his fears, they'd take over.

"His name is Deacon. We sat next to each other on the flight home. Seems like a decent guy. Turns out he's Desiree's ex-lover and Mitch's brother. What are the odds?"

Lily rubbed her hand over her belly and provided, "Ex, meaning former. What's the problem?"

"Mitch thinks it's a problem. He was so upset when he told me. And if anyone knows the history, it would be him."

One not to jump to conclusions, Lily asked, "You and Desiree discuss this?"

Tilting his head, it shook with each word.

"That's the problem. She has not mentioned Deacon at all. And I know she has seen him. He went to the wedding."

She felt a flutter in her belly, smiled at the gentle movement.

He realized, "You look like the cat that swallowed the canary – peaceful, satisfied. That's good for you and Michael."

"You and Desiree can be content, too. If the relationship with Deacon didn't end well, then his being in town may be a sore spot for her. Not something that she wants to bring up."

He nodded.

"I thought about that."

"Ollie, you both have some clutter in your lives. Who doesn't? My advice is to organize what's salvageable, throw out the rest. And stop reading those crazy letters from Marcel."

Not sure if he'd do either, he felt Desiree had a responsibility to share her past with him. Since she didn't, Ollie figured this to be a test for them. He'd wait and see how she'd score.

Chapter 25 – Duty Calling

The emotional storm ebbed through her – delight, wanting, anger, and guilt. When it quieted, who would be the man in her life? Ollie had not called her regarding his meeting with Zoe. And she had not called him after her talk with Deacon the night before.

She remembered how he looked, sounded, and smelled as he sat at her kitchen table, holding her hand, soothing her heart. There were moments hers had stopped beating. And when he left her table, he left her restless. Sleep took hours to fall and it left too quickly.

Morning arrived and duty called. As principal, her students and staff were counting on her to lead, guide, direct. Late, she eased out of bed with a quick prayer on her lips. No time for breakfast, she showered, dressed, and made a few calls in her car– none to Ollie.

She realized on her way to school she could have a comfortable life with Ollie and Olivia – not easy. Having a small child was a 24/7 job, and doing it alone seemed longer. Ollie needed someone.

Until Deacon resurfaced, she pictured that someone to be her. She still could see glimpses of herself in that role but couldn't feel with Ollie what she felt with Deacon.

Deacon's touch sent her soaring. It created a tumult only Deacon could calm. The same satisfaction came close with Ollie, but it didn't completely cover the target over her heart.

Why? Why couldn't she just settle into being wife and mother? She knew Ollie wanted more children. So did she. She thought again, "Lord, it would be so comfortable, even pleasant, but not easy."

She shut down all her thoughts, as her sister Rayne had often told her that was something she was very good at. Besides, she had other children in her care that required and deserved her undivided attention.

Principal Davenport entered Public School 48. The stuffy warm heat slammed into her face. She spoke pleasantly to the uniformed police officer.

He smiled big. Officer Bonner had a thing for her and had asked her out several times. When she started dating Ollie he became her excuse for turning down the young officer. He shouted after her on the way to the front office, "Got my ticket for the fundraiser! You gonna be there, right?"

She turned. "Fundraiser?" she thought. It took a few seconds before she remembered, "That's this Saturday, right?"

The 25 year old squinted, showing off his golden brown eyes, "It's your man's thing. You forgot?"

Trying to shrug it off, she came back with, "I just wasn't thinking of it first thing this morning."

He playfully checked his watch, lifted a brow.

"It's not morning anymore."

Desiree checked her own. Technically, 15 minutes to the hour, it was still morning.

"Very funny, Raymond."

She walked off. It was quiet until she heard Ms. Jones' third grade class shouting out their two times tables. Music to her ears, she sang along, "Two times four is eight, two times five is ten, two...."

She was still singing when Karyn looked up from her social media page and quickly minimized the screen.

"Karyn, I told you, check that on your break."

"Good morning to you, too."

Karyn whipped her saucy attitude on her boss. Desiree noticed her short black hair was spiked, shooting out toward the right, like an arrow of some sort. She had on bright pink lipstick and matching eye shadow. Desiree couldn't believe her school secretary was a 30-year-old woman with two children.

Karyn gave her boss a teasing, chastising look and said, "You're late, Principal Davenport."

"I heard from Officer Bonner."

Karyn perked up like a coffee pot.

"Umph Umph Umph, don't he look good today, Desiree?"

She shook her head, looking at the pile of folders that Karyn still had not filed.

"He looks the same everyday. He wears a uniform."

"It's those eyes and those lips. The man looks good enough to spank. Yeah, Lawd!"

Karyn waved her hands, giving praise for her hormones and Officer Bonner's tight buns.

Smirking, Desiree looked around the office. "No kids, no teachers, just Karyn," she wondered.

"Quiet morning?"

"Thank God, since you weren't here. And speaking of a good spanking, you and Ollie finally get buck wild?"

"Buck wild?" she thought. She also thought about Deacon, not Ollie, and the first and only time they had been together. The moment they shared had been wild, crazy, fast – too fast.

A little annoyed and not certain why, she snapped, "Karyn, what does that mean exactly, buck wild?"

Karyn would have run her tongue over her teeth, but her metal braces reminded her, not such a good idea. Instead, she cleared her throat and spoke in a professional professor's tone, "Buck wild, it is the expression when two throw all caution to the wind, along with their outward garments, producing pleasure beyond their wildest dreams." She smiled, returned to her normal voice, lifted her painted on brow, and commented, "You're late, but not because you got buck wild, you're too touchy this morning. I could hook you up with Brick. That man will...."

Desiree rolled her eyes and rushed into her office. She felt badly for Karyn. Intimacy did not solve the problems in life. No one knew that better than her. She put away her coat and handbag, carried her briefcase over to her desk, sat down, and sulked.

And knowing that, she didn't know why she was so down. "What is my problem?" she wondered. She had a wonderful man and child in her life and all she could think about was Deacon. The one that left, that broke her heart.

Karyn's definition of buck wild raced the images back from 14 years ago. She remembered he wanted her out of her blouse – desperately. He had ripped it away. She hadn't recognized the passion in him, or herself for that matter.

The memory played so vividly, that she hadn't heard Karyn standing in her doorway, raising her voice.

"Principal Davenport!"

She jumped in her seat, reminded herself, "Yes, I'm the principal." Taking a deep breath to calm her pulse, she asked, "What is it, Karyn?"

"Tiona Washington and Mr. Barnes are out here. They want to talk to you."

"Why? What's the problem?"

As she asked, she heard the wails.

Karyn shrugged.

"Don't know. She won't say. Girl's crying her eyeballs out."

Alert now, Desiree got on her feet.

"Tell 'em to come in."

Karyn stepped back and waved them in. She lifted her chin to Desiree as they walked past her.

"Want me to stay?"

Desiree looked at the distraught 10 year old. Mr. Barnes had his hand on the girl's thin shoulder.

"I don't know what the problem is. She asked to go to the bathroom. Came back upset, won't tell me nothing."

Desiree walked up slowly to Tiona, knelt down in front of her. The girl was trembling.

"It's alright," she said, to both the girl and her teacher."

Not once taking her eyes off of Tiona, she asked, "Mr. Barnes, is anyone watching your class?"

"I got Mrs. Simps looking out."

"All right. You can go. We got her. Thanks for walking her over."

The dark-skinned bald man wore a plaid wool jacket, seemed cautious and afraid to leave.

She reassured him.

"Please, let us talk with her."

Karyn opened the door for him.

Desiree tried to get Tiona into a chair. Her rigid little body wouldn't budge. Thinking, "So much for my knees," Desiree knelt in front of the child, reached for the tissues Karyn handed over and used them to wipe the girl's face.

"Sweetheart, you gotta tell us what's wrong."

Tiona managed to hiccup the words, "You gotta call my mother. Please call her."

Desiree looked up at Karyn, who was already heading out of the office in search of the parent's notification list.

"We're calling her right now. But honey, when you're in school, I'm responsible for you. Can you please tell me what happened?"

Tiona threw her body into Desiree, wept even harder. She had no choice but to brace herself from falling backward. Once steady, she then wrapped her arms around the shaky child.

"Go ahead. Cry it out. Cry it out."

Karyn stepped back in less than three minutes.

"She's on her way. Going to take a while."

"Karyn, get her some juice, please?" Desiree asked still holding Tiona.

Karyn slipped out once more, returned with a plastic container of orange juice and a small straw and slipped it into Desiree's hand.

"Honey, come on. Sit with me."

Desiree sat on the floor and tugged Tiona down. Karyn would have sat too, but her black shiny skirt was way too tight to make the transition down without hearing something go...rip. She took the visitor's chair next to them.

Desiree slipped the straw into the juice.

"Here, drink a little of this."

Now only twitching and whimpering, Tiona's shaky hands took the container and sipped a little.

"I don't want anymore."

She returned it to Desiree.

Leaning against her hand, she studied the girl, hoped she could tell her something.

"What happened when you went to the bathroom?"

She lowered her eyes. "I...I...."

"It's alright, go on."

"I...was on my way back to class and then, he...he...."

She was starting to lose it again. Desiree gently ordered, "Look at me, Tiona. Take a deep breath." She did. "Alright, that's good. Now just look at me and talk slowly."

She nodded.

"I was on my way back to class and he saw me, he put his hand…," She paused looked at Desiree and then over at Karyn.

Karyn's heart ached. She thought of her two girls.

"What did he do?" Desiree pulled Tiona's focus.

"He grabbed…."

Karyn jumped up, shouted, "Somebody touched your privates? Who did it, Tiona? Who was it?"

Desiree's eyes enlarged at Karyn bouncing and waving her arms like she was ready to fight somebody -- anybody. A little frightened herself, she begged, "Karyn, please."

Karyn stopped mid-bounce, lowered her arms at her sides. "Sorry." She timidly took her seat.

Desiree removed the creases out of her forehead and turned back to the child. "What boy touched you?"

Tiona hesitated, her eyes flooded again.

"I promise you Tiona; he won't touch you again."

"It…it was Trevor."

The faces and names began floating across their minds for recognition and placement. Karyn asked, "Trevor Walters?"

"Trevor Rendell."

Heads snapped to attention, Karyn and Desiree looked at each other in utter shock. Not Trevor Rendell. He was the sweetest, most well behaved honor student in their entire school.

"Are you sure?" Desiree probed certain of Tiona's uncertainty.

Tiona failed to meet her inquirer's eyes. She looked down. Her tears fell onto the dusty gray carpet, and her voice cracked, "Yes."

Chapter 26 – What Can I Render?

While Desiree had her work, Deacon also had his. Unlike her, he had started very early, walking the streets of Brooklyn, looking for Nicodemus. He searched for him the day prior and found some of his comrades, but they did not know where he was.

Dressed appropriately for the wintery weather, he covered the downtown area during morning rush hour. Walking in the snow dusted streets for two hours made his feet numb. Determined, Deacon trekked on.

The life of a missionary could be lonely. As many as there were, there were few. Why had he been called to care for the homeless, broken, hurt, sick, and dying? He accepted that all human beings had a responsibility to care for others but found a missionary's plight to be more concentrated. It required complete and total surrender without the understanding of his family and friends.

At a whisper from God, Deacon saw Nicodemus and desired to help him. But even the homeless held a level of pride. The man would only accept so much help. Maybe that's why he'd left his *home*, his corner, and alley. Maybe he thought Deacon was some sicko.

Nevertheless, Deacon had an assignment and he walked with the crowd of people -- some going to work, some looking for work, and some going to the social services offices for help.

The crowd, burdened under layers of clothes, protecting them from the brutal wind, just kept going and going. Such was life. It kept going. But not without purpose or meaning, and because he had completely surrendered to his heavenly father, he'd keep going, keep looking for those hurt and lost. Maybe one day, he'd have a companion to share his work with.

"Oh God," he breathed. "Maybe my companion would be Desiree Davenport. Maybe not, Ollie has a ring for her."

And what did he have...the memory of breaking her heart, taking her virtue and running away.

He stopped a minute, finally seeing the fresh fallen snow. He completed most of his work in much warmer climates. The snow reminded him of childhood and Sterling. They had the best snowball fights. He remembered once it had snowed so long, by the time they came outside the next day the snow rose above their knees.

They built forts and all the neighborhood kids played until they were blue. Sterling's parents made them come in, change, and drink hot chocolate. Yet it wasn't long before they were back in the snow, freezing, and loving every minute of it.

"Sterling," he thought.

He knew he had to find Nicodemus, but he also had to see Sterling. Another layer had to be exposed, opened, and then closed properly.

Deacon stood at the curb, closed his eyes, and prayed for help. An elbow in his back, and a grunt, said, "Move, man, the light's red." The woman's directive opened his eyes. He got out of her way.

He didn't cross over, but turned left, into a narrow street.

Walking down that street he found a woman with her back pressed against a wall. Good for her. The location helped protect from the windy snow.

Deacon approached slowly, searching her eyes. He noticed she appeared disoriented, confused, and very, frightened.

He kept his hands in his coat pockets, tilted his head.

"Miss, are you okay?"

She opened her mouth to speak, but she did not answer. He realized she was not homeless. Her hat and coat weren't tattered and her face was bright. This woman had a connection to someone. Regardless, she was terrified.

"Can I help you?"

Her eyes filled with tears.

"I want to go home," she told him in a childlike voice.

Her voice was familiar, but not her eyes. He knew her, but the fear and timid behavior she showed did not belong to her.

"Where is your home?"

"I don't know."

The bell went off. He was looking into the eyes of Ivy Pipman, Sterling's mother.

Chapter 27 – Tell Me Why?

Deacon had to do something. For one, he had to get Ivy Pipman home. Where was home? He moved slowly, careful not to startle the 65-year-old woman.

"I'm calling for help," he told her.

Still in a childlike state, she nodded. After four rings, Deacon sighed when he heard Mitch's voice.

"Man, where does Ivy Pipman live?"

"Who?" Mitch shouted in Deacon's ear.

Deacon realized, like him, his brother was walking the streets of New York somewhere. He heard the wind singing into the receiver.

"Ivy Pipman, Sterling's mother. I found her wondering downtown Brooklyn. She said she's lost."

Deacon could hear the sarcasm in his brother's voice as he said, "What do you mean she's lost? You mean to tell me that...."

"Mitch, just give me the address."

"It's in Cobble Hill...."

"Got it."

Deacon didn't need the street number. He realized it was the same home where Sterling grew up. Tucking his phone away, he looked into her eyes.

"I'll take you to Ted," he said, hoping mentioning her husband's name would put her at ease.

"Ted," she repeated softly.

"Yes, Mrs. Pipman. I'll take you home. How's Sterling?" he asked, hoping to trigger another pleasant thought.

"Sterling." She smiled.

He gently took her arm and guided her in search of a cab. It would take a miracle to get one, considering the snowy morning. It was a good day for cabbies.

It took 15 minutes before they climbed into the back of a warm cab. Deacon rattled off the address. The cabbie engaged the meter.

Ordinarily, it wouldn't take long to reach the Pipman home. Ivy hadn't wandered far from home. However, the weather hadn't helped the traffic.

The cab pulled up to the classic brownstone. The houses stuck together like a fort. A flood of happy memories came rushing back. And one in particular conjured up mixed feelings. He remembered where he and Desiree shared a very intimate kiss. How wrong is it to kiss your best friend's fiancée? But to kiss her, in his house, that had to have been a broken law for sure.

He shook it off, paid the cabbie and helped Ivy out and up the steps. Thankfully, someone had cleared the snow away.

Ted had been waiting and looking. He saw some man dressed for Alaska escorting his wife up the stairs. He swung the door open, pulled Ivy into his arms, and softly cried, "Thank God. Thank God."

Deacon stood outside, watched relief wash over Ted Pipman. It was obvious he hadn't recognized him. At the moment, Ivy held his attention.

Against his chest, she mumbled, "Ted?"

"Yes honey, it's me." She was coming around, remembered her husband. "I...I...couldn't find you."

Ted looked up and at Deacon.

"Thank you."

"You're welcome, Mr. Pipman."

Ted creased his shaggy silver brows. Deacon removed his hat.

"Mr. Pipman, I'm Deacon Stephens."

"Deacon?" His brain made the connection. He let his wife go, reached and pulled the young man out of the cold. "Please, please, come in. Oh my, God. Son, how long has it been?"

"Fourteen years, sir."

Deacon stepped into the hall and followed them into the living room. He noticed, like his brother, the Pipman's had done little redecorating. Things were much like he remembered. Sterling's lifetime photos still graced the mantle along the powder blue walls.

He zeroed in on Sterling and him – their graduation pictures from high school and then college. Next, a wedding picture of Sterling, and his wife and then another of Sterling in cap and gown. It must have been when he got his graduate degree. Even sitting in a wheelchair, his eyes glistened with pure joy. He really missed his friend.

Afraid to let his wife's hand go, Ted Pipman held it while Deacon studied the photos. Ted commented, "He misses you. He still begins a lot of his stories to his children with, "When I was young, Deacon and I...."

Deacon turned, and asked, "He has children?"

Ted walked his wife over to a small table, waved Deacon over. He saw the table filled with all shapes and sizes of picture frames of their grandchildren – Sterling's children. He had a boy and girl. The boy took on the dark attractive Latino features of his mother. The girl surprised him. She had the golden blond hair and piercing green eyes of her grandmother.

He turned to Ivy, told her, "Your granddaughter reminds me of you."

Still in a memory haze, she frowned at Deacon. She had recognized her husband. But Deacon wondered if she knew he was her husband, or just someone she knew.

Ted offered, "How about some tea for you two?" Deacon nodded and followed the couple into the lemon yellow kitchen. He noticed the appliances and the linoleum had been changed to white. Realizing his shoes were dirty and wet from the snow, he stopped. "May I take my shoes off here?"

Not concerned, Ted answered, "If you like. I'm not going to bother with Ivy's. It's just easier to let her keep them on."

To be polite, and since he was use to taking off his shoes before entering certain homes, he unlaced his boots, took them off, and set them aside. He followed up by removing his heavy black jacket and hanging it on the coat hook on the wall.

Ivy sat at the square white table like a guest rather than an owner, still wearing her coat and hat. Deacon smiled at her while Ted started the tea.

Her husband placed a nice serving tray on the table.

"Ivy, we're using your mother's tea set today. With Deacon being here, I think the occasion calls for it."

She blinked, picked up an antique teacup and turned it in her hands.

"It's nice," she said. "Yes sweetheart, very nice."

Ted joined them as the water warmed. He sensed Deacon had questions. Nice to have someone to talk with he began, "Ivy has been having memory issues for a few years now. She retired a year ago from Social Services because of it."

"I remember she use to work there," Deacon commented.

"She loved the job and the people. She never looked down on anyone. She loved helping people." He sighed.

"I try to watch her closely. Today she slipped out while I was in the shower. She thinks she's going to work. She gets downtown and gets disoriented. Once, she was gone until nightfall."

"Did you call the police today?"

Ted jumped up.

"Oh, my, I was so excited about seeing you. I'll call now."

He turned to the matching phone mounted on the wall, called in his wife's return and joined them a second time.

"She's done this...." Ted let his eyes roll, thinking. "Oh, I think this is the fourth or fifth time."

"Is she on medication?"

"Not yet. Maria, that's Sterling's wife. She's helping us. She's a nurse. She found us a specialist."

Ivy perked up at the name.

"Maria? Is she here?"

"No, sweetheart. She'll be by later."

Disappointed, Ivy held her head down and stared at her hands in her lap.

"She loves Maria. You know after Desiree called off the wedding, she grieved. We only had Sterling. Ivy loved Desiree and her sisters like they were her girls."

Deacon didn't understand. Before he could ask his question, the kettle whistled. Deacon selected a peppermint herbal teabag from the dainty sterling silver tray. Ted came back with the water. He let him get his wife's tea prepared before he mentioned, "Desiree's mom and your wife were very close. I don't understand."

"Well, none of us did. Desiree threw us a curve. She literally just called out of the blue, said she couldn't marry Sterling. No explanation. It devastated us. After Sterling's accident, we still believed he would have a full life with Desiree. It wasn't so."

"Is Sterling happy?"

"He is. He has a wonderful family. I guess at that time, we were in love with the Davenports. Simone, William, and the girls were a part of our family. So were you and your brother. Let's face it, in the early seventies, not many African American and Caucasian families accepted one another as we and the Davenports had."

Deacon knew where Ted was coming from on that aspect, but not on the friendship issue.

"Are you saying that Simone ended her friendship because Sterling and Desiree didn't get married?"

Ted held his teacup, shook his head.

"Not just like that, no. It was over time. The relationship was strained. Ivy came to resent Desiree. And although Simone didn't agree with her daughter calling off the wedding, Desiree was still her daughter. They could not be friends anymore.

"The end of their friendship did a number on Ivy. She felt empty and afraid for Sterling, thinking no woman would want her son in a wheelchair. Maria fell in love with Sterling, and Ivy fell in love with Maria."

Deacon drank a little of the tea. It hit the spot. He wondered why Ted hadn't mentioned him leaving, how it affected Sterling, so he asked, "How did he do after I left?"

Ted flushed. He left that out, not wanting to hurt Deacon's feelings.

"It hurt him. He wouldn't let anyone speak ill of you though, not even Desiree. She seemed more upset than anyone. Sterling said he knew your father's suicide really took a chunk out of ya. Said you needed time. He waited to hear from you."

Ted's eyes went hard as he looked Deacon in the eye.

"Why didn't you ever call him? Write him? You and Desiree were the closest people to him, and at his lowest, you left. You two took a chunk out of my son."

Deacon brought his fist to his mouth as his eyes watered. He murmured, "I'm sorry."

Chapter 28 – Don't You Dare

Deacon left the Pipman's residence, and by nightfall he was fuming. He went home, kicked the wheels of the Mercedes that didn't belong to him, and then climbed inside.

His day hadn't been as promising as he expected and prayed for. Granted, finding Ivy Pipman had blessed them both. How awful would it have been if the wrong person had stumbled upon the disoriented woman?

Thankfully, her mental cloud passed after she drank her tea. Deacon drove through the dirty slush filled streets of Brooklyn, considering how the cloud moved. Ivy had looked down and realized she was wearing her coat and hat.

"Ted, are we going out?" She looked up at her husband.

Ever so sensitive with his wife, he answered, "No honey, you just came in from one of your impromptu walks this morning."

He held his hand out at Deacon and added, "And look who you brought back with you."

Sharp and without hesitation, she looked into his eyes and yelled, "Deacon Stephens! What in the world are you doing in my kitchen?" Ivy leaped up and dived into his arms.

Within seconds she had peeled off her coat and announced, "There's no way I'm letting you leave here without a hearty breakfast. It's supposed to snow today you know."

Neither Deacon nor Ted offered that the snow had already begun or turned down the steak, potatoes, and eggs she got to work on.

Before Deacon left the Pipman residence, he inhaled the hearty meal, ate a slice of Ivy's homemade butter loaf pound cake, and listened to an earful of stories – all about him and Sterling.

The warm fellowship fueled him, sent him back into the streets in search of his homeless friend, Nicodemus. The search had been unsuccessful. And the more he thought of Ted's words "You and Desiree were the closest people to him, and at his lowest, you left. You two took a chunk out of my son," the angrier he became.

He went to the traditional nightly women's service with hopes of seeing Desiree and shaking her silly.

The services were the same as he remembered. The elder women wore all white, while the younger women wore white tops and black skirts. The women were not allowed to speak standing from the pulpit. A podium had been provided for them on the floor.

Mother Marilyn was the speaker. She talked of love and compassion for her fellowman/woman. The more he listened, the more he wondered about the events of the past, and how he was going to let

Desiree have it. She didn't come to the night service. He was going to her.

Deacon pulled up to the curb and looked up at her dark house. Her car was not parked out front. He turned off the engine and waited, hoping it wouldn't be too long. The temperatures had dipped down into the 20s. He knew most of the snow and slush would be hard and crunchy by morning.

Five minutes later, she pulled up in a black Infinity SUV, taking her time gathering her briefcase, Bible, and handbag. Careful not to fall, she stepped out of the vehicle.

Ten inches of crunchy snow waited at the front of her house and on the stairs. Desiree sighed and decided to go through the first floor. She knew she might fall if she attempted the stairs. With each step against the blasting wind, she regretted her responsibility to clear the sidewalk and stairs before morning.

Deacon slammed his car door.

She turned her head, barely recognized him with the thick fuzzy hat on.

"Deacon?"

"I want to talk to you!" he shouted, stomping in snow.

She sighed again. Her school day had been long with Tiona's incident. She went to Bible study with Ollie for restoration. However…he had a bug riding his butt. She didn't know what his problem was. And now all she wanted was a hot bubble bath and something sweet to eat.

She already pictured herself eating a slice of German chocolate cake while soaking in her massive tub.

"I don't want to talk tonight, Deacon. Go home."

He trekked over to her, took her briefcase and Bible out of her hands.

"It won't take long. Let's go inside."

He nodded his head.

"Look," she pointed her gloved finger in his face, "you don't order me. I don't know what kind of women you're used to, but you're in America, and we…."

"Shut up, Desiree and open the door. It's freezing out here."

A rush of wind bit through them.

"You shut up," she mumbled, fumbling with her key.

It was freezing, so she caved and he followed her inside. She flipped the lights and climbed up to the second floor where her living room, kitchen, and dining room were.

Resting her briefcase and Bible on the coffee table, he watched her shed her outdoor clothing. He took off his hat, but didn't bother with his coat. He pictured he'd let her have it quick. For the moment, she silenced him with her causal smooth movements.

"What?" she demanded.

He remembered the reason for the visit, popped back.

"How could you, Desiree? How could you let Ivy Pipman and your mother lose their friendship? If you would have just told your mother why you decided not to marry Sterling, maybe they could have remained friends. Did you know what the broken engagement did to Mrs. Pipman?"

Desiree started to open her mouth, but Deacon deepened his voice and fueled on, "You let your mother die without her best friend, Desiree. You're so doggone selfish. Just like you coming to me, to have sex with me, with no intentions of staying with me. You ever think how it would affect me? You ever consider anyone besides yourself?"

Her eyes blazed stronger than his now, her voice trembled, "I made love to you, you self righteous coward! Don't you dare accuse me of selfishness. You left Deacon! You left!"

Her eyes watered as she continued to shout, "I had to look at Sterling! I saw him suffering! I saw him not able to walk. I saw him needing to learn how to do things all over again. I helped him as long as I could."

Exhausted, she took a breath, added softly, "I had to see what my decision cost someone that I loved. And I have to live with those consequences everyday of my life."

Her eyes flooded, before the first tear fell, she declared, "I was *in* love with you. I needed you. You left...and I needed you. You were gone...," she trailed off, sobbing.

He walked up to her and slowly wrapped his arms around her. Touching his lips to her ear, he whispered, "I'm here. I'm here. I'm so sorry, baby."

He held her. She allowed herself to hold onto him, and held until her sobs quieted.

"Deacon, why?"

He pulled back a little, looked down into her incredible eyes, kissed her forehead.

"Why, what?"

"Why are you here? What do you want? I'm involved with someone. I can't hurt him."

He didn't exactly answer her.

"Mrs. Pipman is in the beginning stages of dementia. Your families were so close."

Her breath hitched.

"I didn't know."

"Not many do. Not even the people in their congregation."

He closed his eyes, pulled her in closer and let out a deep sigh.
"I can't find him."
Because it felt so good, she rested on him.
"Who?"
"Nicodemus. I'm worried about him."
His distress amazed and confused her all at once.
She remembered all the years she wondered what country was he in? What was he doing? Was he in danger? Now holding onto him, enjoying the steady beat of his heart, she realized his distress over a complete stranger amazed and confused her all at once.
"Realistically Deacon, you can't help everyone."
"Only those I'm called to help. It's my assignment." His reply was firmly set and Deacon would die for his calling. She considered her life. What was her assignment? "What about Ollie and Olivia?" she wondered.
He felt her body stiffen. His lips drifted to her ear, whispered, "Desiree...."
Trembling, she felt his warm breath grace her skin, his heated gaze, his lips anointing her cheek. He revealed, "I want...."
"Not now, not now," she begged. "Please...don't."
He let her go, decided to focus on another important matter.
"You got a shovel?"
"A what?"
She blinked up at him.
"You better let me clear the snow from your stairs and sidewalk before someone falls."
"You want to clear my sidewalk?"
Baffled, she stepped away, stared into his penetrating eyes.
"For now, yes," he answered, sincerely.

Chapter 29 – Fancy Me This

Against her sane judgment, Zoe sat across from her mother for a late dinner. The unfailing badgering began within the first five minutes of them sitting down.

She contributed to the treatment by purposely choosing the super conservative suit. The jacket had a high ruffled collar that she had pulled up, covering her neck. No skin showed other than her hands and face. She also pulled her hair back into a neat bun and wore her most obnoxious black-framed reading glasses.

The ghastly expressions coming from her mother gave her such sweet pleasure.

Zoe struggled to keep a straight face as she sipped her water. Deliberately provoking her, she carelessly asked, "Problem, mother?"

"How could you, Zoe? How could you?"

Zoe just lifted her brow, angled her head at her mother.

"You know exactly what've you done. You're trying to kill me and I'm only trying to help you."

Marsha Cartwright lifted her purse off the table, took out a tiny silver pill case, and tossed two little white pills down her throat. So use to taking them, she didn't need any assistance from her water glass.

Zoe knew they were only placebos. Her mother wanted to rant, so she let her.

"Your father and stepfather have already left us. I just want to see you happy with someone. Thank God for your sister."

Marsha began fanning her small beautiful face as if a hot flash was coming on. "At least she's found someone. You...."

She stopped fanning and pointed at her eldest child.

"You on the other hand, what you're doing...with that thing...is sacrilegious."

"Oh."

Zoe lifted her brow again.

"I thought you didn't believe in religion, mother."

"I never said I didn't believe in it. I said it's for the weak. And since you do, you should be ashamed of yourself. It's not normal, Zoe."

It was wrong to continue to let her mother believe she and Chelsea were anymore than great friends. But seeing her mother get so flustered delighted her. She imposed, "Mother, you should be happy for me to have someone as wonderful as Chelsea in my life. She looks out for me. I couldn't make it without her."

Marsha whipped her head on her daughter.

"Don't you dare give me details of your twisted affair."

Now, Zoe did smile. She hadn't given any details of any kind.

Her mother propped her elbow on the table and pushed two fingers between her eyes. She was demonstrating an impaling headache.

"At least for my sake, please go to the restroom and take that ridiculous bun out of your hair. You knew we were meeting someone tonight."

"I told you I didn't want to meet anyone."

Zoe quickly did a mental survey of all the men her mother introduced her to. Customary, they were all incredibly handsome. They were also heartless, rich perverts.

Nothing like the man she shared her evening with the night before. Ollie was special. She felt it in her spirit. And if she had shared that with her mother, she would have declared her insane. Maybe she was. She had had a difficult day trying to keep her mind off of his glowing light skin, exotic eyes, and full lips. He had a sly, very inviting look about him, but nothing about him was sly at all.

He seemed sensitive. She remembered how he teared up at her testimony. And that was the clincher -- he shared her faith. They had a commonality she had never shared with any man or anyone in her family. And if she admitted her feelings as Chelsea always told her to, she found herself extremely attracted to Desiree Davenport's man.

She let out a disappointed breath as she refocused on her mother's lips, not understanding any of her words.

"Zoe, are you listening to me?"

"No, not really," she wanted to say. Ready to get the evening over and done with, she inquired, looking around the place, "Mother, where's this man anyway?"

Marsha glanced at her expensive diamond and gold watch. He wasn't late. She told him to arrive 20 minutes after they did. Knowing her daughter, she'd come in looking undesirable. She wanted a few minutes to peruse her, hopefully help her make herself a little more presentable. And as she expected, her most stubborn child would not budge.

"He'll be here," she mumbled. There was no way he'd want her daughter. And this time, she really believed she had found the perfect man for Zoe.

She looked up and saw him making his way over to their table. If she were younger, she might have snatched this one up for herself.

Stunning, he had just returned from holiday, and she noted, he was one that tanned very well. His skin hued a golden flavor she found fascinating. Tall, dark, and well built. He was someone that put immaculate care into his body. He smiled, approaching the attractive women. His white teeth against his glowing skin, took her breath away. She held out her hand in a feminine gesture and thanked him for joining them.

"My pleasure."

He turned to Zoe and saw the flicker of recognition in her eyes.

She cast her eyes downward as a signal for him to not reveal anything. He played along.

"And you must be Zoe. You're as beautiful as Marsha described. I'm Garrett Walsh."

She took his hand. "Zoe Landry. Nice to meet you."

Marsha let out a slight sigh. At least her daughter had manners.

Garrett took his seat between the ladies, said to Marsha, "Excuse my lateness. I had meetings that ran over."

She gave a lazy laugh.

"Oh, it's no problem. You have a very exciting profession. Why don't you tell Zoe all about it?"

He shifted in his seat, turned to Zoe.

"I'm what they call, a legal pusher. I sell drugs to doctor offices, hospitals – that sort of thing.

Zoe took a sip of her water, craved more lemon. "Pharmaceuticals? I assume you travel a lot?"

"The part of my job I've learned to love, as well as hate. I just returned from Puerto Rico."

It showed. She didn't remember him being so tan when they met before.

A couple walked up, friends of her mother's she noticed. As expected her mother squealed -- with grace.

"Trudy, Franz, my, fancy you being here."

Trudy spoke, "Why, I was just saying the same to Franz." She looked at their table. "Good evening."

Zoe and Garrett said likewise and Trudy looked back to Marsha. "Playing the third wheel tonight, I see."

Her mother, such the actress, crossed her legs and looked up at the couple.

"I'm afraid so. Actually, these two are a little out of my league. Mind if I join you? Trudy, we really should catch up."

Franz, a very smart man, Zoe realized, never said a word. He let the ladies have their charade.

Trudy's mouth fell open in false surprise.

"Join us? Why, sure. Franz, you don't mind, do you?"

"We should take our seats." That's all the ladies got from Franz as Marsha stood, apologized, "Garrett, I hope you don't mind?"

He stood as any gentlemen would.

"Of course not, Marsha. Please join your friends."

She nodded graciously, looked at Zoe. "Sweetheart?" She gave Zoe the mother's sad eyes. "Mothers and their guilt trips," she thought.

"Mother, go on. It was nice seeing you Trudy and Franz."

They waved off as Trudy and Marsha put their heads together, with Franz, trailing quietly behind them.

Garrett took his seat and smiled.

"Poor man."

Zoe laughed.

"I was just thinking the same thing. He's also smart. He's not getting into any of that."

Garrett exhaled.

"You look good, Zoe. But what are you wearing?"

"You too, Garrett. I call this design, male repellant."

"It could work, if you weren't so incredibly beautiful," he complimented.

Silence lingered for a few seconds. He disclosed, "I called you a couple times. I spoke with Chelsea."

"She told me, and I was planning on calling you back. I wanted to see you. Ironic, how'd you meet my mother?"

He drank some of his water, explained, "Like I meet most people, working. She had a doctor's appointment. I guess she pegged me for you right away. She struck up a conversation. We only met a couple weeks ago." He'd rather talk about her, not her mother.

"How have you been?"

"Great."

He smiled. She did look great, even with the get-up.

"I'm glad I met your mother."

"If you knew her, you might not be saying that." She joked.

"She still thinks you're a lesbian?"

"I'm afraid so. Told me it's sacrilegious."

He grinned.

"I hate to tell you this Zoe, but you're lying to your mother."

She bit her bottom lip, and whined, "I know, but it's so much fun."

He laughed, deep and rich. She joined in. Tossing her reading glasses onto the table, she realized she was going to have a pleasant evening after all.

Chapter 30 – Are We on Schedule?

Desiree couldn't sleep, she couldn't eat, and she barely focused. And at that moment, all she could do was sit and think while Deacon cleared the snow. He came back inside with a round of wind, capturing her undivided attention.

Watching him stomp the snow from his shoes on the welcome mat, she believed her reaction to this man wasn't normal. After 14 years, and with no contact, how could she still desire him – love him?

He announced, "I sprinkled some salt, but still be careful."

She clasped her hands on the arm of the sofa, dared not move.

"Can I get you anything? You've got to be frozen."

He propped the shovel in the corner, and declined, "I better go. I have to get an early start in the morning."

She didn't reply, he asked, "You alright? You look tired."

"We had a situation at school today. I need to get an early start, too."

Concern registered in his eyes. Deacon took brisk steps, sat with her.

"Anything serious?"

A child had been violated – in her school. Desiree almost blamed herself for being late that day, knowing her lateness held no responsibility for what happened. She replied, "Deacon, it's pretty serious. I can handle it."

Desiree thought about Tiona's distraught behavior. It staggered her, but then when the accused little boy and his father arrived in her office, his delicate behavior landed her flat on her backside. His unreserved distress transcended from his eyes and into his father's, followed by a complete collapse. The boy melted in his seat, wept a wave of tears until he resided in a mumbling noodle, cradled in his father's arms.

Deacon saw all her day's worries in those expressive eyes of hers. He lifted his hand, allowed his icy fingertips to trail along her jaw-line. Her lashes fluttered, sending chills through them both. Keeping his hands off of her was no easy task. Retaining control, he stood with an encouraging smile.

"I know you'll handle it well. Good night, Principal Davenport."

"Why does he smile like that? So…sure, so sweet, so sexy…," she thought.

Finding her voice, she said, "You, too."

When the door clicked shut, whatever filled her, left her empty. Why were things so unbalanced in her personal, as well as, her professional life? Her cell's ring tone said Ollie was calling. That surprised her. He had barely spoken two words to her earlier at church that evening. Wanting to hear his voice, she answered, "Hey."

"Hey, yourself. Why didn't you tell me that a parent called the police on you today?"

She blinked.

"How'd you know?"

"Mitch. Dez, I know…" he paused, not ready to get into it about Deacon. Starting again, he said, "Talk to me."

Curling her feet under her, she asked, "How much do you know?"

"I know a little girl was violated and her mother is blaming you."

It was true. Tiona's mother heated up and then exploded into fiery bits all over the office. Ms. Washington had actually called the police, demanding Trevor's arrest…and Desiree's.

Desiree let out a long tired breath. She heard Olivia playing with her talking teddy in the background. The sweet child sometimes gave Ollie a run for his money at bedtime.

"You should give her some warm milk," she suggested.

"I will. How you holdin' up?"

"I guess if the officers would have taken me to jail, it would have been a good thing. At least I would have been taken away from the madness."

She heard his mouth drop.

"Sorry, sweetie, but I tell you, if I got a call that someone had put their hands on Olivia, especially like that, I'm going ballistic."

She understood a parent's frustration, but still, she had to be fair.

"I know. I am the one who has to step back, find the truth and protect all my students."

"You will. I'm sorry…." He decided to tell her.

"I know about Deacon."

She remained silent. He expected she'd be shocked.

"I met him on my return flight. We sat right next to each other."

"What do you know?" she requested.

"I know we need to talk. Not over the phone."

He wanted to look into her eyes, they'd tell the truth.

Knowing she hadn't been fair, she offered, "I'll stop by in the morning."

He said nothing and she confessed, "I do love you, Ollie. Please know that I'd never hurt you."

Already hurting, because he had to be the one to bring it up, he changed the subject.

"How'd the fitting go, tonight? Are you all set for the fundraiser?"

Panicked, she closed her eyes. She had a fitting for her gown. Thanks to Deacon popping in, yelling at her, wrapping her in his arms and then clearing her sidewalk, she forgot the appointment. She provided, "I'm on schedule, how about you?"

"So far, so good. Lily and I had a meeting today."

She opened her eyes, it sounded like Ollie released a breath.

"Desiree," he said, gently.

"Yes, Ollie?"

"I love you, too."

Her eyes looked at the phone after he disconnected. His voice sounded like a plea, as if he were afraid of losing her.

Chapter 31 – It Feels Like Home

Ollie bolted up in bed. The disturbing dream had him reaching for the lamp next to him. He flicked it on, let out a ragged breath. "What was that all about?" he wondered.

He dreamed of Sapphire, his late wife, but not like before. Usually, he'd dream that she was alive and well, raising Olivia with him and loving every minute of motherhood.

Today, the dream started with Desiree. Their wedding day had arrived and he could feel the joy and excitement of preparing to marry the woman that warmed his heart. She started down the aisle towards him. The walk seemed like forever, delayed and stumbling. She hesitated, searched the pews with each step.

She finally reached him, they exchanged their vows, and he longingly kissed his beautiful bride. And when he opened his eyes, he was staring Sapphire in the face. He nearly jumped out of his skin and the bed.

Now he sat, hands bracing the mattress. He thought again, this time aloud, "What was that all about?"

The clock proclaimed, 6:22 in the morning. Olivia would be up by 7:30. That gave him some time to recover, get his head together.

He walked barefoot toward the kitchen, started a fresh pot of coffee, and sat at the small kitchen table, hands tight together with his chin resting on them. His dream was about Desiree and her distraction. He got up, sighed, found a dark brown mug, added cream and sugar. He poured his java, drank, and thought again, "It's Deacon she wants, not me."

He lifted up a prayer, "Father, now what?"

******

Desiree arrived at Ollie's door at 7 that morning. She knew he'd be up, yet it was late enough that Olivia would still be sleeping. He took a little longer to answer than she preferred. March hadn't quite moved in, and yet the winds were picking up against cold damp air.

Finally, he answered. If Deacon resembled a midnight prince, then Ollie had to be a fiery morning star. Sweat glistened off his exposed muscled arms and shoulders. The man was sculpted and oh so lean.

She looked down at his loose fitting gray sweets and bare feet. She had seen his pretty feet before. From head to toe, he looked good enough to eat.

Hoping to get out of the wind, a truce and a chance to talk, she offered him one of the cups of gourmet coffee.

"Good morning, may I come in?"

He stepped back, accepted the cup, struggling a little to catch his breath. His morning workout had been intentionally extra intense.

Professional and sharp, she walked in, set her coffee cup on the kitchen table and slipped her briefcase off her shoulder. He didn't offer to take her dress coat, so she laid it on the back of a chair and sat on it.

"How've you been?" she said, staring up at him, since he hadn't joined her at the table.

He wrinkled his brow. Still upset about his disturbing dream.

"Give me a sec."

She nodded, giving him time.

He came back wearing a dry wife beater and a towel around his neck and sat.

"Good morning."

She put her fingertips on her coffee cup, fiddled with it.

"I didn't ask for any of this."

She didn't speak for a while, thinking about what she was admitting.

Ollie asked, "What is Deacon to you?"

"I don't know how to tell you."

Having felt this way before with his late wife, he stated, "You mean you don't want to."

She widened her eyes, lifted thick lashes.

"He's a part of my past. He...we...have been talking about some things."

"He must have been pretty important to you. You've been separated from me for a month or more. You told me it was Rayne's wedding."

"Deacon came back because of Rayne's wedding. He's Evan's first cousin."

Ollie felt he had a right to know.

"I think he came back for you. Is that what you've been talking about with Deacon?

She said the words quietly, "I never expected him to come back."

Ollie decided to sip on the coffee she offered. It was warm and tasteful. "Thanks for the mocha blend." He attempted a smile, his lips barely curved, but his voice was soothing. "Desiree, are you in love with this man?"

She couldn't say, not yet, with the weight building in her heart. "I don't know. I have a lot of mixed emotions about what happened between us."

"Tell me, please."

She bit her lip before she began, took a breath.

"Deacon and Sterling were best friends."

Somewhat shocked, he wondered, "When did things get serious for you and Deacon? Was it before you and Sterling got engaged or after?"

Ollie attempted to listen without judgment. She saw him struggle with his thoughts.

"It was after. Not planned, not thought out -- attraction is weird like that. I actually found Deacon annoying and intrusive. He was always with Sterling and me."

His voice soft and probing, he asked, "What changed?"

"He looked at me one day."

Ollie lifted his brow.

"I know." She gave a weak laugh.

"That sounds crazy. But he looked at me, with eyes of admiration and gentleness and he seemed so needy. And he kissed me. Well, it was kind of a kiss. It shocked me. I almost fell backwards. But we both felt something. It wasn't weird or intrusive. It seemed...natural. And it scared the crap out of me."

It hurt. Ollie didn't want to hear this, but he had to.

"So what, you two got buck wild?"

She pursed her lips, thought of Karyn, and shook her head.

"Not like that. No. Things got awkward between us. He stopped being annoying and just stopped talking to me. One day, I went over to Sterling's place and Deacon was there. Sterling wasn't. I was going to leave and Sterling's mom insisted that I stay and wait with Deacon. She had to run out. That left us alone...."

"And that's when y'all got buck wild?"

Desiree whipped her head a little higher.

"Ollie, we did not get buck wild."

She sighed, started up again.

"He started telling me how he felt about me. How it was killing him. He felt guilty. He wanted the feelings to go away, but they wouldn't. He said he never felt that way about any girl. He reached for my hand, and I held his."

Ollie was sitting on the edge of his seat, waiting for the buck wild part. Instead, Desiree laughed.

"You had to know Deacon back then. He was a wild man – had all this unruly hair, which he never combed. His clothes were wrinkled. He looked a straight up mess. But his eyes and his touch were gentle and peaceful."

Ollie interrupted, "What, Sterling wasn't gentle and peaceful enough for you?"

"Sterling was very kind -- sweet. I started to understand why they were best friends. I always saw them as opposites. Sterling was very neat, conservative and by the book. I didn't understand why they connected until Deacon touched me. I felt alive."

Ollie shrugged, knowing he never made Desiree feel alive. That hurt. He waited for the bottom line. She was taking entirely too long to get there.

"We shared our first intimate kiss. It sent us to a place that we knew we could not return from. Knowing that, we both left Sterling's house with a promise not to be in the same place at the same time. Still, we couldn't stay away from each other. We started calling, spending time together at school. My time was spent between Deacon and Sterling."

Ollie lifted his brow.

"You were a busy woman."

Offended, she cleared, "I wasn't sleeping with either one, Ollie. Until...."

"Until when...?" Ollie lifted his voice and Desiree's body perked up.

"Is that Olivia?"

Moving his eyes left and right, he listened, hearing his baby's faint cry for her father.

They both stood, went to her room. Olivia was sitting in bed, whining just a little.

"Daddy's here."

He lifted her, kissed her messy soft curls.

"Is she okay?" Desiree wondered. Usually Olivia awoke all smiles and giggles.

He felt her forehead for a fever.

"She feels fine."

"Rae Rae?" Olivia's eyes opened and her arms instantly reached out. Ollie passed her over.

"Hey, Princess." Desiree kissed her forehead and temple, discreetly testing for a fever as well. Her father was right. She felt fine.

"I've missed you." Olivia nuzzled against Desiree's stiff suit, warming her heart.

"How about I make us breakfast?" she asked.

"Won't you be late for work?"

She smiled.

"Hey, I'm the principal. I can be late."

He lightly kissed her lips.

"We'd enjoy breakfast."

So would she. They tabled the discussion. Holding Olivia in her arms and looking into Ollie's eyes also felt like home.

Chapter 32 – Your Legs – Your Home

Close to 11 that morning, Ollie waited at the door of Zoe Landry's home office. He felt somewhat calmer after sharing breakfast with Desiree and Olivia. They meshed comfortably together, without effort. A gift most didn't find easily.

In the back of his mind and hers, Deacon held his place, pricking his brain like a thorn. Ollie simply wanted to pluck it out and send him away, and knew it just wasn't that easy.

He filed the thoughts and fears away and focused on business. He told Zoe he'd be stopping by sometime that day. Conveniently, he failed to give her a specific time. Pretty sure he'd bring her on board, and yet, he wanted to see her casual at home. Her job working with the children in his foundation held a great amount of responsibility. She had to be nearly perfect for the job. So, what was a day like for Dr. Zoe Landry?

She answered out of breath. With her face wet and flushed, a green towel around her neck, she took in the air that hit her damp skin when she opened the door.

"Ollie, wow, I didn't expect you this early. I'm in the middle of a workout."

"Should I come back?" he asked cautiously, feeling a little guilty about interrupting.

She stepped back, welcomed him in.

"It's fine." She inhaled again, catching her breath. "I'm good."

He couldn't help but agree; good definitely came to mind looking at her. The tight black fitness pants showed off long firm legs, and the tight rounded muscles in her thighs – she was a runner, no doubt. The tank top bared muscular arms, flat abs.

Yes. Good. The good doctor could be a model. She had the height, the body, and that interesting exotic face – wide dark eyes, high cheekbones, pouting red lips – a face that intrigued him. He noticed she was not wearing a mark of makeup.

His staring made them both a little uncomfortable. Clearing his throat, he apologized, "I'm sorry."

"I know you're checking me out."

Ashamed, fear crossed his face.

"I...uh...no...."

She laughed.

"I meant, for the job with the foundation."

He laid a hand on his chest, smiled. Although, they both knew he had checked her out physically. He chastised himself for it. The truth was Zoe was indeed stunning. He gathered women would stop to look at her. Her presence commanded attention.

"Do you need a minute?"

He lifted the folder, holding the contract he had with him. "I don't mind waiting."

She shook her head, waving the long dark brown ponytail that flowed over her damp back.

"Follow me in."

He did. The foyer entered into what he considered a home out of a magazine. The expansive living room had a traditional southern feel to it, the high ceilings, white walls, offset by vivid colors of gold, red, and orange accents, the sofa had a warm red pattern on it. He liked it all.

She sat, extended her hand for him to join her. Beyond comfortable, he sighed, as the sofa seemed to swallow him. He could sleep there after having a fitful night's rest.

He looked down at Zoe's feet, like her face, they were bare. She didn't paint her toenails, he realized, "You workout barefoot?"

Her foot decided to wave back and forth.

"Tennis shoes are restricting. I wear them when I run. I was actually about to get on my treadmill."

"Sorry," he said again, adding this time, "for interrupting. I usually start my morning off with a devotional, a workout and some painting before Olivia wakes up."

His smile became a grin as he looked at her narrow feet.

"I don't wear shoes either."

Interested, she wondered, "You run too?"

His laugh came out quick and easy.

"Nah, at home I do the basics – push-ups, sit-ups, squats, and lunges. When I go to the gym, I box."

She nodded carefully imagining his lean frame under the black leather jacket. Considering, he was as lean as she imagined, she cleared her throat this time. He had a girlfriend. She steered the meeting along.

"May I see the contract?"

He looked down awkwardly.

"Sure," he said, handing it over. "I had my attorney make the change you requested. Your salary will be reinvested into the foundation. Thank you, Zoe."

She took it out of the envelope perused the document.

"It's no problem," she admitted without looking up. "I'm really excited."

Ollie leaned forward, rested his elbows on his thighs and folded his hands.

"I am too. I think you're really going to fit in. You'll help the board select the children and then, monitor them throughout the program."

Reading, she said, "Um hum. When do we start the selection process?"

It dawned on him. Desiree had not provided her recommendations. Her responsibility included working with other principals throughout the five boroughs, compiling the recommendations.

"I'll have to get back to you on that. I was hoping as soon as you sign the contract we could get started."

Zoe lifted her eyes.

"I just need a definite date so it doesn't interfere with my practice."

Fair enough. It annoyed him that he couldn't give her specifics. He and Desiree really needed to focus. He studied the room again, decided, "I should get going. I'm sure you have patients."

She smiled, corrected him, "Clients. And no, I'm off today."

There was a rumble in his belly, a mixture of desire and attraction. Zoe was very close to being his employee/colleague. But when she lifted her head and focused her eyes on him, he saw her fresh face. It allured. *Wow.* He *had* to go and stood up.

"Wait, Ollie. I want to talk to you about the fundraiser this Saturday."

He fastened his eyes on her. She sat comfortably, long legs crossed, bare foot swinging. He really wished she'd stop that. "Her legs – her house," he thought. Putting his wish on hold, he forced his voice to be pleasant, sat again.

"Is it sold out?"

"Unfortunately, we have six seats left."

"May I buy them? I think I can fill them."

He enlarged his eyes. Doing the math in his head, he told her, "Uh, that's three thousand dollars."

"No problem," she simply replied. "My sister's coming in town with her fiancé. I also have a date."

He didn't flinch when she told him she had a date, but considered why he wanted to. He kept his gaze level as she laughed and added, "Against my better judgment, I've invited my mother, too."

"That's nice."

"If you only knew my mother," she warned.

Counting, Ollie said, "You'll still have two seats unaccounted for."

"I'm sure we'll fill them. I'm going to ask my assistant and her boyfriend to join us."

Since she had a solid plan, he agreed, "I'll reserve a table under your name. You have the information to send the funds?"

She didn't and asked, "Can you e-mail it to me?"

He nodded, but asked, "Zoe, just how much money do you have?"

She laughed at the curiosity in his voice, causing him to smile, too.

"Let's just say, I've got enough to share."

He followed up with, "Many of us have enough to share. Zoe, I think you got money to burn."

She frowned at the puzzling comment.

"Why would anyone burn money?"

"It's an expression. You have a lot more money than you need."

"Ollie," she said seriously, "I believe in what you are doing. We're going to make a difference in the lives of so many children. I've seen a child's dream cut down too many times. The kids need this. I don't have any problem giving."

He believed her and the sincerity illuminating from her engaging eyes reminded him; he really *had* to go.

"I need to leave," he confessed a little too abruptly.

Nervous that she had said something wrong, she stood up as well.

He turned, remembering his way out.

Following after his quick strides, she touched his shoulder when they reached the front door.

"Are you offended that I'm rich?"

He couldn't keep the crooked grin from forming. Her timid behavior was cute.

"I feel very blessed, Zoe. I hope this foundation is a blessing to you also."

She smiled.

"See you Saturday, Ollie."

Chapter 33 – Me, Pick Me!

After leaving Zoe's swinging feet, Ollie had a brief meeting with Desiree. He rode the train from Manhattan to Brooklyn and quoted some Scriptures hoping to get visions of Zoe out of his head: "Those who keep their mind stayed on Him; He will keep in perfect peace."

No matter what the future held for him and Desiree, Zoe was a colleague, and a good person. He didn't want to think about her in tight workout gear.

He entered the school and greeted the security guard. Officer Bonner had only laid eyes on Ollie a few times, but he remembered the guy's unique face. He once overheard the school's secretary tell Desiree that he reminded her of the artist Prince.

Ollie remembered him as well and asked, "How you doing, Raymond?"

"Great. I'm looking forward to Saturday. Got a date, too." He winked.

Ollie smirked, signed in for Officer Bonner, and thanked him for his support of the foundation, "I appreciate you joining us."

"No problem. I had to take out a small loan to buy the tickets. I asked Desiree if she'd recommend my niece as one of your students. The girl has real talent. She can dance."

"Her dance teacher says she can be in a company one day. She's really good for her age."

Ollie nodded at Raymond's bragging, enjoying the enthusiasm, he offered, "We'd love to include her in our selection process."

"Really?"

Ollie thought Raymond was about to jump for joy.

"Really."

"I can't wait to tell her. Nyasia's the youngest of four girls. All my sister's girls had kids before they turned sixteen. We're trying to save Nyasia from making the same mistakes. She's different. She has dreams and she's going to go places."

After hearing that, Ollie felt he had to give Nyasia a slot. That's why he needed Zoe. He didn't know how to select. Left up to him, he'd have hundreds of children in the program, when he only had 50 slots for all the five boroughs of New York.

Ollie shook Raymond's hand, stated his belief, "If Nyasia's got dreams and willing to work hard, then she deserves a chance." Raymond swallowed the lump in his throat and nodded as Ollie found the front office.

There were two girls sitting in it. He didn't know if they were in trouble or just needed something. The guidance counselor's door was closed. He could see the light shining through the frosted glass. The assistant principal's office was dark. Desiree's was well lit.

Karyn's head snapped to attention. Ollie noticed her engrossed in something on the computer. She hadn't seen him enter or approach her desk.

"Hey, sexy," she said after he greeted her.

Ollie looked back at the two snickering girls behind him. Karyn pursed her lips.

"I forget I'm in school. You know you have an affect on women." She lifted one brow, and licked her lips.

Use to Karyn's flagrant behavior, he smiled.

"I need to see the principal."

"I see," she said, biting her bottom lip. "Have you been a bad boy?"

He only shook his head and lifted his thick brow.

She couldn't get him to bite, but that wouldn't deter her.

"I'll let her know you're here."

She could have buzzed Desiree; however, that wouldn't have given Ollie a view of her expanding round bottom captivated in tight gray pants – and boy did she shift it.

Ollie turned, smiled at the giggling girls. Karyn had a bottom so big he was certain if someone wanted to, they could set a meal on it.

After transferring the message, she glided back, and eased into her chair, explained, "She's finishing up a call."

Instead of offering him a seat, she propped her elbow on the desk, stuck her pinky fingernail into her teeth, showing off her braces.

"Are you wearing a tux on Saturday?" she asked.

He lifted his brow again.

"Are you coming?"

She smiled.

\   "I'm Raymond's date."

Ollie thought about the young man guarding the school, felt sorry for him. Karyn looked like she'd rip a man to shreds.

"Oh."

He hoped she couldn't detect his fear for Raymond.

"You didn't answer my question."

She ogled him.

"It's black tie. I have to wear one."

"Umm, umm, umm, I can't wait to enjoy that."

Apparently, she couldn't hear or see Desiree standing next to her either.

"Karyn?"

She heard the disdain in Desiree's voice.

Karyn bounced so high in her seat, her arms jumped, knocking over her soft drink.

"Oh shoot!" She scrambled for napkins in her desk drawer.

Desiree smirked.

"Come on in, Ollie."

"Take care, Karyn."

Karyn's eyes followed him into Desiree's office.

"You too!" she shouted after him.

"She's something," Ollie commented, taking the visitor's seat. Desiree sat behind her desk.

"Tell me about it. I don't know how the woman makes it through the day."

Ollie smiled, but it didn't reach his eyes. He wondered about her dilemma, "How are things with Trevor and Tiona?"

She closed her eyes and then opened them.

"I had to suspend him today."

"I thought you said you couldn't, no witnesses?"

He sounded like he was defending Trevor.

"That's not why I had to suspend him. I suspended him for fighting."

He shifted in his seat.

"Tiona?"

"No, thank God. Some boys were congratulating him, for allegedly copping a feel off of Tiona. He didn't like the attention. You know how kids are. They get a hold of something and it's the latest fad. They wouldn't let go, so Trevor went to swingin'. We had to pull three boys off of him."

He widened his eyes, asked slowly, "Three?"

"Uh-huh."

She thought for a minute, looked up at the corner in the ceiling.

"Ollie, how does this happen? We have a prize student here and just in two days, he's accused of sexual harassment, and now he's fighting?"

He sighed, realized, "No boy's going to fight like that unless he's innocent. You gotta get Tiona to give it to you straight. And then you need to discipline her for what she's done to Trevor."

"I know." She let out a deep breath. "Jack is back tomorrow. I need his help with this investigation," she said, speaking of her assistant principal.

He hated that she was under so much stress, but he needed her help, too.

"I met with Zoe this morning. She's on board and wants to know when we can begin the selection process."

She totally forgot, threw her hands over her nose and mouth.

"Do you have anything for me?" He sounded desperate.

She jumped up and rushed over to the table in the corner. Fumbling for the information, she said, "I do," and found an expandable folder.

She took the chair next to him, handed it over.

"These are from the other schools. Actually, I'm the only one that hasn't included my recommendations."

She laughed as he opened and leafed through it. He wondered what the laugh meant. She saw it annoyed him.

"I wanted to recommend Tiona for the art program."

He squinted.

"She draws?"

"She does well. Her mother can't afford lessons. Mrs. Wilson, our instructor here, said Tiona's talent is unmatched. She's light years ahead of her other students, draws and paints."

Ollie considered, "Why wouldn't you put her down?"

Thinking the answer was obvious; she opened her hands and closed them.

"She's having apparent issues."

He didn't hold the psychology degree, but Tiona seemed liked an ideal candidate.

"I think the program could redirect her. Maybe she'll fall in love with her gift and with us offering Christian guidance, she may get it together."

Desiree rested her elbows on her thighs and her face in her hands.

"I'm not thinking straight these days. You're right."

Ollie frowned, thinking about Deacon. It crushed him that Deacon had taken Desiree's mind and heart. He didn't look up. She watched him gaze through the information. A minute later, he asked, "Do you think you'll have your list soon?"

She said softly, "Sorry."

The apology seemed to cover more than just her late recommendation list. She promised, "I'll have it today, Ollie."

She touched his hand and felt things becoming distant between them. Their eyes connected.

"Desiree?" He didn't have to ask, it was evident in her eyes. "You're in love with him."

"Ollie," her voice cracked, "I love you, too."

He put his palm on her warm cheek.

"I know. We'll finish our talk, later. I have a meeting with my sister." He started to rise. She did also.

"You mean so much to me," she blurted out. She couldn't hurt him, not the way she hurt Sterling.

116

He tried to put a smile on his face. It didn't work.

She held her head down, and he lifted her chin with his finger.

"I didn't ask that to make you feel guilty, Desiree. I love you, too. I need to know where I stand."

She didn't expect the sobs to clog her throat, spill out and land on him. He rested the folder on her desk, wrapped her in his arms. She mumbled against his shoulder, "I just wanted a peaceful, comfortable life with you and Olivia. I never asked for this."

Painful to admit, but he found the strength and realized, "Maybe not, but deep down, you waited for him. Our season may be over."

"Can we hold on, just a little longer?"

Her plea surprised him, he leaned back to see her face as she went on, "Saturday, the fundraiser, it is such a special day for you -- for us. We worked hard building this."

He smiled, ran his fingers over her tears. She did work hard. Actually, if it wasn't for Desiree, he didn't think he would have put things in place.

"Dez, I'm not ready to let you go, either."

Leaning in, he brushed his lips against hers, smelled her strawberry lip-gloss.

"I love your lips," he whispered.

Because they both felt needy, they pushed, broke one of their rules, and deepened their kiss. They found themselves seduced by it - no rules, no thoughts, no restrictions.

Within 30 seconds flat, he had her backing up and sitting on her desk. His hands rushed through her soft sassy flipped hairs. Her arms floated, wrapped around his neck, and demanded that he come closer.

For balance, he held, resting one hand onto the desk, the other on her back as she reclined, aggressively angled him forward.

Their kiss never broke contact despite all the maneuvering. On the contrary, the rhythm increased, the sound of their desires drowned out all reason. The last time he'd been intimate was more than two years ago, with his wife. For Desiree, it had been 14 years – with Deacon. Maddened by emotions, they ignored the papers and desk supplies, crashing to the floor.

Neither one knew how long the stormy kissing lasted, nor why it suddenly ended.

Ollie eased upright, searched her smoldering eyes. His own were full of pleasurable disbelief.

"Desiree," dropped from his lips. They had never shared such a careless moment.

Clearing his mind, he stepped back.

"I...." That was all he could say.

Unable for her to say anything more, she replied, "Umph," then slipped off her desk and regained her professional composure.

He gathered up the disarrayed paper and desk supplies off the floor and packed his papers into his knapsack, while she folded her arms around herself, nervously fidgeted.

He abruptly started for the exit. If he didn't leave immediately, he'd beg Desiree to forget Deacon and marry him.

Chapter 34 – I Know It Hurts

Ollie wished for a vicious workout instead of a meeting with his sister. Desiree had awakened his senses, and an hour later, he was still reeling from their office romantics. So…that's what she had kept controlled and hidden from him. The night of her sister's wedding, he had a taste of it. Today she had fed him a little more. Thank God they hadn't moved on to dessert.

He took a look around the Queens neighborhood. At 3 in the afternoon children were returning home from school, excited about the end of another school day. He remembered he never was happy about returning home from school. His grandmother raised him. She was a hard lady that kept him in line with an iron fist. He couldn't say that he loved her, for she never said it to him. And when she passed away, he broke free, leaving his faith. His faith was the one thing she passed on to him that he truly loved.

Vaughn answered the door with an entangled and very happy appearance. Her hair, he guessed was supposed to be swooped up. On the contrary, parts of it dangled freely where others stayed in place. She had one of her sleeping twin sons on her hip. She opened the door and immediately shushed him.

He eased in, closed the door as she glided away in pale pink sweats and a white t-shirt. A couple of minutes later when she walked back in, he noticed the shirt was stained with grape jam.

"Nice design. Can you make me one?" he commented as she sat on the sectional with him.

"This is a Sammy original. You'll have to have him make you one," she replied.

He gave her a smirk.

"The runway model. Look at you. You're a mess and as happy as can be."

She rolled her eyes.

"I was never a model."

"You wanted to be," he jumped in.

"Well, I wasn't. I am happy, Ollie. The boys run me ragged, but I love it. I'm glad that I stopped working and decided to stay with them."

She saw the sadness creak into his eyes.

"I'm sorry."

"Nah, no need." He shook it off. "You know I'm happy for you. I wish Olivia had a mother to be with during the day."

Vaughn wished for the same.

"Well, she will have a mother. Let's see the ring. I heard it's beautiful."

Ollie took it out, regretted what he had to tell his sister. As expected when she cracked the box open, she gawked.

"Great day in the morning!"

"I thought it would suit Desiree. She never told me what kind of ring to get her. I thought it would be something we could pass on to our children."

Vaughn nodded, slipping the ring on her right hand. She admired it as she questioned, "Are you proposing Saturday, at the fundraiser?"

He sighed.

"Desiree's in love and it ain't with me."

His sister's hazel eyes popped.

"Don't tell me you've got cold feet."

Vaughn loved her brother's girlfriend. She was professional, smart, Christian, and great with Olivia. She believed she was perfect for Ollie.

"This has nothing to do with my feet. Dez got a past that she never clued me in on. And he's back with his sights set on her. I ain't getting in the middle of it."

Vaughn shook her head unable to accept his words.

"So…it's over? Just like that? What about everything you've worked on together? The foundation? What about Olivia? You two love each other."

He held up his hand for her to halt.

"Sometimes love is not enough. Vaughn let it go. I am."

She brought her hands to her face. She desperately wanted Ollie to marry his true love. He was a good man and deserved that.

"I ought to call Desiree and give her a piece of my mind."

Ollie smiled and gave his sister a once over.

"The way you look, you need to keep all the pieces of yo' mind."

Seriously changing his tone, he said, "It's all good. I've been praying. And I think I rushed things with Desiree. As much as I love her, I shouldn't be looking at another woman – and I have been looking."

This was over the top for Vaughn's afternoon. Usually while her boys napped, she read her devotional and prayed or napped as well. Feeling overly stimulated, she pleaded, "Ollie, tell me you didn't cheat on Desiree. Is this what the real problem is?"

Offended, he replied, "Please. I told you. Desiree's got a man. I'm talking about Zoe. I think she's got it going on."

Vaughn blurted out, "She's white!"

Ollie looked around the room, spoke between his teeth.

"You gonna wake the boys. Why are you even bringing it up?"

Why indeed? It was the first thing that came to mind. Zoe, too, was very smart, professional, attractive, good with children, and a Christian.

"Sorry. I shouldn't have." After a minute, she said, "When did this all happen?"

Ollie let out another deep breath.

"It sort of hit me out of nowhere. I don't know if I should act on it. She's working with the foundation now."

"That could get messy," Vaughn agreed. She had lunch with her a few times when Zoe first moved to New York. Truthfully, she respected the woman. However, once she met Zoe's mother, she gathered she would not be welcoming of her daughter dating a man that wasn't rich and was African American. Yes, it could be very messy for Ollie. She hated that things were not going to work out for him and Desiree.

Ollie snapped his fingers in her face.

"You done with the inner monologue? You know you women think too much."

Vaughn wondered if she should give *him* something to think about.

"I met Zoe's mother. She's a first class snob. They come from a totally different world."

"I'm not intimated by her world. I'll admit it's overwhelming. I saw her home today. Wow," was all he said.

"Just be careful, Ollie. No rebounding. Wait until you're really ready to move on."

He agreed, "I have no plans for a rebound relationship. It just hurts."

"I know."

She scooted over, rested her head on his shoulder.

"It hurts me, too."

They sat in silence for a while, realizing nothing else needed to be said.

Chapter 35 – Father Says...Protect and Serve

Deacon opened his eyes at the ringing cell phone. He took a breath, trying to remember where he was. His hands were folded over an open book on his chest. He rested one of his legs on the floor and the other on the couch. After hearing the cell go off again, he realized he was home.

He answered without looking to see the caller.

"Yeah."

"Found your man."

Deacon closed his eyes and opened them again.

"Say what?"

"Deacon, it's me, Mitch. I found your man," he repeated, shouting into the receiver.

"Nico...."

"Oh, yeah."

He still sounded dazed to Mitch. A second later, he caught up.

"Oh, yeah. Great, good."

He swung around placing his other foot on the floor, closed his Bible and rested it on the coffee table in front of him.

"Where is he?"

"His usual corner, by the cheesecake restaurant."

Standing, he looked around for his jacket.

"What's he doing, Mitch?"

Mitch looked out of the window of his old black SUV and reported, "He's sitting on the couch, watching football on the flat screen. I think he's got a cold one."

Deacon stopped in his tracks, his jacket in hand.

"What?"

Mitch ranted, "What you think the man's doing, Deacon? He's homeless! He's sitting on the corner, backed up against a building. What kind of question..."

"Dude, chill. I'm on my way. Can you watch him for me? I don't want him to get away."

Mitch said, "Yes" and shut his cell phone. He worried about his brother. What did he hope to accomplish with this Nicodemus?

Seven minutes flat, Mitch heard Deacon's borrowed Mercedes come to a hollering halt. If it weren't his brother, he'd give him a ticket. What? Was he going to kill himself, or someone else trying to save a stranger? "God, help him," he thought.

Deacon jumped out into the cold, thankful the sidewalks were cleared of all snow and ice, but the shelved mounds of it sat on the curb all dirty and gray. He maneuvered around the slushy stuff, taking long brisk strides toward Nico's direction. Mitch joined his side.

"What are you going to do with him, Deacon? Take him to our house?"

Deacon smiled. He had a glow on his face that told Mitch he would if Nico accepted the invitation.

"Oh, boy."

Mitch huffed, forming a cloud of vapor into the bitter chill.

Deacon approached slowly, stuck his hands in his jacket pocket. Mitch glared at the man, letting him know he was a cop. Deacon didn't like that, but what upset him was his brother's crude behavior. Mitch harked, shot spittle out the side of his mouth. Deacon turned to Mitch.

"Thanks for watching him. I can take it from here."

"I'm not leaving you, Deacon. So just do what you came to do."

Deacon let a crooked smile grace his lips. He'd forgotten how protective his big brother was.

"I'm homeless, not a thief." Nico looked up at them.

Deacon squatted, got eye level with him. The man looked weaker than he remembered.

"I'm not a cop."

He looked up at Mitch.

"This is my bother. He's a detective. His name is Mitch. I asked him to help me find you."

Nico took a few seconds and said, "Deson?"

He didn't correct him.

"Yeah, it's me. Where you been?"

"Why do *you* care? Most people throw me something to eat and keep moving. Why? You stalking me? Even got the cops stalking me. I ought to report you."

Nico looked up at Mitch, gave him a warning look.

"Nico, we're here to help. You know, protect and serve?"

Nico squinted.

"I thought you said, you ain't no cop."

"I'm not. I work for a higher power." Deacon lifted his hands flat in surrender. "Hey, just wanna help. You okay? You look... sick or something."

He saw the redness brimming around his eyes, the hollowed cheeks and white specks in the corners of his mouth.

"Can't eat, hurts too much, and nothing stays down. Been staying with my lady friend...in this crack house -- it got busted."

Nico glared up at Mitch again.

Mitch shrugged, rolled on the heels of his feet.

"You had to leave," Deacon softly realized. "Nico, I want to help you, trust me."

"How can you trust me? You don't even know me."

"I know you need help. Let me take you to a doctor."

Nico let out a gruff laugh.

"You see how I'm dressed? You can smell, right? No doctor gonna see me. Plus, I ain't got insurance."

"Let me handle the doctor and insurance. You can come by my house, shower, and change. I brought you some fresh clothes. I've been looking for you for days to give them to you."

Shock and warmth landed in the man's eyes, wondered, "You an angel or something?" Nico then looked at Mitch, thought again.

"Nope. I don't think angels hang out with demons."

"Hey, who you callin'..."

Deacon held up his hand, stopped his brother.

"I'm no angel, but I'm pretty tight with the Father. Nicodemus let us help you."

Weak, Nico struggled to lift himself up off the cold concrete. Deacon gave him a hand.

Mitch thought his brother should be wearing gloves before touching the filth on Nico's coat. He didn't say a word as he watched his brother escort his newfound friend to the car.

Chapter 36 – He's Steady on the Case

The shower had not removed the entire stink. How could one shower remove years of filth and grime? Nicodemus knew he needed more than one. But oh how that one was close to heaven. And who was Deson, as he referred to Deacon. The man looked at him with respect, like a human being. He welcomed him into his home, gave him a bag of new clothes, replacing the only tattered ones he possessed.

Deacon told him to put the old clothes in the plastic bag and he'd wash them for him. Nico shook his head; told him, "Burn 'em. I had on those clothes for almost a year now."

Sadly, he'd been homeless for three years.

God. He scratched his head, as he slumped in the chair of the urgent care facility. What happened to his life? He turned and Deacon gave him a pleasant smile.

"You gay?" Nico frowned at him, scooting over.

Deacon laughed loudly, alerting the other patients in the crowded waiting room.

"You think you're my type, Nico?"

He lifted a brow and then winked at his new friend.

Uncomfortable, Nico shifted in his seat and sat straight up.

"What's your type?"

"Not you. Don't worry, Nico," Deacon answered soberly.

"Murderer?"

"If I wanted to kill you, I could have done it while you were in the shower."

"I locked the door."

Maybe Nico was homeless because he lacked basic common sense. Deacon replied, "You think a locked door keeps out a murderer?"

Nico shrugged.

"I don't get it. I've never met anyone like you. You don't know me from Adam. You buy me clothes; let me in your house. Take me to the doctor in your Mercedes...."

"The Mercedes belongs to a friend."

Nico frowned, creasing his baldhead.

"You got good friends."

He really did. And it saddened Deacon that Nico had to fall into the coldness of the streets.

"I was never really friendly. Friends hurt you."

True, nobody knew that better than Deacon, especially since he was the friend that did the hurting. He let his mind travel over Sterling's face a minute. He came back seeing Nico slump again.

"You're hurting?"

He groaned.

Deacon wondered if he should have taken Nico to the emergency room. He checked his phone calculating the time. They had been waiting an hour and 10 minutes. He wanted to give him something, anything to ease the pain, but he had no idea what.

"God, help us," he prayed aloud.

Nico mumbled through the searing pain.

"That's it. You're a religious fanatic."

"I'm more of a relationship fanatic."

Nico's eyes widened just a bit. Deacon noticed a man on his left who had been reading some kind of report on a very sophisticated electronic device look at him. Since he was listening, Deacon stuck out his hand to the gentlemen.

"Deacon Stephens."

Somewhat sheepish that he got caught, he politely extended his hand.

"Garrett Walsh."

"This is Nicodemus." Deacon pointed to his right.

Garrett reached around Deacon with an inviting hand. Nico stared at it, in wonderment. Someone wanted to actually touch him. Deacon encouraged him, "It's alright, Nico."

Reserved, he took Garrett's smooth large hand.

"Nice to meet you Nicodemus. That's an interesting name."

"Yeah, yeah, heard it all before," Nico brushed him off afraid Garrett would follow-up telling him about Nicodemus in the Bible. Why had his mother named him that?

Garrett smirked at Deacon.

"You were going to say something about relationship fanatic."

Deacon looked at Nico, who had slumped further down, his head resting on the back of the chair. He turned to Garrett.

"I spend quite a bit of my time praying, reading my Bible, worshipping. I have a relationship with God. It keeps me grounded and able to help others."

Garrett liked that.

"You're a Christian."

"Through and through," Deacon reported with conviction.

Garrett looked over at Nico.

"How about you?"

Nico looked up at the ceiling.

"God don't look out for everyone. I'm just on this planet until my pain shuts me down."

Garrett started to tell Nico that he felt badly about that, but before he could, someone called, "Nicodemus Parker?" Deacon stood and helped Nico out of his chair. The calling nurse saw them approaching, went and grabbed Nico's unsupported arm.

"We'll take him from here. You his son?" she asked Deacon.

Insulted, Nico blurted out, "I'm only forty-nine. How could I have a son this old?"

The nurse only smiled. Although to her, Nico looked at least to be in his early 60s.

With Nico on his way back, Deacon took his seat. Garrett lifted his chin toward the door leading to the examination rooms.

"He's not a relative of yours?"

Deacon answered, "New found friend. I'm a missionary. I was walking down the street, saw Nico. He's homeless. I got him something to eat. We talked a minute. The Holy Spirit told me to help me."

Deacon searched Garrett's eyes, wondering if he thought what he had said seemed strange.

Garrett's voice wavered as he slowly questioned, "The Holy Spirit?"

Deacon nodded.

"Did it tell you to help him when you first laid eyes on him, or while you were talking?"

"While we talked."

Garrett permitted the words to marinate a moment before asking his next question.

"The prompting of the Holy Spirit had you help a stranger? That's incredible!"

Easy now, Deacon smiled.

"You're a Christian, too?"

"Not like you obviously. Tell me more about how the spirit speaks. I don't know if I've ever heard it."

"It's not an audible voice," Deacon began providing his understanding. Garrett lifted thick brows against his tanned face, listening with curiosity. The gentlemen talked until someone called Garrett's attention away. Deacon marveled at the impressive looking businessman in the designer suit. He was kind, intelligent, funny, and very interested about Deacon's missionary life. Fascinated, Garrett walked off, but not before inviting him to lunch. Deacon accepted, thanking God for another newfound friend.

The doctor admitted Nico into the hospital. There wasn't much they had shared with Deacon because he wasn't family. The staff agreed to tell him more once Nico signed the authorization forms, releasing the information. Still leery of Deacon, Nico refused to sign the documentation. On the contrary, that didn't stop him from staying with Nico. Deacon stayed until he was finally resting comfortably.

One thing he had learned, do not question God. In time, he'd understand. He learned that his heavenly Father had connected him to many people. And this was a divine connection.

As he watched Nico sleep, he looked around the hospital room and out of the window. Yesterday it snowed, and today it rained. The television flickered; it's light shadowing the room. TV was the first thing Nico wanted to watch. He said he hadn't watched television in years. Even though the man slept, Deacon let it play.

He found it prime time to pray and usher in the spirit of healing. At the moment, Nico didn't have a roommate. Deacon pulled the curtain and began a prayer. He walked the room as he prayed, "Dear Father, thank you. Thank you for allowing me to find Nicodemus when I did. Thank you that he did not die in the cold streets. Thank you that you blessed him with a companion that rode the trains with him at night. Thank you for his compassion for her. Lord, help me to minister to him, and help him see your love and compassion. Bless me with all the finances I need to cover his medical bills and care for when he leaves this hospital. My prayer is that you heal him, completely, healing all the facets of his heart, mind and soul. Use him for your glory and give him a heart's desire to serve you. Lord, you are so merciful and kind. I love and...," he paused, hearing footsteps. Looking down, he saw the blue clogs. A hand drew the curtain back.

"I'm sorry. I didn't mean to interrupt your prayer."

Deacon smiled with his arms folded across his chest.

"It's fine. Do you need to check him?"

"Yes."

The nurse rolled in the monitor to check his vitals.

"I'm sorry," she said again.

"No. Please."

He stepped out of the way as she crossed over.

She wrapped the blood pressure cuff around Nico's arm, commented, "You pray like my father used to. He'd walk and pray. He also played guitar. Dad sang and prayed."

"Your father's passed?" Deacon gathered.

"A long time ago, I was twelve. I remember his singing prayers. Is this your father?" she asked, moving on to his pulse.

Deacon shook his head.

"We just met."

The nurse's eyes lit up.

"Hey, you're the Deacon that brought him in."

Smiling, he corrected her, "My name is Deacon."

She shook her head, checking Nico's temperature.

"See how things get turned around."

She stared down at Nico for a long time. Deacon wondered, "Is he alright?"

She looked up.

"Will you...pray for me? My son got accepted into an MBA program. We just can't afford to help him. He could take loans, but he took a lot for undergraduate. My husband's been on disability for years now. We just...." Her eyes watered.

Deacon walked closer to her with intense sincerity in his eyes. He held out his hands. She held them in hers and they closed their eyes.

"What's your name?"

"Sara."

"Dear Father, you know Sara's need. She has a desire to bless her son. Only you can create something when there seems to be nothing and no options. Make a way for Sara and her husband. And as you do, bless their son to remember the sacrifices his parents made to bless him and others. Our hope is in you. Thank you for Sara's praying father. I believe he is with you in Glory. He planted the seeds of prayer and communication in Sara's heart. Please, Lord, lift the burdens of her heart to trust. You are already on the case. In the name of our Lord Jesus Christ, Amen."

Chapter 37 – As Long as We Breath

That night Deacon did not show for rehearsal.

"Just as well, he wasn't a part of the choir," Desiree thought. As much as she secretly wanted to see his wonderful face, his presence would agitate her, especially after her office antics with Ollie earlier that day. She nearly ate the man alive. "What's wrong with me?" she thought.

The choir needed her. They suspected something off balance when Desiree turned down Mother Marilyn's fried chicken and fish, using a headache as an excuse.

Truthfully, a headache pulsated behind her brown eyes. She squinted in the darkness, walking over to the curb for her car. A midnight blue Mercedes screeched, double-parked next to her vehicle.

Lo and behold, Deacon jumped out, leaving the engine roaring and his hazard lights flashing. He rushed up to her, lifted her off her feet, twirling her around.

"Put me down!" she shouted. "Are you insane?"

He stopped twirling her, but kept her up and off her feet. Looking into her striking and fearful eyes, he teased, "Afraid *your boyfriend* will see us?"

She didn't appreciate his lack of respect for her relationship with Ollie.

"Put me down, or I'm going to hit you."

He sat her down easily, a smirk covering his desirable lips.

"Deacon, I do have a boyfriend and you're...." She scanned the night, searching for any of the choir members that might have come outside. No one was on the block.

"I'm what...confusing your relationship with him?" he probed.

She knitted her brow not pleased with the conquering look in his eye.

So excited, and about to pop, he shoved his hands into his jacket pockets for control.

"I had a really good day today. I wanted to share it with you."

Sarcastically, she replied, "I'm happy for you, Deacon," and stepped away from him.

He kept talking as if she hadn't moved.

"Today put a lot of things into perspective for me. I'm not going to waste another second, reserving my feelings for you."

She whirled her head around, widened her eyes.

"Desiree Raquel Davenport, I'm in love with you. You're in my blood, in my bones. I can't get you out." He gave an easy laugh. "Believe me, I've tried. If that confuses you, shakes up your life, I'm glad."

"What?" she yelled.

"I'm glad," he replied slowly, "glad that you're in love with me, too!"

Once again, he found his hands on her, twirled her around.

"I love you!"

She shook her head unable to declare it to him.

"Put me down now!"

"I thought you were going to hit me," he teased, but did set her down. With his arms fastened around her middle, he whispered into her ear, "Come with me."

Her stomach danced, "Where?" she managed through a mumble.

Concealing the pleasure in his voice from feeling her tremble in his arms, he replied, "You'll see when we get there."

She let out a breath when he let her go.

"Deacon, I'm really tired. I had an awful day. My head is…"

He creased his brow; looked into her eyes, saw the headache beating there.

"Got any aspirin in that oversized bag of yours?"

She frowned at the purse on her shoulder.

"Yeah."

"Take a couple."

"I haven't eaten anything."

He laid a gentle hand on her back, guided her over to his car. She slipped in, against her better judgment. He could see her fighting a variety of reasonable thoughts.

Once he sat in the driver's seat, he took her hand, gazed into her eyes.

"Desiree, will you give me tonight? I know you have Ollie and we both know you can't continue with him with what we feel for each other."

The water building in her eyes only made the headache stronger. He kissed her fingertips.

"We're going to do things right this time. I promise. Tonight, just be with me, please."

Surrendering, she rested her head back against the soft leather, closed her eyes.

"Alright, tonight."

Deacon eased down the street. Desiree didn't open her eyes as she contemplated, "What happened today?"

"I found him. I found Nicodemus."

Desiree had no earthly idea how finding a homeless person helped Deacon float on air, and confess his love for her. She considered that was the mystery of the man driving and she had no idea where they were headed.

******

The drive was 25 minutes, taking them from the Fort Greene area of Brooklyn to East New York. When she opened her eyes, she noted they weren't too far from Ollie's church.

"Where are we going?"

"Almost there," he told her. "How's your head?"

"It's not that bad."

Sitting back with her eyes closed helped. Not to mention, the scent of him, even though it was only soap and Deacon, it relaxed her.

He pulled up to a collection of new condos. They climbed out and walked to about the third one. She heard the beat of drums and the resounding horns before they were upon the gate.

"Deacon, this is not going to help my head."

As they entered the gate, and started up the stairs, they heard singing, she added, "At all."

He smiled, took out his cell phone, thinking they wouldn't hear the bell if he rang it anyway.

Thirty seconds later, a pudgy happy man answered. "*Compadre!*" He embraced Deacon.

"*Hola.Cómo está usted?*" Deacon joyfully asked.

"*Estoy bien.*"

He let Deacon go, followed up with a happy handshake, pulling Deacon inside.

He turned to Desiree, introduced, "*Esta es mi amiga*, Desiree, and this is Marco."

She was greeted with the same warm hug and handshake that shook her entire body.

"*Hola, Marco. Mucho gusto.*"

She managed a smile through the pain.

Deacon lifted a brow at her Spanish as they followed Marco into a large family room. He leaned close to her ear.

"You speak Spanish?"

"Forty percent of my students and their parents do. I wanted to learn. When did you?" she asked, gazing at the set-up of instruments, recognizing the small group was singing songs of praise in Spanish.

"Years ago."

In Spanish now, he explained, "Marco is a pastor of a new church. They worship in his home. Tonight's their choir rehearsal."

He waived at the women who were singing and swaying with the festive music.

She nodded and he saw her squinting all the more.

132

"Too fast? Did you understand what I said?"

She replied, "*Sí, la cabeza me duele.*"

Marco overheard she had a headache. After taking their coats, he held Desiree's elbow, waived over one of the dark haired women, and asked her to take care of Desiree.

She gathered it was Marco's wife that he spoke kindly to.

"Hi, I'm Gladys."

Her Latino accent fresh and strong sounded pleasant.

Desiree looked at Deacon.

"We're in good hands," he assured her with a glorious smile. In the company of his friends, she saw him in his element. The glow on his face suited him and soothed her.

Trusting him and the strangers, she followed Gladys upstairs into the kitchen. They could hear the tempo of the music echoing under them.

Gladys talked, breaking between Spanish and English. She asked Desiree if she would enjoy a meal of chicken, rice, and pigeon peas.

She accepted, sitting at the large table covered by a white lace tablecloth. As soon as Gladys rested a full glass of water before her, she took four aspirins. "*Gracías.*"

"*De nada.*"

She joined Desiree with a small bowl of food as well.

"I think to eat with you."

Desiree smiled.

"Sure."

Gladys graced their food.

"Um, good."

"You like?"

"*Delicioso.*"

Gladys appreciated the praise, stuffed a fork full of food in her mouth. "Thank you. You're Deacon's *amorcito?*"

Desiree shook her head, smiled as to not offend.

"I have a boyfriend. Deacon and I...." She didn't know how to answer.

"Deacon is your true love," she put it bluntly.

One not to believe in love at first sight or soul mates, Desiree remained silent. What did that mean anyway? How could love be anything, but true? She thought about her parents, they had an incredible love. She felt a moment of grief for her widowed father.

Changing the subject and because she really wanted to know, she asked, "How do you and Marco know Deacon?"

"We worked together on a mission trip in Guatemala. We've known him eight years...," she paused, twirled her fork and corrected, "No, nine. Nine years. He's loved you a long time."

Desiree continued to eat. Maybe if it were Rayne, her sister, sitting across from her, she'd free her tongue.

"Do you know that life is short, Desiree?"

She smiled, liked the way the R rolled in her name when Gladys said it. "Yes, I do. I lost my mother a couple years ago."

"I'm sorry," she said sincerely. "We've seen death – a lot of it. Marco and I know there is only one thing that matters to a person before they die."

Gladys saw Desiree's eyes squint, she continued, "Only love – the love of God, and those around you. We told Deacon not to run from his love anymore. We know it was wrong what you both did. It's over. God forgives. If you don't love Deacon back, then you are your own prisoner."

Gladys' frank words sat on her a while. Standing, she yelled, "Oh, no! I need Deacon."

Gladys panicked, lifted her hands as she got to her feet. "I'll get him."

She ran, came back with Deacon on her heels. Still standing, Desiree swiftly asked, "The man? Nicodemus...did he...die?"

Deacon frowned, "No. I took him to the doctor today and they admitted him into the hospital."

"Is he going to be okay?"

He didn't have any diagnosis yet, he said, "That's what we're praying for. Why? What's wrong?"

She felt silly, glanced at Gladys standing behind Deacon.

"We were talking about life, death and love and I thought about my parents and then you," she hesitated, "telling me you love me. I thought...." The tears and emotions welled up and her voice cracked.

Feeling ridiculous, Deacon hugged her, said softly, "I'm sorry. You told me that you had a rough day. I shouldn't have brought you here. I hoped you would enjoy the company and music."

She sighed, closed her eyes as the tears gave way. With him, she felt all her strength deplete. She rested on him, remembering his words, "Tonight, just be with me." She could do that. She wanted to. Holding on tightly now, reservations released, she pleaded, "Deacon, don't let go. Please."

"Never," he declared. As long as God gave them life, he'd hold onto her. "I'll take you home."

She stepped out of his arms, looked at Gladys.

"I'd like to stay, finish my meal."

Gladys smiled brightly.

"You'll sing with us? Deacon says you have a good voice."

Desiree returned the warm smile.

"I'd like that."

Deacon gazed into her eyes, smiled at the peace he saw forming there, and prayed in his heart for the beginning with Desiree he hoped for.

She started to turn back, he grabbed her hand, tugged her back with a whisper. "

Please, wait a moment."

She froze when he took her face in his hands, thinking he was going to kiss her. Instead, he meticulously wiped her tears.

She stood, mesmerized by his gentleness. He mouthed, "I love you."

She realized, "You're never going to stop saying that."

"Never."

His touch froze, while the warmth of his words melted. It took all her will not to buckle and cry again. The emptiness she felt for 14 years was filling up with Deacon.

Chapter 38 - Furry, Fiery, Love

The next day Desiree avoided them both. She had to let Ollie go. He deserved better. She sat in the baby-blue striped pajama pants and a spaghetti strap top. Her legs were folded as she rested her head on the arm of the sofa. Concentrating on the action movie proved impossible. She thought about what she had told Ollie, "I never asked for any of this."

Thinking it over, she admitted that to be a lie. She had prayed for the day when Deacon would return and she could confront him.

It seemed apparent that Ollie had come to terms for ending their relationship – accepting her love for Deacon. What was holding her back from fully embracing it?

Instead of letting Ollie go, she nearly ate him alive, and at her desk! She couldn't believe her unprofessional behavior. Here she was in the middle of a sexual harassment investigation involving 10 year olds, and she, the principal, got it on while the school was full of students. "Oh, God, what if Karyn or someone would have walked in?" she wondered.

Angry with herself, she glared at her cell phone sitting next to her. Her sister Rayne was calling. She didn't answer. Rayne would detect something wrong and she'd be forced to discuss her *buck wild* moment. The ding following the ring meant Rayne had left a message. She'd call her back later – too upset to talk now. Or so she thought, until not even a minute later, she saw Deacon calling. She answered on the first ring.

He sounded cheerful.

"Hey, desire."

She blinked.

"What did you call me?"

Laughing, he slowly said, "Desire. You are my desire."

She pursed her lips.

"Hmm."

"What's wrong?" The laughter subsided.

"Another unusual day."

"You know you never told me what's going on at your work. I'd love to come by, but...."

"Oh, no. Not a good idea," she thought. She cut him off at the pass, firmly stated, "Deacon, no. You're not invited."

She could only imagine what she would do with Deacon. It might be incredible during, but after she would feel isolated.

He hesitated.

"I was about to say that I'd love to come by, but can't. I'm staying at the hospital with Nico."

She had forgotten about that. Feeling selfish, she asked, "How's he doing? What are they saying is wrong with him?"

"It's intestinal. He's got more tests tomorrow. They're keeping him comfortable."

She sat up now, putting her feet in fuzzy socks on the floor. "You need anything?"

"Just your prayers."

She didn't know what else to say, and then thought aloud, "You're staying there, all night?"

"Until he falls asleep. He asked me for a favor. I'm going to try to fulfill it."

Curiosity slipped into her voice.

"What's that?"

"He's got a lady friend. They usually ride the trains all night – to stay warm. He told me which ones they ride, her name and what she looks like. He wants me to find her and bring her to see him."

"You're going to look for another homeless person, tonight?"

"Yeah."

She was picturing him shrugging, as if to say, "What's the big deal?" Fear settled in her gut.

"Deacon, please be careful going out on the streets of New York, looking...."

This time, he cut her off.

"My desire, God's got me. I'll call you tomorrow."

His voice, desire in her ears, made her sigh.

"Good night, Deacon."

"Wait!" He almost forgot. "I got invited to this formal thing on Saturday. Would you like to join me?"

"Saturday?" she pondered. She had to decline. "I have a BOYFRIEND! And we have a thing this Saturday."

He didn't say anything. She explained, "Until Ollie and I settle things, I can't date you."

That stung, but he kept his voice level.

"By settle you mean end?"

She let out a breath.

"Yes."

"Good."

He sounded bold, expecting her to just end her relationship because he had waltzed back into her life.

"Look, I love him. I can't just turn my back, like you did Sterling and me. You got a whole lot of nerve," she ranted.

Building a relationship with Desiree wasn't going to be easy. Whereas he had spent the past years giving his pain and guilt to the Father, Desiree had held hers like a pet -- nurtured it. And now it had transformed into a healthy furry four-legged creature. He'd listen to it bark, but never accept its bite. He pulled the phone away from his ear, looked at it and then spoke into the receiver, "Pray about this situation, Desiree."

She said nothing.

"Desiree, when I held you last night, you asked me not to let you go. Do you still mean it?"

Her hand absently went to the black satin nightcap on her head. She closed her eyes.

"Yes, I meant it!" she shouted.

In kind, he returned her punchy attitude.

"Then fine. Have your *thing* with Ollie. And call me when you're ready. I'm never letting go!"

There was silence again, but he knew she was there, and ordered, "Have a good night, desire."

"Good night to you, Deacon!"

"Wait...." he added.

She held the phone.

"What?"

"I love you. Get some sleep."

He hung up, before she bit his head off again.

Desiree tossed the phone aside and shook her fists. She suddenly remembered something else about Deacon Stephens. He was the only man that could frustrate her to the point of fury.

Looking back at her cell phone, she snidely remarked, "You get some sleep."

She knew she'd have to pray for him half the night while he searched the streets of New York for another stranger.

Chapter 39 – They Are Alike, Yet Different

One thing Desiree could always count on from Ollie – to be treated like a lady. He explained he'd have to be at the gallery early, but would send a car for her. When her doorbell rang, and she stepped out into the windy night air, her mouth smiled at the amazing black stretch limo waiting for her.

The driver escorted her to the vehicle, opened her door and she slid inside. The soft leather seats, fresh linen air freshener, and the sound of smoothing jazz kept her company. She turned, seeing pedestrians under New York's night-lights. Having seen it all before, she decided to close her eyes, rest her head.

The quick nap powered her. She awoke from the rushing wind whipping into the car as the chauffeur held her door open. He held out his hand, and she placed hers in it.

"Thank you."

She stood for a moment, wondering if she should tip him. As if reading her mind, his professional voice replied, "It's all been taken care of. I'll walk you in."

He did, opening the door for her, and whispered something to the young lady that checked Desiree's coat.

"You have a good evening, Ms. Davenport."

Desiree thanked him and smiled again. Anxious about the night, she stood in place a moment.

Ollie appeared in all black under the archway. She'd never seen him in a full black tux. Usually his dinner jacket was white. Her eyes danced over his elegant, yet masculine appearance. He seemed stunned too. Her gown was shiny apple red satin and strapless. The bodice revealed an endowing dose of her breasts.

"If I could get my tongue off the floor, I'd tell you how incredible you look tonight," he finally managed to say. He closed the space between them and gave her a gentle hello kiss. She returned his greeting with another. His eyes traveled down the fabric around her waist that gathered and pulled. There was a dazzling letter "O" looped through the fabric. Tracing his thumb over the rhinestones, he asked, "O?"

"For Oliver," Desiree recited his birth name. The dress had been designed before she knew Deacon would be back into her life. After her fitting she considered having it removed then changed her mind. Ollie had been a significant part of her life for the past year. The thought of that changing saddened her.

He stared into her warm brown eyes and she found the gratitude of the gesture in his. The water came, but he wouldn't let them fall, not tonight.

"Ollie."

She wrapped her arms around him, rested her head on his shoulder. They both knew this would be their last night together. Understanding what was in her heart, he held her.

They heard chatter from behind. It was his sister. She called, "Cut that out and get in here."

Ollie let Desiree go and gave his sister a warning glance not to be hard on Desiree. With the look, he added, "I didn't tell your husband that when he was all over you a minute ago." His sister smiled and held out her hands. Desiree took them and widened them for a better view of Vaughn's burnt orange gown. The strapless sophisticated style wrapped around her breasts, straight and long to the floor, praising her shapely hourglass figure. Her hair was swept up, accented a beautiful face and hazel eyes flattered by green eye shadow.

Desiree hugged Vaughn.

"You always look amazing. You sure you're a mother of two year old twin boys?"

"Yes," Vaughn breathed. "And I miss my babies."

Ollie playfully poked a finger into his sister's bare shoulder.

"Oh, please. You were the first out the door. You practically ran away from home."

Vaughn folded her arms across her chest.

"I know, but now I miss them. I was just about to call home."

She pulled her cell from her matching clutch.

"The kids are in good hands," he commented and knew his reassurance wouldn't be satisfying.

"I still want to call," she stated.

Ollie shook his head.

"Well hurry up and come in here."

He took Desiree's hand, started under the archway. Vaughn waved him off and dialed her cell phone.

"Who's watching Olivia?" Desiree wondered.

"We combined resources, thinking it would be fun for the kids. They're all at Vaughn's house. We've got friends from church watching them, including Lily's two kids."

Desiree thought about his sharp cousin Lily – a very busy woman. She was one of the board members of the foundation as well as the attorney for it. She also held the title of chief legal counsel for her father's multi-million dollar church and her husband's very successful construction business.

Desiree often wondered how Lily held it together, and managed to be so graceful and professional. She considered she'd be like Lily, although busy, but rooted and grounded. With Ollie, she saw herself that way. They would be a power couple. Not that way with Deacon. They'd probably travel the world picking up strangers she thought, as Ollie escorted her into the gallery.

Things were almost ready. The live band on stage ran through some numbers. They caught her attention, she thought again of Deacon and his musical genius. Ollie leaned over and offered another compliment, "If you sing tonight like you look, I don't know if I'll let you go. *You* look amazing."

His raspy voice regained her focus. She kindly replied, "You, too. And so does the gallery. You transformed it into an enchanting five star restaurant. It's incredible, Ollie."

He took that as an endorsement and weaved around the formally set tables to the front of the room.

Ollie had a small platform built for the evening where he placed the gallery's artificial altar. It daily served as a focal point for his business. He kept the flames burning as a reminder of God's grace and strength for him. Hues of orange, blue and white wildly flickered.

Desiree lifted her eyes, and above it hung a large cloth backdrop. The color of sapphire, it held a silhouette profile of the late Sapphire Sparrow. Her eyes were focused onto the stars and in them a gleam sparkled. Next to the gleam, Olivia's name was beautifully scripted.

Speechless, she stared at it in wonderment. Like Deacon, Ollie's talents seemed to have no end.

"What do you think?"

"Ollie, it's so beautiful. *She* was so beautiful." She studied Sapphire's high cheekbones, seductive eyes, inviting charm. If that's how Ollie saw Sapphire, Desiree understood how she could easily captivate any man.

"Hi, Desiree."

A voice had Ollie and Desiree turning away from Sapphire's presence. Desiree smiled at the woman. Opening her arms, she hugged her.

"Hi, Lily."

Lily smiled.

"Isn't this amazing? You and Ollie did a great job."

Guilty, she shook her head, turned to Ollie. Resting her palm on his face, she replied, "You did a great job."

He looked into her eyes, remembering the long days they shared working on the foundation. He corrected, "We did this. We do amazing work together."

It was Desiree's turn to blink back the tears, and since that word kept coming up, Desiree agreed, and turned to Lily.

"You look amazing. Love your dress. Wow!"

A sexy burst of forest green; it flattered her blooming pregnancy.

Ollie agreed and demanded, "Where's your husband?"

"At our table."

He pointed.

"Well, get back over there with him. The last time we had an event here Michael went to beating on one of the guests."

He followed up with a teasing grin.

His cousin grinned with him. Desiree didn't understand the inside joke. Lily shook her head.

"Alright, Ollie, I'm going. And Desiree, you look beautiful."

She turned and Ollie lifted a brow.

"What was that all about?" Desiree inquired.

"Family joke, tell you later."

"Hmm."

She shifted at the sound of Vaughn's announcement, "Guess who I found?"

Her family had arrived. Desiree's sister, father and brother-in-law were following Vaughn. Rayne's steps picked up when she saw her sister looking fabulous in red; she beamed, "Sister, look at you."

Desiree returned, "Look at you!"

Rayne's gown was navy and flowing.

The men shook their heads as the women fussed about who was more beautiful. Finally, Desiree looked at her father, hugged him.

"Dad, I'm glad you came."

His baritone voice replied, "Me too," when she turned and casually acknowledged his date. "You know Marilyn."

Desiree's mouth dropped. She hadn't even recognized the woman, outside of an apron, or the smell of fried chicken and fish upon her. This Mother Marilyn was sharply outfitted in a captivating black suit.

Since she couldn't spit it out, Rayne nudged her with an elbow.

"Uh, yeah. Yes, Mother Marilyn. You look…great."

"Thanks, sweetheart."

Silence lingered while everyone held onto smiles not sure what to say next. It surprised Desiree that her father was dating and she had no idea. Vaughn broke the silence.

"Ollie, it's time to get this party started. People are flooding in."

He glanced around and said, "I'm on. I need to check on the serving staff and cue the band. You sing in an hour."

He looked to Desiree as if asking permission.

"Sure, do what you need to. We'll find our table."

Vaughn offered, "I can help with that. You're right next to my family. I know everyone's excited to see you."

Chapter 40 – Coincidence?

Deacon loved the glide of his borrowed car. He figured in a week or two he'd drive it back to the owner. In the meantime, he listened to his date tell him how much she enjoyed the ride as well.

"Too bad there's so much traffic. I'd like to see what it can do."

Deacon lifted his brow at Natalie Jones, his pastor's daughter. Little Nat, as everyone referred to her, was no longer little. When he left All Praise Church 14 years ago, she had been 12 and he was already legal drinking age. He considered that asking Nat to escort him tonight might be awkward.

She seemed to be fine with his company. Still, he kept seeing a little girl with bangs, braces, long conservative skirts, and a shy smile. In contrast, the adult Natalie knew how to prepare for a formal evening out.

Her hair tastefully swept back into a sleek bun showed off her small delicate facial features. A black Asian gown covered up her petite packed body. He thought she looked very conservative, until she slipped in the car, and he looked over to see her thigh exposed through the deep split running up the front of her gown.

Deacon made a point to keep his eyes on the road. To him, she'd always be, little Nat.

"Maybe you can pick me up for a ride out of the city sometime," she invited, breaking his concentration. He turned, looked at her face.

"Sure."

"So…what's this fundraiser all about?"

He cleared his throat, smiled sheepishly.

"I really don't know," he confessed.

"We're going to something and you don't know what the support is for?"

He noticed she sounded worried.

"I didn't say that. I know it has something to do with children and the arts. I met someone the other day. We had lunch and he offered me a couple seats for this fundraiser."

Pensive, she remembered there was an event posted at their church about children and the arts. Of course, she didn't think any of the members could afford the expensive seats. In focus now, she said, "Maybe this is Ollie's thing."

"Ollie?" Deacon lifted his voice.

"Yeah, Desiree's man. He's starting a foundation for children in dance and art, in honor of his late wife."

Nat thought a crooked smile lined Deacon's kissable lips.

"Why are you smiling?"

"No reason."

He shrugged, thinking, "So Desiree, your thing with Ollie is a thing for me, too. Interesting." He'd get a chance to see Desiree with *her* man, as Nat referred to Ollie. Not something he looked forward to, but considered it to be more than just a coincidence.

They arrived at the fundraiser and Garrett lifted out of his seat and welcomed Deacon as if they had been buddies forever.

"You made it!"

The men exchanged strong handshakes and Garrett started with the introductions for his table.

"This is the beautiful Dr. Zoe Landry. She's a member of this foundation."

Zoe stood, shook Deacon's hand. Deacon politely tugged Nat closer to him.

"Nice to meet you, and this is Natalie Jones."

"Hello," Nat replied, gazing at the handsome couple. The man had piercing blue eyes, dark full hair. He looked like a movie star. The woman, lean, tall, and sexy in a black off the shoulder gown had stunning eyes and full lips. The top of her hair was pinned, but she also let some strains of sleek brown hair hang loosely, anointing her shoulders.

Garrett explained the reason for the two empty seats at their table, "We're waiting for Zoe's sister and fiancé."

Deacon nodded and started to pull out Nat's chair. She declined, planning to keep her hand in his by walking with him.

"I'd like to look around first."

Garrett smiled and Nat saw a twinkle in his eye. She thought Zoe was a very lucky woman. Garrett encouraged them, "Go ahead. It's the social hour anyway. One of the rooms has been turned into a ballroom. I was just about to ask Dr. Landry for a dance," Garrett indicated, lifting his brow at Zoe.

Nat looked at Deacon.

"Do you mind?"

Deacon continued to hold her hand.

"Let's check this place out."

Curious himself, they eased off as Garrett escorted Zoe.

Desiree was laughing so hard at Vaughn's silly antics; she hadn't noticed Deacon or Nat. Although Deacon's cousin Evan had.

Deacon and his date were circling the Gallery admiring the art-lined walls.

Inconspicuously, Evan tipped his finger against his nose -- a little signal for his wife. Rayne frowned, followed her husband's nose. Her eyes bulged. She patted Desiree's leg under the table.

"You mind walking me to the restroom?" She made her voice sound extra casual.

Desiree hesitated, not interested in leaving Vaughn's company. Rayne squeezed her sister's leg. Giving in, Desiree requested, "Vaughn, hold that thought. I want to hear more about your visit to the hip hop exercise class."

They skirted around the tables. Rayne noticed Ollie speaking with Zoe and Garrett along the way. She whispered in her ear along the way to the restroom.

"Deacon's here."

Desiree's eyelashes speedily fluttered at Rayne's announcement. "What?" She started searching the crowd. Keeping her voice low, Rayne repeated, "Deacon's here."

Heart racing, she stood in place, eyes searching. A guest almost bumped into her. Rayne tugged her arm into the powder room, pulled her down onto a cute pink loveseat.

"What's he doing here, Desiree?"

Her voice rose, "I don't know!"

"Did you tell him you'd be here?"

"No," she replied quickly.

Rayne nervously folded her hands in her lap.

"Well, he's here, with Nat."

"Nat!"

Twiddling their thumbs, they sat silently a moment. Desiree realized, "Deacon's not one to start a scene. Why is he here?"

Rayne smirked. "You don't think you have anything to do with it."

"Deacon's *never* been one for confrontation."

"Neither are you," Rayne added and asked, "Does Ollie know about you and Deacon?"

She sighed. "He knows. This is our last night together. As silly as it sounds, I wanted our breakup to be a happy memory."

Rayne laid a hand on her sister's.

"That's reasonable. Emotions are not."

Her words ran away from her, "Tell me about it. I've been a wreck since I heard he was coming back. He gets me so off balance. I don't know what to expect with him. He's kind and giving, he's selfless and brave, he's demanding and over confident. He's...."

"In love with you. And we both know how you feel about him."

Desiree closed her eyes. Rayne touched her hand.

"Listen, go out there and pull Ollie to the side, so he's not blindsided."

Desiree nodded, laid her hand on the sofa, and started to lift herself up. Rayne held her in place.

"And, stay away from Deacon. This is a very special night for Ollie and his family."

Desiree smiled thinking Rayne sounded like the big sister instead of the baby.

"I know, sweetie. And I love his family. I feel like not only am I losing Ollie and Olivia, I'm losing them all."

Rayne considered this to be a difficult night for her sister. She embraced her.

"The family will be wounded. You know how they feel about Ollie, after losing his wife."

"I know," she replied somberly, knowing the family was very protective and only wanted the best for him.

Rayne and Desiree walked out of the restroom, passed the starlight ballroom and back into the dining area. Too late for pulling Ollie aside, he was already talking to Garrett, Zoe, Deacon and Nat. Desiree looked to her sister for advice.

Rayne grabbed Desiree's hand.

"I'll walk with you."

Upon them, Ollie turned and Desiree saw the fire in his eyes. His raspy voice remained cool as he spoke to Deacon and Nat, "Thank you for coming."

"Garrett and Zoe invited me. I think it's wonderful what you're doing in honor of your wife's memory," Deacon remarked.

On the surface, Ollie could see why Desiree would be attracted to Deacon. He came off suave, and yet humble. That didn't mean he had to like him. Even in a weird sort of way, he did. Ollie turned to Desiree, brushed his lips against hers.

"How about a dance, beautiful?" he asked, smiling into her eyes.

Desiree felt her pores open up as thin perspiration seeped through. Before she could oblige Ollie, Nat complimented Desiree and Rayne, "You both look nice."

Ollie put his hand on Desiree's waist, gave it a squeeze.

"Excuse us," he said, guiding her away from Deacon.

Deacon grinned as they walked away and then turned, kissed Rayne's cheek.

"How's my cousin treating the new bride?"

Rayne smiled at Deacon. He was very confident about his feelings for her sister.

******

Secure on the dance floor, Ollie admitted, "Now, what a coincidence."

Chagrin, she explained, "I didn't invite him."

He swayed her, hoping she'd relax.

"He told me that he's Zoe and Garrett's guest. It's cool."

She creased her brow.

"Really?"

"Yep. I'm learning nothing in life is really a coincidence. He's meant to be here. That doesn't mean I have to like him."

He gave her his best crooked grin. She smiled weakly.

"Thank you for not getting upset."

"Not my style, especially not tonight."

He turned his attention to Rayne and Evan, followed by Deacon and Nat as they entered the ballroom.

"Everyone wants to dance."

Desiree turned her head. She looked miffed.

"Jealous?"

She lifted her brow.

"What, of Nat?"

She shook her head.

"Surprised more than anything. She's our pastor's daughter. I've only seen her look…reserved. She doesn't look that way tonight."

Ollie teased, "She's got nice legs." He noticed when Deacon dipped Nat, exposing one very fine leg.

"You're trying to upset me."

Desiree bit her lip.

"Hey, why should I be the only one jealous tonight?" He laughed, and put in, "Don't sleep on the conservative ones. My cousin Lily is a pastor's kid, too. She got some freak in her."

Desiree lifted her voice. "Lily?"

"Well, maybe a small freak. But it's there. She's very aware of her femininity. See."

He tilted his head and Desiree saw Lily and her husband share an intimate kiss on the dance floor.

Ollie took a deep breath and let it out with a jest, "Yep. Deacon might be having a nice dessert tonight." He laughed deeply.

"You're just being incorrigible."

"Maybe."

In one quick moment, Ollie took her hand and spun her out, yanked her closely into him, and gave her a kiss. Their kiss was interrupted from an announcement coming from his sister. Desiree looked at the front of the room.

Vaughn had a microphone in hand.

"Thank you all for coming. We hope you're enjoying your evening. After the next song, please take your seats. Dinner will be served shortly."

Ollie whispered in her ear, "You're the next song."

He believed he heard her eyes grow bigger. He pulled back and gazed into them. She had forgotten she was performing.

"Uh, I better get up there."

As she started off, he pulled her hand back, stood closer, chest to breast. Her breath came out quick and short. He could see it, feel it, the energy she had for Deacon, flowing from her heart. It made him want that – a woman that would fill the room with her energy for him – and him alone.

Chapter 41 – The Past Becomes Present

After hearing the announcement, Zoe gazed into Garrett's baby blues as they continued their dance. She turned her attention on Ollie and Desiree, staring into one another and then Desiree taking her place on stage.

"What are you thinking?" Garrett asked.

"Noticed some tension earlier."

Garret smiled, showing off his pearly whites.

"My guess, it's a woman. That would be the only reason Deacon and Ollie would stare down one another like that."

"You saw that?" Her voice pitched slightly higher.

He chuckled. "Us men creatures -- I picked up the scent."

On to something and curious about hearing it from a male perspective, she probed, "And your take?"

Before he answered, the tempo picked up. Garrett swung them around. Zoe lost her breath at his fancy footwork.

"Oh!"

He grinned.

"We're dancing and Desiree is singing her heart out."

His gaze went to the stage and then back with his observation, "My take...they want the same woman. So first I consider the women, Nat or Desiree. Then seeing Nat showing no signs of distress, I gather it's Desiree. She didn't say a word when she approached us."

She smiled, complimented him, "Very good. Maybe you should be a psychiatrist."

He chided, "I think good salesmen are. We have to be observant, learn our potential client's likes and dislikes in order to provide the best pitch."

Zoe frowned.

"You sell drugs."

"It's still sales. We've got to convince our customer they need what we have."

"Even though they may not."

Zoe sounded a little judgmental.

"I believe in the pharmaceuticals we sell."

A good salesman reply, she smirked.

Turning the tables a little, he redirected, "Your take on the love triangle."

"I agree with everything that you've said. And Deacon already has Desiree. If he didn't, she wouldn't have been uncomfortable standing between the two men. Her heart's not with Ollie."

Garrett's eyes followed Ollie standing alone on the dance floor. His eyes glued to the woman singing. He sighed.

"Poor guy."

"Ollie's incredibly forgiving."

Men creatures and senses, Garrett picked up an admiration in Zoe's tone.

"How well do you know him?" he insisted.

"Not well. But, I can tell he has a sensitive heart."

Changing the subject, Zoe noted, "My sister is very late."

"Maybe she got held up. I'm sure she'll be here."

He thought for a moment. "Happy your mother couldn't make it?"

She let out a breath.

"Truthfully, a little relieved. Plus, it wouldn't have been much fun without my assistant being here."

Garrett realized, "That's right, your mother believes Chelsea is your lover."

Playfully, he scoffed, "How were you both going to pull that off? You have a date tonight. Or am I just a cover?"

She laughed, offered, "I started letting my mother believe that, hoping she'd stay out of my love life. It's fueled her. She's determined to find me a man and cure me."

Garrett laughed. "Lies always backfire."

"Don't I know it."

"So, you're going to confess…to your mom?"

She hummed.

"One day, I suppose."

She gave him a beautiful smile and it pleased him that he basked in her beauty for the evening.

The song ended, he took her arm.

"Shall we have dinner?"

******

As their server placed their plates, Zoe's sister and fiancé swept in. Zoe quickly slipped her chair back and rose to her feet. She hadn't seen her sister in six months, since she had visited her in France.

"Aimee!"

Zoe's arms opened and her sister latched on. Squeezing her strongly, Aimee apologized, "Sorry, we're late. Our flight was delayed."

Zoe released her and admired Aimee's perfect porcelain skin. She was certain God hadn't given her sister pores. He did bless her with incredibly fiery red hair. Tonight the long ringlets were free and glowing, providing a stunning contrast against her gold shiny dress – not a long gown. At 5 feet, 6 inches, only an inch shorter than Zoe, her sister showed off firm legs. Like Zoe, Aimee had the legs of a runner.

Her sister looked healthy and happy. Her cheeks held a rosy color. Zoe replied, "It's all right. The dinner hour just began."

The moment Zoe had been waiting for arrived. She couldn't wait to meet Aimee's future husband. Who would be the special guy to care for her little sister? She took a breath and Zoe looked into the face of the man that Aimee raved about. Excited, her sister did the honors.

"Zoe, please meet Shaw Edwards."

Shaw smiled, extended his hand.

"Zoe, it's a pleasure to meet you."

Zoe immediately felt her breath kicked out of her. She looked at his face, and then her eyes dropped to his welcoming hand. Everyone at their table saw how pale Zoe grew. Her legs felt like rubber. Garrett pounced, gathered Zoe up.

Leaning on his chest, she couldn't speak. Distressed and a medical doctor, Aimee studied Zoe's fading eyes.

"I think…she's….fainting."

And she was. Garrett carried her, searching desperately for help. Where could he take her? Deacon hurried to Ollie's table, bringing him back with him.

There was no way to be discreet. Like a ragdoll, Garrett held Zoe and followed Ollie into his office. Aimee spoke to her fiancé, "Please, let me check her." Concerned, but respectful of her wishes, he nodded.

"Let me know what I can do."

She ran off, caught up with Ollie and the others. Ollie opened his office door, removed some papers off the sofa. Garrett gently rested Zoe onto it.

"May I?" Aimee knelt in front of Zoe, called softly, "Zoe. Sweetie, Zoe."

All the while, she held her wrist, looked at her watch, monitoring her pulse.

She mumbled, "Aim…."

"Open your eyes."

They fluttered before opening.

"Aim…?"

"Sweetie, how do you feel?"

She took a moment, remembered the last person she laid eyes on. A cold sweat poured out of her. Woozy, she couldn't sit up.

"I think I'm going to be sick."

Garrett looked at Ollie.

"You have a restroom in here?"

He pointed to the right.

Figuring Garrett to be her sister's man, she prompted, "Can you help me with her?"

As if she weighed nothing, he scooped her up and into the bathroom. Zoe dropped onto her knees.

Aimee laid a hand on his broad shoulder.

"I'll take care of her."

Hesitant, he left and closed the door. Ollie looked up, his arms folded across his chest, deep fear in his eyes.

"Was it the food?"

"No, no," Garrett answered absently, "We hadn't starting eating yet." He kept his eyes on the closed bathroom door.

Thankful, Ollie sighed. And then they heard the contents of Zoe's stomach, flooding into the commode.

Ten minutes later, Aimee eased out. Both men were still on their feet.

"She thinks she's coming down with the flu. She said one of her clients had it."

Garrett wondered about that. She seemed fine all evening until Aimee and Shaw had arrived.

"Does she want to go home?"

"She does and wants to speak with Ollie."

Ollie shrugged and stepped forward into the restroom. Pale and trembling, she sat on the commode. He took off the tuxedo jacket, draped it around her goose bumped arms.

"Can I get you anything?"

"No. Please, don't get too close," she warned. He didn't step back, but forward and knelt down. Her voice shook.

"I know you wanted to introduce the foundation's board and staff members tonight. I can't stay."

"Don't worry about that."

His hand instinctively went to her clammy forehead.

"You just get well." She wanted to smile and thank him. She couldn't. "Please tell Garrett that I'm ready."

"No problem."

He stood up, stared at her a moment. She looked fragile and frightened.

"You sure there's nothing that I can do?" There was nothing anyone could do. Her eyes filled with tears.

"Please let Garrett know I'm ready," she repeated. Waveringly, he walked off to pass along the message.

Garrett rushed back to her side, prepared to scoop her up again. She lifted her arm.

"I want to walk. I've made enough of a scene."

"Just a little extra excitement for the evening," he teased and held out his hand for support.

They walked back into the dining room to exit. Some of the guests discreetly watched Garrett escort Zoe out. Shaw quickly joined Aimee.

"Is she alright?"

"We're taking her home," Aimee explained.

Zoe stopped, turned.

"No!" she pleaded, almost desperate. "I mean… please stay and have your meal. I don't want *you* to get sick."

Aimee lifted her brow.

"I'm a doctor, Zoe."

"Me, too," she retorted, "and your big sis. Call me tomorrow. I'll let you know if I'm feeling better."

Garrett observed Aimee's hesitation and Zoe's persistence. In the end, Aimee obliged.

"I'm coming over tomorrow, with Mom."

There it was – another wave of nausea. She leaned on Garrett.

"Please, take me now."

Chapter 42 – All Yours

On their way home from the fundraiser, they rode in silence -- something very unusual for them. Their hands were clasped together on the seat – each one staring out of their respective passenger windows.

As the limo halted in front of Desiree's home, she turned to him.

"I don't even know why I'm doing this."

Ollie looked at their hands.

"You do. We both do."

Yes, she was in love with a man that she had loved over a decade.

"Ollie, you're wonderful."

He smiled into her eyes.

"Apparently, so is the Deacon."

"I'm sorry."

"For what? Loving another? Don't be. I'm just glad he came back, before I gave you this."

Ollie sprung the engagement ring from his inside jacket pocket.

Looking at it, he said, "I don't even know why I carried it around. I bought it before Rayne's wedding. I planned to propose to you that night."

He slipped the ring back into his jacket, recalled the past events in detail, "The night before your sister's wedding, Olivia got sick. I couldn't go. You came over later that night and seemed disconnected. I held back on doing it. I started having dreams that you were like Sassy." He referred to his late wife.

Stunned, she lifted her voice.

"Sassy?"

"Yeah, I dreamed that you were cheating on me."

A chill ran along her spine. She may not have kissed Deacon, or even slept with him, but in her heart she was with him. Guilty, she didn't say anything. Ollie continued, "Unlike Sassy, you came to me with the truth. You never finished your story." He inclined his head, hoping she would now.

"Yeah," she remembered.

"So?" He grinned big. "When did you and the Deacon get buck wild?"

She wanted to leave things as they were. If he knew the truth about her past, what would he think? She forced herself to stare into his smiling hazel eyes. He deserved honesty and she gave it, "The night before my wedding to Sterling there was so much buzz going on. My mother was on cloud nine. My aunts were staying with us, my cousins and, of course, my four sisters. It was crazy. They were throwing lingerie at me and making jokes about my honeymoon. At twenty-one, I was a virgin -- believe it or not."

"I don't find that hard to believe, Desiree," he said matter-of-factly.

"I wanted my first time to be special. I knew Sterling would be considerate. But would it be special, you know? What would I feel? I didn't love him like I did Deacon. Once I said my vows, I could never break them. Since I hadn't taken them yet, I went to Deacon. I had one night. One night," she repeated remembering.

"What happened then?"

She frowned, shifted her eyes back and forth.

"We... did it. We...."

He sighed.

"Desiree, I know that. What happened after?"

"Oh. Deacon thought me coming to him meant I wasn't going to get married in the morning. When I told him that I *had* to go through with it, he became furious. Told me to put my clothes on and get out. I couldn't believe how cold he became."

Ollie saw a midst forming in her eyes as she went on, "I begged him to hold me. It was the worst way for me to lose my virginity. He said, 'You're nothing to me.'

Then he opened the bedroom door, screamed for me to get out. Mitch was standing right there, in a panic. Of course, I scrambled, pulled the covers up over my head, but Mitch had already seen me. He told us that Sterling had been in a car accident and that it was bad."

"Man," Ollie breathed.

"It was tragic. Sterling lost his ability to walk that night. We learned later the reason why Sterling was out driving. He was coming to see Deacon. He called my house and couldn't get me. And when he called Deacon...well...we were caught up. I don't even remember the phone ringing."

They both sat silently a moment as Ollie took it all in.

Desiree broke the silence with a questioning thought.

"After the accident, I was sure I couldn't back out of the wedding. We were still going to get married when he grew strong enough. That didn't happen. Sterling ended up cheating on me. I often wondered, even though Sterling never mentioned anything, if he suspected something between Deacon and me. Did Sterling know that I was with Deacon the night he ran a stop sign and an ambulance blindsided him?"

"The dude didn't deserve all that."

The life drained from Desiree's face. Ollie regretted his last comment.

"I've lived with the guilt since. I honestly don't know if I can be with Deacon, carrying this burden."

Ollie looked down at their still intertwined fingers. He proclaimed, "Desiree, if you have asked God and Sterling for forgiveness, you don't have to carry this burden any longer. I wish you would have shared this with me."

He lifted his head, gazed into her almond shaped eyes. It hurt learning how deeply she suffered.

"I put it behind me because...."

"No," he interrupted, "you held it close. I always felt there was something between us."

"I'm sorry," she said.

"Don't be sorry, Desiree. Be happy. I want that for you. I want to dislike the Deacon, but I can't help but like him. Don't get me wrong, he did his boy wrong. So did you...."

"Thanks," she said sourly.

"Hey, he's truly a good guy. After all these years, he comes back for you and is looking to make amends. I thought I was going to have to warn you about him."

Confused, she squinted.

"Yeah. See, after Sassy and I broke up once, I went back to her, for her money. I didn't want to work."

"You?"

"I was way out of my place as a man. Thinking about my past, I thought Deacon might be playing *you*. He's alright. He made a donation tonight," he informed her.

She looked shocked.

"A thousand dollars. The good Deacon gets his tickets for free from Zoe and he turns around and pays for them."

Desiree closed her eyes.

"What am I going to do with Deacon? He's...so...different, open, trusting."

Ollie smirked, kissed her cheek.

"He's all yours."

Rubbing his thumb against the back of her hand, he added, "This is not goodbye for you and me. Anything that you ever want or need, you call. Promise me?"

She stared into his eyes, calculated what she saw – no resentment, remorse or regret, she promised, "I will." Her tears watered her face.

"Olivia," she mumbled.

"You're welcome to visit her anytime. I hope you will."

They held each other for a long time before Ollie walked Desiree to her door for the last time.

Chapter 43 – Not Now, Maybe Not Ever

Garrett followed Zoe into her living room. She fell onto the sofa, motioned with her hand for him to do the same.

"Is there anything I can do for you?" he asked politely.

She shook her head.

"I just want to get out of this dress."

She looked down at all the black flowing fabric.

Lifting his eyebrows, he commented, "I see. You know you didn't have to faint if you wanted to be alone with me."

She felt better and appreciated his lighthearted humor.

"Not a chance, buddy. I'm just not the evening gown type."

He whistled.

"Not a chance? Ouch."

Smiling, she admitted, "I didn't mean it like that."

He knew she didn't.

"I don't mind waiting while you change. You don't have the flu. And if you do, I think you got it from your sister's fiancé."

Garrett had really good perception – a fine quality for a man. She'd tell him some things, not all, not yet and maybe never.

"Can I get you anything?"

Hunger getting the best of him, he asked, "You got some menus. I'll order dinner."

Zoe walked away into the kitchen and came back with a folder, handed it to him.

"All these places deliver. I spoiled your evening. My treat. Choose whatever you like and order me the same. I'm not picky."

She turned to walk off and he gently held her elbow.

"Just being with you made my evening, and since you haven't sent me on my way, I get to spend more time with you."

The blue pools he had for eyes, were full of warmth.

"I won't be long."

Back 20 minutes later, Zoe pounced downstairs. She changed into faded jeans, a red sweater, and matching fuzzy socks. About the third step from the bottom, she slipped the rest of the way and reached for the newel post.

Garrett got to his feet.

"You alright?" he chuckled.

Laughing too, she said, "I'm fine. I normally don't wear socks around the house. They don't work well with carpeted stairs."

"Then why are you wearing them?" he asked, still laughing.

"My feet are cold," she easily stated and walked over to him.

He had removed his jacket and tie, unbuttoned the top two buttons of his shirt. He appeared comfortable and very handsome.

Appreciative she hadn't scared him off, she timidly asked, "Mind if I hug you? I'm glad you were with me tonight."

He cleared his throat, opened his arms and she walked into his embrace. She trembled. She was cold.

"I could get a fire going," he offered.

"That would be nice."

She stepped out of his arms, watched him expertly prepare and light the fire.

"You do that well."

"I have a ranch house in Pennsylvania. When I'm home, which is rare, I like fires, too."

He joined her on the sofa, but sat back in the corner, crossed his long legs, and rested his arm. His respect for her kept him from reaching for her. She seemed vulnerable and very alluring. Careful, he reached over and took her hand.

"I'll listen."

He had been patient, so she began, "I knew my sister's fiancé as Thomas Edwards. I called him Tom."

"How long ago?"

She let out a breath, counted back.

"Eighteen years. We met in college – had a volatile relationship. It ended badly. I hated him for a long time. I thought I was over it."

She shrugged.

"Tough break for you and Aimee," he commented.

She agreed, "I really don't know what to do here. Should I tell her? I don't think he remembers me."

He considered and rubbed her hand.

"Eighteen years is a long time. Yet, I don't think I could ever forget someone like you."

"That's sweet. I was a different person back then. In my rebellion years, I colored my hair bright red."

He jumped in, "Like your sister?"

"Not like Aimee. Rambunctious, the color of fruit punch. It earned me the name, Punchy. I was also thinner, awkward, and lanky back then."

Garrett attempted to get the vision of her in his mind's eye. He smiled, decided, "You must have been cute."

"Not to my mother. To Tom, I was a wild child and just what he wanted...for a little while."

"Years later, you're the beautiful Dr. Zoe Landry, and your sister is the intriguing Dr. Aimee Cartwright, engaged to Thomas Shaw Edwards. *You* are involved in quite a triangle," he said, thinking of Deacon, Desiree and Ollie.

They both didn't speak for a while. Garrett concluded, "Tom must have done something awfully terrible for you to react the way you did after seeing him tonight. You don't want to tell me, do you?"

She didn't. The pain had resurfaced, she requested, "Mind if I don't?"

"I do. I don't want you upset. Maybe after you pray about it, you can tell me."

"Pray about it," she thought. She hadn't considered prayer, wondered why she had forgotten to pray.

The doorbell sounded off.

"That must be our food," Garrett stood.

"I'll take care of it."

Chapter 44 – Something Told Me to…I Didn't Listen

After Garrett left, Zoe spent the rest of the evening praying until Chelsea interrupted with a visit. Aimee might have bought the "I think I have the flu routine," but Chelsea wouldn't pay two cents for it.

A nightlight glowed as Zoe sat absently in an old-fashioned chair in front of the window. A robe tightly covered her up. She held a wooden cross-carved by her Grandpa Joe. Chelsea sat in the other chair next to her.

"You have a very strong stomach, Zoe. What happened tonight?"

Zoe measured the expansive room; the walls were covered by yellow wallpaper with prints of pink roses and streaming ribbons.

"This room reminds me of Texas."

"I know," Chelsea said softly, "you decorated the entire house to remind you of Grandpa Joe."

She hugged her middle, sat back in her chair, placing the wooden cross on her lap against the white plush robe.

"I think I should pay him a visit. I miss him."

"Me, too. He's a very sweet man. Since you're missing him so much, I know what happened tonight shook you up. You turn to Grandpa Joe when you're hurting."

"Not always. I've been praying."

Chelsea nodded. She wouldn't let up. "Talking is good, too. I am your friend, Zoe."

She was and she was grateful.

"I knew him as Tom."

"Who are we talking about?"

"Aimee's fiancé. His full name is Thomas Shaw Edwards."

"When did you know him?"

Zoe admired Chelsea's round angelic face. Her cheeks seemed to hold a powder pink hue.

"It was a long time ago," she finally answered, "in college. I met him in my sophomore year."

Chelsea believed she had figured it out.

"You two fell in love, he left you, breaking your heart. Years later he's marrying your sister…." She tapered off, waiting for confirmation.

A breath of air released from Zoe's nostrils along with a short laugh.

"That's a nice story. I never loved Tom. And I'm certain he never loved me."

Chelsea sat back and listened, carefully.

"We were in similar places," Zoe realized. "Rebellion stages, you could say. We were both Ivy League. That's where our parents said we had to go. At least I got to study psychology. I wanted to. He never wanted to major in law. We hooked up, and found we liked being rebellious and doing drugs together."

Her friend's voice filled with surprise.

"You did drugs?"

"I wasn't always a Christian."

"That I know. I just can't picture you doing drugs. What did you do?"

"Uppers mainly, we enjoyed those. When we wanted to come down, we smoked some things. We moved in together. It made our relationship easy, at first."

Trying to digest what she heard, she asked, "And your grades...y'all didn't flunk out?"

Zoe pursed her lips, shook her head.

"Surprisingly, we did well enough."

"So...how badly did it end?"

"Very, I got pregnant."

More shock and surprise, Chelsea's eyes popped.

"You had a child?"

"A pregnancy. It was very upsetting for Tom. That seemed to wake him up. His parents would have disowned him."

"Well, I can't imagine your mother dealing too well with it either."

Zoe answered quickly, "I didn't care what she thought. My mother married my father for love. He died when I was seven. We had nothing. Mother refused to accept money from Grandpa Joe because he was a Christian. Grandpa put everything in trust for me until college. Until then, we were strapped. Months after my father died, mother married Aimee's very rich father. Aimee secured my mother's financial future, not me. I became the shadow under her nose. Aimee was the star."

Chelsea had heard this from Zoe before. She understood why Zoe had at one time resented her mother.

"Having the child was a way of slapping your mother in the face," she deduced.

"That, and I *wanted* my baby. I was hell bent on having it, and Tom, he was hell bent on me not."

"You had an abortion," Chelsea whispered.

Zoe smiled.

"Will you let *me* tell the story?"

"Get on with it then."

"I'm getting." She took a breath and continued, "During winter recess I told mother I was not coming home for the holidays. That put a bee in her bonnet. She loved all the Christmas parties, showing off her daughters. The pregnancy gave me a reason to put her off and see Grandpa Joe. That was a good time. We talked a lot. He prayed with me – for me. Even though I didn't embrace my faith at that time in my life, it planted a seed."

Chelsea didn't interrupt. She had not accepted faith either. Intrigued, she only lifted her brow, hoping Zoe would finish her story.

"I left Texas, went back to school convinced I could make it as a single mother. Grandpa Joe said he'd come to Boston and take care of the baby and I would finish college."

"But Tom?"

"Yes, Tom. I told him that I had an abortion. I moved out of our house and got my own apartment. He seemed pleased enough. Naturally, my belly began to rise. Someone told him they saw me, still pregnant. He came to my apartment, high, and insanely angry. Something told me not to let him in. I didn't listen. I wanted to talk to him. Maybe help him see the child as a blessing. Our talk became a physical argument. He put his hands on me and pushed me down a flight of stairs."

Chelsea threw her hands over her mouth.

Zoe's voice began to shake feeling like she was back in that time and place.

"The fall knocked me unconscious. My mind was out. My body went into pre-mature labor. My son lived about forty-eight hours. They never let me see him. I woke up three days later with my mother by my side. She told me my baby boy had died and that I'd never have any more children."

Chelsea squinted. "I don't understand."

"Me either. Something went wrong in the delivery. I had a hysterectomy. I was nineteen."

Sadly, they sat in shaky silence for what seemed like half the night. Chelsea finally asked, "Tom?"

"He called nine-one-one. When they showed up, he left. I thought forever."

Chapter 45 – All Mine

Sunday morning Desiree lifted her arms, standing with her back to the congregation, and directed the choir of All Praise Church. The song, a church favorite, had the members jumping. Hands clapped, and feet stomped, as soon as the organist and drummer sounded off the first note.

Desiree's arms swayed as the voices accompanied the music with the words, "He's a faithful God."

When she quickly looked to the left, he seemed to materialize out of thin air. Deacon tickled the ivories of the piano and caught her glance. He winked. She rolled her eyes, turned her attention onto the choir.

The song ended, stirring up the congregation's joy. Desiree caught the organist's attention and signaled for him to play it again. Just as she began directing, she heard a familiar high-pitched voice. Mother Marilyn shouted hallelujah. And like a rush, her praise kindled a wild fire tearing through the building, lighting up the souls it touched.

Garrett and Zoe were Deacon's guests at church. Garrett had never been a part of such an explosive service. He looked up at Zoe for her take and found she was on her feet, clapping, and worshipping along with the congregation. She seemed caught up, yet not lost, understanding exactly where she was and whom she served. His eyes traveled to the choir stand. There, Desiree allowed her feet to dance in jubilant praise.

After service, Garrett had to ask Deacon the reason behind all the demonstrative worship. As a Christian, he never behaved that way in church. He never understood things such as the Holy Spirit. What did everyone feel? Why didn't they seem the least bit ashamed of their jumping, and crying, and running around the small old church. Even Zoe had become a part of this unusual behavior. These were intelligent, rational, upstanding citizens who behaved as if something in them tortured -- in a joyful sort of way.

The church quieted down and the minister took the pulpit. Garrett planned to focus on the message and block out all the questions racing through his mind. Occasionally, he'd look at Zoe. She'd smile and look back up at the preacher. What he retained from the thin older gentlemen in the black robe and purple tassels consisted of a lot of yelling about getting saved and turning from his wicked ways. "What ways? he thought, as service ended and parishioners started hugging and greeting one another. Cordial, their hands reached for his. He smiled and introduced himself and Zoe. He glanced over at Deacon and Desiree, hoping for a time to discuss the peculiar worship experience.

Desiree intentionally took extra time fellowshipping with the members that Sunday. Deacon eyed her with a mischievous smile. Glaring at him, she barely listened to Brother Johnston's praise of the choir. The very large man detained her in a suffocating hug.

"Ew-wee, y'all tore it up this morning!" he yelped.

Deacon slapped Brother Johnston's back, causing the enthusiastic man to turn and face him. Ignoring the annoyance in Brother Johnston's eye, he asked, "Did you enjoy the service?"

Rescued, Desiree took a deep breath, straightened her suit jacket, and smoothed her hand over her hair.

Brother Johnston stuttered, "It wh--- wh--- wh--- was, a good service. Good service."

Deacon nodded toward Pastor Jones standing at the back of the church greeting his exiting flock.

"You should tell Pastor Jones. I'm sure he'll appreciate it," he suggested with a bright smile.

Brother Johnston's hefty body rolled around and sheepishly walked away – in the opposite direction of the pastor.

"That was mean, Deacon," Desiree said, heading for the exit.

He fell in step with her, leaned in and kissed her cheek.

"I don't want these men squeezing my woman."

She repeated slowly, "Your woman?"

"Mine."

He slipped his hand around her waist as they walked toward Pastor Jones.

"Did you end your *thing* with Ollie?"

Her mouth opened with fire in her eyes.

"I got something for you. You just wait a minute."

She swallowed a groan, put the fight on hold a moment and greeted Pastor Jones pleasantly, "Good afternoon."

"Good afternoon, Sister, Deacon."

His golden complexion seemed to glow from the joyful service.

"I just want to thank you for doing such an excellent job with the choir." He held out his hand, shook hers. "Keep up the great work." Reaching for Deacon's hand, he added, "And you really played that piano this morning. You had the thang smokin'."

"Thank you, Pastor Jones. Enjoy the rest of your day."

As they moved along so the others could greet their pastor, Deacon leaned in, asked, "What you got for me?"

"Just wait until we're out of the house of God," she bit out, taking brisk steps to the exit.

He smiled, thinking she sounded like her mother. Since they were on their way out, he asked, "Mind if Zoe and Garrett join us for dinner?"

She stopped, faced him, and clinched her fists at her sides. Deacon braced himself, afraid she might belt him a good one.

"Dinner?" She turned her eyes into slits. His cockiness made her want to cuss on a Sunday. She grabbed his hand and pulled him upstairs and onto the balcony of the old church. No one was allowed in the space, nor was the church ever crowded enough to use it. It seemed like a good place to let him have it.

She pointed her finger into his chest as her head shook from left to right.

"You don't know my plans and you don't predict my day. You don't come back into my life, telling me what to do, or who to have dinner with. I am not your...."

Enough, he yanked her toward him. Fourteen years later, their first kiss was perfect. His mouth feasted as his hands held onto her curvy hips. She matched his hunger, wrapping her arms around him. Pausing, he whispered, "You hear that?"

"What?" she asked, breathlessly.

"Our hearts racing, I like it better than you mouthing off at me."

"Shut up, Deacon," she ordered and leaned in for more.

He did, and sampled her lips with a few more light pecks. Not satisfied, but careful for now, he said, "Desiree, I know you always have Sunday dinner with your father. It's the only reason I invited Garrett and Zoe. I'd like to get to know them better and I wanted you to be a part of my day."

Her breath and mind clouded from his intense kiss. She couldn't articulate that her father had other plans. She just blinked up at him.

Deacon provided, "I'll prepare dinner. So, are we having Sunday dinner, or not? Don't be rude."

Squinting, the only thing that came out of her mouth was, "You make me sick!"

He laughed loudly, taking her hand.

"I know. I love you, too."

They returned to the sanctuary. The remaining members fastened their eyes on them. Some in shock after witnessing their passionate balcony kiss. She gave his hand a tight squeeze.

"You really do make me sick," she grunted out.

Unmoved, he smiled at the gawkers and whisperers as they approached Zoe and Garrett. Deacon exclaimed, "I bet that's the most excitement that balcony has seen in years!"

They burst out laughing. Desiree tried not, too, but couldn't help it. How could one man change her life in just a matter of weeks? And as Ollie told her the night before, Deacon was all hers. But there was more, she was all his.

Chapter 46 – Certain

Just as he promised, Deacon tossed aside his jacket, rolled up his sleeves, washed his hands, and began preparing Sunday dinner. Desiree followed, tying on an apron and offering him one. He shook his head, declining, and began collecting foods for a traditional Sunday dinner – something that he truly missed when traveling. Desiree took note of the chicken, collards, yams, corn bread, macaroni and cheese. She realized dinner wouldn't be ready anytime soon. Since he seemed to know his way around the kitchen, she let him have at it and worked on a salad for her impromptu guests.

Pleased at what she decided to do, he grabbed a cucumber slice from the cutting board and popped it into his mouth.

"Thanks, I started to ask you to make us something to tide us over."

"Uh-hum," crept out of her throat.

"You still mad at me? You're the one that asked for it."

She whirled around, knife in hand.

"Deacon, I don't like your approach."

Dropping the collards into a colander, he commented, "You don't like to be happy."

Turning her back, she went back to slicing.

"So you think the truth is you make me happy?"

He started washing the vegetables.

"The truth is you're in love with me. If you say it, it might make you feel better," he teased.

Deacon could tease all he wanted. His lack of sensitivity disappointed her. Maybe he didn't know her at all. Maybe he didn't realize that she didn't like hurting Ollie. He didn't think how her decision would affect Olivia. There was more than Deacon in her world. She didn't want to forget that. She thought his insensitivity to Ollie and Olivia to be downright cruel. She bent down and opened the cabinets on the island, slammed around bowls until she found the one she wanted.

The noise alerted her sister, who was sitting in the living room with her husband entertaining Zoe and Garrett. Rayne stepped into the kitchen. A puzzled expression covered her face.

"Is everything all right in here?"

Desiree rolled her eyes.

"Everything's perfect. Deacon's an idiot."

He turned and frowned at Desiree with tears flooding her eyes. She squawked, "Rayne can you finish this salad and set out some cheese and crackers?"

She rushed out, using the kitchen stairs. Rayne and Deacon stared at each other. Baffled, he shook his head.

"You don't get it, do you, Deacon?" Rayne asked.

"Can you help me?" he asked, sincerely.

She would, but first, she finished the salad and served their guests.

She came back and found he had the collard greens and yams cooking, while preparing the chicken for frying.

"You work fast," she commented, sitting at the bar. She fixed his salad and asked him what kind of dressing he liked. When she gave it to him, he sat with her.

"Deacon, how long ago were you in a romantic relationship before you came back home?"

"A serious one…maybe five years."

"Well, Desiree and Ollie were pretty serious just yesterday. He was going to propose the night of my wedding. She feels guilty. Not to mention, she's still carrying a lot of guilt from what happened with you and Sterling years ago."

"What are telling me? She needs more time? It's been fourteen years!"

She didn't think so. "She wants you to acknowledge her feelings and understand."

He shook his head. For so long, too long, all he wanted was to love her. He believed this was their time.

"I'm just excited having her in my life again."

"She knows that."

Cautious now, he said, "Will you ask her to come down?"

Rayne did, but Desiree didn't come back into the kitchen until Deacon had almost finished their meal. Frying the last of the chicken, he smiled at her. She had changed into black pants and a long sleeve lavender t-shirt.

She studied the counter. Everything was displayed and smelling divine. It suited her that he didn't need help and believed it served him right to prepare the meal alone. He walked up to her ready to hold her in his arms. She shook her head, pushed him away. He didn't touch her, but whispered, "Desiree, *I* haven't loved Ollie for a year. If I had, maybe I'd have some regret."

She shifted her head, listening as he lifted his voice.

"I have no regrets. Honestly, if I would have come home, and found you would have married him, it would have nearly destroyed me. I made up my mind to come back and ask your forgiveness and pursue your heart. I put my trust in God about it. We let too many years escape because of guilt, secrets and dishonesty – everything that's not of our heavenly Father."

His loving tone captured her presence, he confessed, "I'm not proud of what I'm about to tell you."

He paused and explained, "I met a lot of women in my first few years away from home. I had more than my share. I could not commit to any of them. I used them for one thing and one thing only. In my heart I knew that a woman desired and deserved more than one part of me. I didn't care. I tried filling a void – a place where you left me empty. Only God could have filled the hole you left in my heart. I left New York, you, Mitch, Sterling, God, and everything I knew of him."

He closed his eyes and said reverently, "I'm thankful he found me. Truly, I was completely lost. He's forgiven me and I've accepted that I don't want any other woman but you, Desiree."

He opened his eyes, knelt before her on one knee and took her hand. "Desiree Raquel Davenport, marry me, please? I'm in love with you, deeply."

He had proposed…just like that. It had only been a matter of weeks since he re-entered her life. With her mind reeling, she sputtered, "We haven't had our first date."

Point taken, he agreed, "Have dinner with me tomorrow. We could see a play."

"It's not only that…it's been years between us. There may be things about you…about me…that might make us not want to get married."

He blinked up at her, concurred, "Right," and got up off his knee.

Looking into his eyes, she panicked. "I'm right?"

"Uh-huh."

He turned back to his chicken, afraid he had burned it. He removed it from the pan and placed it on a plate, noticed he scorched it. Desiree stood still watching him with her mouth open.

"Dinner's ready," he announced.

She touched her hand over the sassy flip of hair that had fallen over her left eye.

"You propose, and then bounce up and say, dinner's ready?"

He took his time, washed his hands, dried them on a blue dishtowel, and walked up to her. They stood toe to toe. He rested his hands on her shoulders and his forehead upon hers.

"Desiree, it's called proposing, not begging. I already know I want you. You're the one that's unsure. If you need time, or me to date you, I'm willing. If you want to go through pre-marital counseling, I'm willing."

Lifting his forehead, he wrapped his arms around her, gazed into her eyes. "I'm not letting go until you tell me, but I won't beg either."

With that, he said, "We've been rude to our guests. Will you help me set the table?"

Chapter 47 – You Think You Know Someone…

Their guests had been very gracious. Zoe picked up on Desiree's discomfort. She factored Desiree had mixed feelings about Deacon and Ollie. However, since it didn't involve her, she dared not judge. As a matter of fact, she thought a lot of Deacon from his hospitable dinner invitation. Even after she and Garrett suddenly left the fundraiser, he called and invited them to church and dinner. She figured him to be a certain man -- a fine quality in a Christian.

He didn't waiver on what or whom he wanted. And 24 hours later, he had prepared an incredible meal. They sat around the exquisite table complimenting every dish. Garrett especially liked the collard greens, he wondered, "Is this a Southern dish? I thought you were from New York."

After swallowing his cornbread, Deacon answered, "My father was from the South. He taught Mitch and me how to cook."

"Your mother?"

Desiree held her breath. Deacon hadn't mentioned his mother since he had returned home. It still hurt, it always would, but he answered, "She left us when I was three months old. Drugs. She wouldn't let them go. We don't know if she's dead or alive."

Garrett didn't touch it. If Deacon and Mitch wanted to find their mother they had the resources. He asked, "Your brother is a police officer?"

"That's right."

Garrett looked over at Evan, Deacon's cousin and Rayne's husband.

"And you're an FBI agent?"

Evan on the verge of biting into his chicken leg, admitted, "That's right."

Zoe smiled over at Garrett. Deacon and Evan were men that were of little talk when they were eating and he was full of questions. Although, he was world traveled, he had no point of reference for the day's demonstrative worship service. It somehow seemed to excite him. She bit into her candied yams as he continued to pepper them with questions.

"What do you do?" he asked Evan.

Garrett looked over at Rayne. She just smiled at him. Her husband wasn't happy about all the dinner chatter. Accommodating the guest, he answered, "I work in the homicide division. I used to be a homicide police officer like Mitch."

Garrett nodded.

"Interesting work. It's concrete."

"Not so much. A lot of it is analyzing data."

That's not what he meant and explained, "You work with people and have a superior you can talk to for guidance. It's solid work."

"And you don't?" Evan wondered, devouring his mac and cheese.

"My father's the chairman. But really, he's retired. I'm CEO and I do all the traveling sales. I meet with the pharmaceutical companies. Make most of the decisions."

Zoe chimed in, "Do you have a board of directors?"

"We do. My sister's job is to communicate with the board. And I communicate with her. I'm on the road a lot. She's got a family, seven children."

Rayne looked up from her plate and noticed Desiree didn't offer anything into the conversation, Rayne said, "Seven, wow!"

Garrett added, "She had three, adopted four more."

Rayne nodded, asked, "Garrett, do you enjoy your work?"

"I do. It's a great way to see the world. But I never see the people that take the medication. I read the testimonials, but your work, all of you, is more tangible. You see and touch people's lives." He shifted his head toward Deacon. "Especially you."

Receiving his gratitude, Deacon thanked him.

"No," Garrett offered, "thank you. And thank you for inviting us to your church today. It was quite an…experience."

Rayne laughed. Garrett flushed a little.

"I've never attended anything like it. It really surprised me."

Rayne and Zoe exchanged looks as if they could read one another's mind. Zoe spoke first, "You're wondering how a collection of intelligent, educated citizens could behave in such an expressive way, without reservation."

"Forgive me. Most people in other cultures around the world are not as educated, not as fortunate as we are. I understand their expressive actions. Today's service was almost tribal to me," Garrett said and Evan stopped eating.

Zoe explained, "When you come to know God, understand his love and sacrifice for us, it is not uncommon to show your gratitude in a demonstrative way. David in the Bible was a king; however, it didn't stop him from dancing and praising his God. His wife however, found it offensive."

Zoe turned to Deacon, finding him to be a very intriguing man. His posture was regal, his heart was humble. Smiling into Deacon's eyes, Zoe highlighted, "King David was a certain man. Sure of his position, faith and God."

She laughed when Desiree chimed in, "We also know David's downfall."

To their surprise, Garrett reported, "Women."

"You know the story," Zoe replied.

"I am not a member of a church. I read my Bible."

All forks and knives stopped moving. A Christian without a church?

That information was unknown to Zoe. They didn't discuss their churches, but she just assumed he belonged to one.

Evan wondered, "How's that working for you? A man without a church."

Garrett shrugged his firm shoulders.

"Fine. I'll visit a church or two from time to time. I accepted Christ a year ago, in my hotel room, flipping channels. For some reason, I couldn't sleep that night. On business that week, I had dinner with a beautiful woman. I thought I had the perfect life, money, houses, and women. But the woman speaking on television helped me see I was missing Christ. I said the prayer, picked up the Bible and started reading that night. I send donations to that church every month."

"You have a desire for connection. You don't find it in your work and you don't have a church." Zoe looked to Rayne who made that last statement.

Garrett realized Rayne's words rested on his heart. He didn't reply and his awkward silence quieted everyone but Deacon.

"God doesn't act alone. He has a heavenly host. He designed us to connect, to fellowship."

"No offense, I just can't see myself doing that in public."

Deacon provided, "You don't have to *praise* that way."

Garrett commented, "I didn't see you running around the church." Lifting his chin, he directed to Evan, "Or you."

"I have," Deacon explained, "Evan on the other hand, he has his moments."

Rayne rubbed her husband's back, smiled.

"Yeah, the BIG GUY has brought this big guy to his knees, a time or two."

Although Garrett was a Christian, he believed that he balanced himself on a different level than those surrounding him. Their presence made him uncomfortable. He said to Zoe, "I feel like I've entered into a new world. I thought I knew God.

"The good thing is," Zoe explained, "He knows you and he positions people in our lives to help us see him – to really get to know him."

Garrett was starting to believe that's why he had met Zoe, and now Deacon. He asked her, "How did you come to know God."

Zoe had to mention his name. She looked at Desiree and revealed, "Ollie's parents. I worked on a case in Florida that affected his family. I met his parents then. If there was a couple that knew and relied on God, it was them. I will forever be thankful for his family. It's one of the reasons why I've committed to Ollie's foundation."

Desiree spoke up for the first time and said to Zoe, "Ollie appreciates your commitment. As do I. We started this foundation to bless children."

Deacon gave her a smile, added, "I'd like to help, too."

She shook her head, not because she was upset, but simply because of who Deacon was. Of course he'd want to help. She remembered what Ollie said last night while they danced at the fundraiser. "Deacon's meant to be here."

Suddenly, Desiree remembered the orchestrator of her life. God had a plan for them and he knew what he was doing. Desiree decided to forget the guilt and trust God.

Chapter 48 – No, Thank You

Back at square one, Ollie stood in the middle of his gallery admiring how it had transformed once again. His romantic relationship with Desiree had ended, and considering the energy radiating between her and Deacon, there was no chance he'd remain in that circuit. Not too long ago, he had been an angle in a love/lust trio. The past events didn't go well. In fact, it turned out to be the worst-case scenario. His wife was gone. No matter how many nights he closed his eyes and dreamed of her, in the morning, she was gone. And now, so was Desiree.

Still, he had work. Only a couple of days ago, the gallery served as a five star restaurant and ballroom. Back to normal, it felt like home. The sculptures, paintings, and viewers smiled at him. He returned their warm gestures, hoping his daughter would come to love the gallery as he did. One day he'd pass all of his works on to Olivia. He and Desiree had discussed having more children. He really wanted more, a lot more. At the rate of his experience with relationships, he began doubting if more children were in his future.

Brushing the thoughts aside, he started in the direction of his office. She stopped him. His gaze lifted and locked into those eyes. Oh, she could still do it to him – make him stop, stare and surrender. The large backdrop he created for the fundraiser hadn't been removed. The cloth painting of his late wife slightly waved. Funny, he didn't feel the wind stirring and wondered where the breeze was coming from.

"I miss you, Sassy," he whispered, looking at that incredible face. His daughter held a striking resemblance to him. Yet, she had her mother's daring eyes. He had hoped as Olivia matured she wouldn't give him a run for his money. With a slight grin, looking into his wife's eyes, he had a strong feeling, she would.

He shared with his mother his daughter's daring spirit. She once said, "Sapphire had a gift of bravery. In her tangled world, it distorted her. Olivia has the same gift. With God and your love and guidance, she will be a force to reckon with and a strong Christian." He believed it.

A voice came up from behind, declared, "She's remarkable, the eyes mesmerize you." Ollie turned toward the soft voice, recognized the face. The hair was dramatically different. He replied, "She was."

"I read about your turn-out this morning. You had a great fundraiser Saturday night. I want to make this donation. Congratulations." She extended her dainty hand, offering a check. Ollie accepted cautiously as she went on, "The article painted you in a good light. You're very generous and committed to the foundation – the children. It gave me the courage to see you again."

"Why?" he wondered. Lacy Reid, the spouse of his wife's ex-lover and murderer stood before him again. He stated, "This can't be easy for you…being around me, staring at my wife's picture."

He noticed she had cut her hair really low since the last time he'd seen her, colored it platinum blond. Her caramel small oval face seemed fatigued.

"Answers, I need to know," she confessed.

"Talk to your husband."

Ollie stepped back and turned away. Lacy kept on his heels.

"Marcel is a liar."

Her eyes welled up. "I don't know what to say to my children about their father. I want to write a book about it. I need to understand why all of this happened. Why my husband is in jail? Why your wife is dead? I thought…we could help each other," she pleaded, staring into his eyes. They went cold and she started second guessing her decision of seeing him again.

"Lacy," Ollie sighed, shaking his head.

"I can't help you. Sapphire didn't tell me she was having an affair until she wanted out. I don't have details. I only know how it affects me and Olivia and I wished it never happened."

She smiled at the name, remembered she had a doll years ago named Olivia. "That's a beautiful name."

"Sassy named our daughter seconds before she died."

Holding her head down, she grieved and apologized, "Thank you for sharing that with me." She gripped his arm, peered into his eyes. "I need whatever you can tell me." Desperate, she persuaded him. Ollie had a very kind heart. She felt it.

"My book…might help other women run from a man like Marcel." She held out her hands as if he could see her brokenness. "Look at what he did to me."

He didn't speak and her determined eyes cast downward, focusing on Ollie's long fine hands. She opted against taking one. Instead she provided, "I can't move forward. I can't until I know something. Please. Will you…help me?"

She couldn't decipher the expression in his hazel eyes -- pain, confusion, disgust? Unsure, she handed him a folded sheet of paper.

"This is my phone number and where I'm going to be tonight. Please, meet me." She waved it at him. "Please."

He accepted the paper. She let out a deep breath.

"Ollie, I'll wait for you. This is important." Lacy turned and rushed out before he said no.

Ollie's heart went out to her. And still, he asked himself, "Come on, do I really need this in my life?"

Chapter 49 – I Only Wanted Him to Like Me

The school day was close at end. Desiree and her vice principal, Jack, had decided they were coming to the close of an unsure harassment investigation. They interviewed all their teachers, staff, students-- anyone who may have had contact with Tiona and Trevor and had learned little.

Trevor hadn't violated Tiona. That much she and Jack gathered. Not because Tiona fessed up. Trevor seemed too distraught over his good name being dragged into murky waters. It didn't add up.

Nothing more to be had, Jack and Desiree divided up their notes, decided they'd type them up for submission. As she crossed the administrative office to her office, she passed Karyn. Something held her attention. It stopped her, made her shout, "Oh my goodness, Karyn, your desk! It's…clean."

She replied sourly, "Don't sound so shocked. I do get my work done, eventually."

Desiree pursed her lips, *eventually* meant something or someone had upset Karyn. That was the only time she'd move like a whirlwind, cleaning, filing, organizing everyone and everything in a silent fury.

Since typing her notes could wait, Desiree announced, "I'd like to talk to you."

Karyn got up from her desk, dressed in all back. As usually, her clothes were tightly fitted against her full body, but no hint of cleavage or legs exposed. This had to be about a man, Desiree figured as she held her office door open for Karyn.

She started with an observation as she took her seat at her desk and Karyn filled one visitor's chair.

"You and Raymond looked like you had a good time at the fundraiser."

Karyn barked, "How would you know? You spent the night *highfalutin'* at the high society table, laughing like a hyena with Ollie's family."

Desiree let out a breath through her nostrils. Karyn was on a rampage. However, truthful, Desiree did have a great evening. Ollie's sister kept her in stitches until Deacon walked in, completely gorgeous with Nat on his arm. "There should be a law against a man looking that good in an Armani," she thought.

She'd rather dance around her tangled emotions concerning Deacon and focus on someone else, she asked, "What's wrong, Karyn?"

Karyn's hand sprang up and started swaying with her summary. "Raymond was the perfect guy all night…at the fundraiser. I know there's an age difference, but I was like, so what. Both my baby daddies were my age and stupid. So I think, maybe the younger generation knows a little more. Me and Raymond talked, laughed, danced, and then, he takes me to his place for a minute. I'm like, cool. I don't mind giving him a little somethin'."

Desiree lifted her brow.

"Karyn," she breathed, "you didn't! You and Officer Bonner work together, here at *my* school."

"He wasn't Officer Bonner on Saturday night. He was Raymond. And I liked him, a lot. We got to his place, had a couple drinks, and played cards."

"Cards?"

Karyn eyes enlarged.

"Yeah, I'm like wow, this is different. Anyway, about midnight, I'm thinking, either we're going to do this, or I gotta go. My babysitter was texting me. I tell him, and he says, 'He really wanted to spend more time with me.' So I know what that means. He told me to do *something* for him."

Karyn rolled her eyes. Desiree was staring at her with a blank look on her face. She clearly had no idea what *something* was. Karyn made an explanatory expression. Still blank, she frowned and finally the light came on…blaring.

Desiree cringed.

"Oh! Karyn! Did you?"

Rolling it off her shoulders, but not her heart, she causally admitted, "It's no big deal." Karyn lowered her head and said, "Afterward, he pulled my arms and put me out."

"Oh, Karyn," Desiree sadly replied.

With her heart full and ready to spill over any minute, Karyn said, "Raymond told me that I wasn't worth the dirt on his shoes." She bit her bottom lip as it trembled. Dez, I've been with a lot of guys. None made me feel as dirty as Raymond did. He called me… names. I hate him. I don't even want to work here anymore."

"Names?" Desiree repeated.

She nodded, making her tears roll. "He got, like, mad at me. Called me a trick, said, 'I don't need another 'ho in my life.'"

Desiree took a breath, not sure how to offer any comforting words. She understood rejection from Deacon when they were together years ago. She never, ever, experienced anything like this. Nor, could she ever hate Deacon.

Desiree came up and around her desk, draped her arms over Karyn.

"I'm so sorry. I really am. That was wrong of Raymond. And…twisted."

She considered the man guarding their school.

Karyn decided, "I shouldn't have done it. I just want a good man. He's a cop. I thought it was alright. It ain't easy getting a good man."

Desiree told Karyn something she had learned years ago. "Offering yourself to someone is not the answer. Trust me. This may be hard to hear, but sex outside of marriage is not a *good* decision. It's what the Bible says, and I have to agree. The marriage bed is undefiled. It is a place where you respect one another, express your love for one another."

Karyn leaned back, out of Desiree's embrace, scoffing at her words, she said, "You make sex sound holy. Men don't want that!"

She pointed out, "Besides, it wasn't really sex...."

She stopped at Desiree's serious expression.

"OK, maybe to you, it was. I thought he'd really like me if I took care of him." She wept harder now. Desiree remarked, "The right man will respect you. He'll be a gentleman. Wait for your husband."

Karyn started to say that abstinence was impossible, but the school alarm rang. It had their complete attention. Jack barreled into her office and shouted, "Someone is shooting on the school grounds! The kids are outside!"

Desiree, Karyn, and Jack ran out into the chaos. Teachers were pushing the children inside the school. Desiree started for the front exit and Jack strongly pulled her arm.

"You can't just run out there like that!"

Correct, she screamed at the teachers, "Is anybody hurt?" Mrs. Morrison was yanking her students down the hall and yelled back, "I saw Simon Barnes go down."

Desiree froze, her eyes locked in on Jack's.

"We gotta get to him." With a determined nod, he agreed.

Desiree turned to Karyn. "Follow procedure. You know what to do."

Karyn headed back to the administration office, got on the phone. Help had already been dispatched and the children and teachers were filing into the gym. She got the crisis team together and started notifying panicked parents.

Jack and Desiree rummaged into the cold streets, found teachers, a few parents, and strangers securing the children back into the building. At the front of the school, near the curb, lay Simon Barnes, conscious, but bleeding from his chest.

They knelt in front of him, heard the sirens fighting through the busy East New York streets.

"Hang on, Simon," Desiree ordered, lifted his head onto her lap. The cold sidewalk against her knees didn't bother her, compared to the look of desperation in his eyes.

"Tell my wife...tell my kids...."

Jack cut him off, taking his hand.

"You hang on and you tell them. Stay with us, Simon!"

Jack looked at Desiree and asked, "Where's our security? Where's Officer Bonner?"

Simon gurgled, "He went after the kid. He went running down Pennsylvania Avenue."

"Oh, God!" Desiree thought she'd faint. "A kid? One of our kids did this?'

"Trevor and another kid…," he wheezed and his eyes started to roll back.

"God, please, God, please," Desiree repeated over and over as the paramedics stepped in and pushed her and Jack out of the way. She stood shivering, not from the cold, but from watching Simon fight for dear life.

Chapter 50 – Not Gonna Let Go

Deacon sat in the cafeteria and finished up a turkey sandwich. The doctors had finally come up with a diagnosis for Nico. To fix him, part of the man's intestine had to be removed. Deacon's missionary organization had secured some of the funds for medical expenses, but not all.

He sat silently, praying for God to provide a way to help him come up with the shortfall. His eyes fastened on the flat screen television. The words flashing across the screen, made his heart rate jump. "Shooting at Public School in East New York." When Deacon saw the school number, he realized, "Desiree's school!"

On his feet, running to Nico's room, the hospital staff requested that he slow down. He couldn't.

Nico turned his head as Deacon slid in.

"Practicing your ice skating," he remarked. Deacon lifted his chin to the TV in the corner ceiling.

"Look, that's Desiree's school," he panted.

"Your lady?" Nico's eyes widened.

"Yeah, I…."

Waving, Nico ordered, "Go, go! I ain't going nowhere."

Even in his haste, Deacon had to smile. Nico had been considerate. He hoped by befriending him he would see how much God loved him. He explained, "I'll be by as soon as I can. Can I bring you anything?"

"I'm still waiting on my lady."

Deacon nodded. He hadn't been able to locate his lady friend yet.

"I haven't given up. I'll keep looking," he promised.

******

Having a brother that worked for the police department worked in his favor. He trekked in the frost biting rain, dialed Mitch.

"What happened?"

All over the news and scanners, Mitch understood the short question.

"Some kid started shooting. That's all I know. The situation's contained. The shooter's in custody. One teacher down, critical. Desiree's alright. She's in questioning."

Holding his umbrella, cell phone and pounding the pavement, he considered, "The children?"

"All accounted for and well. A few still haven't been picked up yet."

"I'm about a block away. Can I get through?"

"When you get to the blockade, tell a boy in blue to radio me."

Deacon slipped his cell in his pocket and let out a breath. She was okay. The kids were okay. But one teacher was not.

He began praying in his heart, walked up behind the blockade, stared down at the sidewalk. The crime scene had been secured. The area was marked where the victim had fallen. Most of the rain had washed the blood away but some remnants remained. Spectators pointed and whispered over Simon Barnes' blood. He shook his head, thinking of man's ability to destroy.

He signaled a young officer over, asked him to please contact his brother. It took several minutes before Mitch appeared. Deacon realized just how much of a cop his brother was. His eyes held no emotion. His jaw was set in determination. Mitch was angry. The navy blue windbreaker showing he was law enforcement was soaked as well as the rest of him.

Mitch nodded his thank you at the officer and indicated with a finger for Deacon to walk down to the end of the blockade. They entered the school through a secure side entrance – away from the crime scene. The stuffy heat in the school building warmed them.

"How is she?" he asked a second time as they stood dripping in the hall.

"I don't know. I haven't been in questioning with her. This isn't even my district. I'm here to help, for her. Evan's here, too."

Deacon nodded thinking of his cousin, the FBI agent. He asked about Desiree's sister.

"Rayne is on her way with their father."

Mitch started walking through the halls, Deacon followed.

"I'll take you in a classroom. It's gonna be a while."

Deacon appreciated it. He wanted to be with her. They entered the room. He removed his wet jacket, sat the umbrella aside, folded his arms across his chest, and began pacing.

Mitch studied his little brother. He had grown into a man – no longer a disarrayed wild boy. Deacon held love and compassion, Mitch didn't comprehend. He had cared for women, but never loved them...except one. He never told anyone about her and convinced himself it didn't matter.

Deacon stopped pacing, asked, "Could it have been her? Could she have been the one who took the bullet today?"

"I don't think so. Desiree is usually outside when the kids are on the grounds. Not today. She was speaking with the school secretary when it went down."

A sigh of relief comforted him. Wrong, he knew, and yet, he was grateful it wasn't her in critical condition. "Can you somehow get a message to her? Let her know I'm here and I'm not letting go."

Mitch squinted. "Not letting go?"
"She'll know."
Mitch's face softened, nodded.
"I'll tell her."

Chapter 51 – Consider Happy

That evening the foundation staff meeting consisted of only three--Ollie, his cousin Lily and Zoe.

On paper the selections had been made for students they trusted would benefit most from the foundation. Now the interviewing process needed to get going. The board sat in Ollie's small office, perused the long list of names. Interviewing would be quite the process. Not only would the students be interviewed, so would the parents.

Lily read the names assigned to her. She directed her suggestion to Ollie, sitting at his desk, "Michael's got an offer to use the timeshare in Florida. Can we schedule these for the first half of next week? I can join him and the kids later."

Ollie knew his cousin would do just that -- let her family leave while she worked. He asked Zoe, "You think we can divide up Lily's list? Handle the interviews on our own?"

Zoe smiled.

"We can. I was thinking about Rayne Ross. She's a therapist and works with teens."

Ollie considered Desiree's baby sister, Rayne. Working late hours wasn't something he preferred. It took away time from his child. He liked the idea.

"I'll call Rayne."

"No, I got it," Zoe jumped in. Ollie seemed tired. She looked at Lily on her right and considered, "It'll be good for you to vacation. Between your practice and your husband's construction company, and now the foundation, I don't know how you do it."

Lily admitted, "Michael and I worked out a really good system. But now with baby number three, on the way...," she patted her round belly, "we've been talking about reducing my work schedule."

Before Ollie became alarmed, Lily continued, "I'm not reducing my hours at the foundation. I really want to be a part of this – for you, Sapphire and Olivia. I'm reducing my practice at church. It's time to bring in another attorney."

The fact that Lily had a spouse, someone to discuss work and family with, saddened Ollie. He expected losing Desiree would hit him, and now the hollow feeling had begun eating at him.

As Zoe and Lily continued to discuss the agenda, his mind floated. He heard of the shooting at her school earlier that day, left messages for her. There had been several moments throughout his day that he contemplated going to the school. Yet, after speaking with Mitch and finding out that Deacon was at her side, he stayed put.

The ladies laughter reeled him back. He saw Zoe's hand resting on Lily's belly.

"Wow, that's one strong baby."

"Yeah, he or she is. This one is more active than my first two." His ringing desk phone quieted the room and Ollie answered and then handed the phone to Lily.

"Michael."

"Oh, shoot." She accepted the phone. "Sorry honey, I didn't hear my cell. Everything alright?"

Michael must have said "No" because Lily looked slightly concerned. "I'm on my way. Love you, too."

Having the expression of a concerned girlfriend, Zoe inquired, "Can we do anything to help?"

"No, no." Lily eased out of her chair. "Nicky's throwing up."

Ollie remembered, "Olivia had a stomach bug a few weeks ago. I guess it's still going around." He shoved his desolate feelings concerning Desiree aside, decided to walk Lily to her car.

"Zoe," he asked politely, "will you give us a minute?"

"Take your time." She smiled. "I need to check my messages."

On their way to the front of the gallery, they walked casually. At 6:30 on a Monday evening, viewers gallivanted.

Lily asked, "Have you heard from her today?" He shook his head no.

Lily commented, "I'm sure she's alright. The media reported only one teacher had been injured. She has to be insanely busy – her students, her teachers, her school. It's a fire pit right now."

He knew that, knew she didn't have to go through the fire alone. He admitted, "It's not just me missing her. I'm thinking about my future. I went from getting ready to marry again, to being single."

She quoted a familiar Scripture, "I know the plans I have for you. Plans to prosper you to give you a hope and a future. Trust God with your future."

Ollie did, he also wanted to know if God would approve of him helping Lacy Reid with her book. Deep down, the family would not support the idea. So he didn't bring it up as they moved out into the evening air and approached Lily's vehicle.

Before Lily descended into the driver's seat, she held her cousin's handsome face between her hands.

"I know it's too soon to hear this, but I'm feeling happy tonight."

He joked, "You stay happy."

"It's easier to be happy, than not." She lifted her brows. "Zoe, I really like her. Maybe you should consider...."

He interrupted, "She had a date Saturday night. I don't know."

"I said, consider. She has a compassionate spirit. It's soothing."

"Like you."

He smiled with his face in her hands; lifting his, he rested his hands over hers. She smiled, too, searching his sorrowful eyes. He had been through so much, hurt so much. He needed compassion. "Get to know Zoe…see where it leads."

Concerned, he acknowledged, "She's white."

Frowning, she requested, "Why should that be an issue?"

"Vaughn…," he mentioned his sister.

Lily stopped him, "You know Vaughn's always protective. I can see why she would bring it up. Race is only an issue if you let it be."

She had a point and it wasn't an issue for him.

Chapter 52 – *You* Put *Somethin'* on *Me*

Zoe had checked her messages and was on the phone with Rayne Ross regarding the student and parent interviews. She glanced over, saw Ollie walk back in and take his seat.

"Great. Thanks Rayne. We really appreciate this. Lily can use the time off with her family. How's Desiree?"

He didn't hear Rayne's response, but when he heard Desiree's name, Ollie held his breath. He watched Zoe pace, talking on the phone. He heard her say, "Yes, tell her I'm praying for her. If there is anything that I can do, please don't hesitate to call me. Take care, Rayne." Zoe ended the call.

Taking her seat, she said, "She's alright. Still in questioning, then she has an emergency school board meeting."

He nodded. "Thanks, I figured she has a lot going on."

Zoe tilted her head, to be eye level with him.

"You talk…I'll listen."

Sitting back in his seat, he sighed.

"Dr. Landry, I'm good. Things are the way they should be. Deacon is good for her."

Zoe felt her mouth drying. She took a sip from her water bottle, wished for fresh lemon. "Why do you say that?" she asked.

"Simple, she has been in love with the man for years. We would have never been as close as a husband and wife should. Deacon would always have been in the middle."

She pursed her lips at his healthy attitude. Finding her big brown eyes easy to focus on, he continued, "It must be nice, falling in love and being friends first."

In her profession she would have prompted with a question, but he wanted to talk – she didn't have to ask.

"Sassy and I started out physical," he explained. "I caught her act a few times. She was an exotic dancer. I made myself a regular of her performances. After a while, she noticed me. I didn't think she'd accept my dinner invitation. I wasn't flashy like the guys I'd usually see her leave the club with. But she did. Our physical relationship started that night. The woman put something on me." He smirked.

Zoe nodded slightly. Ollie apologized, "I hope I didn't offend you."

"No." She smiled. "Sounds like a very pleasant memory. Go on," she invited.

Encouraged, he propped his elbow on the desk and pushed his fingers into his temple, closed his eyes, and continued, "I never met any woman like her. I felt guilty being intimate with her. She didn't. See, I grew up in church and knew our relationship was not Bible based.

Trying to justify it, we moved in together for three years. As time went on, I got away from my place in Christ and my gifts didn't work anymore. I couldn't paint. Lazy, I didn't work and separated myself from my family. Sassy took care of me. Whatever I needed, she provided. In return, she wanted me to marry her. I stalled. She left me."

At some point Zoe realized they had reconciled, married, and had a child. What she didn't know, she asked, "Why are you thinking about this now?"

"I thought I had with Desiree what Sassy and I didn't have -- a friendship. Then...she would become my wife – my lover. I thought I was doing this God's way."

"You were and you did have the friendship aspect. I can see that. It hurts losing a friend."

They sat silently for a while. He apologized, "You're not here to listen to me."

"Ollie, I will listen as long as you talk. And I agree, whomever you choose to marry should have you and you only in their heart."

There it was, that compassion Lily mentioned only minutes ago. It enveloped him like a heated blanket. Cozy, he sat on the verge of crossing a line and, finally, crossed over.

"You?" He lifted his chin. "How serious are things between you and Garrett?"

She fastened on his hazel eyes, felt his direct gaze dance shivers along her spine. Powerful, it silenced her.

Unsure why she stopped talking, he regretted the question. They sat gazing at each other until her ringing cell interrupted.

Ollie stood to give her some privacy.

"Wait!" she called after him.

He kept going and stopped at the door.

"I shouldn't have asked that. I'm sorry."

He eased out.

Zoe looked down at Garrett's name blinking on her phone.

Chapter 53 – You Sure You Want the Truth?

Always the gentleman, Ollie secured Zoe in a cab after their board meeting ended. He realized she hadn't answered his question about Garrett and he didn't dare ask it again.

Sitting in his car, he wondered which direction to take. He could go home, spend quiet time with God. Or, he could meet Lacy Reid. Olivia was spending the evening with his aunt and uncle. He didn't *have* to rush home.

His eyes peered at his glove compartment. He opened it. Inside were 20 handwritten letters from Marcel Reid. Why did the man feel compelled to communicate with him? More importantly, he wondered why did he allow him to? He had read every single letter and placed them into his glove compartment.

Ollie sat holding the letters in his hand, thinking about Desiree. *She* had held Deacon for years. In some ways, he still held onto Sassy. Could writing a book with Lacy Reid be a healing process for him? If so, would he forget, let it all go? Returning the letters to their holding place, he steered his car in the direction of Park Slope to find out.

******

Lacy Reid sipped on her second mixed drink and spotted him. The man oozed sex appeal. She couldn't understand why Sapphire had need of her husband. Or why Marcel had need of Sapphire. Ten years ago, Lacy said her vows and meant them. She had been a faithful wife, caring for her husband and children. She rarely denied him intimacy. So why? Why did he have the affair?

Ollie's eyes scanned the room. He didn't see her. It should have been easy with her platinum blond hair-do. She waved until his head turned in her direction. Nodding, he walked in her direction.

She thanked him when he approached her table.

"Can I order you a drink?"

"Water is fine."

He joined her. Calling over a server, she ordered his water and some nachos.

"Long day?" she asked. He looked tired.

Before he could answer, she said, "Hey, your girlfriend, she's the principal at the school shooting today. It's all over the news."

He took in the buzzing bar and grill. Sure enough, there was footage of the incident on television. He could see a distraught Desiree and her assistant principal on the ground – the victim's head in Desiree's lap. Thankfully, the footage didn't show the open wound in the teacher's chest.

He explained, taking his eyes away from the screen, "We're not dating anymore."

She wanted to ask what happened, but she had a list of other questions for him.

"So," she hit him with her first one, "have you decided to work with me?"

Ollie folded his arms across the table. "Lacy, I really don't know how this is going to go. I haven't prayed about it."

She lifted a thin arched brow. Placing his hand on his heart, he admitted, "I'm a man of faith. And right now, I have a lot going on. I need to move on too. That's why I'm here."

Fair enough, for now she'd take it and pulled out her voice recorder. He lifted his hands, waved, "Hold up. You're recording me?"

Shifting her eyes back and forth, she said, "Well, yeah. I need to keep the facts straight."

"Have you written any other books?"

"Yes and no." She smiled. "Writing is a hobby of mine. I never published anything."

"But you want to publish this?" He lifted his eyes as the server rested their nachos and water.

"I think this is worth publishing. Don't you?"

Ollie thanked the server, drank some of his water. "I don't know. Men and women sleep around all the time. What makes this so special?"

Dipping into the nachos, she took a bite and stated the obvious, "Your wife is dead, my husband is in jail."

He kept silent for a while then dug into the nachos.

"Shoot. Ask me whatever you want?"

Hitting the record button, she began, "Who do you think initiated the relationship?"

"Marcel," he said without thinking twice.

"Why?"

"If you knew my wife, you wouldn't ask. She never had to approach any man."

Quiet, as if she didn't like what she heard, a twinge of jealousy took over.

"Marcel told me Sapphire pursued him and that she enjoyed the chase."

Ollie scoffed.

"You're the one that said your husband is a liar."

"But your wife was a stripper."

"So."

He rolled his shoulders, defending Sapphire.

"You think that made her chase men? Please. It may have enticed them, but Sassy didn't have to chase them."

Offended, Lacy explained, "I'm just saying she liked the lavish lifestyle. She may have gone after my husband, for the money." She pointed her finger at him, pushing her point home.

Realizing he was actually very hungry, he gathered up more nachos.

"Look Lacy, do you want the truth?"

She shrugged.

"That's what I want."

"Well, act like it. I'm tellin' you that your husband ran after my wife and she loved every minute of it. And while he was chasin' her, he was sleepin' with other women."

He saw the heat and then pain flash in her eyes.

"That was mean," she told him, "you didn't have to tell me that."

"I did. You want to believe there was some innocence in your husband. There wasn't and there's none now. If you want to write an honest book, you're going to have to accept that."

Hearing that didn't bring her peace at all. It only made her angry. She raised her hand for another drink. Ollie pulled it down.

"If I do this with you, I want you sober."

The server walked over. She focused on Ollie and sent the server away. Her eyes drifted to the warmth of his hand still covering hers.

"You have beautiful hands."

The tone of her voice shocked him. He snatched his hand away. She laughed.

"I didn't mean to make you uncomfortable."

She took a deep breath. "Okay, next question, do you think that you were lacking in any way to cause your wife to have a year long affair?"

He opened his mouth, she halted him.

"The reason I ask is because I blame myself."

He understood, and answered, "At first, yes. I thought that. Sassy made me realize, it wasn't me. Lacy, I don't know you, but I can say it wasn't you."

Her eyes filled with tears.

"Thank you. I needed to hear that."

This time, she reached out for his hand. He took hers and gave it a squeeze.

Chapter 54 – To Whom Honor Is Given

After millions of questions from parents, teachers, the school board, and law enforcement, Desiree looked into the shocking eyes of her staff, her vice-principal Jack and Karyn her school secretary, Officer Bonner, school security, and a few other teachers and staff who stayed by her side.

She gave them a heartfelt thank you and forced all the emotions down that had been harboring in her chest.

"You all knew what to do today and you did it. Thank you. The last report I received on Simon is that he's critical, but stable. The doctors will not let us see him. I'm visiting anyway -- tonight. His family is there."

She took a deep breath, pushed to provide them with direction.

"Tomorrow and the rest of the week, school is closed. However, the staff is required to be here."

She studied the faces, knowing she looked the same way -- shocked. They were running on adrenalin alone.

"Any questions?" she asked her final question.

If they had any, no one said anything. She released them, "Please go home and get some rest."

As they started to file out, Karyn walked up to her and hugged her.

"Call me if there is any change with Simon." Desiree nodded. "I will. You got a ride home? It's late."

"I can walk."

Desiree refused to hear that. "Hold on." She walked out, down the hall and into the room where her family waited for her.

Although they were all there, her father, sister, brother-in-law, Mitch and Deacon, it was only Deacon's eyes that caught her. He walked over and embraced her. With a heavy sigh, he thanked God that he could hold her. She trembled in his arms and when the rush of the day's trauma flooded her mind, her knees buckled. Deacon scooped her up.

After checking her out, they realized exhaustion had overtaken her. Obvious to Deacon, her body and mind couldn't take much more, he said, "Mr. Davenport, I'll take her home."

Her father couldn't let Deacon do it alone. "I'll drive, you sit in the backseat with her," he stated.

All in agreement, Deacon carried her, passing Karyn along the way. "Oh, my God!" Karyn shouted.

"She's fine. We're taking her home."

Desiree mumbled, "Karyn?"

Deacon replied, "She's alright. Just rest, we're taking you home."

"Karyn," she repeated, "take Karyn home."

Deacon looked at Mitch for assistance.

"I'll take Karyn," Mitch offered as they cleared out.

Deacon sat in the backseat of the car, laid Desiree's head onto his lap. He wanted to soothe her and gently caressed her face with his fingertips. It didn't work. She struggled and sat up.

"You fight too much."

He smiled at her, but let her ease up.

"I'm alright."

She felt her head float again as she sat up, saw her father driving Deacon's borrowed Mercedes.

William Davenport looked back.
"Honey just rest. Your body is forcing you to. And I'm enjoying driving this fine piece of machinery."

Mocking her with lifted eyebrows, Deacon smirked, patted his lap. "Lie down and let me care for you."

"No," she demanded, "take me to the hospital. I need to see Simon."

William drove under the light drizzle and listened to Deacon's best argument. Getting nowhere with his stubborn daughter, he suggested, "If you lie down, I'll drive you to the hospital." That suggestion seemed to work. Desiree listened to her father and Deacon let out a breath as she closed her eyes and floated onto his lap. Deacon held her hand. God, he loved this woman and her determination.

They arrived at the hospital 40 minutes later and had to wake Desiree after they found a parking space. The hospital staff was very accommodating when they recognized she was the principal. She found Simon sleeping with plastic tubing down his throat, his wife's face resting on the bed as she clutched her husband's hand.

"Tracy," Desiree whispered before crossing the threshold. She looked up, seeing her husband's boss and an attractive man at her side. She had never seen Desiree look so disheveled. Although she had tucked her blouse into her skirt, it was wrinkled, along with her suit jacket. Her hosiery was torn and she was certain, she saw her husband's blood on her white blouse. She motioned with her hands for them to come closer.

"How is he?" Desiree asked.

After giving her husband a long stare, watching the pressure of the oxygen machine rise and fall, she declared, "He's hanging in there. Thank you for what you did today."

Desiree frowned. What had she done? She wasn't even outside when the shooting took place. Desiree shook her head and Deacon eased his hand into hers.

"I saw the news. You ran outside, helped Simon. You dropped to your knees, held his head in your lap."

She pointed, noted Desiree's legs. "That's how you ripped your stockings. Thank you for not leaving him alone."

Consumed with grief, Desiree nodded. Deacon rubbed his thumb over the back of her hand. Tracy noticed his tenderness.

"Who's this?" she questioned.

"This is my…," she hesitated, but stated, "my boyfriend, Deacon Stephens."

"Are you going to get married?"

Deacon grinned at Desiree's dumbfounded expression, he replied, "That's the plan. How long have you and Simon been married?"

"Twenty-two years. We have three girls. I didn't want them to see their father like this."

She turned, looked at her husband and then back to them. "They cried when they saw him, but they're okay. They're strong girls. I hope one day they find men like their father."

Her eyes focused on her husband again. "He's such a good man. He doesn't deserve this."

"You honor your husband. Do you mind if we pray with you?" Deacon respectfully requested.

Tracy was not a praying woman, religion and prayer stayed out of their household. However, if there was a God, she hoped he'd listen and help Simon now.

"I don't mind," she said.

Deacon walked around to the other side of the bed. He held Simon's hand, and reached across for Desiree's. She completed the prayer circle by taking Tracy's hand and Deacon prayed, "Father, thank you for sparing Simon's life. We thank you that no one else got hurt in today's incident. We thank you that the shooter is in custody and we pray that you'll bring peace and healing in his life. Lord, there is no rule in life that says we get what we deserve. Some things that happen in our life seem to be random. Leading us to ask, why did this happen? But nothing is random God, not to you. Lord, sometimes things happen to give us answers, to bring goodness in the darkness. Please, Lord, heal Simon, strengthen and continue to provide for his wonderful wife and children. Give Desiree and law enforcement guidance and direction. Above all, give us your grace to do your will in every situation. In Jesus' name, Amen."

Deacon touched Tracy's shoulder on the way out. Desiree offered a brief smile and promised she'd visit again tomorrow. Once out of the room, she paused, feeling a violent wave of grief. Unable to control it, her back slammed up against the hospital wall. She wept sorely. Deacon pulled her into his arms and encouraged her spirit, "It's not your fault. You couldn't have prevented this. He's going to make it. Simon is going to make it. Trust God. Trust him."

She held onto Deacon, sobbed, until she had nothing left. Stepping out of his arms, she clutched his hand, pleaded desperately, "Please take me home. I want to go home."

They found her father patiently waiting in the driver's seat. Deacon asked, "May I drive you home and then take Desiree?" William looked up and saw his little girl on the verge of passing out again. "Sure," he complied.

Deacon drove swiftly, wanting her to rest. After dropping her father off, he took her home. If she could have, she would have slept on the floor. Somehow she found her way to the second floor and into her bathroom. She needed a shower and took one. By the time she made it back downstairs and onto the sofa, Deacon had made her some tea and toast.

"Thanks."

She sat next to him, wrapped in a lavender robe, drank a little of the tea and took only a bite of the toast. He didn't have any more words so he decided, "I should go."

A look of panic filled her eyes. "Please don't."

Understanding, he nodded and remained close to her.

She leaned into him. "Mitch gave me your message. Thank you for never letting go."

Deacon took her hand, kissed it. "I love you."

She admitted, "I've been horrible to you. I'm sorry."

No more blaming or pointing fingers, he explained, "You have issues from the past you need to deal with."

"I know," she agreed. "There was another time that I felt like this, terrified, guilty and unsure."

Holding her hand, he gazed into her eyes, realizing the time she spoke of. "The night of Sterling's accident," he said.

"I was such a mess over it. I thought I'd lose my mind. You left and then I felt like I couldn't go on."

Deacon looked down at her hand, feeling awful over how his leaving affected her. He needed to know something. "How did you go on?"

"I honestly believe it was the prayers of my mother. And now I believe that it will be your prayers that will carry me through this."

Her words brought a smile to his sweet lips. He had no idea what was coming next. Desiree told him, "I want you to know my answer is, yes."

Confused, he frowned.

"You did propose, yesterday. In my kitchen...remember?"

His mouth fell completely open. He couldn't believe it. She wasn't going to fight him. "Oh, God. Are you serious? Really? Desiree...."

This time she brought his hand to her lips, kissed it softly. "Deacon, I could have easily been on the school grounds. The only reason why I wasn't was because Karyn and I were caught up in conversation. It could have been me lying in a hospital bed tonight, or worse. We don't know how much time we have left on this earth. The time I do have, I want to spend loving you. Deacon, I love you so much and I need you. Please don't let go."

She stared into his eyes, praying he would say something. Finally, putting his fist up to his heart, he declared, "I hold you here. I'll never let go. I love you. I love you, baby."

He leaned over and they kissed until her eyes clouded. She smiled, and whispered, "Deacon, do you know what you do to me? I want you to stay the night." She slipped onto his lap.

"Uh-oh," he said quickly, "I want to stay, but let me go. If we wait, our honeymoon is going to be so special."

She would wait. She would follow the advice that she offered Karyn earlier. Her heart overflowed with joy. He noticed her tears. "Desiree," he whispered, "please understand."

"I do," she murmured. "You're so honorable."

All those years she wondered why Deacon left. And now she was grateful. The man that returned was not the same. She had a divine treasure.

Not waiting to spoil him, she eased up and off of his lap, and ordered, "Go home."

He saw her smile and smiled also. Standing, he said, "Goodnight, Mrs. Deacon Stephens."

He kissed her forehead and went home to offer God praise for his future bride.

Chapter 55 - Failed to Plan

She awoke feeling refreshed the next day. Desiree rolled out of bed and onto her knees. She needed answers and she had every intention of getting them. But first, she gave thanks for Deacon being back in her life and for the support of her family, parents, and staff.

She finished her morning prayers and readied for work. Then she needed food and coffee. She sat at her island watching the news. The shooting at her school was still the hot topic. The police stated the shooting wasn't random. However, the victim was not targeted. "What does that mean?" she wondered. She would call Mitch, but now she returned Ollie's message.

He answered on the third ring.

"What took you so long," she joked.

She noticed he was whispering and she wondered if Olivia was still asleep. She asked, "Did I wake Olivia?"

"No," he replied. "How you doing?"

"A lot better than Simon."

Easing through his house in bare feet, he commented, "I know. Is he going to make it?"

"Yes," she declared, unable to accept anything less. "He has a wife and three daughters by his side. He'll pull through for them."

Ollie pressed the ON button on the coffee maker. "Good. Do you need anything?"

"Just some answers." She looked up at the reporter, now reporting on a fire just blocks away from her school.

"I wish I had them for you."

He grabbed two coffee cups.

Desiree put her oatmeal bowl in the sink and washed it. "How was the first staff meeting? Sorry I missed it."

"Good." He reached in the fridge for the cream. "Lily and Michael are going away next week. Your sister Rayne is going to help with interviews." She felt out of the loop, but she could not help. "That's good of Rayne. You know once I get things settled at school, I'll be back."

Leaning against the counter, he cradled the phone against his neck and boxed his arms over his bare chest. "Take care of the school. Don't worry about us."

"Thanks, Ollie. And thanks for checking on me."

"No problem." He smiled. "I know the good Deacon is taking good care of you. But you need anything, call."

She nodded as if he could see her through the receiver.

"The same goes here. Is Olivia up yet?"

Ollie paused when he saw Lacy find her way into the kitchen wearing just her bra and underwear. The reality of what he had done smiled awkwardly at him and took a seat at the small kitchen table.

Desiree repeated, "Ollie? Ollie?"

"Uh, no. I mean she spent the night with my aunt and uncle."

"Well, give her a kiss for me."

"I will. Take care, Desiree."

Ollie ended the call and rested his cell phone. He turned his back and focused on the coffee pot, ashamed to look at her now.

"Do you drink coffee?"

"Yes, black is fine."

Pouring a mug for her, he wondered, "Would you like for me to get you a robe?"

"No need. I'm just going to have a quick cup and go. My mother is getting my children to school. And I need to go to the hospital, check on Dad."

Adding a little cream to his cup, he joined her and took a sip. He felt awful. They had talked well into the night. He offered her a ride home, but she said she wanted to see his basement. He had created several large paintings of his late wife for his daughter.

After the showing, they eased upstairs, talked longer. Due to the lateness of the hour, Lacy asked if she could just crash on his couch. He agreed. However, an hour later she had slipped into bed with him. Ollie couldn't believe what he had done.

"I'm sorry," he said. Lacy ran her hand over her short hair.

"You have nothing to apologize for. It has been a really long time for me. I could tell for you too. I don't trust most men anymore. I trust you, Ollie."

"Hmm," he replied and realized, "What now?"

She darted her eyes around his cozy home, then shrugged, lowered her eyes into the coffee mug. "I didn't plan this."

"Lacy...."

She knew he was struggling.

"Ollie, you don't owe me anything. Don't feel obligated. I wanted what happened...just wanted to feel close to a good man. To feel loved, if only for a little while. And you're amazing. Thank you."

He didn't know he could feel violated. It sounded like she said, "Wham bam, thank you man!"

"I see." He stared into his coffee cup.

After taking a few more sips, she got to her feet.

"You mind if I take a shower?"

"Of course not. There are fresh towels in the bathroom."

With her cup in hand, she said, "I hope this doesn't change anything. Will you still work on the book with me?"

"I'll have to think about it, Lacy. I didn't plan this either."

Forgetting Betrayal *Brook Lynn Dorcent*

"I'll have to think about it, Lacy. I didn't plan this either."

Chapter 56 – Play with Your Guard Down…

Before heading to the gallery, Ollie met Mitch at the gym for a boxing workout. Boxing with Mitch was always intense. Mitch fought like a warrior. There had been several times Ollie reminded him that he was not fighting some street criminal. Today, he didn't mind getting his butt kicked.

"So…," Mitch said through quick jabs. "You hit some last night?"

Ollie bobbed and weaved. "Don't say it like that."

"Well, is the woman your wife?"

"No."

Mitch threw another jab. "Then, you hit some. She didn't charge you, did she?"

Appalled, he raised his voice, and took one in the jaw. "No, she didn't charge me! I told you, I don't even like her like that."

Mitch grinned. "You liked her last night.

Ollie circled with a scowl on his face.

"Why are you so uptight about it? You finally got some. Good for you."

"Mitch, you know what the Bible says."

After landing a few more punches and knocking Ollie off balance, he said, "Yeah, tell that to your hormones. Did you quote some Scriptures to your hormones last night? They didn't listen, did they?"

Angry, Ollie landed some fierce punches into his opponent.

"Oh, you mad now?"

Mitch came at Ollie with excessive force. Ollie landed on his back. Dazed, he looked up. He should have prepared himself, instead of getting angry. He knew Mitch's style.

Getting back on his feet, he decided, "The Bible is very realistic. I got caught off guard. I didn't find her attractive." Mitch squinted as Ollie explained, "She is an attractive woman, but what I'm saying is, I ain't planned to get with her. She just got up in my space and I didn't think."

"You got played. Women know how to take down your guard." Mitch said and pulled off his gloves.

Ollie thought about Lacy's sweet face and soft voice. Did she really play him?

Chapter 57 –Grace Feels Wonderful

Zoe ran with the joy of the Lord in her heart. She wore a red windbreaker that covered her bottom and black shiny skintight biker's pants that helped protect her skin from the wind. The voice of a Gospel artist bellowed out God's praises in her ears. She felt the grace of her God upon her as every muscle received His oxygen.

The feeling was simply exhilarating. Being a part of a life-breathing city like New York increased her energy level. Central Park lived for its citizens. Particularly, in the mornings, it gave them their first jolt of electricity. After living in the city for a year now, she couldn't imagine living anywhere else.

She pounded the pavement, her breath escaped, and mingled with the crisp air. She cherished the invigorating feeling, pushed harder, and ran until her legs sang. She could have pushed further. Regardless, she knew when to stop and allow her heart rate to return to a gentle pace. Taking a bottle of water from her backpack, she walked, listened to her music, and watched partakers of nature.

Already mid-March, spring teased the air. She flirted back, closed her eyes a moment and took in its sweet scent. When she opened them, she had clarity – clear mind, clear heart. She felt certain about her future, but first she wanted breakfast. "Just cereal and fruit," she thought as she headed home.

Several steps away, she spotted her neighbor Dr. Gina fumbling with his newspaper, morning coffee, cell phone, and overcoat. She smiled, always finding the distinguished gentleman in a rattled state. "Why didn't he get himself collected before coming outside?" she thought. A hasty character, she was thankful he wasn't her doctor. As they came face-to-face, she offered, "Can I give you a hand?"

Amazed that someone asked, he looked up.

"Oh, Zoe, good morning. I'm late." "As always," she thought. Holding out her hands, she offered, "I can hold your things. You can get your jacket on. It's a cool morning." She noticed his unkempt hair and waited for him to hand over his necessities.

"Thanks," he agreed shyly.

"My pleasure," she said and meant it.

"You enjoy your run in the park this morning?" he asked, slipping into the tan jacket.

"Loved it."

She beamed and he could see the workout did her good. Her skin radiated, glowing against the rosy color of her cheeks.

He replied, "I wish I had your practice and you had mine. Babies come when they want, and they don't stop."

He popped his collar, giving her a dashing smile.

She grinned big and said, "I'm sure they do, Dr. Gina," and handed over his items.

He took a sip from his cup and a fresh deep breath.

"Thanks for the help. Have a great day." He trekked off, whistling.

She smiled as she watched him from behind. Her little assistance seemed to make his morning. "Lord, bless him."

Zoe walked a few more houses down and reached her own. She climbed the stairs, went inside and into the kitchen.

Chelsea looked up from the morning news and her cereal. She didn't say anything as Zoe floated around the kitchen, gathering up her breakfast.

As Zoe poured raisins and bran into a bowl, Chelsea squinted. "You're singing."

"Am I?" She glanced up, reached for the milk on the table and smiled. Zoe hummed a little more and sat with Chelsea.

Hesitant, her friend added, "And you look great." Her bow shaped mouth made the perfect "O."

She asked slowly, "Zoe, what did you and Garrett do last night?"

Zoe shook her head, picked up her spoon. "Not a thing. It was great."

Chelsea wasn't buying. Using the remote, she muted the television. "Come on. I know that look."

Zoe lifted her brows. "Which one?"

She exaggerated with a seductive breath. "I feel so good and relaxed look. Your cheeks are flushed."

A grin lined Zoe's lips.

"What you see upon me my dear is the grace of God. I do feel so good and relaxed."

Puzzled, Chelsea pushed, "So, what's the story with you and Garrett?"

"Garrett is great. I mean, so nice. Really, I like him. There's just...."

She pounced on it.

"Just what?"

Zoe let out a loud laugh.

"Look at you."

Chelsea pointed out, "Hey, you haven't had a man since I've known you. I'm starting to think, maybe you are a lesbian."

Zoe scooped cereal into her mouth. "Well, if you think I'm a lesbian, no need to tell you...."

Practically whining, she pressed, "Please...there's just what?"

"No sparks between Garrett and me," she announced, matter-of-factly.

Chelsea's eyes scanned Zoe and then she felt her forehead for a fever. "The man is absolutely HOT. He's like something out of a magazine. Dark hair, blue eyes, great smile and his rock hard body... not to mention, he's loaded."

Her friend's observation was accurate. However, something else held Zoe at bay.

"Spiritually," she said, "Garrett and I are on another level."

Chelsea butted in, "He's a Christian, right? Now there are levels of Christianity?"

"No. We see things differently. For instance...he doesn't have a church home. And doesn't think he needs one, right now anyway. And finally, he doesn't agree with the way I worship."

Not getting it, she said, "Huh?"

Zoe explained carefully, "He thinks that shouting and dancing before the Lord is tribal or primitive. He doesn't believe intelligent, educated people should behave that way."

Chelsea agreed, "I think it is crazy, too, Zoe. But you're my friend, and I know you're not crazy. You've explained the joy and love you have for God, so I don't question it. Maybe you and Garrett can agree to disagree."

Zoe had considered that at dinner last night. But when he kissed her goodnight for the first time, she realized there wasn't any chemistry between them.

"Chelsea, we're just not compatible and we both know it. We're going to remain friends."

Chelsea knew her friend, that was final and a closed deal. However, she saw a smile frame her mouth.

"There's more. Give."

She used her hands, beckoning for more.

Zoe lifted her eyes from the bowl.

"I am feeling some sparks for Ollie. I think he does too, he asked me about Garrett at the end of our meeting last night."

"Really!" Chelsea shouted. "What about Desiree Davenport?"

Zoe brought Chelsea up to speed on Deacon and Desiree.

"How sweet for them, terrible for Ollie," she remarked.

Zoe replied, "I think he'll be alright. I'm praying for him."

Chelsea thought for a minute. She had never seen her friend excited about a man before.

"Seeing you glow like that, I think I'll start going to church with you."

Zoe smiled. "You're always welcome."

Actually, she had been thinking about it since Zoe gave her a job, a home and a friendship. "What are you going to do with these sparks?" she asked.

Zoe rolled her shoulders and decided, "Be a friend. He needs time to heal. He's still grieving over his wife, and now Desiree."

Chelsea shook her head.

"A friend? Girl, you need to date more." She sighed. "It's just as well. What do you think your mama is going to say about you dating a black man?"

Zoe hadn't given any thought to her mother.

"I really don't care what she thinks. She should be happy. At least she'll know we've ended our relationship," she said laughing.

Chelsea chimed in, "That's right...I won't be your lover anymore. I've been replaced."

She pretended to pout and they laughed until their bellies ached.

Chapter 58 – I Failed Again – Why?

Guilt ridden, Ollie didn't know how to come to terms for what he and Lacy had done. Where she had no regrets, his heart was full of them. He remembered all the negative thoughts he had toward his wife because of her affair. And now he had slept with another man's wife. It mattered to him, even if she was legally separated from Marcel. She was still his wife.

He thought about Mitch's comment that he had "hit some." That seemed only partially true. Yes, he fed his physical desires, but he fed something even greater and it frightened him. Deep down, sleeping with Lacy gave him a devious satisfaction. He had done to Marcel, what Marcel had done to him – had sex with his wife.

As he sat in his office at the gallery, he questioned if Marcel would have cared. Marcel believed if he invested in a woman, he owned her. And his greatest investment was his wife.

Ollie had no intention of disclosing to Marcel what he had done. In an odd sort of way, concealing it felt like a delicious secret. What was happening to him? He felt himself twisting in a web of rejection and recompense. He took a breath and checked his desk clock since he had a meeting with a new artist. The new display would have the place buzzing.

A knock at the door alerted him. He stood to meet the artist. His curator stepped inside, he asked, "Hannah, is he here?

She shook her head. "Running late."

She saw the twinge of annoyance upon him. Ollie had learned over the years the fate of punctuality. Hannah informed him, "It gives you some time. Dr. Landry is here."

His eyes lit up.

"Zoe?" he questioned.

Careful not to smile at his excitement, she explained, "Said she's passing through."

He shook his head in compliance. Hannah left to get Zoe.

Just weeks ago he had noticed how attractive Zoe was. Cautiously, his recent actions made him feel obligated to Lacy. A week had passed since they were intimate. After beating himself up about it, he returned her calls. She was ecstatic to hear he'd continue with the book project.

Zoe walked in showing off firm arms and an elegant little black dress. For the first time, he saw her great legs. The dress cut slightly above her knees.

Stepping closer to him, she extended her hand and apologized, "I hope I'm not barging in." Embracing her hand with a gentle squeeze, he replied, "Not at all. What's up?"

She smiled, turned and looked at the white sofa in his office. "Can we sit?"

He found his hand touching her elbow. "Sure."

Zoe sat and crossed her fine legs. She appeared gallant, as well as humble – a fine combination. Ever more appealing, his eyes swept over her. She had her hair pinned up, showing off her feminine neck. Stunning, she made him feel insecure.

"I won't stay long," she explained. Ollie shifted in his seat, tore his gaze from her face and neck. She noted his discomfort and went on, "I'm meeting my sister for dinner. She wanted to meet me here, see your gallery."

"Your sister…," He landed his eyes on her again, thought for a minute. "I'd offer a tour, but we have a new artist coming in tonight."

"That's not why I'm here. I wanted you to know I'm almost done with my interviews. Rayne has been great. We should have our final selections by the end of the week."

Remarkable, she was proving to be a great asset to his foundation.

"Zoe, you're more than competent. I know you've got it under wraps."

She nodded and smiled.

"I'm also here because you asked me a question a week ago and I didn't give you an answer."

Squinting, he waited for her to explain.

"You asked me about my relationship with Garrett. He and I are good friends. I wanted you to know that."

Unable to pull his eyes away from her beauty, he marveled, "Why do you want me to know?"

"Why did you ask?" She smiled at him.

Ollie wanted to kick himself for getting involved with Lacy. What would Zoe think if she found out? He asked, "Can we be honest with each other?"

"Of course."

"I find you to be an incredible woman. I realized that when I was dating Desiree. I felt a bit guilty over it and it caused me to wonder if I would commit myself to her. I guess Deacon's timing was perfect."

Zoe's heart began to speed up, thrilled with his honesty. He continued, "There's still a void. Desiree had been an important part of my life. Right now, I feel…" He feared telling her that he felt low, and unsure of himself. "I feel…romantically handicapped. I can't get involved with anyone."

The flash of disappointment swept into her eyes. Then he saw understanding. "You've been through major loss. It's not my style to be so direct. I admire your sincerity and your heart. You're a man of integrity. I trust you. I'm here for you...praying for you."

He blinked, remembering Lacy said she trusted him the morning after their encounter. His eyes welled up, but he held on. Confident he couldn't share his farce with her; he stood and cleared his throat. She rose with him.

He thanked her; "It means a lot that you're praying for me. I need that now."

His evident pain drew her to him. She didn't stop her feet from taking the few short steps and embraced him. "If there's anything I can do, let me know."

How could he be so close to her and not hold her? He had to, and he held on tightly. If he would have just been stronger, wiser, really been a man of faith and integrity, maybe he would be free to receive what Zoe offered. He let go, stepped back and she saw it in his eyes. He wasn't ready for her.

She ran her hand smoothly down his arm and warmly said, "Ollie, God's a comforter, let him comfort you."

Chapter 59 – Take the Truth and Shove it

Aimee absolutely adored the gallery. As their heels sounded against the marble floors, her eyes fastened on a piece by Ollie. It rendered her speechless, the colors shouted from the painting. He even captured the vitality and joy in the eyes of the children. Zoe beamed as her sister admired the painting.

"Innocent," Aimee decided.

"Yes, he is very talented."

Aimee heard her sister's voice flow like silk. She recognized the sound. "Oh…" she whispered as she turned to look at her sister.

"Oh, what?"

Aimee grinned. "I thought Garrett was your guy. I see I was wrong."

"Ollie and I are colleagues. I hope we're on our way to becoming friends," Zoe corrected her sister and turned so they could move on. The gallery was busy with the introduction of the new artist.

"Tell me about him."

Stopping in front of a sculpture, Zoe began, "He's a widower and single father. He was planning to marry. However, his girlfriend had some unfinished business. It didn't work out. He needs time. He's not ready."

Aimee nodded listening to the confidence in her sister's voice. She hoped she wasn't setting herself up for disappointment.

"And you're just going to wait patiently in the wings?" she questioningly stared at Zoe.

"No." They began walking again. Zoe realized, "We better get a cab. I have reservations for seven."

Aimee agreed. They turned and headed out to collect their coats and then into the nighttime streets. She stated, "What if Ollie gets involved with another woman? Where does that leave you?" She took a breath as the wind barreled into her.

"You're too beautiful to wait on a man with baggage."

They approached the busy intersection, Zoe lifted her arm.

"He's not a man with baggage. He's a man that has had a loss. There's a difference."

Aimee failed to agree.

"It's just a different bag. He's still carrying something."

Zoe had planned to have this conversation over dinner with Aimee. She had delayed it for a week after she learned who her sister promised to marry. She wanted to pray, to make sure she wasn't carrying any baggage – that she had her sister's best interest at heart. Since Aimee brought up the baggage, she shared, "I knew Shaw years ago."

Aimee blinked, wind sweeping into her eyes and her red ringlets flying behind her.

"Knew him? When?"

Zoe threw her fingers into her mouth and whistled loudly. A cab came to a stern halt. Aimee smiled.

"Impressive."

"Thanks."

Once snuggled inside, Zoe rattled off the address and the meter began running.

"Aimee, we met in college."

Aimee heard a shift in her sister's voice. The silky tone transformed into a coarse fabric.

"Were you involved?" Aimee asked.

Zoe met her sister's eyes in the dark cab.

"We were. It was serious, but we were not in love." She paused, afraid to share the hurtful past.

"Go on," Aimee prompted.

"Aim…we did drugs in college."

Aimee held her hand up over her mouth in shock. The cab driver entered, "Hey, what college kid don't do drugs? Don't be so surprised."

Zoe shook her head, decided, "We'll finish this over dinner."

Desperate, she demanded, "We'll finish now. Were you intimate with my future husband, Zoe?"

The cab driver lifted his brows and reclined his head back for better listening.

Lowering her voice, she said, "We did drugs and we moved in together. Yes…we were intimate and…"

"And what!" the driver shouted.

Aimee shouted back, "Sir, please!"

He just shrugged and turned a corner.

"And I got pregnant."

Aimee was surprised her sister would make up such stories.

"You're lying, Zoe. You were never pregnant. You never had a child. I would have known."

"No," she replied firmly, "you would not have known. I was in Boston. You were in Florida. Mom was keeping you occupied with ballet and debutante balls. I got pregnant; the only person I told was Grandpa Joe. Shaw wanted me to have an abortion. I refused and he pushed me down a flight of stairs. I lost the baby."

"Stop…stop!" Aimee didn't want to hear anymore.

"Aimee, I'm telling the truth. Shaw was a very violent man."

"It wasn't Shaw. You're mistaken. I know him. He would have told me something like that."

Neither one had realized the cab had pulled up before the restaurant. The cab driver listened intently as Zoe went on, "He wouldn't have told you. He's a coward. He hurt me and our baby died because of it."

Unable to accept it, Aimee insisted, "He would have told me. We're engaged."

"I agree, Aimee. Why didn't he tell you? Maybe you need to find that out. Maybe the man you're about to marry is not who you think he is."

Zoe didn't expect the ice to come from her sister. Yet it did, Aimee blasted, "Maybe you're exactly what Mom always said you were…trouble. Why didn't you tell me, Zoe? I sent you pictures of Shaw and me. Didn't you recognize him?"

"You sent me pictures on my phone, which I told you I could not open. I knew him as Tom, not Shaw. When you said things were serious, I left the states to meet him and he suddenly had to go out of town on business. I didn't see him until the fundraiser."

Aimee recalled how Zoe buckled after laying eyes on Shaw. She sat dazed and confused.

Zoe laid a hand on Aimee's shoulder.

"Hey, you deserve to know. I only want what's best for you. If Shaw kept this to himself, he's all wrong for you."

Aimee refused to accept the truth.

"He's not the same man. He's not. You say he pushed you…I don't believe he's capable."

Convincing herself, she shook her head. "No, he couldn't have. I need to hear his side of the story. I can't have dinner with you tonight." Aimee rushed from the cab.

Zoe started after her, but the driver shouted, "Pay the fare! Pay the fare!" She huffed, digging into her purse for money. By the time she paid and stepped onto the streets, Aimee had disappeared.

"Oh, God, did I do the right thing?" she thought.

Chapter 60 – Winner Takes All...

Lacy Reid had been telling herself for a week, "I am not going to fall for this man!" The reasonable inner argument did not change what she felt for Ollie. She replayed their intimate encounter over and over in her mind. It made her body relive it, and her mind did not understand that Ollie provided exactly what her body needed. It was just sex, she kept telling herself. Her heart said it was much more. Ollie was so much more. She was in fact, falling.

She stared at her father. Thankfully he was sleeping at home in his own bed. She hoped his rest was comfortable. He had recovered enough to be released from the hospital after the debilitating stroke.

He could not speak or walk, but he agreed to rehab. Lacy spoke for him, and created his rehabilitation process at his home.

They always had money, so she ordered the necessary supplies, equipment and hired 24-hour nursing care.

For some reason watching her father sleep in his black silk pajamas made her think of her husband. Marcel reminded her of her father. He had been that safe place for her. There was a time that she adored him – his power and confident attitude.

Lacy had been shielded in her life, first by her father, and then her husband. But when she learned of her husband's unfaithful ways, she left both men, taking her children out of the country.

She never imagined she'd get a call from her estranged mother with news of her father's illness.

Watching him sleep made her chest tighten. His muscles were already breaking down and the flesh on his bones began sagging. Her father had always been lean and in good shape – much like Ollie. Her brain could not stop thinking about him.

The night she slept with him was not planned. He glided into the restaurant that night just being his honest and sensitive self. She could tell he had no idea how attracted she was to him. She didn't want the evening to end and asked if she could see his home paintings. He warmly agreed.

Afterward, he offered to drive her home. She replied with an unreasonable suggestion. Surprisingly, he permitted her to sleep on his couch. Sleep never came. However, fantasies of hearing him passionately whispering her name did.

Two hours later, she gave in to her desires, peeled the clothes off burning flesh, and eased into his bed. At first, he squinted, taking in her face and body. Before their time was over, she was the one repeatedly breathing out his name.

Her memory flash ended when her mother waltzed into her father's bedroom. Even though she didn't live there, she failed to knock. That was to be expected from her mother.

Gracelle Yorkson was 58 years old. The years and her lifestyle added great stress to her face; however, with help from a good plastic surgeon, she looked to be in her mid-40s. And, of course, she never dressed age appropriate, wearing a short red mini skirt. At her age, she still had great legs. She eased off her jacket revealing a sleeveless white blouse and her bare loose skinned arms. Taking the other gold and navy striped chair, she sat next to her daughter.

"He said anything yet?"

Lacy looked into her mother's face.

"No, still mumbling. I thought you were going to Hawaii?"

"Slight delay. Enrique can't leave until morning."

Lacy couldn't believe the men her mother dated. Enrique was 27 years old. What was worse than that, he knew her mother was HIV positive. Her diagnosis didn't stop their sexual relationship. Gracelle crossed her legs and brushed off her skirt.

"How's the book coming?"

Normally, she wouldn't discuss her life with her mother, but Gracelle had much experience with men.

"I slept with him," she blurted out.

Gracelle's oblong face lengthened.

"You did? That's wonderful."

"How can you say that? You know who he is."

"So what," her mother said with a wave of her hand. "Your husband slept with his wife. You slept with her husband. Revenge sex is the best kind." Her mother's grand smile showed off artificially sparkling white teeth.

Lacy sighed, covered her face with her hands.

"He's feeling guilty over it. I'm feeling…scared."

"Of what? You did use protection?"

She couldn't believe her mother asked that question. Yet, they hadn't.

"That's not why I'm afraid. I'm afraid because I want him. And I know that's not what he wants."

Lifting her voice and one painted on eyebrow, she asked, "What does he want?"

"I don't know much about him. He had a girlfriend. They broke up. He's a great father. He's active in the community and with his church…" She paused trying to remember. "Oh, and he's very close to his family. The family runs a mega church in Brooklyn."

Gracelle's wheels began turning. Since Howard's stroke, they began talking again. She wanted to keep the lines of communication open and help her daughter.

"You gotta hit 'em where his heart is. Sounds like church and family first. Go to his church. Take the children with you."

Lacy didn't agree with that.

"My husband killed his wife, his daughter's mother. I don't think they'll accept me."

She had a point. This would be a test.

"Go," she persisted. "Go and see if they are really who they say they are – Christians or cowards… There's just one thing."

Hanging on her mother's every word, she waited.

"Why are you still married to Marcel? He's incarcerated?"

Lacy turned her head, looked at her father.

"Oh, nooo," her mother bellowed. "You want to hurt Marcel and you're using Ollie to do it."

"You're the one that called it revenge sex," Lacy replied.

"Yeah, I thought the sex was for *you*. It's for Marcel, too. You did it all wrong my dear," Gracelle explained, tapped one long finger on her daughter's shoulder. "You let your heart into the bedroom."

Lacy's eyes pleaded. "What do I do?"

"I have a great therapist. I'll set it up."

Lacy believed therapy would help, but her mother's therapist? Gracelle couldn't keep any commitments – not to her, or her father. Looking at her now, all she saw was the queen of denial.

"Your therapist can't help anyone, not even you. You haven't accepted your age. How many times have you gone under the knife? You have HIV…you're going to Hawaii with your lover?"

Gracelle Yorkson never felt offended.

"True. I've been honest with myself. I *know* how old I am and Enrique *knows* about my condition. You're sitting here, lying to yourself."

Feeling a surge of confidence, like the night she presented her unencumbered body to Ollie, she admitted, "I want Ollie and I want to crush Marcel."

Gracelle flashed a grin and swatted her daughter's arm.

"That's my girl!"

Chapter 61 – The Relationships We Build

Sitting before Deacon at the Starlight Ballroom in mid-town Manhattan, Desiree felt like she was sitting on top of the world.

The view was spectacular and so was Deacon. His smile in the dimly lit room absorbed her. He acknowledged, holding her hand in his, "I'm loving you in that dress."

Her dress was royal blue. It seemed to her that blue was his favorite color. The fabric danced off her shoulders, giving him a warm view of her subtle skin. She smiled into his twinkling eyes, and told him, "I'm loving you."

"I like it when you relax."

Stroking her fingers over his strong hands, she professed, "I plan on being more and more relaxed with you. It's easier."

She closed her eyes, and for a moment, exhaled. When she opened them, he said, "Are you alright?" Full with excitement, Desiree barely touched her seafood dinner. They were on their first date.

"I never knew that I could be this content."

It seemed he couldn't stop smiling.

"Well," he decided, "I think it's a good time to give you this." Reaching into his jacket pocket, he retrieved a black velvet box.

She gasped when he slid the box across the elegantly dressed table. Deacon continued, "A token of my promise and intentions."

She stared at the box, eyes glistening.

"Sweetheart, open it," he prompted.

"My hands won't stop shaking," she replied.

He opened it for her. The ring had a gold band and sapphire chips encased the heart-shaped diamond.

"I had it made while I was in Africa two years ago."

Shaking his head, he lifted the sparkling ring out of its former home, and explained, "Talk about faith. I didn't know if you'd accept me. I just knew you were all I wanted. When I met the village man and saw his work, I immediately thought of you."

Reaching for her unsteady hand, she held it out to him.

"My desire, be my wife. I promise to be a good husband."

"Yes," she breathed. "I promise to be a good wife."

After easing the ring on her finger, he asked, "Your choice of color for a dress tonight is perfect."

She looked at her shiny dress and the glittering stones on her hand. "I thought you liked blue."

He recalled, "I love blue. Do you remember you wore royal blue underwear the night we made love?"

"Oh, my," she thought. She put her head down as heat rose in her cheeks. She hadn't remembered that. But he did.

"I remember everything about that night, Desiree. It changed my life. That night I learned that intimacy mingled with desire and love is powerful. I spent years chasing, running after it. I learned you can't get that from any woman. Our power was created from the relationship we built, the friendship that we had. I cherish you, Desiree."

As they held hands, her eyes clouded.

"Dance with me," he invited.

There were no other couples on the floor. And in that moment, she and Deacon were the only two people in the room anyway.

Placing her hand in his, she let him guide her into the center of the room. He slowly wrapped her in his arms and let out a breath.

She rested her face onto his shoulder, inhaled him. "You smell so good."

He grinned. "I'm not wearing any cologne."

"It's just you," she remarked, "fresh and warm. Your scent thrills me. I can stay here forever."

Letting his hand trail up and down her back he didn't want to rush, but he knew he didn't want to wait to marry her. Needing to know, he asked, "What kind of wedding do you want?"

She lifted her face and gazed into his eyes. "I don't know," she whispered. Odd to him, he frowned. Just about every woman that he met knew exactly what kind of wedding she wanted.

"I don't know," she said again. "I spent so much time planning to marry Sterling. The wedding was going to be perfect, traditional. After you left, I had no hope, no desire. I really haven't thought about it."

Biting his lips, he realized, she was being honest. He had a plan. "Trust me?" he inquired.

A hint of a smile touched his eyes. Curious, she asked, "What do you have in mind?"

"Let me plan our wedding. But promise we won't have a long engagement. I can't take waiting much longer."

She felt the same way and offered, "Pre-marital classes are for six weeks. We can get married right after that."

Shrugging, she decided, "It can be on the day of the last class, if you want."

Yes, he wanted. Boy did he want. He angled his head for a taste of her sweet lips, then, noticed a couple entering the ballroom.

She turned her attention to his gaze and felt an immediate rush.

"Does that bother you?" Deacon wondered.

It surprised, more than bothered. She couldn't believe it. Ollie held the waist of an attractive petite young woman, with a caramel complexion and short platinum blond hair.

Sensing her cool attitude, he asked, "What are you thinking?"

"He didn't wait to start dating again."

"Why should he?"

She squinted, observed the way Ollie held his date's chair. After he sat, he eased in, whispered something in the lady's ear that made her blush.

Gazing at the couple, Desiree said, "I don't know what to think."

Deacon asked, "Are you jealous?"

She thought for a moment, looked Deacon in the eye. She was not. "No, worried."

He took her hand. "Let's meet the lady."

Desiree did not have time to decline. Deacon was already forging ahead. That was Deacon. And she had to admit she was curious about Ollie's date.

They reached their table. Dumbfounded, Ollie looked up.

Deacon extended his hand. "Good evening."

"Good evening," Ollie replied. He turned nervously to his date. She gave him a pleasant smile. Lacy stated to Desiree, "You're the principal of that school where the shooting occurred."

With finesse, Desiree reached past Ollie and offered her hand to Lacy. "Desiree Davenport." She hesitated, hating to break the news to Ollie this way, but added, "And…this is my fiancé, Deacon Stephens."

Ollie swallowed the lump in his throat and offered his congratulations. "You two didn't waste any time."

Desiree could say the same for him, but she wouldn't be petty.

Lacy shifted in her white clingy dress, slightly cleared her throat. Ollie accepted the prompt and spoke up, "Oh, this is Lacy Reid."

The name rang a bell for Desiree. But…it couldn't be. Could it? Maybe it was a coincidence. As Desiree's thoughts traveled speedily through her mind, Lacy invited, "Join us?"

Lacy grinned when she saw Ollie's discomfort, and said, "Ollie, I've yet to meet any of your friends."

He didn't want the fellowship. He accepted the relationship that had developed between him and Lacy, but not enough to share it with anyone close to him.

Deacon provided the exit, "Actually, we were just leaving." Extending his hand again, he said, "Ollie, it was good seeing you, and Lacy, nice meeting you."

Desiree nodded as Deacon guided them out of the ballroom.

Chapter 62 – Pay the Fare!

The next day Deacon couldn't believe where he was headed. God really was radical. He questioned, "Why me?" Could not someone else be better suited to deliver the message God had for Ollie? He certainly didn't believe Ollie would accept the words he had for him.

Deacon had learned in his line of work, not to question God – just obey. So he walked into the gallery and asked the curator for Ollie.

While he waited he scouted out the place. He loved the work and what Ollie had built. He hoped Ollie cared enough about his future to keep it.

Deacon was admiring a picture of siblings playing when Ollie approached. "This is a nice piece," Deacon complimented.

"Thanks, the artist is only fifteen years old. She's very gifted."

Deacon looked around and observed a group of high school students on their class trip. "You mind if we talk in your office."

Ollie felt like he was suffocating. He ran into the man last night on a date he didn't want anyone to know about, and now, he showed up at his place of business. He suggested, "How about a walk outside?"

Deacon agreed. "Sure. That'll work."

They stepped out into an early spring afternoon. Deacon stuffed his hands into his pockets, struggling with his assignment. "God", he mumbled to himself.

"What brings you by? Want me to be your best man?" Ollie joked, but the humor failed to be sincere. Ollie was very different from the man Deacon met on the airplane several weeks ago.

"I have something to tell you." Deacon began.

They stood at the intersection. "Tell me then."

When the crosswalk sign changed to walk, they stepped onto the asphalt. Deacon remarked, "My brother is very particular about his friends since he's a cop. I know if he calls you a friend; that makes you an Okay guy. And I know Desiree would never date someone who didn't have a good heart."

Annoyed, Ollie pushed, "Your point?"

"Alright." Deacon took a heavy breath of air into his lungs, let it out slowly. "The woman you're with will destroy Olivia."

They stopped walking. Overhead, a tree bloomed. Ollie looked up at it and then back at Deacon. "What?"

"She's hurting you. If you stay with her, she'll destroy Olivia."

The guy wasn't making any sense. Lacy hadn't even met his daughter. Ollie doubted Desiree's choice for a sane husband. "English would be helpful."

Deacon reported, "Lacy is going to separate you from your family, your support system, your church and your faith. You're going to lose sight and Olivia is going to lose the father and future that God wants her to have."

Ollie shook his head. "How?"

Because he really did not have the answers, Deacon shook his head.

"I don't know. I only know what I had to tell you."

"You are absolutely insane!" Ollie spouted, "You don't know me."

"You're having sex with Lacy."

Touching his fingertips between his eyes, Ollie barked, "Why is that your business?"

Deacon shrugged.

"It's not. You have no right to intimacy with Lacy. You're hurting her, too. The longer you sleep with her, the more connected she wants to be with you."

Deacon felt the words now entering him with fluid ease. He knew God was speaking for him. He continued, "You don't love her and you are only interested in her body. You're going to tire of her and she will snap. She'll feel betrayed by you. She trusts you, believes you're safe. And when you end this, she won't be able to handle it mentally."

Ollie wanted to turn to walk away from the gibberish.

"First you tell me, Lacy will destroy Olivia and to leave her alone. Next you say, if I turn her away, she'll snap on me."

Deacon followed up with a question.

"Does your family know about you and Lacy?"

They didn't. Ollie didn't reply. Deacon unveiled, "See, she has already begun pulling you away. What I'm saying is…walk away and then be prepared. Your behavior has consequences."

Offended, Ollie brought up Deacon's painful past, lashed out, "What about the consequences of you sleeping with Desiree? She was your best friend's fiancée."

Deacon considered those words and replied, "I paid for them."

Placing his hand on Ollie's shoulder, he provided, "God gives grace, even during our consequences."

Chapter 63 – Never Hurt the Children

Zoe loved her new job as guidance counselor for the Arts Foundation. Classes had begun after school on Tuesdays and Thursdays. Her first task required her to develop trusting relationships with the students. This came by simply observing them and encouraging their gifts.

She sat and watched the dance class as the students worked in teams of two. They walked across the floor, arms held up gracefully, backs straight, and legs extending in black tights and leotards. They looked intent, yet peaceful. The sound of a classic piano and the instructor's voice played as accompaniment.

She found the staff did a solid job of selecting the appropriate students. Zoe believed that before her eyes were the world's most talented professionals. Their lives would be changed.

She looked down, checked her watch and eased out of the room. It was time to observe Ollie's art class.

His class had 12 students that day. Compared to the dance studio in the next room, his class was completely silent. She regretted creeping in. Ollie looked up from some sketching he was doing and signaled for her to join his table.

"Sorry," she apologized, gripping her teeth. Shaking his head, he replied, "You're supposed to be here." He pulled out her chair.

Zoe whispered, "Still life?" She looked at the bowl of fruit at the front of the room.

"Yeah, once they're done, I told them to go crazy. Draw whatever they feel."

Turning toward her brandy-colored eyes, he said, "I thought you'd like to analyze their creative side." Hearing the lighthearted humor in his voice, she smirked. "Sure."

He noticed Kalvon peep up at him. The young talent began his creative piece, and found Ollie's and Zoe's whispering distracting.

Ollie tapped her hand, indicating they should step out. She followed him into the hall, leading them into the adjoining art gallery.

"The students are really serious," she commented, once they were inside the gallery. She noted the quiet evening. Only a few viewers appreciated the art.

He nodded and she saw the strain of dark circles under his eyes. His skin didn't hold its normal glow.

"Are you feeling well?" Zoe inquired squinting.

Ollie looked up, saw her hair was piled high into a bun encircled by a thick braid. He never saw her hair like that. "Who did your hair?"

"Chelsea," she said, referring to her assistant and friend. "Madison, one of the dance students, advised me that with my neckline and bone structure, this style would flatter me. She has fashion talents as well."

"She's right." Ollie nodded again. "The style makes you look younger."

With a curve lining her lips, she stated, "I know I looked so old before."

He let out a breath as they continued to stroll.

"Let me get you a cane." He smiled. "What did Madison say when she saw your hair?"

"Told you, Dr. Z."

That got a deep raspy laugh out of Ollie. "I knew you were the right woman for this job."

She thought so as well, and wanted to know what was going on with the man.

"You're looking a little worn down. Working too hard?" She thought of his business, foundation and his daughter.

Actually the late nights he put in with Lacy were taking their toll. He cared not to disclose his sex life. He diverged, "How was dinner with your sister? Enjoyed catching up?"

Answering before she could think, she explained, "It didn't go well. She's not speaking to me."

They walked in front of an iron park bench that was positioned against a wall of painted trees. Extending his hand, he invited, "Wanna sit?"

"Yeah, thanks."

Grateful for the distraction, Ollie asked, "Why isn't she talking to you? Didn't she just get back to the states?"

A long story, but she trusted him. Besides she was curious how he would react to her dysfunctional family drama. "Long story short, I dated her fiancé in college. I got pregnant. He got mad, pushed me down a flight of stairs, and my baby died. We never spoke again until the night of your fundraiser. I told Aimee. She doesn't believe me, and my mother's upset with me for telling Aimee. Mother is always upset with me for one reason or another…that's nothing new. The end."

"And I thought I had problems," Ollie blurted out. She laughed. "We all have problems.

What's that Scripture about a man's days being full of trouble?"

Ollie recited, "Man that is born of a woman is of a few days and full of trouble." He thought for a minute. "You say…the end. Is your sister going to marry the guy?"

"I say the end, because I know my mom and her manipulative behavior. She will convince Aimee to marry this man. He comes from a political family. They're very influential people. For my mother, it's all about social circles, money, power, connection."

Ollie cringed as a couple walked passed hand in hand and noted, "Sounds pretty cut-throat. Isn't she concerned about your sister?"

Zoe turned to him, lifted her brow. "One would think. Mother is more concerned about what people will say if Aimee calls off the wedding. When I lost the baby, I just wanted her to hold me. She came to Boston with a plan to make sure no one found out. She almost had a nervous breakdown over it."

Ollie didn't know how to reply. Zoe continued, "She doesn't love us. She can't. She doesn't know how to accept and love herself."

He would have never guessed behind Zoe's intelligence, beauty and bank account, there was so much emptiness. He asked, "Do you love your mother?"

"I do. I try to see her as God does – a person created for a divine purpose."

She reached over and placed her hand on his.

"I admire you, Ollie. My mother had great resources for us. Yet, she had no idea how to love her children – that's what we really needed. You, as a single father, you love Olivia and all these children. You'd never do anything to hurt them."

Ollie thought about Deacon's warning and considered if that were actually true.

Chapter 64 – Bring Us to a Common Place

"I have to leave."

Desiree's eyes lifted from the cup of clam chowder soup she held as she slipped the plastic spoon from her mouth. She felt an immediate drop in blood pressure and prayed she would not fall from her chair. "Was it like before...suddenly leaving as he did fourteen years ago? No!" she thought.

Deacon regretted giving her the wrong idea. Softer now, he said, "Desiree, I have to return the Mercedes. While I'm away, I'm helping with a teen mission trip in South Carolina."

"Oh," slipped from her lips as her heart rate slowed. "I thought...."

He knew what she thought watching her from where they sat at a little conference table in her office. Deep fear gripped her when it came to Deacon having to leave. He couldn't live with her feeling that way. Taking the soup cup and spoon out of her hand, he rested them onto the table, tugged her onto his lap, and kissed her – deeply.

His hand lovingly caressed the side of her face. She opened her eyes, as his voice softly soothed, "I don't want you living fearfully. I'll get assignments. I'll have to go. There will be times I'll invite you to come with me. With your responsibilities here, that will be difficult. Like now." He leaned in, pressing his lips against her warm neck.

Her eyes involuntarily closed, feeling her heart rate speed up once more. She swallowed hard with hopes of slowing down the racing emotions flooding her body. He felt her tremors. With her eyes still closed, she rested her face on his.

"Why?" Her breath was choppy, releasing with passion. "Why, can't I go with you this time?"

"The investigation, Simon...the children," he reminded her. And there was one more reason. He'd tell her about it later.

Deacon had the power to make her forget everything that rested upon her shoulders. What an unselfish man he had become. He would not expect her to drop all for him. She asked, "When do you leave?"

"Tomorrow morning. I'll be back in a week. I honestly forgot I was supposed to go. You have that effect on me."

Because his lips mesmerized her, she traced her thumb over them. "You have that effect on me, too," she commented and tasted his lips until she felt his tremors match hers.

When she stopped her torture of him, he cleared his throat. They had to talk about something else. "I need a favor. Will you visit Nico for me?" he requested.

Desiree remembered the homeless man Deacon had been caring for. "What can I do?"

"He's had his surgery. He's recovering well enough...."

He sighed.

"What?" she prompted.

Shaking his head, he explained, "I haven't fulfilled my promise of finding his lady friend. AND...I haven't secured all the funds to cover his expenses."

Pensive, she shifted on his lap. "I don't understand. I thought your agency covered it."

"They provided a good portion. It's not enough. They can only issue so much. We try to partner with other agencies to meet the short fall. Donations haven't come in like they have in the past. With the recession, people have slowed on their giving."

She nodded, witnessing the weight of the problem upon him. "What are you going to do? Are you responsible for the short fall?"

"God is and He will provide."

Desiree expected that reply from Deacon. He accepted faith at a level that made her uncomfortable. She slipped off his lap and into her seat.

"It's not going to be like that, Desiree?" He easily knew her thoughts.

"I wouldn't take on assignments that would put our family in a bind. I do not live carelessly. I save and invest, generously. I've learned as a traveling missionary, you've got to. However, there will be times that I'll take on something radical. It is not I, but God that decides those tasks and I trust him."

Desiree trusted God too, but this man just asked to marry her. He was talking about thousands of dollars for a stranger. Not to mention, Deacon would run into a dangerous situation when God called. Maybe she wasn't ready for life with Deacon. But God, she loved him. She had lived life without him, and she could not imagine doing it again. A fresh flow of tears filled her eyes.

He reached for her hand and held it – firmly. He thought a little distance between them would be good.

"Father, help her to trust you," he prayed.

Chapter 65 – The Stench Still Stirs

Later that day, Deacon rode the 5 and 6 trains as Nico had instructed. He barely made the 10 o'clock schedule, but he was there. He walked through the subway cars. Nico explained Lady always sat in the last car, in a two-seater near the door.

He searched, praying he'd find her by morning before he had to leave. As he walked, grabbing and balancing himself with one long metal pole after another, he remembered what Nico's doctor said. Nico needed surgery to remove part, almost all of his large intestine. He also needed follow-up care and, of course, a place to stay.

The bills were piling up. Thinking and walking, he pulled the next subway car open, stepped into the brief darkness that linked the train and then into another brightly lit car. He prayed in his heart, asked God for the remaining $20,000 he needed to cover Nico's medical expenses. He knew they'd come from somewhere.

Then, there was Lady, Nico's friend. He wondered if Lady was her birth name, or just a street name. Nicodemus had an unusual birth name, and so did he. Deacon's mother named him after his late grandmother. She was a deaconess in the church. Really all his mother ever gave him was a name. A drug addict, she left them when he was only months old. If he passed her on the street, he wouldn't know her. Was that one of the reasons he wandered the streets? Deep down, did he hope to find her? Was his calling in life, unusual, like his name? No, he accepted it to be fitting. He marveled that he was a chosen vessel -- a servant for the highest authority.

He didn't find Lady on that train and stepped off, waiting for the next in order to continue his search. Thinking, walking, praying, he got to the last car of the third train of the night. The foul smell hit him before his sight took in the scene.

There were one or two passengers seated on one end of the train and then in the back, humped over on a two-seater, in layers of thin coats, rested a figure.

He approached slowly, leaned back against the wall. When the train made its next stop, he lifted his voice, "Lady! Lady! Lady!"

No reply, he knew this wasn't going to be easy. When had he ever received an easy assignment, he smiled a little at his heavenly father. Shouting louder now as the doors closed, "Lady. Hey, Lady, Nico is looking for you."

She opened her eyes, lifted her head. She hadn't been sleeping. She thought a cop was about to hassle her to get her off the train. "Nico?"

"Are you Lady, his friend?"

She nodded quickly. Her face smeared with dirt and weariness smudged her paled yellow skin. Her red-brimmed eyes were tired, but warm. "Yeah, who are you?"

"My name is Deacon. I met Nico a few weeks ago. He's in the hospital. He wants to see you."

Her eyes shifted nervously.

"What's wrong? Is he dyin'? He's been sick a while."

"I'm praying for his recovery. I've been helping him."

Gripping the subway seat, she remembered, "Yeah, he told me about you. You're really strange."

He let out a breath, laughed.

"Thanks. Do you wanna go see him?"

She looked down at herself, immune to the smell of her filthy flesh, but not the sight of it.

"I can't go into a hospital. They'll kick me out."

A lady is always a lady. He understood.

"I can help you get ready. What size clothes do you wear?"

She frowned.

"You're going to give me your clothes?"

He smiled. "I'm going to buy you new clothes. You can come to my house to shower and change."

A bubbling surge of tears flooded her eyes and then it wailed out of her.

"What did I say?" he wondered.

When she pulled it together, she mumbled, "You'll let me shower? At your house?"

"Oh, God," he thought. Her reaction gripped him. He couldn't imagine how long it had been since she had showered. Holding his own tears, he replied, "Yes. I stay in Brooklyn. You can shower, stay the night and in the morning, I'll get you some new things."

He paused looked at the whiteness of her lips. "Can I get you something to eat?"

"I don't care what it is. Anything would be good."

Deacon looked up, they were well into the Bronx now, and he didn't know the restaurants. They'd have to get on a returning train. Scanning his memory, he thought about some places in midtown. "Alright, let's get off at the next stop and cross over."

She didn't hesitate, getting up in anticipation of the next stop. She wasn't reluctant, like Nico had been. She trusted him instantly. For Deacon, that was strange, but welcomed. They exited the train together, and although her smell repulsed him, when she smiled up at him with those warm eyes, she melted his heart.

As they walked, he recognized she had a limp. "Are you okay?" He pointed to her leg.

"I was born like this. I've always had a limp."

He smiled and when they reached the stairs, he took her arm and assisted her.

Another wave of tears, gurgled out of her. She pulled her arm away. Deacon backed off, but she told him, "I know I smell bad. No one except Nico has ever been this close to me, let alone touched me, Deson."

He could not help the grin from leaving his heart and filling up his face. She called him Deson, like Nico had.

"You're welcome, Lady."

******

Close to midnight, Deacon opened the gate of his house and let Lady through. She didn't walk through, but paused. Staring up at traditional brownstone, she inquired, "How long have you lived here?"

"Since I was born."

Her eyes roamed the structure, then the neighborhood. It was quiet, late and cold. "Maybe this is a bad idea."

Deacon squinted, but took a chance and touched Lady's arm.

"I promise I won't hurt you."

She didn't doubt that. "Who do you live with?" she wondered.

"It's only me and my brother."

"No wives?" She lifted a fluffy grey eyebrow.

"I'm not married, but working on it," he replied, smiling.

"She looked at the small square yard, there was a bench. "I could sleep here. In the morning, I'll come in and shower."

Deacon touched his hand to his heart. "Would you do *me* a favor? Please come in?"

Her red eyes watered. "You a favor?"

"It would be an honor for me."

Lady took several seconds to deliberate. Finally, she mounted the stairs.

Deacon followed slowly, opened the door. They turned left and entered a dimly light hallway. Deacon didn't particularly appreciate the sounds he thought were coming from the television. He considered his brother was watching one of his many adult movies.

When he lifted his head and looked at the old worn sofa, he realized the entertainment was live and in color. He shouted, "Oh shoot!" Turning an about-face, he barreled into Lady, almost knocking her down. "I'm sorry."

No time to consider her feelings, he grabbed Lady's arm and took her back into the hall. "I'm sorry," he repeated.

Her eyes weren't shocked, but dancing, with a smirk, she asked, "Your girlfriend?"

He shook his head, looked over his shoulder.

"Oh, your boyfriend?"

"What? No, my brother!" he shouted.

She lifted her brow.

"Lady, I apologize, this is not the kind of thing that goes on…"

"Where I come from," she interrupted him, "I see things like this all the time. That's what human beings do. At least they're indoors." She lifted her chin at the opening into the living room.

Deacon was certain Lady had seen quite a bit living in the streets. As a missionary, so had he, but he didn't expect *this*.

"What's that foul smell?" Mitch shouted, before he stumbled into the hall wearing his boxer briefs and nothing else.

Deacon fired, "What you're doing smells worse than anything else in this house."

Mitch looked at the tiny woman. He gathered she was 5 feet 2 or 3 inches tall. Her eyes were hazel and he factored she was biracial, pegged her to be of Latin and African American descent. And based on her scent and clothes, his brother had dragged yet another homeless person into his house. "Can I talk to you a minute Deacon?"

He had a long day and he let Mitch know it. "I own half of this home. This is Lady. She's my guest. I see you have one of your own tonight."

Deacon turned to Lady. "I'll show you around."

Lady smiled at Mitch, before she limped away after Deacon who was walking way too fast for her to keep up.

While Lady washed away years of filth, Deacon went into the kitchen for a drink of water. Mitch found him still wearing his jacket, arms folded across his chest, his back leaning against the sink and his legs crossed at the ankles.

"I'm sorry you had to see that," Mitch started and sat at the kitchen table still just wearing his underwear.

"Nat's only twenty-six years old. Mitch you're forty! And for God's sake, she's Pastor Jones' daughter!"

He didn't need Deacon to do the math or define the relationship. He knew. "It's not what you think. Nat and I have…an arrangement."

"What's that supposed to mean? She's another one of your booty calls."

Mitch didn't appreciate the tone coming from his little brother, especially after having their home smelling like a zoo. He bit out, "I'm Nat's booty call, since you want to accuse somebody."

Deacon held up his palms. "Hey, I'm not the accuser. What? You mean to tell me Nat's the one that called you?"

"That's right. Nat and I have hooked up before, on and off a couple years now. But she stopped calling me. She started messing with Elder Atkins."

"Elder Atkins is older than you!" Deacon shouted in frustration.

With his elbows on the cool table, Mitch relayed, "She likes experienced men. But the reason I think she called me tonight is because you insulted her."

Confused, Deacon wrinkled his forehead.

She said, "You're not paying her any attention. You told her you only have eyes for Desiree."

"Sounds like Nat has issues, and you know I'm here for Desiree." Deacon shrugged. He wasn't getting into any drama.

"And let's not forget the homeless people," Mitch added sarcastically.

Deacon quickly retorted, "I'm taking care of Lady and Nico."

Mitch let out a breath. "Lady and Nico. Whatever, man. Just be careful. You're an easy target to be taken advantage of."

"So are the homeless."

They remained silent a minute. Mitch stood up. "Nat's waiting."

Deacon frowned. "She's still here?"

Mitch sucked his lips to the side.

"You thought it was over, because you walked in? Yea, right. I don't know what world you live in little brother."

Offended by Deacon's disapproval, Mitch's bulky chest puffed up.

"Mitch, you're disrespecting Nat."

Pointing to himself, he reminded Deacon with a wink, "I didn't make the call. I'm simply giving the lady what she wants."

Deacon didn't care what Nat told Mitch, he knew women wanted more, they often times settled for less.

"Dad didn't teach us to be that way, Mitch. He never brought women home and he...."

Mitch's voice lowered, dripping with disgust, his finger pointed in Deacon's direction.

"Don't you ever mention that man to me! He did his dirt, and you know it. It doesn't matter that he didn't do it at home. And what I do has nothing to do with him."

Deacon took a breath and backed off, realizing how much of what Mitch did stemmed from their father.

"Alright, man. We'll talk about this later."

"We won't. You've chosen your life, looking after the pitiful. I've chosen to look after myself."

"You're a detective, Mitch. You look after the hurt and the hurting, too. We just do it in different ways, we have different bosses."

After a long pause, he advised, "A woman deserves more than one part of you. If you can't give her that, take Nat home."

Mitch walked away, and with his back turned, he advised, "You should get the Lysol and deodorize this place, now Deacon!"

Chapter 66 – Oh, Snap!

Ollie's sleepy eyes turned toward the clock on the nightstand. At 4:30 in the morning, he recognized the faint cry coming from his daughter's room. He pulled on a pair of sweats and drifted across the hall.

The opened door casted a nighttime glow on Olivia's sleeping face. He noticed she whimpered in her sleep. He watched, debating if he should wake his 2 year old. She seemed distressed.

He walked over slowly and knelt at the toddler's bedside. Closer now, he saw little lips smiling in between baby talk. Cute, he grinned, grateful she wasn't having a bad dream. He stood, started easing out of the room. As he approached the door, he heard her whisper, "Rae Rae." The sound of her precious voice rested an ache in his heart.

Of course his baby girl missed Desiree. So did he.

He left, keeping his baby girl's door ajar, in case she called for him.

Ollie eased back into his bedroom, carefully shut the door, and engaged the lock. Lacy hadn't stirred as he got back into bed with her.

They had a working arrangement. Two nights out of the week Lacy arrived after 10 when Olivia was already sleeping. The couple spent one hour working on her book. The rest of the time was spent in his bed.

Since Olivia was home when Lacy arrived, it worked in his best interest that she loved quietly. Her expressions were soft sighs and moans. She was very physical, however. He figured different women had their ways in bed. During their heated exchange, Lacy clawed, scratched, and bruised his arms and back. And after, she'd become very emotional, crying. Ollie ended up holding her until she slipped into sleep.

Lying in bed next to her, he considered how quickly he allowed the emotionally erotic situation to manifest in his life.

A nagging thought gnawed at his baseline. What if Olivia did wake and call for him? Her sleep was so animated…for some reason. He didn't want to confuse her. Olivia was dreaming about Desiree and she'd awake to a stranger. No, he wouldn't allow that. He turned, rocked her shoulder, "Lacy, Lacy."

She stirred.

"Is it five already?" she mumbled.

"Olivia…she's a little restless."

Lacy rolled over, saw his tense face in the nightlight. "What's wrong?"

Quickly, he sat up against the pillows. "I don't know. I'm afraid that she'll wake early today."

As the sleep haze loomed, she realized, "You want me to go, now?"

"I think it would be best."

She thought a second, told him what she thought, "It's time that I meet her and you meet, Marcel Jr. and Michelle."

He cringed at her son's name…Marcel's son. Marcel, the man that had an affair with his wife…killed her? The reality of the chaos engulfed him.

"Lacy, we have to stop."

She knew one day Ollie would end their affair. It didn't matter how sweet and tender he was with her.

She believed she loved him, and understood their relationship didn't sit well with his faith, his family. He had no intentions of introducing them to her. That hurt. It was her body, and only her body that he wanted -- nothing more, nothing less.

Feeling a hole expand in her heart, she pleaded, "I can't take your rejection. I'm a good woman, Ollie. Truly, I am. We can make this work. We can be a family."

Ollie didn't want to hurt her, his voice cracked, "Lacy, you are a good woman. But this, us…." His first tear fell as he continued, "Us being together, it's eating at me. It's just a constant reminder of my past. I promised God after Sassy and I married that I would be the man that he wants me to be. I'm not doing that. And I have to. Not only do I have Olivia depending on me, I also have the children at my foundation. I need to be strong for them."

Lacy lifted her nude body, turned, and sat on the side of the bed – her back turned from him. She whispered, "You're saying I make you a weak man. I don't think that of you. I have so much respect for you. I'm in love with you."

Disgusted by his irresponsible actions, he felt bile rising in his throat. He wanted to purge himself. "How could I use her like that? How could I accept her body over and over again with no desire to care for her, or her children?" he thought. Yes, he believed he had become a disgusting, vile creature.

He looked at the feminine curve of her back, desiring to touch her, yet knowing it wouldn't bring her comfort. Restricting his hands from moving, he revealed, "I care for you, Lacy. I'm sorry, so sorry."

His pity filled the gaping hole in her heart with an icy spirit. The chill gave her a nefarious strength. Silently, she stood, walked proudly to the bathroom, and dressed. She reentered the bedroom for her jacket and purse and walked elegantly for the exit.

Ollie jumped out of bed after her. Lacy turned slowly, held up her hand and shook her head no.

Almost afraid, he obeyed and saw a glint in her eye. It wasn't pain. It wasn't sadness. It was fury.

Lacy lowered her hand, turned and continued her slow, steady walk. She seemed to be in a trance. Ollie remembered Deacon's warning, "She'll snap."

Chapter 67 – Mitch Match

As promised, Deacon left early, but not before stopping in and making breakfast for his fiancée.

The distance between them was different this time. This time, she wore his ring. Desiree admired the stones and counted the number of times he had called during her school day. So far, it had been three.

A tap on her door lifted her gaze from the ring. Mitch stepped in. "Working late on a Friday?"

She checked the time; saw it was a quarter to six. "You too," she stated.

"Police work is never done." He drew a breath, eased his large frame into one of her visitor's chairs.

"Principal's work, too." Not feeling like the principal, she got up and sat in the lonely chair next to Mitch. "What brings you by?"

"Two things." He shifted in his seat. Desiree noticed how much Mitch looked like a detective – the tweed brown jacket, tan polo, black jeans, and thick black boots. He lifted his finger.

"One, Deacon wanted me to check on you."

Desiree felt a blush coming on. She attempted to hide it, failed. Mitch grinned.

"And two, your investigation."

Anxiety replaced her blush. She had been waiting weeks to find out while Simon was still recovering from a bullet wound to the chest. "Finally," she replied.

"Police work is slow business. It's not like they glamorize it on TV."

"I know. Please tell me."

It would be difficult for her to hear. But Mitch heard stories like this all day long. He disclosed, "The shooter is Corey Rendell, Trevor Rendell's cousin."

Her ears perked up even taller, she remarked, "Trevor's the young man that had been accused of sexually harassing a fellow student."

Mitch turned his chair and the legs struggled against the gray carpet. Face-to-face with Desiree, he revealed, "That's what this is all about. Corey didn't like his cousin being accused for something he didn't do. He told Trevor he was going to threaten Tiona, and force her to fess up. That method didn't work. Guns and kids equal chaos…you know how it played out. Kids screaming and running, someone ran into Corey, the gun fired, and left a bullet in Simon's chest."

This couldn't be. Someone almost got killed because of a lie, because a minor had his hands on a gun. She hadn't gotten to the bottom of who really touched Tiona. And why not? Was she so consumed with

Deacon being in her life that she failed to do her job – to keep her staff and children safe?

Mitch could see her deflating under her thoughts. "Hold on."

He pulled out his cell phone, dialed. When someone answered, he handed Desiree the phone. "Baby, it's not your fault."

She heard teens chatting in the background. Deacon's voice traveled through her like electricity.

"Isn't it?" she questioned.

"Don't do this. You couldn't make Tiona tell the truth. You didn't put the gun in Corey's hands. Baby, don't blame yourself, trust God with this."

There he was again – telling her to trust God. Disgusted, she handed the phone back to Mitch, he said, "Hey, I'll hit you back later," and tucked his phone away.

Mitch stated, "I remember that night."

Desiree stared at Mitch then lowered her eyes. She knew the night he spoke of and didn't want to discuss it. Really, what did that night have to do with her current issue?

"Desiree?" She looked up. Mitch reported, "I've known you for years. The night of Sterling's accident changed you. You blame yourself for every terrible thing that is connected to you. You know I ain't half the believer that Deacon is, but I think…maybe you ought to trust God."

She noticed Mitch's pensive face. "In my line of work, sometimes we just can't solve a case. We run out of leads and we don't have a clue. There are moments; I whisper a prayer and out of nowhere, we get something. I don't even know why God would answer my prayers. I know that you've been serving him since you were this high."

Mitch lifted his hand for indication. "Trust him. I promise I'm going to find out who touched Tiona. And we're going to need God's help."

Mitch couldn't believe what was coming out of his mouth, and yet, he believed they couldn't learn everything without divine help.

Desiree took a deep breath. What was trusting God? The situation seemed to be so big – beyond her control and understanding. It frightened her. The parents and children looked up to her, counted on her. At that moment, it clicked. She knew who she needed to look up to and whom she needed to see.

She asked Mitch, "Will you go someplace with me tonight?"

Chapter 68 - Forgetting Faults

The *place* was Sterling Pipman's house. Mitch and Desiree approached the home under the crisp black sky. She felt her heart rate increase, thinking about seeing Sterling in his wheelchair. Her breaths came out short and rapidly. Mitch took her arm, told her, "This is good."

Yes, good and way overdue. She listened to her sensible black pumps click against the concrete walkway, the sounds of Mitch's black boots, supporting her every step. She rang the bell and held her breath.

They hadn't called ahead. She didn't know if she was intruding. She didn't know what she'd find. She just came with a desire to face her fears.

Desiree saw a little girl with dark hair looking through the thick glass door. "Dad!" she yelled.

She heard a muffled response and the little girl ran away. In the distance she heard the sound of a powered wheelchair, rolling in their direction. Desiree looked down and into the man's eyes she had promised to marry long ago.

Sterling smiled and opened the door.

"Well, it sure took you long enough."

He maneuvered his chair backward and he pulled the door wider. She took a step forward, unable to control the shaking in her legs. Mitch rested one large hand on her back and extended the other toward Sterling.

"Good to see you, man."

"Same here."

As Mitch shoved Desiree into the foyer, Sterling closed the door. With expert precision, he wheeled his chair around, leading them into his family room. The little girl was cuddled on the couch watching a television comedy. She looked at Sterling and asked, "Daddy, who is this lady?"

Desiree watched as Sterling parked his wheelchair and answered, "Juliet, remember the man that came here last week? Well this is our other friend, Desiree and Mitch is his brother."

"Yeah, Mr. Deacon, he was fun. You played basketball together."

Mitch laughed. "I know you whipped him. That boy can't play no basketball."

Juliet smiled proudly. "Yes, my daddy beat him."

Sterling asked, "Can we take your coats?"

Juliet was already standing and prepared to accept. Mitch declined, but Desiree slipped out of the wool coat, grateful to shed some weight.

He motioned for them to sit. Desiree asked, "How've you been?"

Sterling answered, "I'll tell you, once you have a seat." Desiree didn't realize they were still standing. Juliet came back, scooted past her, and sat in her father's lap.

Mitch and Desiree sat on the sofa. "It's really nice seeing you, Desiree."

Mitch scoffed, "What am I? Chopped liver?"

"Yep, and you've always been. Besides, I see too much of you," Sterling teased.

"Oh," Desiree realized, "you've stayed in touch?"

Mitch nodded.

Desiree added, "And Deacon's been by to see you?"

"He has," Sterling replied. "He told me that you weren't ready. I wanted to call you. But the way things ended, I didn't know if that's what you wanted from me."

His daughter turned to him, touched her father's face. "How did things end?"

He smiled at his curious angel. "Desiree and I were very good friends. And then one day, we weren't."

"Didn't you want to be my daddy's friend?"

Desiree never envisioned her reunion with Sterling and the bright eyed little girl. The child's presence made it more difficult for her to get comfortable.

Clearing her throat, she replied, "I thought your father wanted other friends."

"Did you, Daddy?"

Sterling smiled. "Alright sweet pea, go watch TV in the kitchen. I'll be in soon."

Juliet hesitated and received a nudge from her father. "Go on."

Mitch and Desiree smiled as she slowly sauntered out of the room.   Sterling commented, "She's a curious one."

"She's cute," Desiree admitted. "She looks a lot like your mother."

Sterling agreed and added, "My son looks like my wife. I get nothing," he joked.

Desiree inquired, "Are they here? Your wife and son?"

"No, she's visiting my mother. Jason went with her."

Mitch eased up and announced, "I'm going to wait in the car." Feeling Desiree's panic, he explained, "You don't need me here."

He leaned over, gripped Sterling's hand. "I'll see you Saturday and will show you no mercy. I don't care about your wheelchair." Mitch made a stern face.

"Whatever man, talk is cheap. I'll see what you bring on Saturday."

Desiree remained quiet until Mitch cleared the room. Because it was true, she said, "You look really good, Sterling."

He did. She could tell he put a lot of time and effort into his upper body. It was buff and strong.

"I can say the same about you," he commented, reaching over, he lowered the volume on the television. The sounds of the characters whispered in the background. He spoke up, "What other friends?"

She squinted.

"You said, you thought I wanted other friends."

"It's nothing," she said.

Sterling rested his hands on each side of his chair. "Desiree, you didn't wait fourteen years to tell me nothing. I want to know...why did you leave...without a word or explanation? Please, I need to hear it from you."

She owed him that and paid up – in full.

"One afternoon, I came in and found you and Maria having sex."

His eyes widened to the size of two 50-cent coins. "No way!"

"Way. I saw Maria riding you like a wild cowboy."

Sterling shook his head. "That would be girl."

Desiree blinked.

"Maria would be a cowgirl," Sterling clarified.

"Girl or boy, it doesn't matter...you were the horse."

This time Sterling let out an easy laugh. "At least tell the truth Desiree. Come on...why'd you really leave?"

Feeling slightly warm, she forced, "I told you what I saw."

"What you saw was virtually impossible. I was not physically able to have sex – not back then. Along with my legs, other things weren't working."

Instinctively, her eyes went to his crotch. Embarrassed, she snapped her head back.

He laughed again. "So... I couldn't have been the horse. Was I even awake? The medication barely kept me conscious."

They sat quietly.

Desiree was a lot of things, but crazy was not one of them.

"I know what I saw."

But she thought back to that day and remembered she never heard a peep from Sterling as she watched Maria with him.

Sterling recalled the awful time of his life. He lost the function of his legs and his two best friends. Maria became his nurse and protector. She often was very controlling of him. Could she have made it appear that they were intimate? Played it precisely right so that Desiree would get the impression? He wondered aloud, "Was the door open?"

"Wide open."

There would be no way he'd have sex with a woman in his parent's home with the door wide open. The reality was despicable. Would it have really mattered? Desiree wasn't in love with him then, and he knew it – so did Maria.

Time to confess, he explained, "I did a horrible thing to you."

Peering into his sharp eyes, she said, "You couldn't have."

Getting it out, he said, "No, I did. I knew you were in love with him and my ego wouldn't let you go. I was going to *make* you marry me, knowing Deacon held your heart and you held his."

The emotions welled up, filled her eyes with water as she listened.

"I knew," he admitted softly, swiped his hand through the thick black massive hair. "I knew. I don't know when it happened – your feelings for him. It hurt…like crazy. I planned to marry you and take you away from him and over time I prayed you might forget him. I was wrong, you two never forgot. Did you?"

The first swollen tear fell from her eyes, she replied, "We tried."

He went on, "The night before our wedding, I knew you were with him. I drove to his house. I saw you standing, waiting for him to open the door. I watched you fall into his arms. You kissed him like your life was at stake. I drove off, cursing you both. I never heard the sirens coming in my direction or felt the impact of the crash. I remember waking up in the hospital and praying for death."

A chill embraced her. Desiree threw her arms around her.

"I'm sorry," he told her. "I should have let you go. I knew you didn't have the heart to break our engagement. You wanted to please your family. You didn't want to hurt me. And even after the accident, you were going to marry me. I saw you broken up over Deacon leaving. Still, my ego wouldn't let you go." He kept his next thought silent. However, he thought maybe Maria's actions did them a favor.

He let her sit and sob. While she did, he startled her. Frozen, she watched him reach over behind a chair and grab two supports – one for each hand. Using all his upper body strength, Sterling lifted himself out of his wheelchair, shuffled over to her.

When he reached the sofa, he pointed out, "This is the part I need help with. Can you help me sit down?"

It took several seconds to comprehend his words, she whispered. "Oh, my God, you can walk." She jumped to her feet.

"This is the best I can do."

She supported him. "It's wonderful, Sterling."

After she helped him settle down, he lifted his fingers, tenderly wiped her tears away. She let him soothe her.

"Deacon told me how much guilt you held all these years. My accident wasn't your fault, or his. I shouldn't have allowed you to believe that."

Desiree explained, "You wouldn't have been out driving that night Sterling if it wasn't for me and Deacon."

"No," he said firmly. "If I would have been honest, instead of trying to hurt him and make you marry me, I would not have."

He took her hand, shook it. "We all should have been honest. Come on -- no more blame. I've missed you both, so much."

She embraced him.

"I've missed you, too, Sterling."

Chapter 69 – Renew

Ollie had to get his act together. Deacon's warning stayed with him: "She will snap when you reject her." He recalled the coldness coming from Lacy when he told her they had to end their affair. What had he done? Why had he done it?

With the foundation getting underway, it wasn't the best time for him to be going away. But mentally, spiritually and emotionally, he needed the getaway. He put his confidence in his staff, and left Zoe in charge. She didn't ask why he was leaving, only assured him that she'd oversee the children and the activities of the foundation.

Ollie pulled into his cousin's driveway and unstrapped Olivia from the car seat. The drive from Brooklyn to Long Island rocked her to sleep. She stirred briefly, clutched one of his shoulders as she rested her head on the other. He kissed his princess' forehead, pushed the car door closed, and started for the front door.

Lily didn't answer right away. When she did, he saw his pregnant cousin with a dishtowel in hand and a warm smile on her face. "You're early," she remarked stepping back, letting him in.

His 6-year-old nephew ran up to him.

"Cousin Ollie, dad and I are building a tree house. Wanna help?"

That sounded like fun and something his cousin-in-law would do well being an architect and construction business owner. Maybe another time, he had to get on the road. He replied, "Can I take a rain check, buddy? I'm taking Olivia on a holiday."

Nicholas squinted. "What's a rain check? What holiday is it? Is it time for Christmas again?"

The adults laughed. Lily explained, "Rain check means he will help you another day. And holiday means, he's going on a vacation."

"Oh," the little one nodded.

Lily offered, "I'm making dinner. You're staying, right?" She wanted to talk to him. Lately, he appeared weary.

"I want to get to Pennsylvania. Get Olivia settled."

She looked at the sleeping beauty.

"Alright." She wouldn't push. "Have a seat. I'll get the keys to the house."

Leaving the family room, her husband passed her, and lovingly rested a hand on her growing belly. Michael stopped in front of Ollie with a grand smile and extended his hand. Ollie gripped it. Michael's clothing was tattered jeans and a t-shirt. It was clear he had been working, and loving every minute of it.

The child jumped between the men. "Dad, Cousin Ollie is going to help us with the tree house on a rainy day."

Michael looked down, laughed at his son. "He is?" He lifted a brow at Ollie.

"A rain check," Ollie repeated.

Michael nodded, understanding. Lily came back with the keys and their 1-year-old daughter in her arms. She released the keys to Ollie.

Michael reached for the little darling.

"You're already carrying one baby. Let me take Leah," he commented, lifting the toddler. "Lily explained, "She just woke up. I shouldn't have let her sleep this long."

Michael patted the child's back as she fussed and explained to his wife, "It's alright. You were cooking, and Nicky and I were outside. If she doesn't sleep tonight, I'll stay...." He paused, saw a frown cross Lily's face. "Your back?"

She nodded, placed her hands on her back, shuffled over to the sofa, and sat. Her men followed and Ollie stood, feeling slightly out of place, he asked Lily, "You okay?"

"Yes, back pain goes with the territory. I'm fine."

Seeing her smile through the pain and her men at her side, he decided, "I should get going."

Ollie shuffled nervously from foot to foot, waiting for them to see him off. Michael and Lily exchanged looks and Ollie gathered they were setting him up. They wanted to talk. He decided to indulge them since they were letting him use their vacation home in Pennsylvania.

He took the empty seat by the sofa and studied the Carraway family. They were solid, happy. He wanted that...warm evenings with his family...to comfort his wife during her pregnancy.

Ollie shifted his sleeping child onto his lap so she could be more comfortable and asked them, "What's up?"

Michael spoke to his son; "We're finished for today. Wash your hands and wait for me in your room. I want to go over some designs with you."

Excited about talking to his dad over building the coolest tree house ever, he didn't balk as he left the room.

Ollie spoke, "He's getting big."

The proud parents smiled.

"Smarter by the day," Michael added. "I hear there's a new woman in your life."

Ollie wasn't exactly sure how Michael had heard that. He did his best, keeping Lacy away.

Ending his curiosity, Michael said, "One of our church members mentioned they saw you."

"The relationship was brief. Not something to talk about," Ollie replied.

Lily and Michael felt his tension. Lily inquired, "Who ended it?"

Ollie barked, "Does it matter?"

Both Lily's and Michael's backs stiffened. They recognized the rigid spirit – a result of guilt and anger. Michael offered, "Olivia can stay with us. Do you need some time alone?"

He shook his head. "No thanks, I got her."

Lily spoke softly, "We know you've been through so much. What can we do while you're away?"

"Help Zoe. I left her in charge. You can check on her…see if she needs anything."

"We can do that. How long will you be away?" she asked.

"Two weeks," he answered, standing on his feet.

They stood, too, realizing he needed this time.

"Drive safely," Lily ordered.

Ollie looked at his cousins. They really were good people, only wanting to help. He just couldn't talk it out – not now.

"Thanks."

He turned; hoping all the emotions strangling him would release him.

"Stop," Lily directed another order while pushing her self up. "We want to pray with you."

Like a protective shield, they surrounded him. Michael still held Leah. Even still, they each rested a hand on Ollie's shoulder. Michael prayed, "Father, you love us enough to call us back to you. Every last soul is precious in your sight. Please rest your divine strength on Ollie's heart. Lift the dark cloud in his life and enforce a hedge of protection around him, his child, and businesses. Allow him to complete the work that you have assigned to him. We trust you, love, and honor you. In Jesus' mighty name, we pray. Amen."

There was no use in trying to stop them. The tears flowed tenderly from his heart and then his eyes. He nodded his gratitude and stepped away, anticipating a cleansing moment with his heavenly Father and child.

Chapter 70 – Take a Stand! – Destroy that MAN?

With her feet in stirrups, Lacy laid back against the thin white paper. As the doctor examined her, she acknowledged that something new in her had grown. She didn't know if it was a thing or a person. Whatever the being, it wanted to claw and rip Ollie's eyes from his sockets.

"How dare he have sex with me in every possible way that pleased him. He used my body again and again. And now he decides it's wrong. He cannot dismiss me and go on with his business and his little brat. NO WAY!" she thought.

She had enough of being tossed aside, disregarded as if her heart didn't matter. Her husband had considered her for a fool with his long-term affairs. Ollie told her about the condo he bought for his lover, the clothes, and the jewelry. Ollie gave her all the facts she needed to complete her book.

But it wasn't over. It was far from over. "Does he think I'm weak? Is that what Marcel thought?" she pondered.

They were both wrong. Lacy Reid was nobody's fool and she certainly wasn't weak. To prove it, after Ollie tossed her aside, she went home, sent her children off to school, and checked on her father. Her dad still couldn't say one comprehensive word. She saw fear in his eyes. Was that fear for her, or him?

No time to figure it out. She found a rape crisis number, wept throughout the phone call and reported a rape – her rape. The counselor set someone up to meet her at the hospital. As she endured the humiliating exam, answered all the questions, falsely, she thought of Ollie's arrest.

Strategically, Lacy had all the evidence. The technician retrieved Ollie's flesh from underneath her fingernails, from where she scratched him. They removed his semen from her body.

That trick was more cunning to portray since he started using condoms with her. Determined, she found a way to capture his bodily fluids and inject them into her body. A low, vile and disgusting move, she knew. "Doesn't he deserve it? He did rape me, stripped me of all dignity and hope. What I do now is not only for me. Not at all!" she thought.

She believed his rejection and callous attitude required punishment. Not just for her, but also for every woman, and any woman, that had given her body to a man, only to be used and discarded.

The white paper sheaf she wore ruffled as the technician allowed her to get up. And as she did, she resolved to bring the artist to his knees.

Ollie was a man that was rising in their community. People began to admire him.

"Do they know the real Oliver Sparrow? It's my job to show the world, he can't be trusted," she thought.

Chapter 71 – Releasing the Weight

Desiree rested in the solace of her bedroom, thinking about her meeting with Sterling. The spacious room was a powder blue. It complemented the heavy brown duvet she rested upon.

She had no desire to get comfortable and change her work clothes. She just wanted to think. So she curled up in a ball, considered if Sterling really did share any responsibility for her affair with Deacon. Yet Sterling confessed that he had.

Finally, they had all faced the truth. It was ugly, learning three loving friends had all been deceitful, prideful, and self-serving. Not one of them had consulted with the Lord for his direction. What a horrible way to live. She wouldn't live that way any longer. She welcomed the cleansing water from her eyes. With every washing tear, she released the dishonesty and failure. "No more. God, help me to please you in all areas of my life. Help me to be the leader you planned for me to be," she prayed.

She had a job to do. She had a man waiting to marry her. No longer would the guilt of her past hinder her. She turned over, looked at the clock in the dimly lit room. Only a little after 9, she was already falling into a calming sleep.

That night she slept fully clothed and found it was the best sleep of her life. She typically had a habit of waking in the middle of the night, never feeling secure. Seeing Sterling again cleansed her soul and infused her spirit.

Undressing on the way to the shower, she realized she never felt secure because she never fully trusted God with her faults. Forgetting that way of life, she prepared for a new day. Desiree turned on the shower and stepped underneath the steaming water. She didn't bother to cover her head with a cap. On the contrary, she let the water saturate her tresses from the crown of her head to the soles of her feet.

By the time she had showered, dried her hair and pulled it into a sleek long ponytail, she was smiling at her reflection. She looked younger with her hair pulled back. It made her think of her youth, her parents and sisters – and of course, Deacon.

Back in her bedroom, she lifted her phone, dialed. His answer was brisk and he stuttered into the phone.

"Deacon?"

"Get out of here," she heard him say.

"What?"

Smiling through the receiver, he replied, "That's my friend, Nathan. He's trying to take my phone."

"Why," she asked as she looked into her closet for something casual to wear. She found khakis and a light-blue striped collared shirt and laid the clothes on the bed. Deacon answered, "Nathan said it's distracting me. I keep watching it, waiting for your call. I hoped that you would call last night. I left you messages."

He had, but last night, she just needed quiet time. "I was thinking. I just...."

He knew where she went last night and whom she finally saw and explained, "I didn't tell you I had been by to see Sterling. Seeing him for the first time after all these years was a good thing. It was also very personal. I planned to tell you. You had so much going on with the school shooting."

Desiree understood what needed to be done couldn't be accomplished as a couple. Each one had been responsible for their actions and they had to confess it individually. She let out a breath and moved on.

"How's it going?"

"The kids are great. We're building a home for a family of eight. I wish you were here. We could use your help."

The joy in his voice brought a smile to her face. "I love you, Deacon." He paused, caught off guard at her easy tone. Was God healing her?

"Deacon?"

He replied, "I'm here. You sound so peaceful. I love you, too, Desiree."

They both just held the phone and smiled. Deacon asked, "What are you doing today?"

Checking the clock, she had to move and unbelted the black robe.

"Right now, I'm getting dressed."

"You're naked!" he shouted at her with mischievous excitement.

"Wouldn't you like to know?" she teased.

Someone tapped him on his shoulder.

"I really would. I've got to get back to the building site." She let him know, "I'm going to see Nico today." Walking off, he thanked her; "This means a lot to me."

"Deacon, you mean a lot to me. I'm ready for our future together. Finish your building project and come back to me, soon." Her sincere words filled his heart.

"Baby, I'm already there. I'll call you later."

Desiree tossed her phone and hopped into her clothes. It felt liberating to trust God and love Deacon.

Chapter 72 – Nothing Is Really Random

Zoe admired Ollie's frugalness and respect for the foundation's resources. Her office was small, yet quaint. Ollie made it inviting for her with the antique desk and classic refreshment cart. He painted lemons and vines on the refined piece. The walls were also painted a cheery lemon yellow. His artistic sense made the limited space appear bright and open. Each time she walked in it, she smiled at his consideration.

Sipping on a fresh tall glass of lemonade and thinking about the man, her desk phone rang. She answered; learning one of the students had twisted their ankle. The student and instructor were heading to her office.

She waited in the doorway. The dance teacher escorted the child. Both teacher and student wore tights, leotards, and ballet slippers. The only difference in attire was the student wore black; the instructor wore white and a tiny dancer's skirt. Zoe took notice of the woman's stern and absorbed expression.

Zoe smiled as they approached and said, "Ms. Joni, I'm sure she'll be fine." Not certain of that, the teacher and student tightly gripped one another with each tender step. Zoe held out her hand.

"Let's get her to the couch and take a look."

Keeping her eyes warm and anti-accusatory, she looked at Joni, the dance instructor. "You'll need to fill out an incident report."

Joni nodded, feeling a terrible ache in her belly.

"We were just doing a combination. It's pretty fancy footwork, but I didn't think anyone would get hurt. I've taught the routine before…in my other job."

Zoe laid a hand on Joni's thin shoulder. "Accidents happen. That's why they call them accidents. I'm sure she'll be just fine." She studied the child's face first and saw more fear than pain. She knelt to examine the ankle and found Joni kneeling with her.

Zoe lifted the girl's right foot and slipped away the ballet slipper. She saw slight swelling. She asked, "Nyasia, can you circle it around?"

The girl shook her head. "I don't think so."

Zoe was certain it was only a sprain. Still, they would need an x-ray. She explained, "I'll call her mother and take them to the doctor."

Nyasia clutched Zoe's hand. "I don't want to go to the doctor. It takes so long. Can't you fix it, Dr. Z?"

Zoe looked up, creased her brows. "I will take you to my friend's clinic, it won't take very long. I promise."

She added a smile, hoping to release the tension in the room.

Joni pleaded, "You think it's broken?"

"It may not be." Zoe looked up at Nyasia who was hanging on her every word.

"A sprain can swell immediately and they truly hurt. If she stays off of it, ices it, she'll be good as new."

Zoe lifted her tall frame. Joni followed, standing with her concerned arms folded against her chest. Zoe moved swiftly. First, she went into a tiny supply room and came back with an ice packet and gently secured it around the agitated ankle. Then she called the child's mother. Uncertain of what to do, Joni stood over Nyasia, hoping for the best.

Zoe walked over. "Your mother is sending your uncle Raymond to get you," she told Nyasia.

She replied, pointing at the ice pack, "This is really cold."

Zoe got one of the guest chairs, positioned it before Nyasia and lifted her foot onto it. "Is the cold numbing it?"

It was. She became more focused on the coldness on her ankle, rather than the thumping pain. Turning to Joni, Zoe motioned for her to come into the hallway. She kept the door open so the child could see them while she provided, "I truly believe it isn't broken. It isn't your fault. So stop beating yourself up."

Joni closed her eyes and opened them. "We just started this program. I don't want the other parents getting worried, or Mr. Sparrow thinking I'll hurt the children. I wouldn't have them doing anything they aren't ready for."

Laying a hand on her shoulder, Zoe added, "Ollie knows that. That's why he hired you. You're young and have great insight with the children. Go, finish your class. I'll leave an incident form on my desk for you to fill out."

Joni lifted her arms and hugged Zoe. "Thank you."

Receiving the affection, Zoe realized something. Ollie selected instructors who would not only offer their talents to the foundation, but would in turn build character and confidence from it. Another smile had filled her heart as Joni walked away.

Still smiling, Zoe reentered her office and sat with Nyasia.

"Are you thirsty? I've got some lemonade."

"This time of year?" The child's eyes widened.

"I love it all year round. Want some?"

She nodded yes. Zoe got up and poured a cup for them both. "I've seen you dance. You are already good. You're only going to get better.

"Yeah." She took the cup from Zoe and studied her foot.

"I won't be able to learn the dance. It's so cool. Like the videos of the famous dance companies Ms. Joni showed us."

Zoe sat, enjoyed the child's enthusiasm.

"And in a couple weeks you should be alright. You'll catch up. Hey, how about this? I can record the classes for you and you can watch at home while you recover?"

She smiled brightly at the idea, showing off very crooked teeth then asked, "What if it's broken? It might take more than two weeks to heal."

"I don't think that it is."

"I hope not. I don't want to let my Uncle Raymond down. He spent a thousand dollars to go to Mr. Sparrow's fundraiser and he personally asked him to let me in."

Offering some confidence, Zoe explained, "You let yourself in. I saw your audition. You were great."

Nyasia remembered that glorious day. She did well and loved feeling proud after doing her very best. She didn't mind telling Zoe her biggest hope.

"I don't want to be like my four sisters. They all got babies from different daddies. Uncle Raymond said, I ain't gotta be like those whores."

Zoe recoiled. "Did her uncle really say that?" she thought. "You can be different and make better choices."

Nyasia looked at her injured ankle. "I will, Ms. Zoe. I am going to make my uncle proud."

"I can see that. You really love your uncle."

"Yeah, he's a cop you know. He chased the boy that shot a teacher in East New York."

Zoe began to connect the dots. "Oh, he's the school security there. Yes, it was on the news. Your uncle is very brave."

Nyasia looked sadly at her foot. "Yeah, he is. Since that day, he's been real sad. I heard him talking on the phone to the teacher who got shot. He was crying and said he was sorry for what happened...that it was his fault. It's not. We get drive-bys in our neighborhood all the time. It's random. Innocent people just get shot...sometimes they die. Cops can't help that."

Zoe didn't have a reply for the awful and true observation made by a child who had witnessed such horror.

Nyasia went on, "Uncle Raymond said the shooting wasn't random. He said it was his fault. He won't tell me how."

Zoe's wheels began turning as she listened to the child speak of not so random shootings.

Chapter 73 – Common Ground

Friday night Desiree's car pulled into the church's dirt parking lot. Her car phone rang, startling her. She didn't recognize the incoming number and answered professionally, "Desiree Davenport."

"Zoe Landry, how are you Desiree?"

"Surprised," she replied. Her mind began questioning before Zoe had a chance to explain. "Is it Ollie?" she had thought.

Zoe laughed softly. "I know this is a surprise. First, let me thank you for the recommendation. I love working for the foundation. And because of my new responsibilities, I believe I have some information that may prove helpful."

Desiree hadn't turned the car off. She looked at the old church, thinking her choir members were waiting. One in particular got out of their mini car and waved. She waved back and replied, "I am at choir practice now. Can we talk after?"

Zoe remembered the dynamic voices from her visit with Garrett a few weeks ago and offered, "I can swing by. I'd love to hear you practice."

Desiree heard an edge of urgency in Zoe's voice. She surveyed the desolate neighborhood and with the day approaching dusk, she asked, "Are you sure?"

Certain, Zoe had already climbed into her Infinity and turned it towards Brooklyn. "Positive."

Desiree decided to be honest. "Zoe, no offense, but...maybe I should come to you."

"What? Afraid a white girl might get jacked up in the hood?"

Stunned, Desiree didn't reply and Zoe laughed. "Hey, it's cool."

The woman had backbone. Thinking about Zoe's past as a social worker in Florida, Desiree figured she had to enter all kinds of neighborhoods. Abuse and neglect didn't discriminate.

"Alright, just call me when you get here. I'll have someone walk you in."

"Agreed."

Zoe drove on the heels of a flying cab. She hated traffic. "I'll be there in thirty."

She arrived under 20 and drove into the moist earth of the parking lot. As her tires sank, she questioned why the parking lot was not paved and called Desiree, announcing her arrival. A dark-skinned man wearing a dashing smile approached her car and held out his hand.

She apologized as she stepped out and took his hand.

"I'm sorry to interrupt your practice."

"I'm sorry your pretty shoes are going to get mud on them." He looked down at her feet and so did she. "It's alright. They're old."

"And I'm Webster. Welcome back Zoe."

She blinked at him, he explained, "I remembered you and your friend visited recently. We don't have many visitors with your complexion."

Zoe followed him inside. "That's shameful. The music is so powerful and everyone is very friendly."

Based on everything she had seen, the church was struggling. The walls needed painting, the pews replacing, and, apparently, they were saving on the light bill. She saw that only the front of the church where the choir gathered was illuminated.

Zoe decided to wait in the shadows and started entering the back pew. Webster tugged her arm. "No. No. Join us."

Her face reddened with a protest. "I don't sing."

"You don't have to. Not tonight." He winked at her. "Come up closer. You don't want people getting distracted, looking back at you. It'll throw off our harmony," he teased.

Webster led Zoe up to the third pew and lifted his voice with a directive, "Everybody stop being so nosey. This is Zoe. She visited a few weeks back. She's a friend of Desiree and Deacon."

Hands came in all directions and squeezed Zoe's.

"Thanks," she accepted the hospitality and sat. "Please, I don't want to intrude."

Desiree smiled.

"No intrusion."

And in minutes the smile was gone and Zoe noted Desiree fell into teacher mode. "Alright, let's sing the lyrics without the music. Altos first."

The rehearsal lasted about an hour and Zoe enjoyed every second of it. This was something she craved more than analyzed. The choir had a commonality, a love of music, God, and unity.

She envied them.

Many of the members were teens, some young adults and a few seniors.

"Family," she thought. Zoe never had that. She thought of her sister, Aimee. After Zoe shared her past with her sister, she decided to marry Shaw anyway. And with the help of their mother, they cut Zoe out of all wedding plans. She was told she could attend the wedding, *if* it pleased her. She hadn't made a decision yet.

A young man slid into the pew beside Zoe.

"Hi, I'm Parker." She accepted his hand. "Nice to meet you."

"The pleasure's all mine." He pushed his small-framed glasses up on the bridge of his nose. She gathered him to be about 20. He inquired with a smirk, "You're not afraid being here."

She looked at him. Yeah, he was young. He looked like he wanted to bite her, or something. "Hormones," she thought. "Should I be?" She lifted one brow.

"Your car should be. What you drivin'?"

"Parker, go downstairs and get your pizza. This woman is old enough to be your...."

"Big sister," Zoe finished for Desiree.

"Okay, big sister. Get out of here." Desiree shooed Parker away and slid in next to Zoe.

"That boy is in every woman's face. He doesn't care about age or race." She touched Zoe's hand. "And your car will be fine. You parked in our lot, right?"

"I did." Zoe turned and watched Parker bounce away. "I like his style. It's welcoming."

"You got that right. You want to go somewhere and talk."

"Here is fine, unless you'd rather not."

Desiree scanned the church. It seemed everyone had skedaddled and headed downstairs for dinner. "Here is good."

Zoe started, "Nyasia Bonner is a student at the foundation. Her uncle is Officer Raymond Bonner."

Desiree was aware Raymond had quite a few nieces; one attended the foundation. She waited for more.

Zoe gave it. "Nyasia sprang her ankle during dance class. It's not bad. While we waited for Raymond to pick her up, she shared that he blames himself for the shooting. He said it wasn't random and that it was his fault."

Desiree squinted. She knew the shooting wasn't random. It had to do with Trevor and his cousin, forcing Tiona to confess. How was Raymond involved? What did he know?

Zoe touched her hand, pulling Desiree back. She replied absently, "This thing gets weirder by the second. I thought it was just a kid fondling anther kid. I don't know what to think. I need to talk to Raymond."

Zoe quickly shook her head. "I thought of that. Not a good idea."

Desiree frowned at Zoe's response, "He's an officer. He's not going to confess any wrongdoing."

"What wrongdoing?" Desiree blurted.

"That's what you don't know yet."

She could see Desiree had a difficult time receiving the information. Zoe explained, "I've seen some horrible things happen to children. And when children lie, it's because they are covering for someone that they love, or they're terribly afraid of. You've been looking for the child that molested Tiona. I don't believe it's a child. And I do believe Raymond knows that."

The information began to rip at her heart. Her eyes swam in warm tears. "I can't believe this."

"I want to help. We've got to protect the students in your school."

Until she had more, she didn't want the information to leak. "Have you told anyone else this?"

"No," Zoe replied.

"Not even Ollie?"

"Ollie's out of town with Olivia."

"Thank you." Both ladies turned their heads when they thought they heard someone lurking in the shadows. They saw no one.

Desiree shifted in her seat.

"I'll call Mitch. He's helping with the investigation. We can trust him."

Zoe laid a hand on Desiree. "I'll make a statement. Whatever you need, I'll do."

Desiree nodded, listening to the ringing in her ears. "Oh, God, a child molester, in my school?" she thought.

Thankfully, her words from earlier rang louder. "Lord, I will trust you to help me in this."

Chapter 74 – Ready for a Real Woman

Mitch instructed the ladies to go to Desiree's home and wait for his arrival. There were just too many itching ears in All Praise Church. The last thing they needed was for someone to compromise the investigation.

Desiree led Zoe into her home and flicked on the lights.

"Can I take your jacket?"

"Sure, thanks."

Zoe untied the belt of her short black jacket and slid it off her shoulders. Handing her jacket over, she began to peruse the family photos lining the walls.

"I love family photos."

She stepped slowly studying each one.

Desiree stood watching. She noticed Zoe's regal height, lean, yet shapely body. She was wearing an emerald green round-neck sweater, flattering dark blue jeans, and dark brown expensive flat shoes. She looked...relaxed.

Keeping her eyes focused on the photos, Zoe asked, "How was it growing up with four sisters?"

Desiree walked up, looked at a Christmas photo from when she was 12.

"Crowded," she replied. "We had a fairly nice size house. Still...," she sighed, "girls and all their stuff take up a lot of space. My father had no problem spoiling us. It drove my mother crazy."

Zoe sidestepped, looked at Desiree's parents.

"Your mother probably had a difficult time denying your father."

Desiree smiled.

"Oh yeah, she did. Dad's a charmer. He loved my mother."

"It shows. He's like Deacon, perhaps?" Zoe turned to Desiree with a faint smile in her eyes.

Lifting her brows, Desiree asked playfully, "You trying to get in my business."

"May I?"

Zoe really did have backbone. Desiree invited, "That meat lovers' pizza from church really made me thirsty. Let's go into the kitchen for a drink."

Following Desiree, Zoe sat at the large table.

"Water?" Desiree offered.

"Yes, please."

Desiree rounded up two bottles and joined Zoe. She figured they could get this over with before Mitch showed up.

"I know how it looks, but my break-up with Ollie was amicable."

"I can see that. Ollie doesn't seem like one for drama. Besides, I've deduced that you and Deacon have a history. You're both very comfortable around each other. Was he your high school sweetheart?"

Desiree smirked, then turned up her water bottle, and took a deep drink. "How 'bout we put our professional degrees aside. I'm not a principal and you're not a psychiatrist. We're just two women talking."

Zoe shrugged. "Alright, shoot."

"*You* find Ollie charming. You want to make sure I'm long gone and out of the picture."

Honesty always served best. "I didn't plan on it."

"Who does? I didn't plan to fall for Deacon. I was engaged to his best friend." She rested her hand on her chest. "Once my heart locked in on Deacon, he had ownership. After he left, I could only offer men a fraction, not the whole."

Zoe crossed her arms on the table. "Not even Ollie?"

"Not even Ollie," Desiree repeated. "I wanted to give it to him. Ollie's so wonderful. He's kind, funny, sensitive, and easy. He's simply down to earth. Even with all those great qualities, it still wasn't enough for me."

"Facing the truth must have been difficult."

"Very. I love him and Olivia."

"And you're in love with Deacon. And after all these years, you've been waiting."

Somewhat ashamed by that, she admitted, "Pathetic."

"You knew what you wanted. There's nothing wrong with that. I allowed myself to be violated once. It cost me a great deal. I don't get involved with just any man, either."

Zoe thought of her sister's fiancé, her former lover and father of her deceased child. Desiree nodded unaware of Zoe's history, but understanding of the determined look in her eyes. She added, "Ollie's not just any man to you. Does he know how you feel?"

Zoe shook her head, took a sip of water – craved some lemon. "Somewhat. It's too soon. He's getting over you."

Desiree didn't reveal the woman she saw Ollie with a couple weeks ago. Was it just a rebound thing? Unsure, she rested a warm hand on Zoe's arm.

"Then give him time."

"I know he's seeing someone, intimately, or was." Zoe shrugged. Desiree squinted.

"I am very good at analysis." She smiled at the shock on Desiree's face. "I don't expect the relationship to last long. He's not at peace with it."

Desiree had one question. "Do you know who the woman is?"

Zoe did not. "Considering my feelings, I cared not to find out."

Desiree noted their shared interest. They were two women who were very concerned about the welfare of children and the welfare of one man. It made it easy for Desiree to bond with Zoe. She cared enough to share what she knew.

"It's Lacy Reid, Marcel Reid's wife. Marcel killed Ollie's wife." She watched a fearful look register across Zoe's face.

Several seconds later, Zoe said, "Desiree, your break-up was hard on Ollie. You basically left him for another man. His first wife cheated on him. I can see he's lost confidence."

She wanted to retrieve the words when Desiree flinched.

"That wasn't meant to hurt you – only an observation. He'll find his way back. I've been praying for him. It's good that he suddenly took a couple weeks away."

Desiree felt awful. "I haven't prayed for him."

"You've got a lot to deal with, too."

"Still...."

She rested her hand on Desiree's.

"No, don't go there. Just start praying now."

They sat quietly for a moment and realized they both felt lighter after their talk.

Zoe sat up taller and rolling her shoulders she playfully declared, "Besides, when Ollie's ready for a real woman, I'll be here."

Laughing while admiring Zoe's confidence, Desiree swatted her arm.

"I like you, Zoe."

Chapter 75 – Will You Make Me Do It?

Officer Raymond Bonner had to be discreet when visiting Simon Barnes. That was, if he wanted private time with the man. And he desperately did.

He waited in the lobby of the hospital, shooting the breeze with a fellow officer, discreetly eyeing Simon's wife as she exited the building. He used the look on her face as his indicator. She appeared less strained and Raymond took it as a sign that Simon was finally getting better.

Casually ending his talk, he shifted to the elevator and rode up with hospital staff. He anxiously shoved his way off and took long focused strides to Simon's room.

He knocked and stuck his foot over the threshold, cautiously holding the door open with one hand. "You up?"

Simon turned toward the familiar voice. Raymond always looked so official in uniform. He said, "I'm still alive. My wife just left."

Simon's voice sounded like he was under water. Raymond didn't like that, but at least he was talking, breathing. Thank God, he *was* alive.

Raymond stepped all the way inside, crossed over to the bed and seized the empty chair.

"I saw her leave, but I know how fast you fall asleep," he joked.

Simon didn't smile. Not about this, not anymore. There was a gaping hole in his chest struggling to close. He gazed up, thinking about his life decisions. God didn't let him die and he had another chance to make things right.

Raymond held his fists to control them and inquired, "What are the doctors saying?"

"I'll live. They really don't want me having many visitors. I had to call Desiree and ask her not to come today."

Raymond loved hearing that. He didn't want Desiree sniffing around. He took Simon's hand and squeezed it. "I've missed you."

Simon weakly tugged his hand away and turned his head to the stark white ceiling. "Janet has stuck by me. I owe her." He laid a hand on the bandaged wound covered by his hospital gown. "I can't lie to her anymore."

Uncontrollable joy built up in Raymond's eyes. "Are you saying...you're leaving her? I've been waiting for this day for us to finally be free."

Blankly, Simon turned to face him. "I'm not going to be with you anymore. We're through Ray."

Raymond ruthlessly shook his head. He had to make him understand. "Do you think being gay is something you can turn off and on? You can't. We're gay men and you want me. We've been together five years for a reason."

Simon opened his mouth to speak. Raymond wouldn't let him. "I know you've been close to death." He shook his head once more, blaming himself for Simon's near fatal condition.

"You've been lying to Janet since day one. You're gay, man. The minute you accept that, the happier we'll both be."

Turning his head to the ceiling, a tear rolled out of his eye. Raymond demanded, "Look at me!"

Simon wouldn't turn. "Simon, if you don't want to tell Janet, I will. I'll take care of you."

"I can't Ray. My place is with Janet and the girls. I'm a husband and a father."

Raymond banged his fist into his chest. "What about me? You know what I did for us, Simon?"

Simon's head returned quickly to Raymond's emotional gaze. The man could be so irrational. He asked slowly, "What did you do?"

He didn't want to say, but his flailing emotions wouldn't keep quiet.

"I sent that little whore and her mother a message. It might cost me my job, or worse. I did that for us man."

Simon knew who and what he was talking about. It was one of his worst fears. "Tiona, oh God," he thought.

He spat, "You didn't touch a child, Ray? Tiona's mother is an old friend."

"Yeah, an old friend that you bang."

"I told you that only happened once. Besides, you go out with women, too. What about Karyn? You took her to the fundraiser!" he argued.

A sour taste filled his mouth. "She was just something to do. I gave the whore just what she craved."

Simon started fighting, lifting himself up. "You didn't hurt Karyn, did you?"

Raymond sucked his teeth. "Please, I didn't do anything that she's hasn't done a million times. You know Karyn."

Simon fell back down and closed his eyes. They were getting off topic and he needed Raymond out of his life. He wouldn't accept his impulsive, angry, misguided behavior any longer. He said softly, "No more, Ray. No more."

Raymond stood and stared down into Simon's stern face. "Don't make me do something to change your mind."

As painful as it was, Simon pushed himself up again. Sweat began flooding his pores. The intense effort sent the heart monitor blaring. Soon, they expected medical personnel to rush in.

"Are you threatening me, Ray?"

"You better tell Janet to keep those three precious girls of yours locked up. I wouldn't want anything unfortunate to happen to them."

His three girls, oh no! He attempted to reason, "If you love me...."

"I'll do it out of love for you. Seems that bullet has clouded your thinking. Don't make me do something you'll regret."

Simon stared at the man he secretly shared his life with for the past five years and wondered, "Why."

"Ray please...."

Just as they suspected, white coats and green scrubs raced into the room. Raymond eased away, hoping Simon wouldn't force him to hurt another little girl.

Chapter 76 – Holy Antibiotics

It took a couple days in the mountains with God and his little girl to cast away some of the guilt he kept over his relationship with Lacy. The scenery was absolutely breathtaking and a reminder that God truly did exist in all things. He and Olivia stood at the edge of the lake, skipping rocks into the water.

Every time she made a ripple, her joyous laughter infected them both. He loved the sound of her innocent voice as it bounced and landed on the trees and trailed through the air.

Ollie laughed as she jumped up and down, clapping her hands. It didn't take much to please her – time alone with Daddy, nature, and a few rocks. If life was complicated at times, it had been because he made it that way.

"Why," he wondered. Why didn't he come here first after his break-up with Desiree? Instead, he pretended he wasn't hurt by it. He thought about turning to Zoe. The attraction was strong, but he denied it, becoming intimate with Lacy.

He wanted to reason, justify the entire affair. He and Lacy had much in common. They knew what it was like to be deceived by someone you trusted, loved, and desired. They knew what it felt like to lose. Lacy lost her husband to the justice system. Ollie lost his wife to death. Then they were left to pick up the pieces, raise their children, and provide answers to questions that neither of them could ever fully know the truth about.

Then there was the anger, resentment, and desire for revenge. Their flesh feasted on it, making their intimate encounters intense – and at times, he knew they were riding on the verge of violence. Who were they battling? Each other? Their spouses? Themselves? Maybe all of the above.

Ollie accepted he really would have to give himself over to prayer to rise above the guilt and shame. He had to. It wasn't optional.

He looked down at Olivia, hearing her laughter call him back. It helped cleanse him. His child deserved the best of him.

Thank God that he took the first step toward healing by removing the pain in his flesh. He ended things with Lacy, and now, he wanted the wound to close and leave a scar – a reminder.

He realized he could have a relationship with God, go to church every Sunday, Bible study once a week, and still be infected with darkness, uncertainty and fear. The negative emotions infected him and seeped in quietly. Although he was well aware of its consumption, he gave in to it.

Olivia pulled his hand; he knelt down, giving into her.

"It's time for breakfast. Hungry, sweetie?"

"Rocks." She opened her tiny hands showing him she was out.

He picked her up with a smile, kissed her cool cheek. They had been in the morning air long enough. He turned for their cabin. Olivia protested, "More rocks, Daddy!"

"Later, sweetie. Food now. We'll take another walk later. I promise."

She continued to pout, making him laugh.

"Wow," he stated, "you look so much like your mother when you make that face."

Chapter 77 – The Scar

While Ollie enjoyed breakfast with his little girl in Pennsylvania, Zoe and Lily feasted on croissants and tea in his downtown gallery. Both ladies sat in the visitors' chairs so that neither sat in the authority seat.

"It's really nice of you to rearrange your schedule and look out for Ollie's business," Lily commented.

"My pleasure," Zoe replied, "The kids are great. In my practice I have more adult clients than children. My first love has always been the children."

Lily could see that. She said, "Ollie made a good decision bringing you on board." She found she cared for Zoe and understood that Vaughn, Ollie's sister, had her concerns about Zoe being white. Lily did not, however. Not that she was naïve about interracial relationships. Any relationship in particular had challenges. Certainly, when you added cultural, ethnic and racial concerns to the mix, it did make things more interesting. It also built strong relationships.

She considered Ollie and Zoe would be a well-bonded and stimulating couple. Zoe could be the woman for Ollie. As Lily considered the possibility, Zoe detected her analytical silence. "Care to tell me what you're thinking?"

"Why not?" she thought. Picking up her plate, Lily took a bite of her croissant and felt her baby in her womb make a long stretch. "Whoa."

Zoe's eyes widened. The movement was noticeable through Lily's thin white sweater. "How does that feel?"

"Incredible and weird," Lily answered, placing her small plate onto the edge of the desk and rubbing her belly.

Zoe remembered being pregnant in college. She never got further along to feel her baby move so strongly.

Lily answered, "I was thinking about you and Ollie, getting together."

"Huh?" Zoe had forgotten that she asked the question.

For the first time, Lily saw Zoe a little off her game.

"You asked me what I was thinking."

Quickly coming back, she replied, "Really, why Ollie and me? I'm assuming you mean romantically?"

"I'm probably getting ahead of myself and too personal with you. I just see something special in you, for him." She shrugged.

Zoe smiled, remembering how she got into Desiree's business the night before – all about Ollie. She confessed, "It's no secret I find your cousin attractive. I admire him a great deal. I'm not jumping his bones or anything like that. My plan is to do the job he hired me for and see how our relationship develops."

Smirking, Lily said, "Interesting theory. Strong emotions are not that easily controlled. I think you'd do just that, however. You would do it for the children, the foundation and for Ollie. You care for him."

"I do," she admitted. "He's a considerate man. A little too trusting if you ask me. I'm a more skeptical person."

"Ollie can use a skeptic in his life. Someone cautious that thinks before she acts."

Zoe perceived Lily wasn't referring to Desiree, but Ollie's late wife. "You and Sapphire were close?"

Lily nodded. "I came to love her. She was getting her life in line with her faith -- a wonderful transformation to watch and then...," Lily trailed off. Zoe reached over, touched her hand. Lily finished, "Sapphire was gone. It seemed too soon. She never held her baby in her arms."

Zoe felt that pain flood her. She never held her baby in her arms either.

She listened as Lily provided, "Sapphire's infidelity began because she hadn't dealt with her childhood issues. Ollie was caught in the middle of it."

She had to ask. "Are you upset that things didn't work out between him and Desiree?"

Relieved felt more like it. "Honestly, Vaughn and I were on the verge of planning their engagement party. Now I'm pleased that Deacon came back. His timing was perfect. Things worked out just as they should have." She joked, "If Desiree would have gotten Ollie involved in another love triangle, Vaughn and I were going to have to fight somebody."

Zoe's bright brown eyes widened as she laughed with Lily. The ladies turned when Hannah knocked and walked into the room. Her face was pale, eyes frighteningly moving left and right. Lily pushed up out of her chair, moved to her. "What is it?"

Almost whispering, Hannah revealed, "The cops are here for Ollie."

Lily placed her hand on the young woman's shoulder, brushed away her long honey blond hair. The 20 year old was normally shy, now she was terrified.

"Did you tell them that Ollie is out of town?" Lily questioned. Hannah shook her head no, made some sort of grunting sound.

Lily understood why she came to her. Hannah trusted her. She had done temporary work and babysitting for Lily from time-to-time. Ollie snatched up the young talent as his curator when his gallery opened.

Zoe slowly rose to her feet as Lily comfortably maneuvered into attorney mode. "You did good, Hannah. Bring them to me, please."

Hannah nodded and scurried out, happy to have the officers out of her hair.

"Can I do anything?" Zoe volunteered.

Lily looked around Ollie's office.

"We have no idea why they want to talk to him." Lily made an apologetic face, "You mind if you allow me some privacy with them?"

"Oh, sure," Zoe hiccupped and started gathering up their plates. "I'll just be down at the foundation if you need me." She made a quick exit, just as the detectives came in.

Detectives Kris St. Laurent and Dee Spelling identified themselves and flashed their badges. Lily nodded, doing her best not to exhibit any protective behavior for her cousin.

Instead of crossing her arms against her chest, she kept them loosely at her sides. "I'm Lily Carraway. Oliver's cousin," she used Ollie's birth name.

Dee added, "And his attorney."

"That's right. I'm on the board of the Sapphire Arts Foundation. How can I help you, detectives?"

"You can tell us where he is," The male detective answered.

"Why?"

"He needs to be taken in for questioning, immediately."

"What for?"

Kris tilted his head. He was cinnamon brown, incredibly handsome, tall, and skinny. The dark black curls danced all over his head. But his eyes were annoyed. "Mrs. Carraway. I'm going to advise you of this once. Find your client, get him to the station."

He handed her his card and continued, "And inform him that it would be in his best interest to cooperate."

"We have no intentions of not cooperating. My client is out of town on holiday."

"Holiday over," he fired.

Lily returned fire, "Charges?"

"If you like, we can do this the hard way," the male detective barked.

Dee chimed in, "Lily, Ollie's been accused of rape."

Lily felt the air in her lungs flee. She struggled not to show it. "There must be some misunderstanding."

"That's what we hope," Dee provided. "So, to move this along, get your cousin back in town today."

"Of course, I'll get him here ASAP. We'll call when we're on our way to the station."

The detectives turned to leave and Lily asked, "Who's the alleged victim?"

Kris started to reply that they couldn't provide that information when Dee interrupted, "Lacy Reid, spouse of Marcel Reid."

Kris cut his eyes at Dee and she shrugged off his disapproval and directed to Lily, "This doesn't look good."

"Thank you," Lily struggled to stay on her feet as they exited. "Oh, God, is Ollie capable of rape? Was he that distraught over Marcel and Sapphire's affair? No, this did not look good," she thought.

She turned and plucked up her cell phone from the desk. She barely heard him answer, when she instructed, "We have an emergency here. No questions, Ollie. Just get home."

"Where are you?"

"At the foundation."

"I'm on my way."

Lily sighed and finally let her wobbly legs lower her into a chair. She considered it best for him to believe the issue was related to the foundation.

"Rape, good God," she thought.

The next call she made was to Mitch -- a detective, and Ollie's friend. She needed information and Mitch could access it.

Chapter 78 – Mad, Crazy World

Mitch sat in Desiree's office reading through the notes Zoe had put together. Without looking up at Desiree, he commented, "These are good."

"Nyasia Porter is a 10-year old fifth grader and student of the Sapphire Arts Foundation. In speaking to the minor on March 29, she provided that her uncle was Officer Raymond Bonner, School Security for Elementary Public School in Brooklyn, New York. Nyasia provided the impression of a young girl that has a close bond with her uncle. She cares for him and has shown concern for his happiness. She stated lately her uncle had been unhappy, depressed, and at times, she found him crying. He had complained about the shooting that occurred and verbally claimed self-blame. Nyasia had no point of reference and could not provide reasons why her uncle accepts responsibility. Nyasia further explained that she comforted her uncle by expressing to him that random shootings frequently take place. Sadly, this is true. Officer Bonner replied that the shooting was no random shooting, however. Officer Bonner may have insight to this terrifying event. Additionally, it is my professional belief that Tiona Washington, if molested, was molested by an adult in her school, as opposed to another minor. Particularly, when children are dishonest about traumatic events, the reason is to protect a loved one, or they are paralyzed by fear. It is my urgent recommendation that further investigation is required," the notes read.

Eyes still glued to Zoe's report, Mitch inquired, "Nyasia is not a student at your school?"

Desiree replied, "No, only Tiona, the child who was molested. Will you need to question both Tiona and Nyasia?"

"Not yet." Mitch lifted his head, rolled the report into a cylinder and used it as a pointer. "We have a couple things going on here. One, your school security is correct. Not a random shooting. Trevor's cousin pulled that trigger to clear Trevor's name. And Zoe's right, Tiona lied. Who do you think your offender is, Desiree?"

She rested her elbows onto the desk, pushed her hands onto her face. "I've been praying about that all night. I can't believe someone on my staff would hurt a child."

Mitch shrugged, asked, "Why not? This is a perfect place for a pedophile."

Desiree folded her hands together on her desk and leaned forward. "Mitch, you know the extensive background checks we have to go through."

"I do, and people are still able to get around them."

Letting out a deep breath, she asked, "Now what?"

"We hunt. I'm not lead investigator on this. You know I'm homicide. So...I'll have to share this information. You think Zoe can break Tiona – get her to tell the truth?"

"I don't know. If she's traumatized, I don't know what Zoe will get out of her." Desiree paused, feeling a ball of anger in her belly. "I can't image what coming to school day after day is like for Tiona. The child is coming to a place where she is supposed to be safe. Trust adults."

Feeling the anger rush him as well, he stated, "I'm going to help you contain this. We need to protect the other minor, Raymond's niece. I don't want her to get the backlash for speaking with Zoe. Here's what I'll do...."

Desperate to find the truth, Desiree sat taller in her chair, straining to hear, as if something clogged her ears.

Mitch explained, "I'm going to keep a watch on Officer Raymond Bonner. We'll put an undercover in your school as a substitute teacher. We'll have eyes on him in and out of school."

"Won't Raymond recognize the undercover?" Desiree asked.

He shook his head no. "We'll get someone out of the area. I'll also pay Tiona's mother a visit."

"Her mother?" she asked, surprised. She remembered how upset Ms. Washington had been over Tiona being violated.

"Yep, I want to see what she knows."

Shaking her head, she replied, "That woman was so upset, if she knew anything, she'd be in my office screaming about it."

Mitch angled his head to the left. "You'd be surprised at what parents know and pretend that they don't. The homicide that I got called into last night, a 16-year-old girl killed her father. The father had been abusing the child physically and sexually for years. So this kid finally snapped and slashed him up real good. It was a blood bath...blood everywhere. All over the kid, in her hair and eyes...."

Desiree held up her hand. "I got it."

"Sorry. I forget not everyone can stomach the details."

She nodded, wondering how anyone could, but was thankful that someone did.

"Anyway," Mitch made his point, "come to find out, the mother had knowledge and never did anything."

Desiree frowned. "That's awful. Why?"

"The father was loaded. He kept the mother in her cushy lifestyle. And all it cost the mother was to sell her daughter. Sick, right?"

On the verge of agreeing, she closed her mouth when Mitch's cell sounded.

"Stephens."

"Mitch, hi. This is Lily Carraway. Ollie's cousin."

"Hey." He lifted his thick brows at Desiree.

"I need your help," Lily stated and filled him in on recent events.

Mitch replied, "Deacon said something like this could happen."

Now Desiree lifted her brows as Mitch continued, "I'll see what I can find out. Is Ollie on his way back?"

"Yes."

"Alright, good. I'll call when I've got something." He hung up.

Before she could ask, Mitch said, "Ollie's being investigated for a rape allegation."

Desiree's blood grew cold, gripping her thighs as they started going numb. "Ol..Ollie would never hurt anyone. I dated him for a solid year. He never showed any signs of violence. That's not Ollie. Mitch, you know that!"

Mitch stood, pointed to himself. "Hey, I'm not accusing him of anything. I will find out what's going on. You people are keeping me busy," he joked.

Desiree held her head down. "Thanks for everything. I didn't mean to snap at you." She looked up at him and asked, "Has the world gone mad?"

"Unfortunately, being a cop, that's my world. I'll get back to you when we have the undercover ready."

She stood up, too, walked around her desk. "I really appreciate it." Lifting up on her tippy toes, she kissed his cheek.

Mitch held her hand, studied the engagement ring and lowered his voice. "Sweetheart, you know you can't marry my brother."

She saw the hint of mischief in his eyes when he stared into hers. Baffled, she squinted.

"Well first, my cousin Evan marries your sister, and now my brother marrying you...there are no more good women," he teased. "I guess I gotta remain a bachelor, forever. Oh, well." He shrugged and began stepping away.

She swatted his arm. "You're just afraid of commitment."

"Hey, we all have our fears," he said and left.

Desiree watched Mitch's large presence exit the room. Even with his fears, he was a good man, taking on extra work for his friends.

She took a deep cleansing breath and thanked God for his help. She started to walk around her desk, when someone rushed in and grabbed her from behind and attacked her neck.

Her heart nearly leapt onto the desk. Catching a whiff of him, fresh soap and Deacon, she squealed, "You nearly gave me a heart attack!"

Keeping her close, he turned her in his arms and kissed her for a great length of time. Neither of them saw the assistant principal and secretary peeking into the office.

His heart racing too, he managed to say hello with a grand smile on his face.

"Hello, to you." She rubbed her hands over his firm back. He felt so good in her arms. "You're home a day early."

"I love you, Desiree."

Squeezing tighter, she replied, "I love you, too," and rested her head into his chest with an exhale. Holding on to the man she loved, Desiree prepared to face the mad crazy world.

Chapter 79 – I Believe

Ollie had no idea what the emergency could be. It had to be pretty serious. Lily directed, "Don't ask, just get home." He resisted putting the pedal to the metal, considered his baby's safety. He did, however, allow himself the opportunity to do five over the speed limit.

As soon as he was back in New York, he dropped Olivia off at his sister's house, rushed over to the foundation. When he arrived, he found Zoe and Lily in his office.

Frantic, his white shirt was damp with perspiration. His eyes, that were typically wide and exotic, stretched for answers.

Zoe wanted to provide them. But Lily had shared little with her. She got up ready to make her exit and Ollie stepped up to her. "Zoe, what's going on?"

She laid a hand on his arm, squeezed it. "Lily will explain it to you. Let me know if I can do anything to help."

She started to walk off and he grabbed her hand, tugged her back and inched closer into her personal space. "That's not acceptable, Zoe. I left you in charge. I expect you to tell me what's going on here. What's the emergency?"

Lily stood, opened her mouth and Zoe lifted her hand, signaled for Lily to hold off a second. Just as tall as him, she gave him direct eye contact.

"The emergency is about you. It's personal. Two detectives were here to question you today. That's all I know. If there was an emergency within the foundation, you would have had a full report before you stepped foot into this building."

The flushed look over Ollie's face began to pale against his light complexion. She noticed his forehead was damp. She wanted to comfort him, to run her fingertips over his head. Instead, she lowered her gaze, started out of the room.

He called after her, "I'm…sorry."

Before closing the door behind her, she offered, "I meant what I said: If there's anything I can do, just say the word."

He nodded and turned to Lily for answers.

Extending her hand, she invited him to sit down.

"I don't want to sit. The drive was long and frustrating. What did the detectives want? Does it have anything to do with Marcel?"

Lily bit her bottom lip, thought of the man who shot Ollie's wife. "Why do you ask?"

"He's been writing me, taunting me."

"You're still reading his letters? Ollie!"

She fisted her hands and shook them, began a slow pace around the office. His cousin was smoother than this. Nervous now, he demanded, "What?"

"Lacy Reid, Marcel's wife, accused you of rape. I've been in touch with Mitch. He found out there is physical evidence. The detectives want to question you and get a sample of your DNA."

If he hadn't gripped the chair in front of him, he would have fallen. The air in his lungs fled. Lily saw him go completely pale and ordered, "Sit down, Ollie."

He did and because she needed to do her job, she sat at the head of his desk. She pulled out her leather-bound notebook and began, "We have to go down to the station. Let's get this out of the way." Picking up her pencil, she asked, "Do you know Lacy Reid?"

"Yes."

"How did you meet?"

"She came to the gallery one morning. Upset, crying...said she was back in town to care for her father. He suffered a stroke. When she returned home, she found all the newspaper clippings about Sassy...that Marcel had shot and killed her."

"What did she want?"

"Answers, she asked me to help her write a book about what happened."

As professional as his cousin was, he saw her thoughts radiate over her face. She had the look of "You believed that story? "

Ollie provided, "Lacy seemed very upset. I thought by helping her, it might help me too. You know...find closure."

"Opening up all those wounds Ollie would not help you. You knew your wife had an affair before she died. And you basically knew why. Did you really need to relive the details with Marcel's wife?" Lily sighed. "Alright...did you two become intimate?"

"Yes, but not until after Desiree and I broke up."

"Why is she now accusing you of rape?"

"I ended the relationship. The morning I left for Pennsylvania. She wanted me to meet her children, start coming to church with me. I didn't want to be a stepfather to Marcel's kids. I didn't want Olivia to grow up with that."

"How did she react when you ended it?"

Ollie took a deep breath, rubbed his sweaty palms against his black slacks. "Weird. At first she protested. Then her back straightened, she went to the bathroom. Took a while in there, but she finally came out, fully dressed. Without a word, she walked out."

"Did you use condoms with her, Ollie?"

Ashamed, he looked at the wall. "Not the first time we were together. She was staying the night. We talked a long time and she asked if she could sleep on the couch. I agreed. About two or three in the morning she got into bed with me. That's how it started."

Lily didn't want to judge. But with no questions asked, he had sex with a complete stranger. She took another deep breath. "Alright, how long ago was the first time?"

"A few weeks. I don't know how there could be any physical evidence."

"Think hard, Ollie. Mitch said their evidence is pretty solid."

He put his hands together in prayer motion, brought them to his full lips. It took a minute and he confessed, "Things were a little physically rough between us...especially at the height of things. She'd scratch me. She bit me once. I think I bit her back."

Lily lifted her brows. "Are the scratches evident?"

He nodded.

"Show me," she demanded.

Ollie stood up, lifted his shirt over his head and exposed a tight chiseled chest, rock solid abs, and muscular arms. Lily could see Lacy being impressed. She swallowed hard at the bite mark on his left chest muscle. He turned his back toward Lily. She gasped at what Ollie allowed to be done to his body.

Lily rose slowly, walked around the desk and with her fingers she traced the visible deep scratches on his arms, back and shoulders. "Lacy drew blood," she noted.

This did not look good at all.

Lily walked around the desk, sat, and made notes. "You can put your shirt back. "I never raped Lacy. Never. She always came to me – after Olivia was asleep. She never once said, "No," or "Stop," or that I was hurting her. She's not very verbal. But she's aggressive...wild...that's the best way I can describe her. Afterward though, she'd always cry."

Lily lifted her chin. "You didn't think that was odd? That you might have been hurting her?"

"I asked if I hurt her. She'd always said, 'No.' She asked me to hold her. I would until she'd fall asleep. I'd wake her early so she could go before Olivia got up. Later in the day we'd talk. She'd tell me how she liked being with me. She said, 'She felt safe with me.' I'm telling you it was never..." He shook his head for emphasis. "NEVER, rape."

She believed him, but how could she make a jury of his peers believe him?

Chapter 80 – Write and Tell

After being questioned by Lily, they headed over to the station for additional questioning. Ollie permitted the thin male technician to take the DNA samples they wanted and photograph his body. He didn't know if Mitch had anything to do with it, but he had met them there and everyone he came into contact with was pleasant enough. Nevertheless, the entire process humiliated him.

Common criminals surrounded him. He had been lied on, accused, and placed into a horrific nightmare. He focused on Lily's instruction as she drove them away from the station.

"If the DNA is a match, Ollie, they'll issue a warrant for your arrest."

Ollie glanced over at her and felt weak. Lily was five months pregnant. Because of his choices, she had spent her day preparing, prepping and protecting him. At least he should have driven. "Pull over," he demanded.

"Why?" She gave him a puzzling look.

"It's late and you're pregnant."

She shrugged, "Being pregnant doesn't affect my driving ability." She kept the Jaguar going.

"Look, I don't want Michael saying I'm wearing out his wife. Come on, let me drive."

She double-parked on a side street. At a quarter to eight, the sun had settled, leaving the streetlights to guide them. Ollie waited for her to come around, after she eased into the passenger's seat, he shut the door and walked to the other side.

She strapped in, and it hit her -- the exhaustion of the day made her recline her seat back and close her eyes.

Positioned into the driver's seat, he looked over. "You Okay?"

"My back. That's all. I'll be fine. Let's go. Dad's waiting for us."

Ollie signaled, pulled out into the street. They were heading over to Lily's parents house, for family prayer and dinner in Long Island. Already late, it would take over an hour to get there, he said, "I think I should take you home. You need your rest."

She shook her head in disagreement. "I'm fine."

He came to a stoplight. "You're not, but you're going to fight me. We'll go; promise me when we get there, you'll lie down. You can pray lying down."

It sounded reasonable.

"Deal." She opened her eyes and smiled at him.

Because the situation seemed hopeless, he asked, "How much time do you think I'll serve for this?"

Lily turned her head slowly, hearing his acceptance of defeat. "None Ollie, you didn't rape her."

"I didn't, but she's saying I did. From the looks of things, it appears that I did. Everyone is going to believe the jealous, angry husband got revenge on the man that slept with his wife. Since he screwed my wife, I screwed his."

She agreed as they pulled onto the Long Island Expressway. "That's the defense they will use. Lacy was distraught, she came to you for help, believed that you shared a common interest. But you...full of rage over your wife's death and losing your girlfriend to another man, you turned that rage on Lacy. Oh...it's a good defense. Now I have to ask this, because they will..."

Ollie braced himself. "What is it?"

"How much of what we're saying is true?"

As the car glided along, Ollie admitted, "Of course, I was angry, hurt by what happened to Sassy. And, yeah, I was disappointed things didn't work out between Desiree and me."

He stumbled on the next comment. Speaking the truth aloud, hurt even more. "I did get satisfaction out of sleeping with Marcel's wife. In a way, I was getting back at him. Since he enjoyed writing me so much, I started to write him a letter and tell him what we were doing."

Lily's heart jumped. "Please, Ollie, tell me you didn't. That you didn't even start writing one!"

He shook his head. "No...no...," he stuttered, "I thought about it. But no, I didn't start one."

Taking a deep breath, she said, "Good. That's good. But what you said helps."

Confused, he looked over. "It does? How?"

"Lacy was just as angry and hurt over her husband's infidelity. I bet you Marcel was writing her letters. And if she's a writer, I'm betting the farm, she wrote him back – told him about you. Maybe she gave him explicit details about your encounters."

Ollie squinted as she continued her argument, "Think about it...he's locked up. Lacy knows her husband, how arrogant he is. It would further destroy him knowing you're intimate with her...to the point she's animal like, scratching and biting... See where I'm going?"

He was seeing it move into focus. He slammed his hand against the wheel. "I'm so stupid!" he shouted.

"Naïve. Not stupid. You're too trusting."

"I did trust her." Ollie lowered his voice in disgust. "Lacy was using me, to get back at Marcel. What did she want, for me to marry her, raise his children as my own?"

Lily closed her eyes, rested her head against the seat, and tried to think like Lacy – enraged, emotional, and tormented.

"Maybe. She said she trusted you. Truth be told, women aren't wired for revenge sex very well. We get hooked, bonding easily after we've been intimate with a man. We...."

"You didn't. Not with Rick," Ollie cut her off, mentioning a man from Lily's past.

Lily opened her eyes, looked over. "That wasn't like this. Me sleeping with Rick was about wanting to feel desired. I just plain ole fell into temptation. As soon as it was over, I knew it was wrong. Lacy's situation is different. She targeted you for one reason, to cause Marcel mental anguish. In order to do that, she had to keep sleeping with you. However, the more she did, the more she started to fall for you. You're a good man, Ollie – successful, loving father, attractive. What's not to fall for?" She lifted her shoulders.

"Well now that's all about to change. I could be in jail right along with Marcel."

She shook her head. "Eh, eh, eh...not if she wrote Marcel a letter, told him about you two. It could help our defense."

Lily turned and closed her eyes again. She needed to talk to Mitch. How could she get her hands on the letter she believed held the key to Ollie's freedom?

Chapter 81 – My Heart Will Protect You

Sharing his work with the woman he loved fueled Deacon. After he rushed into Desiree's office and swept her off her feet, they went to the hospital *together*, and collected his newfound friend. The doctors released Nicodemus from the hospital into Deacon's care.

Desiree watched the compassion flow from Deacon's heart into Nicodemus. Even after all the time that Deacon spent with him in the hospital, his sincere kindness still amazed Nicodemus. Desiree would occasionally find the once homeless man staring in awe at someone who cared enough to stop on a cold winter day and have an exchange with a stranger.

She had to admit to herself, as Deacon slowly assisted Nicodemus up the stairs and inside, she'd probably never get use to it either.

The type of love that Deacon exhibited was undeniably unique.

He rescued a dying human being from the bitter streets of New York, purchased him new clothes, accompanied him to the hospital, accepted responsibility for the medical bills and, now, brought him into his home for recovery.

She held the door for the men, as they eased in, thinking," Who does that?" Then she answered, "God."

Yes, she saw first hand; only God can open a heart to love and care for mankind the way Deacon did.

In that defining moment, she never considered it possible, but she loved Deacon even more. She found being a witness to his incredible heart planted a seed of protectiveness in hers. The more time she spent in his presence, the more the seed grew. She accepted Deacon would always protect the weak, sick, and homeless with his life and she would protect Deacon with hers.

He would be her husband, and she would provide that safe place for him, where he could be weak and vulnerable. And she would hold him; strengthen him with her heartfelt prayers. She would love him, comfort, and, yes, even obey him. She found no shame in obeying and submitting to a man after God's own heart. It would be a pleasure and honor to be Mrs. Deacon Stephens.

Standing just inside the door, the sound of Mitch's voice welcoming Nicodemus alerted Desiree from her intense emotions. As Deacon supported the man with his hands, everyone paused, looking into Mitch's face. They saw he really meant the sentiment.

Nicodemus said, "Thank you for lettin' me get better at your place."

Mitch bit his tongue. He wouldn't confess that Deacon didn't give him a choice. Instead he said, "No biggie," turned, and went into the kitchen.

Deacon reached over and took the small bag from Desiree that held Nicodemus' worldly possessions, a hairbrush, toothbrush, pajamas, robe, and one full change of clothes. "Thanks, baby. I'll take him from here." To Nicodemus he said, "Got a room for you, Sir."

They trekked slowly through the old house down a narrow hallway, turned right into the small space that served as a guest room. To the left, a small full bath would make an easy transition for Nicodemus when he required the services. Deacon pointed out the lavatory and then helped his friend onto the bed.

With a grunt from the tender organs in his belly, he eased down, planted his feet onto the floor and studied his shoes. "I'd be dead, if it wasn't for you."

Deacon didn't interrupt him. He knew a man needed to express his gratitude. He wouldn't take that right away from him.

Nicodemus continued, "My intestines were rotted. You saved my life." He thought for a second and redirected, "Well, I know you said it was God. I wonder why God don't use more people. There are a lot of homeless sick people in this city."

Deacon didn't judge, only replied, "Not everybody opens their heart to what God tells them to do."

Looking up and into Deacon's eyes, he declared, "Thank you. I want to know more about this God and where was he all those years I was down on my luck, eating out of trash cans."

Deacon nodded. "Sure, I'll tell you whatever you want to know. Right now, I'm going to get your dinner." A sparkling smile radiated against Deacon's handsome face. "Guess who's coming to dinner, Nico?"

Nicodemus' eyes twinkled. "Lady?"

"Yeah. She should be here soon."

Deacon reached over onto the nightstand and picked up the remote, flipped the television on and handed the device to his friend. "Make yourself comfortable."

Deacon left and closed the door, allowing his guest privacy. He found Desiree had joined Mitch in the kitchen. Her silver business jacket was draped against one of the old kitchen chairs. Her ice blue silk blouse was sleeveless and her full flowing trousers moved around the kitchen.

Mitch was straddling a chair, gnawing on a toothpick. The New York newspaper spread out in front of him. He looked up, smiling. "Desiree is making lasagna."

As she browned the ground beef, she commented, "I thought I could get a jump on dinner. Nico settled?"

Deacon opened a cupboard, pulled out a large can of soup for Nicodemus' liquid dinner. "Yeah, doing good," he replied.

Mitch's eyes perused the paper while he questioned Desiree, "You sure you wanna marry my brother? You'll probably always have a stranger under your roof. It could really ruin the romance."

Desiree smiled, stirring the meat. "It only makes me want him more." Deacon stopped opening the canned soup, caught the mischievous look in her eye. "Come here, darling." Stepping closer to her, he leaned in, took a kiss.

Mitch shook his head. His life went from living alone, to having a homeless man recover under his roof, and his brother smooching right under his nose. He started gathering up the newspaper to make a clean getaway, when his cell beeped.

This time, he recognized the number. "Lily."

"Hey, Mitch." He noted her voice sounded tired. "We need your help."

As Mitch listened he filed the thoughts and angles she mapped out for him. It was a good strategy. He wondered if the evidence she sought actually existed.

He hung up with a promise to look into it and see what he could do.

Desiree added the spaghetti sauce over the meat filled with green peppers, garlic, and onions. The water for the noodles began to lightly bubble. "Is it about Ollie?" she asked.

Mitch plopped his elbows on the table, folded his hands, looking over when Deacon joined him at the table. "I thought you were fixing Nico's dinner?"

Resting his forearms on the table, Deacon replied, "Waiting for Lady to get here. She's going to eat with Nico."

Mitch shook his head. "She better smell better than she did the last time she was here."

"I hooked her up with a new private shelter. She's good. What's going on with Ollie?"

Desiree turned, boxed her arms over her chest anxious to hear it, too. Mitch explained Lily's theory about Lacy writing her incarcerated husband, detailing her consensual affair with Ollie, and the importance of having that evidence in their possession.

Desiree let out a shaky breath. She had read some of the letters that Marcel had written to Ollie. They were full of hate and disdain. Why would he help Ollie now? She remarked, "If Marcel has it, he's not giving it up. I don't see it."

Deacon set his elbows on the table, rested his face in his hand. "Let me talk to him."

Mitch pulled back. "Marcel? He doesn't know you."

"I know. I'm neutral to him. If I can build a trusting relationship with him, maybe he'll open up."

"You don't know what you're dealing with. Deacon, the man's delusional, demented. Trust me. This is not your area of expertise," Mitch advised.

Deacon pushed, "Has anyone in Ollie's family gone to see him, to tell him that they have forgiven him. Shown him love?"

Mitch felt a surge of heat building. "Do you know what that lunatic did? He shot a pregnant woman while in labor. She died, Deacon." His voice deepened with disgust. "Don't give me that forgiveness bull. Could you honestly forgive if it was Desiree?"

He slanted his head, demanding an answer.

Thinking, Deacon covered his hand with his mouth. "It would take some time, but I would have to."

Mitch shook his head. "I can't let you go into that prison, Deacon."

Desiree walked over, took the last chair at the table and asked, "Why not, Mitch? You know Deacon has a gift with people. Let him do this, for Ollie, please."

Deacon reached over and squeezed her hand.

Desiree and Mitch cared about Ollie. Deacon didn't have the history they shared with him. Mitch stated to Deacon, "Ollie had a ring for your woman. You're all gung ho about helping him. Why?"

Insulted, Deacon snapped, "He's a man who's been falsely accused. He's a single father and his daughter needs him. He has a foundation for underprivileged children. He's got a purpose in life and I'm not going to stand by and watch an innocent man go to jail. That ain't right."

Hmm. A good argument, but no cigar. Mitch fired again, "And what makes you so sure Ollie's innocent?"

Deacon asked Desiree, "Do you think he is?"

"Yes," she said without hesitation.

Deacon turned to Mitch. "He's your friend. And you're the cop, what do you think?"

Relenting, he proclaimed, "I know he's innocent."

The doorbell rang. Deacon rose to open the door for Nicodemus' dinner guest. Before he took a step out, he pleaded, "Let me help."

For Ollie, he'd do it. "Alright," Mitch caved. "I'll call Lily and we'll come up with a plan." He shook his head as Deacon left them. With a skimpy laugh, he started, "That man...."

"Is all mine," Desiree added and got up to finish their dinner.

Chapter 82 – Purpose, Planning, Preparation

An arrest would soon be underway. Lily explained it might be in the next day or two. She had already prepared Ollie. They would need to get bond ready. He nearly lost it when she told him it could be as high as a hundred thousand dollars. The most he had available was twenty-five grand.

Thank God for family. After their prayer they started fishing. By evening, they had pulled the money together.

Next order of business, Ollie sat in the foundation meeting room and explained things to the board members – Lily, Michael, Zoe, and Desiree.

If someone would have told him he'd be sitting on the eve of arrest for a rape charge, he'd called them crazy -- simply because, it was.

His relationship with Lacy was just about medicating his pain – not control, not violence. He had been an emotionally discouraged man that had become intimate with an emotionally disturbed woman.

And now, she cried wolf. He could not process the hunger for revenge. Would it truly satisfy the woman to put him behind bars? Could she actually live with that untruth?

He pushed his unanswered questions aside and began, "Thank you for coming. I know you're all aware of what I'm facing."

Michael interjected, "If it's alright, maybe we should begin with a word of prayer?"

Ollie nodded, closed his eyes with the rest of the room, and waited for Michael to take the lead. Michael declined and realized, "Ollie…you got this."

Accepting his place, Ollie led the prayer, "Our most gracious Father, I will not ask you how I've got to this place in my life. I know my actions and choices create the consequences I face. Lord, I take responsibility for what I have done. And for what I have not done, I ask for your justice and presence to intervene and heal the pain and hurt that I have caused Lacy. I confess I had no right to her body, even if she gave it willingly. I need you now, Lord. Shower your blessings upon everyone in this room. In the name of our Lord Jesus Christ. Amen."

Amen went around the room and Ollie led his team, "The public is not going to take these rape charges lightly. The parents of the children in our foundation trusted me. Even though I'm not guilty, they don't know that yet. And when the news hits, all they'll hear is a rapist directs this program. So Lily has already created a press release, detailing that I will be stepping down as director. In the interim, Michael will take my place."

Slightly afraid he had offended Zoe, he glanced in her direction, remarked, "I made this decision because I believe a strong male should lead our organization. Zoe, you were in charge while I was away. I hope you're not...."

Zoe sat up taller in her chair, crossed her long legs under the table. Her long dark brown hair danced off her shoulders. "Ollie, I agree with your decision. Michael should be in place. I'm surprised there aren't more men on this board. And for the record...." She scanned the room. "I don't believe you raped anyone. I'm standing by you and this foundation."

Because she was sitting next to him, he reached over and held her hand. "I need you to work with the children. Not to tell them that I'm innocent. Help them understand that this is an adult situation, and God and the law, will show the truth."

"You got it." She squeezed his hand back.

Lily noted for the duration of the meeting that Ollie and Zoe held hands. She smiled, wondering if they realized it, too.

Desiree suggested, "I think it would be a good idea to have a parents' meeting as soon as you're released on bond. You should be present to address the parents and assure them until the matter is settled you will not be on the premises."

Lily liked that idea. "I'll work on communication as soon as...."

An interruption had Lily stopping. Michael directed toward his pregnant, overworked bride. "How about allowing the other board members handle communication? You're taking on the legal side of things – superwoman."

She smiled and received his point. For consensus, she asked, "Everyone okay with that?"

All in agreement, they nodded.

Looking directly across the table at Lily, Zoe said, "Please don't take this the wrong way....but, I know you don't specialize as a criminal defense attorney and I know someone that is very good."

Not offended in the least, Lily replied, "Who's your referral?"

"Kendall Carter."

Lily knew the name. "I've heard of Kendall. She represents the powerful and elite."

"Sounds expensive," Ollie chimed in.

"Worth it," Zoe commented. "You should set up a meeting with her, test her out." She pulled out her smart phone, forwarded Kendall's contact information to Lily and Ollie.

Lily recapped the meeting and their assignments and they wrapped it up.

Desiree checked her watch and started for the exit. She had to run. The undercover officer had arrived at her school and was waiting to meet with her. Ollie didn't let her leave without thanking her with an embrace.

She whispered in his ear, "It's going to be alright. I don't believe for a second you hurt Lacy Reid."

He pulled away, boxed his lips in for a second, and admitted, "I hurt her, but not the way she's professing. How are things at the school?"

"A lot of updates. We can talk later."

"Well, call me," he said.

"Sure." She gave his hand a gentle squeeze. "How's my little princess?"

That brought a smile to his lips. "She's great. For the little time that we were away, she was beside herself. She had Daddy all to her self."

"As soon as this is all over, take her on vacation again."

He actually had been thinking the same. "I will. Be good," he said, as he kissed her cheek. She waved. "I'll be in touch."

Zoe was next in line heading for the threshold. She stopped, feeling the tips of his fingers on her elbow. "Sorry, I didn't want to interrupt you and Desiree. I have to get going. I have clients today."

He smiled at her. "I won't keep you Dr. Landry. I was short with you yesterday, and today I put Michael in charge."

"Ollie, I told you, I agree with your decision. And you have my support. No apology necessary."

He gazed down, noticing for the first time what she was wearing – a smart black pants suit with a ruffled white blouse. "Well," he fumbled at her large welcoming eyes, "you've done so much for the foundation. I feel like I should reciprocate."

He saw a pleasant smile on her lips. Her eyes transformed from welcoming to mischievous. "I have the perfect thing, but seeing you're about to be arrested and all, that won't work."

"What?" He raised his voice.

"My sister's getting married this weekend…in Florida. I need a date."

He took a small step back, stuck his hand into his pockets. She saw him relent. Fine, she wouldn't push. Regardless, he could use a night out. Keeping her grin plastered on her fine face, she teased, "Have a sense of humor and believe in the God you serve. You're not going to jail."

He wanted to believe that.

"If you're not locked up later tonight, have dinner with me. My sister and her fiancé will be there."

"Where?"

"My house. Seven tonight."

Hmm. As he considered the invitation, she revealed, "I could use a friend."

He agreed, "Alright."

She turned. He watched the regal lady walk away, thinking he had just ended a really bad relationship. So far, his relationships didn't end happily.

One dinner he told himself, he could do that – for his friend. Zoe needed that. He could offer no more than friendship.

Until he had a handle on his life, romance was off limits. He couldn't take the backlash of unstable women in his life. Zoe seemed solid, but there was entirely too much at stake for him to risk even the possibility of more drama.

Chapter 83 – Know Who I Am

The smell traveled sweetly out of the kitchen, upstairs, and into her bedroom. It then lifted her out of bed and guided her along. She found Zoe in the kitchen. Her hands were covered in heavy red mitts as she retrieved a prepared dish from the wall oven.

Chelsea exclaimed, "Oh, my God!" She rushed to the island counter, surveyed the contents. "You're making roast prime rib with pink and green peppercorn crust in red-wine pan sauce!"

Zoe placed the steaming dish on to the counter, pulled off her mitts, and took a sip of her lemonade. "Made it."

Chelsea, Zoe's best friend and personal assistant, searched for her favorite. "Where's dessert?"

Zoe pointed to the chocolate bread pudding. Chelsea inhaled it with her eyes and pouted. "You make this and you know I can't stay for dinner."

After checking the plain watch she wore, Zoe sank down into one of the oversized comfortable kitchen chairs. "You are welcome to stay, Chelsea."

Hoping by sticking around Zoe would take pity on her and let her do some tasting; she sat next to her friend. "You really want me and Cotton to join your sister and fiancé for dinner? The fiancé that pushed you down a flight of stairs and made you lose your baby? I can't believe you cooked for him."

Zoe decided to take one point at a time. "You're always welcome, whether I like Cotton or not...."

"Which you do not," Chelsea interrupted.

"Let me ask you this, would you like someone who enjoyed using me as his punching bag when he got frustrated or for what ever excuse he chose to provide?"

Zoe expected the defense, as Chelsea answered, "Cotton doesn't enjoy it He's always so remorseful afterward. It is difficult for him being a musician. He's trying to get a deal."

She lifted her hand, halted her.

"Deplorable. I love you too much to allow you to lie to yourself. Regarding your second point, I also cooked for my sister. I told the truth concerning the man she has chosen to spend the rest of her life with. She's made a decision and she has to live with it. Still, I don't want to alienate her. So...I've invited them both. This dinner is really therapy for me. It will help me see if I can spend an evening with them and show me what emotions will resurface."

Looking over her shoulder at the meal, Chelsea turned with pleading eyes. "Can I have a little, please...."?

Zoe chuckled. "Help yourself."

Literally pouncing, Chelsea snagged a dish from the glass-covered cabinets. As she dug into the prime rib, practically drooling, she remarked, "Always the psychoanalyst."

Zoe lifted her glass, before she drank deeply, she confessed, "I'm cheating. I invited a buffer."

Without looking up, Chelsea asked, "Who?"

"Ollie."

She had enough on her plate, grabbed a fork, and sat with Zoe. She forked in a healthy mouth full, closed her eyes as her taste buds exploded with joy. Zoe considered she had done an acceptable job and smiled.

Chelsea opened her eyes and asked, "Ollie know about your past? The baby?"

Zoe shook her head lightly. "There's no reason to tell him."

"Hmm." Chelsea nodded, feeding herself another bite. "I thought you liked him," she said with her mouth full.

"I do."

"And you're using him as a buffer. You think that's fair?" she added.

She didn't think it unfair. "It's only dinner."

Chelsea laid her fork down, but only for a few seconds. "I won't let you lie to yourself either, Dr. Landry. It's more than dinner. You're using yourself as a test specimen, preparing for the wedding this weekend. You say Ollie has a lot going on, then, maybe he needs a break from his turmoil. Talk to him about your family situation. Be honest with yourself and tell him how *you* feel. It might help take his mind off his problems." Finished making her point, she lifted her fork again.

Zoe considered it. Standing, she announced, "I need to dress for dinner." She added, sternly, "Do not touch dessert. We can't have holes in the bread pudding."

"Can I lift a piece of chocolate off the top?" she asked, smiling.

Zoe scowled, turned, and began up the back stairs.

"Chelsea pleaded, "Pleasseee!"

Zoe shouted from the top of the stairs, "No, Chels!'"

******

The grandfather antique clock chimed and Zoe smiled. Ollie had arrived early, just as she requested. She laid down her Bible and devotional onto the coffee table and eased up to answer the door.

She opened the door and the smell of early spring slipped into her nose. At 6:30, the air was crisp, cutting into her bare arms and legs. She saw him smile, but noticed it didn't reach his eyes. She decided that she couldn't use him as a buffer. He had too much weight on his shoulders. "Please come in."

284

He handed her a pie dish. "Chocolate pie. I made it."

She accepted and realized, "It's still warm."

Closing the door, she lifted it to her nose. "It's smells wonderful. You made this?" she repeated.

He grinned. "I have more than artistic skills."

She led him through the foyer, family room and into the kitchen. "I didn't mean it like that," she commented as he followed her. "It's just with everything you're facing, I didn't know you had time to bake a homemade pie."

Ollie stood in the kitchen, admiring the country feel of the house. One could tell from the layout, Zoe had deep pockets. Yet, her home seemed to envelope him into a cozy embrace. "Thanks for inviting me. Making the pie took my mind off things. Olivia helped. It allowed us to spend time together."

Zoe, intrigued by the pie, inhaled the aroma as she slid it from the decorative bag and lifted the plastic wrap covering it. He smiled. "Have a slice now," he offered.

She gleamed at him. "Don't tempt me. I made chocolate bread pudding and I had to fight Chelsea off of it."

Ollie asked, "Where is it?"

Waving him over to the blue and cream-colored tile island, she lifted the cover away to show him.

"That looks really good."

"It is." She suddenly wished it were going to be just the two of them for the evening. They could talk and indulge themselves in chocolate. She wondered, "Are you a chocolate fanatic, too?"

"Yeah," he admitted, stuffing his hands into his pockets. He really wanted to taste the bread pudding. "Since I stopped smoking, it has become my weakness."

Zoe's eyes shifted between his dessert and hers, with her hands on her waist, she realized, "The only way we're going to make it, is if we get out of this kitchen. How about a tour of the house?"

He chuckled. "Lead the way."

Ollie couldn't help but notice how attractive Zoe was, wearing an elegant sleeveless dress.

The color of jade, it captured her slender curves and stopped just above her knees. Her black suede heels were tall, giving her long fine legs a sexy stride with each step she took. Her deep brown hair matched the color of her eyes. Tonight her hair was full, loosely curled, and somewhat untamed as it anointed her shoulders. Her cheeks held a healthy pink glow. She looked earthy, exotic, and lush.

He walked with her, listened to her point out the different rooms. Many of which were small. However, he could tell the room that held her heart - the library. He liked it, too, and admired the dark wood walls, heavy draperies, and rich carpets of deep burgundy, green, and gold. The rich colors added warmth, not power. He stood, and then turned in a circle. After taking in every angle, he commented, "I'd like to paint this room. Or maybe paint in this room. It's soothing. I can see how reading in here would be easy."

"Really?"

"Really." He noted the surprise in her voice. "You are surprised by me. I bake pies, and I like to read."

She lifted her hands. He saw her fingers were elegantly long and thin -- hands of a musician. "You play?" He lifted his chin.

"Play what?"

Smiling, he asked, "The piano. Your hands…I notice hands. I'm an artist. You look like you play."

Maybe an artist was just as observant as a psychologist. "Yes, I do. I don't have a piano in this house."

He lifted his shoulders, let them fall. "Why?"

"The one I love to play is in Texas with my grandfather."

He nodded, understanding her passion for a place, person and thing – a place of comfort, without pretense. He longed for that, especially with what challenged him.

Ollie turned away, moved toward the shelves. The books seemed to call to him. He laced one leather bound book with his fingers. "Now here's a philosopher for you."

Joining his side, she asked, "You read philosophy?"

He pulled the book from its holding place, opened it. "I did, in college. Art History major. I enjoyed the class discussions, the school of thought. This guy had interesting views about the natural rights of mankind…life, property, liberty."

Her full lips, bursting with their natural red color, parted. Ollie turned to her. Smirking, he advised, "You know, you gotta stop doing that."

She blinked. "What?"

"Acting so surprised that a man enjoys cooking and reading. Or is it just me, and not all men?"

Feeling a bit chastised, she clasped her hands behind her back. "I apologize. And I'm embarrassed. And I'm probably going to regret this. And if I make you uncomfortable and you want to leave, please go. I won't be offended."

Ollie held the book in one hand; with the other he skimmed her arm. "Say what's on your mind, Zoe."

Her eyes met his. "I feel connected to you. From the first time we met and you were dating Desiree. I've prayed for a mate, someone that shares my faith and my interests, even my love for books and chocolate. I had hoped he'd have children…."

He interrupted her, "Children?"

She couldn't tell him about losing her baby. Not yet. She just said, "Yes, I love kids. Through the foundation you started, I can be a help to them. Ollie, I don't want to pressure you, or push you away. It's just how I feel. And if you don't feel the same way, please don't feel obligated. I'll never...."

Her mind went completely blank as his mouth crushed onto hers. She tasted his passion, and found her arms scooping him in, pulling him closer. They faintly heard the book that he held fall to the floor as he returned her embrace.

When Ollie pulled back, he didn't want to open his eyes. "Oh God," was he dreaming? The feeling so surreal, unlike anything in his normal life, terrified him. Had he found her, right under his nose – his companion for life?

Afraid she'd disappear, he kept his eyes closed, placed his forehead against hers, and felt her energy travel through her body and into his. "I'm afraid. My relationships haven't done well," he confessed.

She kept her eyes closed too, declared, "I'm not Sapphire, Desiree, or Lacy. My name's Zoe."

"Zoe," he whispered her name. "Oh, Zoe...."

Holding tighter now, she wondered, "Can I ask you for a favor?"

"Sure, anything."

She whispered, "Let's not rush this. Let us...let this be."

He replied softly, "I want it to be." He lifted his head, opened his eyes and asked her to do the same. She did.

"It's not going to be easy, these next few months. Zoe, anytime you want to go, just step back. I'll understand."

"Shhhh." She brushed her lips over his. "I'm not going anywhere."

"I didn't rape Lacy."

"With everything within me, I know that you didn't. You couldn't." She closed her eyes after his lips moved in to join hers again. The doorbell chimed, interrupting them.

Invigorated, they walked out of the library hand-in-hand. His hand tightly gripped hers. Zoe realized he wasn't her buffer. They had each other as a shield.

Chapter 84 – We All Fall Down

Simon waited until 7 in the evening. He invited Raymond for a visit after his wife and children left the hospital. Ten minutes after the hour, Raymond glided in wearing plain clothes – a white collared shirt and khaki pants. He looked like he had plans for the evening and a twinge of jealousy shot through Simon.

He pushed it away, laid a hand on the bandage that covered the healing hole in his chest. "Thanks for coming," he said, as Raymond sat.

"I assume you've come to your senses," he stated without pretense.

"Yeah," Simon agreed, staring into Raymond's deep-set eyes fitted under neat brows. "I panicked," Simon added, "I don't want things to be over between us. You gotta understand…my wife, she's been great. I feel guilty lying to her."

Raymond reached over, rubbed his hands against Simon's. "Your hands are cold." Raymond held them, warming them. "It's time. Come home with me when you leave this place."

Since he had planned for that response, he followed with, "Let me go home first and get stronger. Then I'll tell my wife I'm in love with you. I'll leave her. But not now…when I leave here, I'm sure the press will be involved. We don't want a scandal. Think about it. You're a cop. You don't want people to know you're gay."

He had a point, holding his head down, he relented, "You're right. I can't risk that. I don't know if I can wait that long, but I'll give you thirty days. Thirty days," he repeated, locked in on Simon's eyes. "After that, you'll come to me. You'll come, right?"

Simon nodded. "Yes, I'll come to you. I promise."

Raymond lifted in his seat, bent forward and reaching over, prepared to kiss Simon. Their lips were only inches apart, when a woman pulled on the door and stepped inside the sterile room. Three dozen red roses in her arms covered her face.

Too quickly, Raymond snapped to attention, feeling a crack in his back. Stifling a curse, he nodded at her as she shifted the roses and saw the man standing there.

Sensing something, yet not sure what, she looked down at her husband and then into Raymond's cold eyes. She remembered him, the officer that chased down her husband's shooter.

"Hello," she greeted him warmly.

Sliding his hands into his pockets, he provided, "Hello, Mrs. Barnes. I just dropped in to see how your husband's recovering." Looking at the massive set of flowers, he remarked, "That must have cost a fortune."

She set them down, leaned over and kissed her husband. "Happy Anniversary."

Raymond cringed.

Simon rebuked his wife, "Honey, I told you not to get me anything."

Her eyes dancing now, she looked at Raymond. "He's feeling guilty about being shot. Can you believe that?"

Raymond cleared his throat, but couldn't focus on her words. He thought back to the previous year when Simon and Tracy celebrated their 22nd anniversary. After work, Simon went directly to Raymond's place for a quick fix before he left for the Bahamas with his wife. He had confessed he wished it were them who were going to the Bahamas together.

Raymond swallowed the sweet urge to spill it and replied, "That's ridiculous. The shooting had nothing to do with him. Nothing at all." He looked coolly down at Simon and then at Tracy. "The flowers liven up the room," he forced.

"I think so," Tracy agreed as she fussed with the flowers. Smiling big, she added, "When Simon comes home, I'm going to have the house covered in red roses for our vow renewal."

Lifting his voice and eyebrows, Raymond asked, "Vow renewal?"

"Yes." She beamed. "Simon called this morning, actually at midnight, to tell me happy anniversary and that when he gets home, we are going to renew our vows. He asked me not to get him anything now, that we'd exchange gifts then. But I couldn't do anything. So, I ran out and came back with three dozen roses -- one dozen for him, one for me, and one for our children."

She paused; Raymond saw her eyes well up.

"We're so blessed." She reached down, grabbed her husband's hand and reported, "Baby, your hands are so cold. You feeling alright?"

The fear in his belly bubbled up and extrapolated him. He lied and Raymond knew it. And with Raymond, revenge would be hell to pay.

The freakish relationship that he had shared with the man for five years wasn't because of his uncontrolled desires. No. He was also very afraid of Raymond.

Simon had witnessed first hand the level of his cruelty -- his hatred toward women. Every time he ended things, Raymond would find a woman and make her think he adored her. Then, he'd take her home and unleash his sickness. He always made them cry. Without his victims knowing, Raymond would record their sessions, and then he'd send it to Simon. He never could figure out why the women never said anything of his torture.

Simon learned that many of the women he hurt were married and could not tell their husbands. Others had low self-esteem. They believed Raymond when he told them they had deserved and asked for it. But now he was hurting little girls? Simon hadn't known him to hurt children. After learning he had sexually assaulted Tiona, he certainly believed Raymond was capable of every vile evil.

Lifting his eyes, Simon connected with Raymond and saw the rage barely holding steady. Yet, whom could he tell? Could he tell his wife and law enforcement? He considered it as Raymond took a stiff step back and congratulated them, "Happy Anniversary. It was nice seeing you, Simon."

Before walking out, Raymond forced himself to round the bed, walked up to Tracy and pecked her cheek. "You're a very lucky woman."

She understood where the chill was coming from; she looked into Raymond's eyes and said, "Thank you."

On his way out he shouted, "Get well soon, Simon!"

When the door closed, Tracy looked concerned. "That guy is weird. He's school security."

Simon couldn't explain Raymond's eerie mood. "He uh...said he had a rough day."

"Oh." Tracy shrugged, went to the other side of the bed and took the empty seat. She immediately started revealing plans for their upcoming wedding. Simon's head shifted left, his eyes planted on the door. Was the man on his way to his house? Would he hurt his three girls?

Tracy leaned forward, tapped her finger on Simon's shoulder. "Am I boring you with this wedding stuff? You know how I am about details."

He looked back. Tears flowed down his boney cheeks, wetting his ebony skin. "Tracy, I need to tell you something," he whispered.

Alarmed, she pleaded with her eyes and waited for her entire world to shatter.

Chapter 85 – Staging and Raging

In disbelief, Raymond drove the police cruiser from the hospital with tears streaming down his round caramel face. The night was as dark as the hole in his heart. He could find no light, no hope.

He had given Simon Barnes five good years. "And for what?" he asked himself. To be duped and lied to while he planned to renew his wedding vows. He thought he had loved him.

Hadn't he tolerated Simon having a wife? Yet, he refused to tolerate any other women. To prove it, he sent a message by way of Tiona to her whore mother: "Stay away from my man, or I'll do worse to your child next time."

The message boomeranged, came back with a bullet in Simon's chest. Then, Raymond saw it as a plus. Maybe, just maybe, they could finally be together. Simon could come to him after leaving the hospital.

He couldn't accept Simon didn't want that. Instead he wanted to live with that talking fool he called his wife. Oh how many times did Simon complain about his wife to him? Raymond couldn't even count. The things he did for Simon, Tracy would never do – not in a million years. And he chose her over him?

Well he was going to make them hurt worse than he did. He pulled up in front of the house Simon shared with his wife and three precious girls. The lights were on. He knew that they were inside, waiting for their mother's return from the hospital. He could easily bypass the locks, go in, and shoot each one at point blank range.

But no, that would be too easy. No, that simply would not do. He had to take one of them.

As he looked up, he saw the flicker of a flashing light and gathered they were watching television. "Yeah," he nodded to himself, wiped his tears with the backs of his hands. He could take their oldest, Carmen – their pride and joy.

Carmen Barnes was a senior in college and would be leaving for medical school in the fall. She was the oldest and probably the strongest, still he could overpower her, and get her into his vehicle.

Thinking out his plan, he had it. He'd kill the two youngest and kidnap the oldest. That would hurt Simon and Tracy. "Oh, yeah, it would destroy them," he decided. He exited the cruiser, began crossing the residential street. It was quiet. "Good," he thought.

As he pulled open the gate to approach the front door, the next-door neighbor walked out with a black trash bag. "Hey?"

Raymond's hands twitched, he wanted to reach for his weapon, shoot the intruder. He smiled instead, "I'm a friend of the family. Just came for a visit."

The neighbor angled his head; studied him. He looked familiar. Raymond rethought his plan and considered shooting the man in his big bloated belly protruding out of a white t-shirt.

"Hey," the man acknowledged, "you're the cop who chased down the kid that shot Simon. I saw it on the news. Yeah, that thing really hit home. I've known Simon and his family for over ten years. Thank God, you got the shooter."

Annoyed and careful not to show it, Raymond agreed, "I did my job."

"You sure did. You guys are heroes. You know…." The neighbor rested his trash bag and went on, "I used to want to be a cop. The wife, she wouldn't go for it. Told me, it was the badge, or her."

"Let me guess, you chose her."

"You darn skippy. A badge can't keep me warm at night. You know…."

Taking in the neighbor's extra flesh, Raymond thought the man's wife had to be one big heater.

The neighbor looked up at Simon's house. "Tracy ain't home. She called, said she was running out to the hospital. Asked us to keep an eye on the girls. It's their anniversary you know."

"Really?"

"Yeah, twenty-three years. The wife, and me we got twenty-one. Anyway, Tracy ain't home. It's just the girls. Come back tomorrow about seven, that's when she gets in."

Raymond bagged the rage and knew it was better to walk…for now. There would be another chance to destroy Simon and his babbling wife.

"Thanks," he said, turning away.

When he eased back into the driver's seat, he thought of another woman he'd like to destroy. Desiree Davenport. She just couldn't leave it alone. She kept pushing to know who touched Tiona. She had private meetings in her office with that arrogant Detective, Mitch Stephens.

He and the entire staff had been questioned and re-questioned. He held his own, knew no one suspected him, and he had convinced Tiona to keep her mouth shut. But all Desiree kept talking about was her responsibility to the students, parents and the staff.

What did she know of responsibility? Her school secretary was a whore and that's what he treated her like. Desiree's sense of judgment was so flawed. While he waited for another time for Simon's family, he'd focus on Desiree. It was time.

Chapter 86 – See Beyond

Marcel Reid read the article with pleasure, "International Art Dealer, Gallery Owner and Founder of The Sapphire Arts Foundation for the Adolescent Charged with Rape."

He loved it. Yes!

Ollie should be the one serving time in prison, not him. He never meant to murder Sapphire. He only wanted to convince her that they were meant to be – to have a future together. But along came Ollie and Marcel panicked and aimed the gun at him. Sapphire struggled, redirected the gun, it fired and killed her.

Marcel sighed, believing what goes around, comes around.

He continued to read the paper, blocking out the sounds from his prison mates. He wasn't like them. THEY were common low life criminals; he was simply a man who was misunderstood.

There was card playing, television watching, and some Bible reading and discussions buzzing in the recreation room.

For some reason he couldn't explain, everybody wanted to get religious after being confined. He clenched his fists, reading on and feeling that whoever wrote the article, made Ollie sound innocent.

"So what if Ollie did a lot for the community? He raped a woman. He's no different than the low life criminals that surround me," he thought.

"You got a visitor." A call from one of the incredible hulk looking correctional officers lifted Marcel's head. He hated that officer and narrowed his eyes.

Seconds later, his brain processed what his ears had heard. "I have a visitor?" he thought.

Excitement filled him and his eyes softened. No one came to visit the once successful oral surgeon. Not any of his colleagues, friends, patients, staff members or family.

He wrote them all -- the father who had abandoned him when he was 10 years old, his four brothers produced from his father's second marriage, his father-in-law, estranged wife, and his children. No one came.

Marcel even wrote letters to his deceased mother. Every letter was apologetic. His arrest had strained her already weakened heart. Six months after his imprisonment, her heart gave in.

Wondering and hoping it would be his father, he stood in the orange jump suit and followed the officer to the visitor's center. His butternut brown skin beamed with a sense of curiosity as his boyish looking eyes searched the man sitting behind the glass.

His visitor had a deep complexion with sharp eyes and defined bone structure. His features looked noble. Marcel gathered the man's look to be a cross between the celebrities, Idris Elba and Morris Chestnut. And sadly, he didn't recognize him. A pain hit him in the gut. The visitor was not for him. Defeated, he repositioned himself.

Deacon tapped the glass, called him back, and picked up the phone. Reluctantly, Marcel dropped into his seat and picked up the receiver. "What?"

"Marcel Reid?"

"Who's asking?"

For three days, Deacon prayed for God to give him the precise words and condition his heart. He needed to demonstrate God's love and compassion, even for a murderer. He introduced himself, "My name is Deacon Stephens. I'm a missionary."

"Please," Marcel thought. "I'm not interested." Marcel started to rise again.

Deacon couldn't explain why he blurted out, "When was the last time you had a conversation with someone on this side of the glass?"

Marcel claimed his seat and widened his eyes and expressed with emphasis, "You're not going to convert me."

Deacon gave him a bright smile. "You're not going to convert me either."

"Why are you here?"

"You have a desire to be heard, Marcel. I came to listen. You had a relationship with a married woman; it ended her life and changed yours...."

"How do you know?" Marcel squinted.

Lying, not an option, he confessed, "My fiancé is friends with Ollie. I know about the letters you wrote him. You wrote those letters because you want to communicate. I'm here."

Almost bursting, Marcel shook. "He killed her. He did. And that's what I put in my letters to him."

Deacon expected the anger. His reply was only a nod.

Marcel asked, "You're not going to tell me to take responsibility for my sins?"

Deacon humbly replied, "I came to listen. I'll come everyday, if you want."

Marcel barked, "I don't trust you."

"You shouldn't – not yet. That may change. We might become friends."

Amused, Marcel began to laugh. "Yeah, right. You're going to come and see me and listen to me everyday, if I ask you."

Skeptical, he scrunched his face. "How much money you want? I spent everything I had on my defense. When I leave here, I can't practice anymore. I got nothing."

He waited a second before he replied, "You can't pay for friendship."

Marcel shook his head. "Come on, man. Everybody wants something."

Truth rested in Marcel's words. Deacon felt awful.

Ollie's attorney believed a letter existed that would help free Ollie, and that letter rested in Marcel's possession. He almost felt like walking away. Instead, he realized this wasn't just about Ollie. It was about Marcel's soul. He requested a deal, "How about an exchange?"

Marcel flashed a grin against his handsome face. "Now you're talking."

"Say I do want something, but I don't want it now. If I come here everyday, and we become friends, you promise to give me whatever I ask for."

Stabbing a thumb into his chest, he asked, "You think I have something you want?"

"You may...I'm not certain."

"What?"

"I'd rather not say."

Considering it, he recapped, "You think I might have something. You don't know if I do, and...you'd rather not say what it is. You're willing to come out here and see me everyday and persuade me to give it to you, if we become friends?"

Simple enough, Deacon nodded. "That's it."

"You must be smoking something that makes you crazy," Marcel commented.

"What I take in, is all natural and it helps me see beyond the surface."

The comment intrigued Marcel, he said, "I see."

Deacon shook his head. "Not yet, but I have hope that you will."

Baffled, Marcel stared at Deacon.

"See you tomorrow, Marcel."

"Wait, that's it?"

"Don't you want some time to think over our deal?" Deacon waited.

Marcel thought, "Don't leave, no one talks to me," then replied, "Come back tomorrow."

Fighting for composure, Marcel swallowed the anxiety, careful not to show any signs of his disappointment of Deacon leaving. He hastily hung up the phone and turned before Deacon stood.

Chapter 87 – The Search Begins

Regardless that she had no new information, Desiree sat at her desk with faith that God would help her. As Mitch promised, Alaina Martin served as an undercover police officer. So far, nothing surfaced.

Spring had officially arrived, sending the children running with excitement about outdoor play.

Desiree ate the last bite of her turkey sandwich, started up from her desk to join the children. Her short walk was interrupted when Karyn tapped on the door and entered. Rarely did her secretary wait for an invitation before entering.

Karyn wouldn't let Desiree surrender a rebuke for her invasive behavior and she quickly announced, "Tiona's mama is here. She's been crying."

"What now?" she thought. Stopped in her tracks, Desiree perched her fingers against the edge of her desk. She thought aloud, "Get Jack, then bring her in."

In less than 30 seconds, her assistant principal stepped into her office. His salt and pepper hair needed smoothing down. He pulled on his tweed jacket while failing to roll down his shirtsleeves. She realized he was just as stressed about the situation as she was.

"Thanks for coming so quickly, Jack. I don't know why she's here...."

As Desiree spoke, Karyn led Wanda Washington in. Curious, she hoped Desiree would invite her to stay. No dice. Desiree gave a subtle headshake. Disappointed, Karyn sulked as she ducked out and closed the door behind her.

Jack extended his hand. "Jack Dorsey, assistant principal."

Wanda gave him a flimsy hand and then sat the same way --- hunched down, legs apart. She wore a hot pink t-shirt two sizes too small and faded hip hugging jeans. Desiree noted her braids were freshly done as she swung lengthy blond twists over her shoulders.

Jack took the dingy gray seat next to the parent and Desiree positioned herself behind the desk. "How can we help you, Ms. Washington?" Desiree began.

Wanda let out a watery sniff. "You gotta promise me something. You don't tell the law everything about me. I'm about to save this school a lot of headache, but you gotta make me a promise...."

Her large baby blues extended, waiting for the answer she urgently wanted. Staring into those pleading eyes, Desiree wondered did the African American woman have naturally blue eyes.

Creasing her brows, Desiree looked at Jack and then at Wanda. What kind of promise did she want? And what would it cost? Desiree required, "Tell us what this is about and then I'll see about making you a promise."

Jack nodded, that sounded fair to him. Wanda bit her lip, then let it rip, "I know who rubbed up my baby. I know who touched her. He works in this school."

Desiree and Jack's hearts pumped double time. Without thinking, Desiree demanded, "Tell me now."

"First, you promise me!" Wanda pointed a shaking finger at Desiree.

Defeated, she looked at Jack and caved, "We promise."

Wanda revealed, "It's your so-called security guard, police officer. The last thing that man does is protect and serve."

Jack and Desiree exchanged looks. Wanda went on, "The man is gay and he's been hitttin' up your teacher Simon Barnes."

Desiree's hand absently went to her heart. "How do you know this?" she quickly requested.

Getting over the hump and letting it all go, Wanda shifted and crossed her legs. "Simon and I go way back. We grew up in this neighborhood. From time to time, he'll hit me up for some."

Desiree lifted an arched brow under her flipped hair and her voice pitched higher. "Some what?"

Getting the picture, Jack chimed in, "You're a prostitute."

Wanda shook her head. "Not like that. If he has an itch, I scratch his back and he scratches mine. I got bills – he helps me pay them. Simon helps a sister out. His boyfriend don't like that...."

"Simon? The man's been married for more than twenty years! He's gay and sleeps with prostitutes?" Desiree lifted her voice in disbelief.

Wanda twisted her thin lips. "Bisexual and I am not a prostitute."

Desiree's vision blurred from disbelief.

Wanda picked up, "Raymond gets really crazy when Simon and I hook up. So to get back at me, he rubbed up my baby and then scared the life out of her. He told her he'd arrest me if she told anyone what he did. She didn't even tell me at first."

Head spinning, Desiree scratched her head as her brain organized the information. "Are you sure about Raymond?"

"Simon called me. He told me that his boy fessed up. He said I had to tell you the truth."

Jack started to ask a question, but Wanda flung her hand.

"You ain't gonna get me in trouble. I'm doing what I need to take care of Tiona. I'm saving for a house -- trying to get us out of the hood. I work hard, but it ain't enough. I do what I'm good at."

"Good God," Desiree thought and let out a shaky breath. "Ms. Washington, you're going to have to give a statement to the police."

Practically jumping out of the chair and her own skin, Wanda shouted, "I ain't gotta do nothin'. I told you! Now it's on you! You gotta get Raymond Bonner away from this school and my child. He hurts women."

"How?" Desiree needed to hear it.

"When he's with you, he makes you hurt. He likes to make you feel bad. He calls you names."

"Names," Desiree thought and about the night of the fundraiser, how Karyn said Raymond treated her. She picked up her smart phone, sent a text message.

"Who you talkin' to?" Wanda asked.

"I'm working on getting someone to talk to Raymond."

"He wasn't at the door when I came in," Wanda remarked.

Once again, Jack and Desiree exchanged looks.

Chapter 88 – You Ask for a Very Hard Thing

They waited anxiously for Deacon's arrival. Lily sat at her desk, one hand toyed with a pencil on her desk, the other rested on her rising belly. Ollie stood at the window, looked out with his hands tucked deeply in his pockets. Zoe sat on the small leather sofa, her eyes planted on her laptop.

Ollie looked to his right, asked Zoe, "What are you reading?"

She shook her head. "Looking at photos from my sister's wedding."

He grunted, swallowed his frustration. He couldn't join Zoe in Florida for the wedding. Over the past weekend he was arrested, arraigned, and released.

Zoe didn't ask him if he wanted to see the pictures. Nor did Lily look up from her rolling pencil. It wasn't right that someone could lie and cause so much grief in your life. It wasn't right that everything seemed to work in Lacy's favor. Yes, it was his DNA under her fingernails and his semen found in her body, but it was not a result of rape. Could it be true? Had Lacy contradicted herself, wrote a letter to her estranged husband rubbing their affair in Marcel's face?

Lily believed it to be true. When her phone rang and her assistant announced Deacon's arrival, she exhaled and told them, "Deacon's on his way up."

Ollie turned around and faced the door. Who would have thought his ex-girlfriend's fiancé would be so valuable to his freedom? Deacon breezed in, closing the door behind him. Not giving him a chance to sit, Ollie, questioned, "Did you get it?"

Deacon walked up to Ollie, explained, "I can't just get it like that. I'm going to have to develop a relationship with Marcel first."

Ollie sighed. "I don't know how much time I have. This thing will go to trial."

Lily pushed herself up and walked over, rested a hand on Ollie's shoulder. "We're preparing for trial, Ollie."

He shook his head. He didn't want the media circus. He didn't want his church members and parents looking at him like some violent criminal. He was the victim here. "I don't want a trial."

"We have no choice, Ollie," Lily replied. "We have a good defense team now that Kendall Carter is on board."

Zoe nodded. "She's good. You're innocent and she'll prove it."

The defeated expression on Ollie's face told her he didn't believe it – not yet. He asked Deacon, "How long is it going to take for you to develop a relationship with Marcel?"

Deacon estimated, "A few weeks. I've got to get him to trust me. Pray for him." He looked at each face, and added, "All of you."

Ollie scoffed. "The man shot my wife."

"I know he did," Deacon returned.

Shouting, Ollie said, "No! You don't! *You* weren't there."

"I wasn't. But God was. Ollie, Marcel still has a soul and we need...."

Ollie pushed Deacon aside, began pacing while pumping his fist. "Don't preach to me. Everyday Olivia grows up without her mother."

He stopped pacing and looked at the three of them. "If my fate rests in this man's hands, then I'll take my chances. Lily, you said we have a good defense team now, right?"

"We do. But that letter will break down her credibility."

"You don't even know if a letter exists. We could be wasting our time."

Deacon declared, "It's not a waste, if Marcel gives his life to the Lord."

Waving his hand, before shoving it into his pocket, Ollie delegated, "That's your department. Not mine."

Zoe added, "Ollie, Deacon's right. It's not a waste and you've got to forgive Marcel. I told you my brother-in-law and I had a thing years ago in college. I got pregnant by him and because of him, I lost my baby."

She paused, failing to tell him the rest. After a few seconds, she picked up, "I never thought I'd see him again. And now, here he is, in my face. I asked God, why. It almost seems like a cruel joke that we're related. I truly thought I had forgiven him. I know now there's still work to do."

Ollie asked, "So you think this chaos is about forgiving Marcel?"

Softening her voice, Zoe explained, "I believe the Bible and it says all things work together for good for those that are called according to His purpose. This *chaos* will be a blessing for you. I have a suggestion." She smiled at him.

Even if he wanted to, he couldn't force his gaze away from her appealing face. "What is it?"

"Let's spend the next few weeks praying...praying for Marcel and my brother-in-law."

"You ask for a hard thing, Zoe."

"The harder the challenge, the greater the reward," she countered.

Deacon lifted his hand, laid it on Ollie's shoulder. "Let's start now." They lowered their heads. "Father, I know that it is a mystery that the man who took your daughter's life may also have a place in Heaven with you. However, you love all of your children. Thank you for this opportunity to receive your love and share it with Marcel and...Zoe what's your brother-in-law's name?"

Without looking up, she answered, "Shaw."

"...Shaw, give us your heart and your mind. In the name of the Father, His Son, and the Holy Spirit. Amen."

Emotional silence filled the room. In that moment, Ollie had a revelation and his tears flowed. They *were* God's children – truly brothers and sisters. He realized that on earth they had definitive relationships. In heaven, all that remained was spirit and soul, and those fleshly connections did not exist. He wanted to forgive for all the times God had freely forgiven him. The task just seemed unattainable.

Chapter 89 – Stand Still and Pray

Many would think it odd that Deacon would stand by Ollie. Deacon didn't happen to be one of them.

He gripped Ollie's shoulder, supported him, understood the man was being broken and rebuilt, and when it all ended, he would be stronger.

Zoe stated truthfully; all things work together for good to those that love the Lord, who are called according to God's purpose. Deacon lived by that statement. The journey that he walked some times seemed lonely, frustrating and uncertain.

However, to be a true follower of Jesus Christ, an effective ambassador of God's kingdom, he had to set himself apart from the ways and beliefs of the world.

Deacon removed his hand from Ollie's shoulder in order to read a text message from Mitch. "Desiree's school is on lock down. Search in progress for missing student," it read. Perceptive, Zoe lifted her head and questioned, "Everything alright?"

"Not sure." He moved for the door. "I'll be in touch."

Outside, he searched the streets for the fastest way to get to the school. He wished for one of his motorcycles to zip through the traffic.

After a quick assessment of his transportation options, he decided to walk. Approaching the school, he heard the sirens; saw the flashing lights, officers directing traffic. A block away, he realized even with Mitch's assistance, he wasn't getting through – no one was.

He lifted his cell phone, dialed, and shouted into the phone, "Are you there?"

"No. I was in midtown when I got the call. Traffic's a beast. You can't get in."

"I know," he said to his brother while still moving forward. He pounded the concrete with long steady steps. "What's going on?"

Mitch knew what he wanted to hear, he reported, "She's okay. One student can't be located. The suspect is...."

Deacon could barely hear. "Who is it?"

"I said...."

Someone shoved Deacon. He dropped his phone, and looked down, praying that no one would step on it. He found the screen cracked and the call dropped.

The facts were clear. He couldn't get through. He couldn't use his phone. He had limited information.

With the crowd pressing into him, Deacon closed his eyes and prayed.

Chapter 90 – Ignorance Is Not Bliss

The school auditorium was filled, every student and staff member accounted for – minus two. Desiree and Detective Alaina Martin stood on the small stage preparing to speak with the staff and children. A serious problem set in Alaina's eyes, she reported, "We can't locate Tiona Washington and Officer Bonner."

Desiree's heart nearly stopped. "What do you mean?"

"She was on the playground when I got your message to report to your office. I had her in my sights. I asked Ms. Knight to keep an eye on her. She said she did until two girls started a scuffle."

She wanted to hear everything they were doing, but Desiree held up her hand, and Alaina shut her mouth. Desiree asked, "Are you serious? Tiona's mother is in my office, giving a statement to the police. She doesn't know her daughter is missing."

Straight and to the point Alaina replied, "The building is being searched a second time, as well as an All Points Bulletin ordered for Tiona and Officer Bonner. We're confident they will be found within the hour."

Desiree was glad someone was confident – she wasn't. Her mind quickly evaluated what she recently learned and realized how little she actually knew. Two of her staff members, one a dedicated teacher of 10 years, and a New York Police officer of eight, had an illicit affair. The officer had an issue with women and the sick desire to sexually assault them. A parent was an "unofficial" prostitute and also had an illicit affair with the schoolteacher.

And who was caught in the middle of it all...an innocent 10-year-old child. The child and that mentally unstable teacher were MIA.

At that moment, Desiree's confidence seemed shaky and people were depending on her. She stepped forward, turned on the microphone, and addressed the frightened faces before her. She had no choice but to trust God.

Chapter 91 – He Knows, He Cares

Tiona set in the dark quiet closet, her back pressed against the cold wall, her legs folded up against her chest. She squeezed her arms around her legs, hoping to stop her trembling. She had been good, very good. When she saw him walking towards her on the playground, he ordered, "Come with me." He walked fast and she kept up. Afraid if she didn't follow all of his instructions, he would arrest her mother. She remembered his words, "Your mother is a whore and whores go to jail forever."

That was true, her mother *was* a whore. There were at least three different men a day that came through the doors of their projects' apartment -- sometimes more. Some arrived while she slept -- some before. Her mother never lied. She knew what her mother did and why. And one day they would buy a nice house, with a backyard. In the summer, they would plant flowers, buy a grill, and a pool. She would have parties and sleepovers. And there would be no more men coming in with their smiles, flashing their money, pretending they cared about them. None of them did, none of them stayed, and none of them cared. Not even Mr. Barnes – her schoolteacher.

At 10 years old, Tiona knew more than many adults. She knew what her mother did was wrong, but accepted it. Still, they adored each other. She also knew men in uniforms promised to protect you, but really, they didn't have to. They could do whatever they wanted as long as they carried a badge.

Officer Bonner was cruel. She remembered her mother's cries when he came over and conducted his business. Her mother always told her that no matter what, she wasn't allowed in her room. That day, Tiona turned up the television louder, but she could still hear her mother's screams. When he left, Tiona gave him a long disapproving glare, prayed for the strength that one day she might hurt him back. He smiled, said he'd see her at school tomorrow. Hours later, her mother came out of the room looking weak and lost.

That day really frightened Tiona. Her mother never spoke a word about it. Never told her how much she hurt. During the night, Tiona listened to her mother cry from her bedroom. She promised herself that she'd protect her mother, because no man or law ever could.

Her head snapped right when she stopped thinking, remembered she was in the closet. She listened to Officer Bonner have a conversation with himself. His muffled voice was angry as he made mention of destroying people.

She wondered why he had taken her from the playground and put her in a black van with only a passenger and driver's seat. He told her to lie on the floor. Then he quickly ripped off his uniform and changed into casual clothes. He took off and drove them for a long while through the city. As the van bounced against the battered streets, she rolled back and forth against the hard floor. Then he took her into an abandoned house. She didn't have a watch or a cell phone, but gauged it was getting late. He hadn't offered her food. And the fear that filled her stomach started to gnaw on her insides.

Hungry, afraid, confused, Tiona decided she would not beg. Men never freely gave and they always wanted something in return for their generous gifts. She wanted nothing from Officer Bonner.

She closed her eyes. Her mother took her to church once a year and that was on Christmas. She remembered the preacher talking about the Savior. Well, that's what she needed. Did He know where she was and would He find her?

Chapter 92 – Needing a Family Moment

Desiree's day had been beyond long. Escorted by her fiancé and future brother-in-law, she lifted herself out of her car, staring blankly into the unsure night.

Mitch unlatched the short gate, pushed it back for her and Deacon to walk through. Just needing to touch her, Deacon took her hand as they mounted the stoop. He didn't have time to ask for her keys because the door swung open the second they reached the landing.

Rayne, Desiree's baby sister, greeted her sister in a long quiet hug. When they stepped through the door, her father stood in line for the next comfort hug. Desiree rested her head on her dad's shoulder, knowing the hug was more for him than her. The quiet in the room ended when a surprise guest swung the kitchen door open, carrying a steaming cup of soup. It took her a minute to register who she looked at. Desiree slowly lifted her eyes into her sister's face. "Beautiful? You're here?"

"Hello to you, too," Beautiful bit out the greeting and shoved the warm cup into Desiree's hands. "This craziness is all over the national news. It's my sister's school. Of course, I'm here."

As if no one in the room was present, Beautiful took Desiree's elbow and directed her over to the sofa. As they sat, she announced, "Sparkle's coming, too."

The soup's aroma helped bring back the appetite she lost. She held the cup with both hands, lifted it to her lips and said a quiet prayer. "Thanks for this, Beautiful."

Beautiful nodded. "What's going on, Dez?"

She looked over, seeing Deacon, Mitch, Rayne, and her father closing in and taking seats around the coffee table.

Desiree asked, "What about Melody? Is she coming, too?"

Annoyed that Desiree didn't answer her question, Beautiful blurted out, "She's pregnant."

"May be pregnant," her father said, correcting her. "They went through a procedure. And she may be. She's on bed rest, can't fly right now."

Desiree lowered her eyes and looked into the chicken and noodles. Why hadn't her sister shared any of this with her?

"You know," Desiree began, "just because I'm not married, y'all don't have to keep these things from me. I care about what Mel is going through."

Beautiful snapped, "This ain't got anything to do with you being married or single. You've been dealing with so much we didn't want to burden you."

She retorted, "My family is not a burden, Beautiful! Y'all always leavin' me out."

Beautiful lifted her finger to drive home a point. Rayne rolled her eyes as the men held their breath.

"Us, leaving you out!" Beautiful swung her finger toward Deacon sitting next to her. "You leave one man and now you're engaged to another. When were you going to tell your sisters, Desiree?"

"I told Rayne," she weakly replied.

"Is Rayne your only sister? Your life is such a screw up, Desiree. That's why all this drama is going on in your school."

"Ouch," she thought.

Desiree's hands trembled and her father broke in, "Beautiful, don't blame your sister. She has dedicated her life to her school."

Ashamed by her father's rebuke, Beautiful jumped up, smoothed her hands over her red fitted pants. "Well, I know when I'm not wanted."

As she prepared to make her dramatic exit, Mitch soothed, "No one wants you to go, Beautiful. I know I don't."

He winked at her. Desiree and Rayne shook their heads at their blushing sister. On the contrary, Beautiful pretended her feelings were hurt. "I only flew out here to help."

Mitch crossed his long legs, folded his hands in his lap and tilted his head. "Then stay."

Not ready to concede, she dipped her hips and fixed her hands on her waist. "Is that what you want, Desiree?"

Desiree lifted her lashes from the cup.

"Girl, nobody asked you to leave. I'm glad that you're here." She looked to her left at Mitch and then looked up at her sister with a directive, "Stop flirting. Remember you're a married woman."

Beautiful's mouth fell open. The room burst with laughter. Before Beautiful could rattle off a defense, Deacon pulled her down onto the sofa and wrapped his arms around her. "Come here. You act like you don't know nobody but Mitch."

"Look," Beautiful said, "y'all better leave me alone."

Deacon gave her a charming grin.

"Well, say hey. I'm going to be your brother-in-law." He followed up with a loud smooch on her cheek.

Desiree saw her sister's eyes light up. Deacon and Mitch certainly had a way with the Davenport women.

Chapter 93 – A Little Higher

Deacon, Mitch, Rayne and her father went home. A couple rooms away, Beautiful slept in a spare bedroom. Tonight she had arms to hold her, voices to comfort and hands to provide for her. But who comforted Tiona?

Desiree sat up in bed, gripped the sheets with her hands. She had prayed with her family, and by herself and still, restlessness choked her. Somewhere there was a mother crying for her child. It ripped at Desiree's spirit.

In the glow of the nightlight, she got up, removed her pajama pants, and stepped into a pair of jeans. She rummaged in her drawer, found her old college sweatshirt and pulled it over a t-shirt. On her way to her sock drawer, her cell phone vibrated. She answered it.

"I didn't wake you," Deacon stated, knowing she wasn't asleep.

"No," she croaked, her voice tired from tears and dread.

"Why are you calling?" she asked and started pacing.

Lying in bed, Deacon looked up at the ceiling. He remembered years ago how he would stare into space, thinking about Desiree. "I want to be with you. I wish we were married."

"Deacon, how can you think about that at a time like this?"

Realizing she misunderstood, he provided, "I'm not talking about having sex with you. I know you can't sleep. I wanna hold you." She stopped in her tracks, closed her eyes and pictured being in his arms. "I want that, too." Knowing her thoughts, he said, "You're not her mother, but you can't be still about this." So true, her bare feet began pacing again.

He felt the same way, nevertheless, he reminded her, "The police are on it."

She shook her head. "We failed this child – me, her mother, the police... We all failed. I want to walk the streets like you do. I might find her. I could tell the police I'll donate a monetary reward to anyone that helps us find Tiona."

He liked the second idea much better than the first. "How much?" he asked.

"I have five thousand."

"I'll add to it."

"Deacon, I didn't ask...."

He didn't want to hear her rebuttal. "I *want* to. I'll make some calls and get more. We'll find her, Desiree."

The warm, salty tears started to pour from her eyes. "I want to believe that."

"Then believe it. Don't go out tonight." She stopped pacing, looked down at her clothes. "I need to do something."

"Do something useful. Pray."

Insulted, she replied, "You know I have been."

He took a breath. "I know, baby. But you walking the streets at two in the morning, with no leads, isn't a good idea. Come on." He rolled out of bed and onto his knees.

"Where are we going?"

"Up a little higher. I'm on my knees, get down on yours. If you want to spend the night doing something, we'll do this, together."

Desiree knelt at the foot of her bed, closed her eyes, and sobbed into the receiver. Deacon prayed as she sobbed. When the cries subsided, she joined him in prayer until sunlight filled her bedroom.

Chapter 94 – Send Me, I'll Go…

After a night without sleep Desiree thanked God her sister hadn't burned the coffee, too. It was an odd feeling of physical exhaustion, but spiritual refreshing. She was preparing to sit down on the sofa and enjoy the java when the doorbell rang. She changed direction and let Deacon in.

He looked down at the mug in her hand. "No thanks, I had a cup already."

She smiled. "Not on your life buddy. I won't make it through the day without coffee." As he kissed her cheek and eased passed her, she wondered how the man managed to look better and better by the day.

Neither one of them received much sleep after spending most of the night praying over the phone. With or without sleep, his appearance charged the room. Feeling like she just received a gift on Christmas morning, she mumbled, "I could play for hours."

"What?" he asked, watching her eyes become cloudy with desire.

She stepped close to him. "You look really good."

"So do you. How do you feel this morning?"

Closing the space between them, he stepped closer, admiring her captivating brown eyes. She replied, "Encouraged, thank you for last night."

"Anytime, prayer and our faith will be the foundation of our marriage. I hope…." Deacon paused, and took in a couple sniffs. "What's that?"

"Slightly embarrassed, she said, "My breath?"

He sniffed again. "Something's burning."

She turned her head towards the kitchen and then looked back at him. "Beautiful's burning breakfast." He lifted his brow and smiled.

She invited, "Wanna stay?"

"Ohhh, no…but I'll feast these." He nibbled on her lips.

She smiled, enjoyed his morning kiss and whispered, "Coward."

"Just trying to live as long as possible and I said feast, not snack."

Deacon aggressively wrapped her in his arms. Her coffee spilled onto the hardwood floor as he kissed her into a state of delirium. She was convinced her man had a Ph.D. degree in kissing.

Beautiful swung open the door and watched them until Desiree's free hand lifted Deacon's navy V-neck sweater and stroked his very fine abs. To break up the intimate scene, she cleared her throat, announced, "Breakfast is ready," and went back into the kitchen.

Deacon lifted his head, opened his eyes, and she knew he saw only her, he said, "Have your breakfast. We'll catch up later." He kissed her cheek, turned for the door and she tugged him back with a question. "What are you up to today?"

"Nico has a follow-up appointment. Later, I am going to the prison for a visit with Marcel."

He didn't ask her about her day. She'd be facing the school board, police, local politicians, and parents. He left her with a piece of advice. "You've got a lot of eyes on you. The way you handle this situation represents not only who you are, but who's inside of you." With that, he kissed her forehead.

The door clicked shut and Deacon stepped out to fulfill his day.

"Amazing," she breathed, staring into the half full coffee mug that had spilled coffee at her feet. He trusted her to handle her day and she trusted him to handle his.

Beautiful stood in the door once again. "Were you going to take the man right here in the living room?"

"I wanted to. Unfortunately, he had to go." She shrugged and started for the kitchen. "Maybe later," she joked.

Beautiful shook her head. "Be careful, Desiree. You're not...."

"Married," Desiree finished. "And why are you so concerned about me? Is it because you want Mitch so badly and you ARE married?"

Touché.

Her sister flinched. "I do not."

"Girl, physical attraction is something else. Maybe you should go home to *your* husband."

"I have self-control."

Upon her sister, Desiree bounced and shouted, "Ah-ha! I knew it! You have to fight for self-control. What is it with you and Mitch?"

"I don't know. I can't get him out of my system."

"That's called lust, Beautiful."

Her sister shook her head as tears began gathering in her eyes.

Desire inquired, "Beautiful, everything alright with you and Big John?'

"We're perfect," She absently replied and boxed her arms across her ample breasts. Seconds later, she decided, "I feel like I'm missing something. And Mitch, he's so sure, you know...exciting! He's a homicide detective and he's so...smooth. The last time we were together we almost crossed the line. I can't stop thinking about if we had."

Thinking about the power of the forbidden fruit, Desiree proclaimed, "You and Big John love each other."

She held her sister's words, considered if Mitch was what she really wanted, or could it be something else?

Both ladies turned at a knock at the door. Beautiful asked, "Expecting someone?"

"Not this early." She began a quick stride toward the door. "I hate when people knock. I have a doorbell." She peered through the glass, didn't recognize the man on the other side and shouted, "Can I help you?"

"I got a letter for you!" he returned the shout.

"Leave it at the door, please."

He did and she watched him walk down the steps and out of the gate. She shook her head. The messenger didn't latch the gate back either. She opened the door and swiped up the letter. Beautiful rushed over as she ripped it open. Eyes scanning the words, they read together.

Principal Davenport:

Let's keep this short and sweet. I have your student, and you want her back. Why not a trade? You, for her. You'll be hearing from me with further instructions. Careful...don't share this information with anyone. Not even your fine new boyfriend or his brother. Detective Mitch. We wouldn't want anything to happen to Deacon while he's out tending to the homeless and incarcerated.

It wasn't signed, but she knew it was from Raymond. She looked up from the letter and into Beautiful's eyes.

"I'm calling Mitch," were the first words Beautiful declared.

Desiree grabbed and held her arm. "No! I wanna see if he contacts me."

Beautiful knew her sister could keep a secret. "You're not going to tell Mitch or Deacon are you?" Frustrated and fearful, she sighed. "Desiree, that man might kill you and the little girl. I am going to tell Mitch!"

Desiree argued, "He might not. He may free her."

Beautiful twisted her face. "Please, and what do you think he'll do with you?"

"I don't know how else to help Tiona."

"You're willing to die for this child?" Her sister's eyes enlarged, waiting for an answer.

She wished Beautiful hadn't been there when the letter arrived. Desiree rationalized, "Mitch puts his life on the line everyday. Deacon, as a missionary, goes into dangerous places. Why? Because we need people like Mitch and Deacon."

"And you? You think you're some sort of hero?" her sister retorted.

"I *have* to do this. I want Tiona safe and sound. If something happens to her, I won't be able to live with myself. She was taken while in my care. I don't care *if* you tell Mitch. I am going for Tiona."

Already late, Desiree shoved the mug into her sister's hand and walked to the coat closet for a short white jacket. Sticking her arms into the sleeves, she requested, "Please, I hate to ask you this, but can you clean up the coffee I spilled? I'm late."

She picked up her briefcase, put the letter in it, and rushed out. Beautiful shouted, "I'm telling Daddy, too!"

Chapter 95 – Embracing Simple Things

At Zoe's suggestion, she and Ollie prayed for their past perpetrators. She prayed silently on her knees, while Ollie prayed and paced the floors of her home office. Even in their different praying styles, they shared many commonalities.

They understood loss and hurt. They understood being reared in a household, receiving adequate food, shelter, and clothing, yet the provision by which they received those needs did not stem from what they craved the most – love. She grew up in a non-religious home, and he, an insanely religious home. And somehow, their past created a hunger in them to love God and others.

She knew when people saw them; they'd see their racial differences. And those who knew them would be aware of their financial differences. Moreover, in her heart, she knew those differences would enhance their relationship; bring diversity to their lifestyle and a spice in their lives that many could not share. Yes, challenges were ahead. For one, his impending trial would challenge them. Two, her mother wouldn't take her relationship with Ollie easily.

As Zoe continued to kneel, she meditated on these things, understanding her past perpetrator had the ability to affect her future, however, why would she allow that? Her future was far too important for past hurt. So what if her future nieces and nephews would be the children of a man who deeply hurt her?

The great thing she rejoiced over was he wasn't *her* husband and no longer her problem. She hummed then, "Thank you, Jesus," eased out of her throat. Ollie quieted, turned, and saw Zoe rock on her knees. He recognized the body language as she rocked, understood the humming and the verbal gratification. She had entered into another phase of prayer and meditation, traveled to a higher plane.

He didn't want to intrude and decided to back up as she soared.

He sat, closed his eyes, and waited for her to come back to him. It was 20 minutes later before Zoe took a seat on the pretty upholstered sofa.

"You're glowing." he realized when she sat and smiled at him.

"Is it brighter in here?"

He laughed. "It's still cloudy outside but, yeah, I think it's brighter in here. I know you are. You're radiant, Zoe."

His compliment flushed her checks, matched the natural red color of her lips. Folding her hands in her lap, she stated, "Life is as complicated as we make it. I want a simple life, Ollie."

His chest tightened, she didn't want to pursue a relationship with him. His life was anything but simple. Ollie replied, "I understand. You don't have to explain."

She squinted at the disappointment in his deep raspy voice, and said, "I meant that I'm not going to let Shaw complicate my life. And we shouldn't let this trial define us. We should display a unified front, trust God. I'm ready to fight, if you are."

He knelt on one knee, and covered her folded hands with his. "I want the same. I've got to be smarter and I don't want to use you as a crutch."

She lifted her hand, extended the long dainty fingers, and rested them on his cheek. His eyes closed, enjoying her tender touch. She whispered, "Use me as your crutch, because in life there will be times I'll need to lean on you."

He could barely speak, but managed, "Zoe…"

Full of conviction, yet soft and sweet, she answered, "Yes."

He stared at her. "Why are you so kind to me? Are you naive?"

She stroked his face with her thumb. "Ollie, you were created to be loved. Treating you kindly, does that make me naive?"

With all his unwise decisions, past hurt and impending challenges, he had forgotten he should have true love and kindness. He promised, "Not a day will go by that you will not feel my love and admiration for you."

Her eyes filled with warm tears. She allowed the cleansing liquid to drift away, accepting she had to share a very intimate secret with him. She took his arms. "Please, sit next to me.

He did, clasping his hands around hers. "What's wrong?"

"You need to know this before we make a commitment."

He blinked at her.

"Ollie, not only did I lose my baby, I lost my ability to have children. The doctor performed an emergency hysterectomy. I'm sorry."

He understood her desire for a man with children. Ollie released her hands, lifted her chin, and studied her wet face. He whispered, "That doesn't matter to me." He pulled her close, held her in his arms. "It changes nothing for me, for us," he emphasized, tightening his embrace. "You're meant to be a mother. I know that in my heart."

The simple things; that's all she wanted. Leaning on him, Zoe shared another concern, "One more thing, there is nothing simple about my mother."

He let out a breath, gave her his infamous crooked smile. "Yeah, my sister Vaughn told me she's something else and a half."

Because he took it lightly, her smiled turned into a big grin. "You have no idea."

Chapter 96 – Be Ready For Anything

They had her surrounded. Desiree sat at her dining table receiving direction from New York City's finest investigating officers, negotiators. When appropriate, Mitch and Evan added their assistance.

Her home looked and sounded like a police station with all the unfamiliar lingo, equipment set up everywhere and coffee and donuts on the island counter.

To her surprise, and Beautiful's dismay, Desiree held law enforcement's support. Desiree Davenport was deputized and going in after Tiona. She even received a call from the mayor with a promise that they would hold off the media. Raymond couldn't have any indication of their plans.

Desiree looked up from the circle of professionals as a young technician with wild blond hair and a nose ring ordered her to stand. She helped Desiree slip on a black stylish blazer.

Evan, FBI agent and brother-in-law, pointed at the buttons. "You're connected. Those are cameras. We'll hear and see what you do. You'll stay connected to us. I promise." The computer screen on her desk lit up, displaying Evan as he talked to her. She even heard his voice coming out of the computer. "Pretty high tech," she said.

She believed his promise and took her seat to sponge up more information. This was their best and only shot. They would leave nothing to chance. They had no leads, even with the $12,000 reward she and Deacon offered. Raymond's note and invitation gave them the best lead they could hope for. Yet they kept in mind, he was a cop and knew how they thought. At all times, they had to be one step ahead.

In the living room, Beautiful pouted, asked her father, "You're really going to let her do this?"

"She's a grown woman, Beautiful. I support her decision."

Bad answer. She pointed at Deacon who had been pacing. "You!" she snapped, "you're her fiancé. If you want a wife, then do something!"

Deacon stopped moving, pushed in hands against the sofa and looked down at Beautiful. "I am, I'm praying."

She dismissively waved her hand. "You really think he's going to let Desiree go once he gets her? Hello, this guy is crazy!"

Beautiful reasoned with her baby sister, "Rayne, you're the shrink, does this make sense? He goes from homosexual to molesting children and now he wants Desiree. Why?"

Rayne sat back. "He is a homosexual. However, he has a problem with women, especially women in a position of power. My guess is that he was hurt pretty badly by a mother figure. It affected his sexuality. He turned to men to comfort his sexual needs. Their comfort cannot deal with the deeper issues. Raymond has a burning desire to punish his mother figure. That's why he hurts women, demeans them sexually. He uses name-calling and pain to strip their power for self-empowerment. My guess is he hasn't touched Tiona."

Deacon asked, "Why do you think that?"

"She's a child, weak like he still sees himself. The only reason he touched her at school was out of anger. His lover had once again been unfaithful to him. And the reason he kidnapped her was to lure Desiree to him. It is adult women he wants. Desiree would make his perfect victim. To him, she possesses all the power – leader of children and adults. And she has rejected him. She believed Raymond had a crush on her. He asked her out a few times. She always declined. I'm sure that built up more resentment."

"But he didn't want a relationship with her," Beautiful put in.

"He wants to disgrace her. Had she given him the chance, she would have had to face him daily, look him in the eye, and see what he did to her. He'd hold the secret over her head, strip her of her power. Thank God she never took him up on his offer."

Beautiful huffed. "She's falling for it now. She's going in."

Rayne folded her hands in her lap. "I trust Mitch, but Evan's in there, too." She lifted her chin toward the swinging door that led into the kitchen. "I know my husband will not put our sister in harm's way. We have to trust God and support Desiree." She reached up and Deacon gave her hand a squeeze.

He agreed, "She'll be alright. I'm proud of her."

Beautiful sat with her hands in her lap. "See, this is why I keep my behind in California. You New Yorkers are crazy."

William Davenport smiled, but Beautiful spoke truthfully. They were dealing with a mentally unstable human being. One trained in law enforcement, with a life purpose to hurt his baby girl, or even worse, take her life.

It seemed like days before the law finished briefing Desiree. Deacon waited until the last uniform left, but William gave Deacon a holding glance. He accepted it as William went into the kitchen to speak with his daughter.

The large man took in a healthy breath and pushed the swinging door. He found her sitting incredibly still, wearing the black surveillance blazer.

She didn't look up or acknowledge her father. She knew his scent. Her dad had been wearing that cologne for years. "All set to take this man down?" he asked, sitting and rubbing his hands over the red tablecloth covered with little white flowers. He remembered it belonged to his wife.

"Yeah," she answered his question with her eyes staring at her hands.

"Really?" he asked. His right fist snapped out, jabbed her in the cheek – not hard, but enough to get her attention.

Her head turned. "Dad!"

"You're not ready. You should have seen that coming."

She furrowed her brow. Her sassy flipped hair fell over her left eye. He remarked, "Start wearing your hair back. You need your full vision."

She feathered her fingers through it, pushed it away. "I know what you're trying to do, Dad."

"You have to be ready. You're on an assignment. You can't be distracted. You don't know how he's going to contact you."

She shook her head. "The investigators told me that. I was just taking a minute to process it."

"Process it later," he directed sharply. "If my daughter is going toe to toe with a psychopath, I need to know she's ready. You remember those self-defense moves I taught you?"

She frowned. How does anyone prepare to battle with a psychopath? She answered his question, "Dad, I was a teenager when you taught us self-defense."

That was years ago and William probably wasn't the best one now to give her a refresher. He called Mitch and Evan in over his shoulder.

They came quickly, a look of action on their faces. "We're okay," William said. "Stand down men. Show her some self-defense moves."

Evan and Mitch exchanged glances. "That's not a bad idea, Desiree. How do you feel about that?" Evan asked.

She stood up and stepped behind her chair, pulled off the blazer and gripped the chair. "I need some time guys."

She turned. "Dad, I've gone from principal to rescuer. Things are moving too fast."

He stood too, took her arms firmly in his hands. "We don't expect certain things in life. Your mother was a healthy woman…never drank, smoked, and she ate healthy. Then one day she dies of a massive heart attack. I didn't expect it. I certainly didn't want to live my retirement alone. I wanted to end my life."

Desiree gasped, hearing her father share his heart. He went on, "It was so much so fast, no warning -- here one night, gone in the morning. I went on …for you – your sisters. Your mother would have never forgiven me if I'd taken the easy way out. You have a giant to face and…" He angled his head toward the door. "…Deacon's pacing the floors, praying for you. We're expecting you to come back to us. Don't let us down."

Her bottom lip trembled, but she sucked it up before her father ordered her to. She looked up at Mitch and Evan. "I'm going to change and then you can show me what I need to know."

William came back with, "Don't change. You don't know what you'll be wearing when he contacts you. You have to be able to defend yourself wearing anything." He ordered the guys in the living room and they began shoving furniture out of the way.

Desiree squared her shoulders, followed the men. When she positioned herself, Deacon gave her his amazing smile and then winked at her. His confidence strengthened her. She tossed aside all distractions and prepared for the unknown.

Chapter 97 – Heart to Heart

"What the hell was that?" Kendall Carter's eyes blared disapprovingly at Ollie. He had no earthly idea what angered her. Kendall was recommended by Zoe as a good defense attorney. However, she described herself as better than good. She never took on a challenge that she didn't overcome.

When she received the call from Lily Carraway, heard the evidence, and the charges, she grinned. The prosecution would have no problem putting together an airtight case. That was the thing about air, things could seep through it, escape – allow room for flaws.

Nothing was perfect. In addition to the challenge, the case would get quite a bit of media coverage. Actually, it already had. She had seen the reports on television, heard it on the radio, read it in the paper – "International Art Dealer, Local Gallery owner and Founder of The Sapphire Arts Foundation for the Youth arrested on rape charges.

The negative backlash from the public was already upon him. Parents were pulling their children out of the foundation, and investors were holding back any additional funding until the verdict. Even so, his new attorney did not bat an eyelash. Kendall Carter exuded confidence. It made Lily easily like her. But now, as the woman glared at Ollie, Lily had second thoughts.

For Kendall, winning meant everything, and she wouldn't let anyone stand in her way, including her client. She slammed the palms of her hands against the pinewood conference room table, asked Ollie a second time, "I said, what the hell was that?"

Not following, he gripped Zoe's hand tighter. They had held hands on the way from the car into the courtroom, and then out of the courtroom back into the car, and now, hand-in-hand, they stood in the conference room of Kendall Carter's office.

Kendall's finger wagged downward, pointing at their hands. "That, that," she stuttered, "what are you doing?"

Ollie slowly lifted their hands. "This? Our hands?"

"It's not about your hands. It's my ass," she snapped. Lily blinked, placed her hand on her belly as if she were protecting her baby from Kendall's wrath. And since Ollie and Zoe clearly were in the dark, Lily enlightened them, "You know I am happy you have found each other, but now is not the time to go public."

Thankful that someone in the room had half a brain, Kendall swiftly concurred, "That's right. What are people going to think? You go from dating Desiree Davenport, to Lacy Reid – who claims you raped her by the way, and now Dr. Zoe Landry. Ollie, you appear cold and uncaring. The public is not going to like this."

Kendall placed her hands on her full hips that she carefully camouflaged with a black tailor-made jacket that covered her bottom. She added one more variable, "And she's white by the way. The sisters are definitely not going to like this."

Without intending to, Ollie squeezed Zoe's hand again. "Hold up. This is my personal business. I don't care who likes it, or who doesn't, especially the sisters. It's a sister who is accusing me of rape."

Kendall retorted, "So you've written off black women?"

"No," he shook his head at her ridiculous inquiry.

"What? Is Dr. Landry your rebound woman?"

"No."

"Wasn't Lacy? After Desiree dumped you…it insulted your ego…so you went after Lacy, forced her to be intimate. You got to screw her and her husband at the same time, didn't you?"

No!" he shouted. "She came to me, initiated our relationship, and when I realized it was a mistake, I ended it. She got mad and did this. That's all."

Zoe held her breath as Ollie's panted out of him. She knew what Kendall was doing. "Ollie." She turned her head. "She's right. Maybe I shouldn't have been at the jury selection today."

Ollie glared back at his attorney. She had a round caramel face. Her flawless complexion popped against the close cut hair that she flaunted. Not many women could get away with hacking off all of their hair. Kendall Carter did, and it made a statement -- confident, strong, warrior.

She was the shortest person in the room, but her presence felt like it towered over Ollie. Zoe shook his hand. "Look at me." He did.

"I don't want to do anything that would hurt you. I thought presenting a unified front, would help. I'm sorry."

He shook his head, believing she had nothing to apologize for and turned to his cousin for advice. "Lily, what do you think?"

Lily's arms boxed over her chest. "I think Kendall makes a good point. I believe…."

Ollie interrupted her and stated to Kendall, "I don't care about her point. Zoe isn't going anywhere because of what the public thinks, or what the sisters like."

"Let me finish, Ollie. You asked," Lily demanded, "I believe the public may think you were on the rebound with Lacy and upset about losing Desiree. However, you decide to rape a woman two years after your wife's death? You're a gentleman and it's out of character for you."

Lily turned her head slightly, glanced at Kendall. "That's how we'll spin it. As for Zoe, since you've stated that she's not going anywhere, we've got to be ready for the backlash."

"I don't need complications," Kendall said, harshly.

Ollie sighed. "I didn't rape Lacy Reid."

Kendall walked up to him. "Good, keep saying that. You sound convincing."

Zoe realized something. It frightened her. "Kendall, you don't believe he's innocent. Why'd you take the case?"

Her eyes flat, she replied, "My job is not to believe him. It's to make the jury believe him. I'm not sure if I can do that with you hanging all over him."

Ollie lifted their hands, interlaced their fingers in Kendall's face. "Then you have a choice to make. I'm not letting her go. Unless..." He faced Zoe. "...you want out?"

"I'm here to stay," Zoe informed them.

Kendall threw her hands up. "Fine. Ollie, you better make the world believe that you love this woman and you're not booty hopping."

Ignoring the fact that Kendall stood only a few feet in front of them, he turned, stood toe to toe with Zoe. They gazed into one another's eyes until Kendall turned on her heels, directed toward Lily, "You've got to help me with this." She waved her hand over at Ollie and Zoe.

Lily smiled. Her cousin had found his match. She would never tell him to back off. She declared, "Awww, come on Kendall, have a heart."

"Heart, fart," Kendall bulked, sitting at the conference room table. She pulled out her legal pad. "We have work to do counselor." She looked up at Lily. Still smiling, Lily joined her and pulled out her notes from the jury selection.

Kendall kept her eyes on her notepad, listening to Zoe and Ollie's kissing lips. "Stop that in my place of business. We do have this pesky business of a rape trial. Care to join us?"

Ollie lifted his hand, careful to finish their kiss. Done, he said, "Let's get to work."

"You go ahead," Zoe prompted. She knew Kendall wasn't just concerned about the public backlash. She was one of those sisters who didn't like black men with white women. The last thing she wanted to do was damage Ollie's defense.

"I've got clients," she said and stepped back. Ollie held her hand. "You don't have a car."

She gave him a sweet smile. "This is New York. I'll get around. Call me later."

With love and kindness Zoe captured his heart. He leaned in for another kiss.

"Do not kiss her in here again," Kendall ordered.

Ollie turned his head and Zoe encouraged him, "Go on, work." She left quickly and Ollie watched the door close.

He had to be cleared of the charges. He wanted to live the rest of his life with Zoe and his baby girl. With conviction, he walked to the table and sat next to Kendall.

Ready, he asked, "What's next?"

98 – With All Thy Getting, Get Understanding

She did have clients. Zoe had Chelsea schedule her appointments later in the afternoon, allowing her time with Ollie for the first day of his jury selection. Her presence in the courtroom wasn't just for him; it was for her as well. Having a gift of reading people when their mouths were saying one thing, but their body language and tone projected another, she would determine their thoughts.

She could see the selection process would not be easy. The prosecutor had dismissed three jurors and the defense five. She had to admit she agreed with Kendall's choices. Zoe would have dismissed those jurors as well. As it stood now, they had two male jurors, one that reminded her of her Grandpa Joe. She really believed he would be fair and listen. The second male was older than Ollie, younger than Grandpa Joe. He seemed to be fascinated with the legal process. Zoe hoped his enthusiasm would allow him to focus.

They had also selected three female jurors -- one in her late 20s, the others were late 40s and 50s, a divorcée, and a widow. They both had adult children – males. She knew it was wrong, but she hoped they'd see Ollie as their son – a young man who got involved with the wrong woman.

She asked the cabbie to let her out a few blocks from home. The weather was crisp for a spring day. She called it false spring. First, it would warm up and everyone would peel off the coats and jackets, then you'd wake up one morning, step outside, and the wind would bite you in the backside. She heard the wind declare, "I ain't leavin', nah, not just yet."

Thinking about it, she imagined the tone of the wind sounding like Ollie's raspy voice. It made her laugh. *He* made her laugh. She considered the socially acceptable relationship rules. There had to be one that commanded "No falling in love in three and a half weeks."

"Oh well," she sighed. They had broken that rule and would break others as well.

For one, Kendall Carter didn't like her. As she stepped into her foyer she thought, "You break a rule and you find out what others truly think about you. Interesting." Kendall liked Zoe fine as a colleague. They had worked together on a couple of fundraiser events. Then, her race didn't matter. "But now...."Zoe thought. She walked in the open family room, tossed her chocolate brown coat, crossed to the window, and picked up the fresh lemonade from the refreshment cart.

After taking a nice long drink, she rested in a gold antique chair and picked up on her thoughts. According to the social rules, her dating Ollie was a "no - no." The sisters wouldn't like it and would withdraw their support. What if the jurors felt Ollie violated the social rules?

Would it impact him negatively? She could only imagine if her mother were a juror. What would she say? How would she react? She had a pretty clear idea.

When she heard the click of her mother's pumps, rushing in from another part of her home, her pretty clear idea would soon be manifested. Marsha Cartwright had a look of total shock. Zoe would normally antagonize her mother; make light of her overly dramatic behavior. Today she wasn't prepared.

Her mother's suit was spring yellow, fitting her elegantly. The jacket's trim held a double layer of small ruffles and the skirt was classically cut to cover her knees. The pumps that sounded against Zoe's hardwood floors matched the pale yellow.

Zoe's eyes traveled back to the raging fire in her mother's eyes, she asked, "Has it been on the news already."

"Yes," she snapped, "it has. I didn't see it, because I was having lunch with friends. Can you imagine what it's like discussing one daughter's wedding, while you get a phone call that your other daughter is walking into a courtroom, hand in hand with a rapist?"

Zoe processed the information. So her mother was bragging about Aimee's wedding. Of course, she was. That would be the highlight of all her social gatherings for the remainder of the year. Her baby girl married into a prominent political family. "Hoo-ray," she thought.

"Sorry I interrupted your bragging rights."

Her mother cocked her head, nearly bared her teeth. "I am not going to let you destroy this family. I have worked too hard to keep us in good standing."

"With whom, Mother? You really think those people care about us?"

Arms stiff at her side, she replied, "What you do, and who you do it with, is very important, Zoe."

"Really?" Zoe lifted her brow. "It didn't matter to you that Aimee married Shaw, after what he did to me?"

"Pish, posh, Zoe. That happened ages ago. And besides, I had no idea of her choice for a groom until they were engaged."

"Liar!" Zoe got on her feet, stood, glaring down at her mother. "You were the one who told Aimee that Shaw was in Paris the same time she was. You encouraged her to look him up. You set this up. Kept it from me. And that's why you didn't come to the fundraiser the night they came home to the states. Don't you dare pretend like you're innocent."

The fire that raged in her mother's eyes transferred to Zoe's. Marsha didn't blink. "You and Shaw were kids back then. Why should Aimee not be happy with him?"

She absently threw up her hand. "Yes, I set them up. I did *not* make them fall in love or get married. It's a good match, Zoe."

"Yeah, for you and Shaw. What about Aimee? He's going to hurt her."

"You have always been jealous of your sister. It's distasteful."

Zoe lifted her palm. "Save it, Mother. I watched Shaw very carefully the weekend of the wedding. He doesn't only have eyes for your precious baby girl. And when she finds him out, he is going to turn on her."

Her mother did her best to calm her breathing as she glared at her daughter. Zoe did the same, closing her eyes, she took a deep breath.

"Mother, you're here about me and Ollie. Just tell the truth, you're so afraid of what your *friends* are going to think of me dating an African American."

Chomping out every word, her mother shot, "Don't you dare make me out to be a racist. The man's a violent criminal and you've latched onto him as if you've lost your mind. I've been trying to give you the benefit of the doubt, but you are forcing my hand."

Making a face, Zoe wondered, "What now?"

Marsha placed her hands on her thin waist and tossed her head back. When she brought it back up, she announced, "Shaw and I have been talking. I don't believe you are mentally competent – first, you are a lesbian and now, you're dating a criminal. You are not capable of managing your percentage of the estate. If you don't stop this nonsense, I'll take legal action, freeze all assets left to you by my late husband."

Zoe gasped. "Charles Cartwright left me that inheritance. Unlike you, he loved me as his own."

"Charles did the proper thing and I will not stand by and watch you squander away everything he and his father worked for. This man you're seeing will waste every dime. How much are his legal fees costing you?"

Offended, she shook her head. "Get out!"

Marsha leaned in. "Zoe, I'm warning you...."

"I said, get *out*! You and Shaw want MY money, try and take it!"

Marsha couldn't move, frozen by her daughter's challenge.

Zoe predicted, "Mother, while you and Shaw are scheming, Aimee is going to be miserable and Ollie and I will be living peacefully. May God help you."

Rolling her eyes, Marsha mocked, "You think God's going to provide for you, through this man? After what he's done?"

"Ollie's innocent. And unlike you, God is kind, loving, and merciful. Without Him in my life, I question where I'd be." She gave her mother a long head-to-toe look. "You're pathetic. May God show you kindness."

She brushed her hands at her mother. "Now, go run to your lawyers and financial advisors. I have clients to see."

With that, Zoe lifted her shoulders and walked out of the room.

Marsha shouted after her, "You'll be sorry."

"Yeah, yeah, Mother." Her mother simply didn't understand. Her financial status did not define her. Climbing the stairs, she prayed, "Lord, please help my family."

Chapter 99 – Firm - Not Fair

Zoe stayed in her bedroom after meeting her clients, grateful for the quiet. Her assistant, Chelsea, was out with her boyfriend so she couldn't get in her face, demand Zoe talk about her troubles. In her profession, she understood the importance of verbalizing your issues. However, her mind was ready to release her tongue.

Her mother made her argument clear. If she were to pursue her relationship with Ollie, she would fail to have a relationship with her mother. "Really, would that be so bad?" she thought.

As soon as she was old enough, Zoe learned that rebellion was the only way to get her mother's attention. Interesting how that worked. Zoe rebelled because she refused to be the perfect little girl her mother wanted society to see. And as a result of her behavior, it captured her mother's attention. To further aggravate her mother she'd make light of the situation, antagonize her with humor. And this pattern became the foundation of their relationship.

Was she doing that now? Was she involved with Ollie to upset her mother? Deep down in her subconscious, she asked, was she using him? Realistically, what sane, educated, mature woman became involved with a man she barely knew, who was up against rape charges?

She had to give it to her mother. On the surface, it appeared insane. She rolled over on her back at the sound of her phone ringing, debating whether to answer Ollie's call.

******

Kendall released Ollie from her office at about 3:30 in the afternoon. He had confidence in Kendall and Lily, but the law had "physical evidence" to arrest, charge and try him for a crime. On his way to pick up his daughter, he called Zoe. She didn't answer.

It was a little after 9 before Ollie realized Zoe hadn't returned his call. He slipped his hand in his pocket, found his cell phone, crashed onto the sofa, and dialed. It took her awhile to answer. When she did, he didn't like her tone of voice. "Baby, what's wrong?"

His sweet sincere question made her see she couldn't verbalize her thoughts. She didn't know how to explain her dependent/rebellious relationship with her mother. In her profession, it would be an embarrassment.

"Nothing." She sniffed. "Just tired. How'd the rest of your meeting go with Kendall and Lily?"

Instead of answering her, he apologized, "I'm sorry for the way Kendall treated you. She had no right."

For Ollie's sake, she defended her. "Kendall is doing her job."

328

He concurred, "Yeah, but not for me. This is another notch in her reputation belt."

"That's why she'll fight tooth and nail to clear you. You're in good hands."

"We're back in court tomorrow…more jury selection. I called you earlier, left you a message. Are you coming?"

She heard the anticipation of hope in his voice. She didn't want to let him down.

"Ollie, I'm not certain I should. Kendall made some valid points."

Ollie played with his imaginary goatee before he asked, "Did your family see the news?" His had. They saw Zoe and Ollie walking close together into the courthouse, hands tightly held as the media pressed their microphones into their faces.

Zoe made a humming sound and replied, "My mother heard about it. I'm sure she's seen it with her own eyes by now."

"Let me guess. It didn't sit well with her."

"That's an understatement."

"Zoe, I wish you had introduced me to her."

Before thinking, it rushed out, "It wouldn't matter. She wouldn't like you. You're not in her social circle."

He added, "I'm neither, rich, or white."

"Ollie…."She could not deny him the truth about her mother.

"She's upset with you, because of me, right?"

"Furious. She threatened to freeze my monetary assets. Deem me mentally incapable."

"Can she do that?" He raised his voice.

"She could try. I don't care."

"Don't say that."

"Excuse me? You think I care about the money."

"You care about something. You've been crying. Zoe…" He paused. "Look, if you want to end this before it really gets started, that's fine with me."

"What happened to him telling me we would have a family; a future?" she thought. She couldn't believe his weakness. Just like that, he'd end it? Simply because she took a time out, a moment to think, he opened the door, offered an invitation for her to walk away.

Her eyes flooded, poured warm water down her flushed cheeks. She guarded what little was left of her heart, stiffened her voice.

"Ollie that's fine with me, too. Will this change my standing at the foundation?"

Ollie felt his heart stop. "What am I doing? Why am I letting her go?," he thought.

He cleared his throat. "Nah, nah. Please stay on."

"Fine. You take care, Ollie."

It took a few seconds to register a reply. Finally, he replied, "You too, Zoe."

The call ended with Ollie staring down at the phone in his hand -- willing it to ring, hoping that she'd call back. Maybe he'd tell her he was afraid she'd end up leaving him one day anyway. That maybe he'd never fit in her social circle.

A fairly grounded woman, he knew, she wouldn't call back. He liked that most about her. Considering his unsettled future, he decided letting her go was for their best interests.

Chapter 100 – Lord, Teach Me How to Wait

Desiree waited in the dark room, listening to Raymond's laughter washing over Tiona's whimpering. "Come closer, Desiree" she heard him say.

In the darkness, she refused and shook her head. "I'm here for her exchange Raymond, please let her go. Please let Tiona go."

She didn't know how he'd done it, but within seconds, he was upon her. The evidence, his warm breath collided with the hairs on the back of her neck. He replied, "You really thought I'd let the little whore go. You're just in time to witness her death."

The awful cry she heard opened her pores as cold water seeped through her skin. She remembered the self-defense moves Mitch and Evan taught her, but paralyzed by fear, she failed to attack.

Was the child dead? After the one terrifying cry, dead silence followed. Suddenly, she lifted her head as if the child's voice floated above her. "Principal Davenport, make him stop hurting me. Please make him stop!" she screamed.

"I will, baby. I will," she promised and Raymond laughed. "It's too late. She's on her way to hell and soon, you'll join her." And then she heard rapid gunfire.

"Noooooooooo!" she cried out as her body quaked with unparalleled fear.

"Desiree, it's alright, wake up baby. It's just a dream." Deacon soothed, rubbed her legs that were draped across his lap as she slept on the sofa and he watched television. Four long anxious days went by and Officer Raymond Bonner hadn't made contact. It was his strategy they knew. He'd take Desiree by surprise, try to contact her when she least expected. The waiting, anticipating the unknown, tore her nerves to pieces. Of course, that's what the enemy wanted -- torture and destroy her mind.

It appeared to be working. Worse, she wondered how much mental damage Tiona had endured. Would the child ever recover?

She closed her eyes, slowed her breathing.

Deacon took her hand, tugged her onto his lap. "I got you."

He wrapped his arms around her trembling body, ran his hands up and down her back, attempting to warm her. He hated what the waiting was doing to her, to them. He wanted to be the substitute. He wished Raymond would call for him, leave his desire alone. She didn't deserve this torture, no one did.

Surrounded by her family didn't keep the nightmares away. Her father moved in, since Desiree refused to leave her home. And her sister Beautiful took up temporary residence.

During the day, Desiree squared her shoulders; met with the Board of Education, law enforcement, and concerned parents. School hadn't reopened yet, and children were terrified. She did what she could, worked as hard as she could.

In the evening, Deacon escorted her home, had dinner with her, and stayed in hopes of her falling asleep. Unfortunately, she'd end up fending off a nightmare before he'd leave.

He shifted, removed her head out of the crook of his neck, and ran his fingertips against her cheek. "I won't think you're weak if you want to cry."

"I don't want to...," she lied as water filled her eyes.

"Go ahead, baby. Your spirit needs a break. You're holding too much." Deacon pressed his lips to her temple. She followed his advice and gave the tears permission to fall.

"It's been days," she murmured, "maybe he's not going to call. Maybe it's too late for Tiona."

He shook his head, kissed her tears. "That's what he wants you to think. He's trying to disarm you. He knows you've contacted law enforcement. He wants you off your guard."

She looked up, her eyes rested on his incredible face. "I'm not afraid for me. Only for her."

He knew that, admired her face since she began wearing her hair in a sleek long ponytail. He kissed her lips. "You'd make a good missionary," he told her.

"If this were you, I'd be freaking out. You've been so calm."

"Because...." He ran his hand across her back, realized she stopped trembling. Thankful, he went on, "I know you have a host of divine help at your disposal. You're coming back to me and Tiona's coming out."

"She gripped his shirt, studied her fist. "You sound so sure."

"I am."

Leaning in, she kissed him softly and gave into the burst of passion that flowed from her heart. She maneuvered, straddled him, forcing his head backward with her eager lips.

He fervently responded. His hands gripped, dug into her round hips. Fighting for self-control with Desiree proved to be the most difficult danger he ever faced. Groaning, he commanded his hands to let loose of her hips, forced them to travel up her back, and then pulled her head back in order to break their intimate kiss. "Desiree." His eyes softened at the pleading in hers. "We can't," he verbalized.

Her body didn't care, pleasure and pulse controlled. She rose and rocked against him. "I want to make love with you, Deacon. I've waited for you for fourteen years. What if...."

"No."

He wouldn't let her believe it, let alone confess it.

"Get this in your head. You're coming back to me. When we make love, it will be as Mr. and Mrs. Stephens."

He wasn't rejecting her. His voice was much too gentle for rejection. He truly and wholeheartedly believed she'd be victorious. Wrapping her arms around his neck, she buried her face into his shoulder.

"I love you. God, I love you so much."

"You are my desire. And with my whole heart, I love you, too."

Chapter 101 – Hope For The Unjust

Marcel sat with a pensive expression covering his face. What did this man think he had? He had to be a quack. The man introduced himself as a missionary. "A missionary!" he shouted in his head. What kind of person travelled the world, sharing the Gospel, taking care of the less fortunate?

And really, what did he care? He had a visitor that had been coming regularly since the first time he laid eyes on the stranger. Marcel began looking forward to their talks, especially since he did most of the talking. But at the moment, he stared through the glass, held the phone to his ear. "What is it?" Deacon asked.

"I think about you," Marcel replied, squinting.

Awkward, Deacon lifted his brows, poked out his lips. He asked, "Think about me in what way?"

"When you hang up that phone," he gestured through the dividing glass, "walk out of here, what do you do?"

Deacon sighed. "Well, right now, I'm not really doing much. Kinda on a vacation. I came back to New York to visit my brother and for the woman I love."

He said it so easily. It didn't sound corny. Marcel wanted to know more. "Does she love you?"

He nodded. "We're in love."

"When will you leave?" Marcel asked. He held his breath, afraid that his one and only visitor would go away.

"My lady has serious work issues. Until she irons them out, I'm not going anywhere."

"You plan on taking her with you. Where will you go?"

Deacon grinned. Oh, he did have plans for his future bride. "I'm taking her to an exotic island. We'll get married and honeymoon there. Then, I'm taking her to Africa and Jerusalem, two of the most spiritual places that I've ever been to."

"That's what I miss the most, traveling. My wife and I use to travel often. After she had the kids, we didn't travel as much. She changed."

"Is that why you started having affairs?"

Marcel smiled. "Do you think that's a good reason to start?"

"No. Just wondering what makes a man that loves his wife turn to other women."

"It's not rocket science." Marcel shook his head. "It's exciting. I never lied about being married. On the contrary, it turned women on. They'd do anything that I'd tell 'em. I guess in hopes they'd turn my loyalties and I'd leave my wife. It never happened. When Lacy found out about Sapphire, she left me. I'd never leave my wife and kids."

Deacon did not reply. He didn't know how to. The man spoke of loyalties and affairs in the same breath.

"She never asked me to leave my wife," Marcel reminisced a moment. "Sapphire never wanted that. She just wanted the adventure, the gifts, and sometimes I felt like she wanted me to love her. There were moments she'd get really quiet, almost depressed. I'd buy something expensive, give her some cash and she'd perk back up."

After another long pause, he admitted, "I think I did love her. I loved her and Lacy. Sounds crazy, doesn't it?"

Deacon answered honestly, "I don't know. You loved both women at the same time for different reasons."

Lifting his voice, he exclaimed, "You understand!"

"I don't understand killing. I do understand unfaithfulness. I understand betrayal. It's selfish and painful for everyone involved."

Marcel detected disappointment in Deacon's voice. "You've had an affair."

"I had one," Deacon confessed, looking in Marcel's eyes. "With my best friend's fiancée. The night before his wedding, she came to me. My friend got suspicious…went looking for her. I guess me, too. He found us kissing in my doorway. Furious, he drove away. He never heard the ambulance's sirens. It sideswiped his car."

Completely engrossed with the story, Marcel jumped in, "He died?"

"It almost killed him. The impact left him paralyzed – waist down." Marcel witnessed a sincere remorse in Deacon. Usually, his visitor's eyes seemed to dance with joy. His deep voice was kind and gentle, but now he saw and heard the pain.

"Tough break, man. See, that's why I never slept with any of my friends or colleague's women. Trust me, some wanted me to."

Marcel sighed, stared up at the ceiling. Silence lingered a beat before Marcel wondered, "Your best friend must be your enemy now."

"He's not. Sterling's incredible." Deacon swayed his head. "He takes responsibility for what happened. He was aware of my feelings and his fiancé's. Back then, he felt like he had the upper hand. She wore his ring. He kept what he knew in his heart and it made him bitter. He was going to punish us. He planned to marry her and take her away from me. Things didn't work out like that."

Marcel grunted. "Then I guess he's the one that got punished…serves him right."

Deacon flinched. "Sterling didn't deserve that."

"That's not how I see it. He knew his woman wasn't faithful. I would never tolerate that. And any man that does deserves it."

"Is that how you felt about Ollie? That he deserved your betrayal?"

An anger rose in Marcel's body and it stiffened. "That's right. Like your friend, he wanted to turn Sapphire against me. She pushed me away, went back to him. I hate him for it. He's the reason she's dead."

"I understand that you pulled the trigger."

"The bullet was for him. No jury would see it that way."

"You're a man who believes it is acceptable to have affairs with women and kill their husbands for trying to save their marriage. Marcel, let me tell you something...." Deacon checked his watch. Marcel feared the visit would end soon.

"Go on," he pleaded.

"It took me fourteen years to come to terms with what I did to my friend. Don't let that be you."

"Why, he...."

Deacon shook his head, stopped him. "Look at where your betrayal put you. You have children. What's gonna happen when you get out of here? What kind of relationship will you have with them? Do you want them to follow your pattern, end up like this one day?"

Marcel considered the weighty list of questions, thought about the father that never cared for him. "I want my children to be better. I love my children and I haven't seen or heard from them in two years. Lacy will never let me near them."

Deacon closed his eyes, silently thanking God. When he opened them, he asked, "Do you want a second chance at life, Marcel?" Hope rushed through Marcel, pumped his heart with joy. He did his best to hold the tears, watering his eyes. They choked him, left him speechless.

Deacon witnessed the gripping emotions. Speaking gently into the receiver, he announced, "Think about what I've said. And if you want a second chance, I'll teach you how to have one. See you tomorrow."

Marcel's shoulders slumped, their visit was over but he wanted to hear more. Sitting behind the glassy barrier all this time, no one had offered him hope. No one except Deacon.

Chapter 102 – What You Do To You, You Do to Others

Since Ollie had given Zoe the invitation to walk away, he had been miserable with a capital "M." She had been a soft illumination in his life. Instead of holding that light up for all to see, he darkened it.

His pastor and uncle called him to church and gave him an assignment. He had no desire to do it. Nevertheless, he sat in Pastor Desmond Rose's office, palms flat against his legs, staring steadily in his handsome face. His uncle was moving into his late 60s and still he had a glow and strength about him. His broad shoulders stood tall. His skin held a glow against the wise eyes and salty colored hair.

Pastor Rose was like a father to Ollie. It pained him, knowing that his arrest and charges had hurt him and their church.

Before they began, his pastor's assistant knocked and walked in carrying a bag from Ollie's favorite restaurant. "Here you go, pastor," she said, resting the bag and laying eyes on Ollie. "How you holding up?"

"I'm good," he answered, even though he didn't feel that way, he certainly knew he had to feel better than she. The young woman was 24 years old and had recently been diagnosed with lupus. Her most recent attack affected her hip, which resulted in a limp. Even with the debilitating effects on her body, she worked hard for the church. "He asked, "How about you, Ellie?"

"Blessed," she replied with a smile. The smile warded off some of the fatigue around her eyes. Turning to Pastor Rose, she inquired, "Need anything else?"

"No, thank you. We have drinks in the mini fridge."

She limped out of the office and shut the door behind her. Ollie realized, "She's strong."

"Very, she gets her strength from the Lord. I appreciate her dedication and the members seem to really like her."

Ollie lifted his brow, thought of his sister that used to be his uncle's assistant. "What? The members didn't like Vaughn?"

Pastor Rose cleared his throat, dug into the bag, and pulled out two gyro sandwiches. "I didn't say that. The members liked Vaughn. She was efficient and professional. But Ellie has a humbling quality."

"Cuz she's sick?" Ollie asked.

Passing a sandwich to his nephew, he quickly shook his head. "Cuz she can be a little more sensitive to their needs. Now, don't get me wrong, Vaughn could handle a boatload of work better than Ellie can. Vaughn also has a sense of humor that I miss. She resigned to take care of the twins, so we have Ellie now. We're delighted she cares for this ministry so faithfully, even with her illness."

Pastor Rose looked at his meal like he could devour it in one bite, but he digressed. "I didn't call you in to talk about your sister. So stop deflecting."

Ollie lifted his brows. "Not deflecting, just wondering, that's all."

Pastor Rose nodded. "Alright, son. I know you have extra time since you stepped down as director of the foundation. Some of the areas in this church could use a facelift."

Thinking about his skills, he thought about his brother-in-law. "Kyle is the one with the construction business."

"I don't need construction. I need a painter." He handed Ollie a sheet of paper, listing all the offices and centers in their church they wanted painted.

"This is a boatload of work," he stated, using his uncle's term.

"It would be good for you and Olivia. You'd be here, at the church and her day care center is here, too."

Ollie glanced at the list again. It would take a considerable about of time. He calculated the trial could start, the jury would deliberate and he might be convicted before he'd finish the assignment. "Do I get a team to help me?"

"You pick one person to help you and we'll pay them."

"What about me? I don't get paid." He grinned.

Pastor Rose pointed to the sandwich. "That's your pay."

Ollie ducked his chin down at the sandwich. "One sandwich?"

"Free lunch. The church will provide your meals."

He shifted, sat higher in his chair. "Uncle Desi, I know what you're trying to do. It's almost embarrassing. I'm a grown man and you feel like you need to keep tabs on me."

Slightly aggravated, Pastor Rose provided, "No one is happy about this. The world is looking at *my* nephew," he pointed his thumb towards his chest, raised his voice, "as if he's a *rapist*? I know you didn't rape Lacy Reid, but that doesn't stop the gossip…what people think about our church and me as your pastor."

Ollie started to apologize and Pastor Rose silenced him. "I'm not finished, son. We can handle this. I've been leading people spiritually for over twenty years. I know you can't change what they think. Only they can do that. My job is to offer the facts – the truth about God's word. You must make better decisions. Was your relationship with Lacy worth it?"

Thinking about the brief intimate relationship, he declared, "Nothing about it was worth it."

Pastor Rose took another look at the meal eyeing him, and corrected Ollie, "Don't say that. Even this can lead to a blessing in your life. And if nothing else, you'll be better for it. Learn from it. You have an incredible gift. And I'm not just talking about your artistic talents. People and children are drawn to you. I wanna tell you something."

Pastor Rose looked down at his lunch and then lifted out of his seat. He sat in the empty chair next to Ollie. "Remember when you and Sapphire separated she moved in with your aunt and me? Your wife told us as an exotic dancer she met a lot of men. Yet there was something about you she couldn't explain."

Pastor Rose laid a hand on his heart. "It is my firm belief that Sapphire is in Heaven today because of your connection with her. Your life is not just about you. You connect with people and your decisions affect your child, family, church and business."

"I know," he replied, humbly.

"Good. Now, you have free creative reign over that list I gave you. Don't let me down. Let's pray and have our lunch."

Ollie slowly shook his head. "Thank you, Uncle Desi."

Pastor Rose put his hand on Ollie's thin shoulder, gave it a firm squeeze. "You're a good man, son and we're going to make it."

Chapter 103 – The Waiting Is Over

"Get in." Two words, one command. Desiree looked over at the silver SUV as she stepped out of her car. She didn't recognize the driver and it was difficult to see his shaded face in the dark. She waited in the street, turned and looked at her house and then back at the SUV. "I said, get in. It's time for the trade, you for Tiona."

The fear overtook, pushing the perspiration through her body. She remembered how to activate the systems built into the black blazer she wore. With an undetected gesture, she bent her fingers and pressed the button under the sleeve. "Lights, cameras, action," she thought. If it worked like her brother-in-law and Mitch told her it would, they would know it was time.

They had also added a tracker into her cell phone. Unfortunately, her purse rested in her car. "Can I just get my bag?" she asked.

The man with the dark skin and thick coarse braids replied, "You don't need it."

"Where's Tiona?"

"Last chance, lady. Get in."

She took a breath. "Okay, Lord, here we go." She opened the door, stepped up and into the SUV. He was speeding away before her door closed. Desiree looked back at her house, hoping her family would get suspicious and call law enforcement when she didn't show.

Seconds after Desiree activated the surveillance; Mitch's cell phone and communicator went crazy. He rolled away from the woman under him, and read the transmission. He swore. "He's got her." He leapt up, found his pants, and jumped into them.

Dazed, Beautiful noticed he didn't bother with his underwear. She lifted up on her elbows. "What?"

Really no time to explain, he searched frantically for his shirt, pulled it on, and started with the buttons. "Damn, it was my turn to follow Desiree home."

Beautiful looked mortified. The men had started taking turns, escorting Desiree. She invited Mitch over, told herself that they were just going to talk. Somehow, she couldn't remember exactly what they talked about. They ended upstairs and in bed. She closed her eyes. Not only had she broken her marriage vows, she had put her sister's life in jeopardy. On her feet now as well, she started looking for her robe.

They both almost jumped out of their skin, when the door burst opened.

Evan stood in the doorway, panting and in shock. His deep voice barreled, "What the hell are you two doing?"

Mitch shook his head, strapped on his harness and holstered his weapon. "It's obvious, Evan. We don't have time for the drama. He's got her."

Disgusted, Evan turned his back and allowed Beautiful some privacy. "I know that. You messed up, man."

Beautiful scrambled into her robe. "What can I do to help?"

Keeping his back turned, Evan directed, "Tell your father and Deacon, no one else. We don't want the media reporting that we know he has her. The transmission is working. We can hear and see what she sees, for now."

Mitch grabbed his brown tweed blazer, rushed out the bedroom door. "Come on. We planned for him to take her."

"Yeah, but you were supposed to follow through." They ran down the stairs and out of the house, Evan added, "The whole world is on this and you're banging her sister. If something happens to Desiree, Deacon is going to kill you."

"Shut up." Mitch sighed at his cousin and thought about his brother. Deacon was not going to take the news lightly.

Chapter 104 – Remembered for Your Last Act

Deacon rushed over to the command center after receiving a frantic call from Beautiful. When he arrived at the station, he was taken into a holding room with a tiny window, a table, and four chairs. He didn't sit in any of them as he wondered, "Where was she? Why hadn't Mitch been there and what was she going through?" He stood gazing though the window, feeling the torture of waiting.

Deacon understood what the waiting had to be like for Desiree. Now she no longer waited, but lived it. He only hoped she wouldn't experience her worst fears.

He swung around when the door opened. His brother and cousin walked in looking official, faces tight and eyes intent. Mitch wore a New York's finest dark blue jacket and Evan a similar one with FBI on it.

Deacon took notice of the weapons that peeped through. Lifting his eyes, he searched their faces. "Tell me something, please."

Mitch held out his hand toward a chair. "Have a sit, Deacon."

Immediate fear gripped him, as if to contain it, he boxed his arms around his chest. "Don't handle me. Just tell me."

"Alright." Mitch placed his hands on his waist, stood taller and took a breath. "Someone picked Desiree up in front of her house. A man, we got his description, voice."

Deacon asked, "Not Raymond?"

"Not, Raymond." Mitch looked at Evan on his right and explained, "Raymond's got help."

Deacon couldn't imagine someone working with Raymond to kidnap a child and a woman. He shook his head. "A sick individual."

Evan said, "It could just be about the money. People are desperate. They'll do anything."

"Apparently," Deacon realized. "Mitch, you witnessed this?"

"Uh-oh," he thought. "I was at the house but, no, I didn't witness it." No need to make him ask more questions, he spilled it. "I missed my turn to follow Desiree home. I...."

"You just said you were at the house...."

Mitch held his head down then snapped it back up. "I'm giving you the facts. I was at the house with Beautiful. We got distracted...."

Another interruption came from Deacon, "Tell me you didn't sleep with Big John's wife."

It was not the time for humor; however, Evan adored the mousy behavior coming from Mitch. Evan was the tallest man in the room and he felt like he was growing. He did his best to control the grin from lining his mouth, tucked his hands in his pockets, rocked on his heels, while his cousin squirmed.

"That's private," Mitch replied.

"Nothin' is private with you, Mitch. What is the matter with you? I swear...you don't care about nobody but yourself."

Insulted, Mitch's hands seized Deacon's arms and pressed him against the wall. "Don't say that. I messed up. But don't say that."

Mitch was bigger built, taller, and stronger than Deacon, but he was no match for his brother's wrath. In less than a second, his arms came up, around and pushed Mitch down onto the table. The table screeched against the floor as Deacon pushed it and Mitch.

Enjoying the show, Evan didn't move, let alone, say a word.

Deacon argued, "First, I find you having sex with Nat, and now Beautiful. These women are nothing to you. And I guess neither is Desiree."

Mitch closed his eyes and shook his head. When he opened his eyes, Deacon was certain he saw tears in them. "I love Beautiful. Always have. I never wanted her to leave New York with Big John. I know what you've been going through all these years...loving Desiree and being separated from her. I know what she means to you. We'll get her back Deacon. I promise you."

Deacon's anger didn't dissipate with Mitch's tearful plea. He gripped his arms tighter, pressing his back further into the table. "You promised to watch over her, Mitch."

"I know I did. I'm sorry. Let me up. Let me do my job now."

From behind, Evan said, "Come on Deac, let him up. We've got more to tell you."

He released him, took a step back. "What?"

Evan reported, "We have her location. Way up in the Bronx. A dilapidated city-owned three-family house. They're on the top floor. When she arrived at the location, Raymond made her strip -- completely -- clothes, jewelry, hairpins, and shoes. We can no longer see or hear what she does. As soon as she arrived, he announced the location is wired with explosives. He knew we'd be watching. He's sending us a message -- stay back or we all die."

Deacon quickly asked, "Do you believe him?"

"We'll treat it as fact for Desiree and the little girl's sake."

"Tiona?" Deacon whispered.

"She's okay. He had her handcuffed to a chair, but she's okay."

Doubtingly, Deacon asked, "He's not going to release them. Is he?"

"Not willingly, no." Evan shook his head. "My wife believes Raymond wants this to be his last act. He doesn't believe he has anything to live for. His career is ruined, and the man that he loves doesn't want him."

Deacon boxed his arms around himself, looked up. Evan slapped his hand down on Deacon's shoulders. The contact made him look Evan directly in the eye.

"Deacon, Raymond's challenging us. I assure you we've got some of the best explosive experts on this. We've got the best negotiators in the world."

Deacon listened and said, "None of that will work. Raymond doesn't want to negotiate."

Chapter 105 – Light in Darkness

Desiree woke up on a cold floor. Something fast and furry crawled across her legs. In a panic she jumped, leapt up off the floor and fell backward into the wall. She felt disoriented as if she were dreaming. "There are rats in here." Desiree's head snapped left to the sound of Tiona's voice. "Tiona?"

"You okay, Ms. Davenport?"

Her body and breath trembled out the words, "I'm fine. Are you alright, Tiona?" Complete darkness filled the room, just like the nightmares she'd been having. Their voices gave them sense of direction. Pleading for more sound, she asked again, "Tiona, are you alright?"

"Just hungry. He hasn't given me any real food – only water and chicken broth."

Desiree counted the days. "You've been here five days. Oh, my God."

"Six," Tiona replied. "You've been sleeping for a day. I called your name, to wake you. Did the rats bite you? They were biting me. I screamed and cried so much, he let me have this chair, but I'm handcuffed to it."

Desiree's hands instinctively went to her body. She remembered now. She was wearing Raymond's uniform shirt and nothing more. He had injected a drug into her arm. The results of it numbed her. She rubbed her hands over her legs and feet. Yes, there were bite marks and dried blood on them.

Her voice full of defeat, Tiona stated, "They did bite you."

After letting out a shaky breath, she declared, "It's alright. We're all right. People are coming for us."

"No," Tiona declared, "they won't. He'll kill them. He's going to kill us. I know he is. He told me so. He told me how and he told me all the things he's going to do to us."

Desiree blocked out the words and only listened to the sound of Tiona's voice. Her bare feet stumbled and staggered against the gritty floor, feeling the dirt and rodent droppings under her feet. She found Tiona, rested her hands on her bony shoulders. The girl had lost weight. She gave her arms a gentle squeeze. "You say I've been sleeping a day now?"

"Yeah."

He was waiting for something. Why hadn't he followed through -- destroyed them? "What else has he said, Tiona?"

"He fusses a lot. When you were sleeping, he stood over you, called you names. He kicked you in your back." Desiree's hand went around, felt for pain. She couldn't feel anything, thinking the drug had blocked the pain, for now. "Then he cries," Tiona continues. "He cries a lot at night and he takes drugs."

"Has he touched you…" she hesitated, but she inquired, "Has he touched you privately?"

"No."

Desiree shook her head, acknowledging that her sister Rayne predicted correctly. Raymond didn't want the girl for his sick behavior. No. He was saving that for her. "Why the delay? Why hadn't he fulfilled his plan?" she thought.

She couldn't think about that now. They had to get out. She needed a plan. "Tiona, tell me everything about this place – how many rooms and doors there are, and if people have been in here."

"There are bombs. He's going to blow us up."

She lifted her hand, stroked the little girl's face. "No, he's not. Tell me everything."

"You don't have anything. He's got guns and he's stronger than us. How can we get out of here?"

That, she couldn't answer. "We have a Heavenly Father and his mighty angels."

That, she could declare. Desiree thought of Deacon and his incredible faith. He believed even during situations that appeared completely hopeless. "I need you to trust God."

Tiona nodded. "I do. I've been praying and praying, and you came."

"Good. That's good. And more are coming."

Chapter 106 – Watching, Waiting and a Lot of Praying

Deacon lifted his body by pressing his hands into the cold floor for support. He squinted in the dimly lit room, gathered his thoughts, and assessed his whereabouts. A moment later, he realized he was still at the police station. He lifted his arm, checked his watch. More than 24 hours had passed since Desiree had been taken.

Mitch, Evan, and two other detectives opened the door and came in.

"We could have found you a more comfortable place to sleep," Mitch sounded remorseful over his brother sleeping on the floor.

Deacon stretched and yawned. "I've slept in worse places. Any news?" His arms went to his face, massaged the remaining sleep from his eyes.

Evan handed him a hot cup of coffee. "Not yet. These are the lead detectives on the case."

Deacon stared into the black liquid and back at Evan. "What, you and Mitch are not leading?"

"Deac, I'm FBI, Mitch is homicide. Due to the sensitive nature of this case, they've allowed us to help. We can't lead."

He gestured toward his left. "This is detective Raquel Thompson and detective Tessa Fields, they're going to notify Tiona's mother."

The coffee cup in his hand began to shake. "Notify her of what? What's happened?"

"She's alive, Deacon. As far as we suspect. We thought it might be comforting for Tiona's mother to know that Desiree is with her now," Detective Thompson, the first female detective of the team spoke.

Deacon noticed she had sharp green eyes and long blond dreadlocks against a light yellow complexion. She looked like she had slept well, unlike Evan and Mitch. Their eyes were drawn and darkened under the stress.

Deacon regarded the green-eyed detective's partner. Her short auburn hair spiked in all directions. She appeared pale and thin. Deacon noted the women standing against the enormous men made them look twice as small. He wondered why they had been assigned.

Mitch prompted, "Deacon, you alright?"

He shook off his thoughts. "It's good that you want to offer the mother some comfort. I know what she's going through." He scanned all four faces. "So that's it? You're not able to get in after them."

"Not yet."

"What about the accomplice? You got 'em, right?" Deacon anxiously waited for a small positive reply.

Thompson, the green-eyed detective replied, "I want to watch him. See where he leads us."

"And?" Deacon lifted his shoulders.

"He burned the victim's clothes and went home. We'll see where he goes today and then we'll bring him in."

"Desiree's not a victim," Deacon provided sharply. Thompson made a frown.

Deacon didn't understand police work. All they were doing was watching and waiting. He couldn't stand it. He shoved the Styrofoam cup back into Evan's hand, started out of the room. His cousin shouted, "Where are you going?"

"I've got to do something useful."

Fields, the redhead, walked over, and touched his shoulder. "Don't do anything that would interfere with our investigation."

Deacon lifted his thick brows that covered intense eyes. "Why would I do that? I have people that I can help. I can't do anything more for Desiree that I haven't already done. I've put her in God's hands. I've got to get back to work."

Fields understood. "Staying busy is a great way to cope."

She gave him a review, sized him up to be at least 5 feet 9 inches tall, 190 pounds. He carried his muscular build nicely. The long sleeved navy tee showed strong biceps. His jeans seemed to fill out nicely. She took pleasure in that remarkable face of his. His deep dark skin and carved bone structure created a superior masculine appeal. She bit her lip, reserved the desire to stroke his face. Instead, she asked, "What do you do?"

He didn't like the dance in her eyes. "I'm planning a wedding. Your job is to bring my fiancée back to me, in one piece."

Shaking his head, he walked out.

Thompson walked up to her, plucked her in the back of the head. "Ow." She turned and her partner chastised, "Detective Ho, must you flirt with every man?"

"I was just testing him. Your brother is pretty solid," Fields turned to Mitch.

Pointing her finger at Fields, Thompson ordered, "You, let's go see the mother. Men, y'all need to get out of here. Keep an eye on the accomplice. Notify us when he moves."

She strode out, leaving Fields to trail behind. The men could hear her blubbering, "I was testing him. Just wanted to see where his head was."

"We both know which head you had in mind," her partner snapped.

Evan watched the women and said to Mitch, "Women are just as bad as men. I chewed you out about Beautiful. She's just as wrong as you are."

The men strode through the station, passed a couple of young teenage boys being dragged in. One had blood dripping into his eyes from his unkempt hair. Disgusted, Mitch pointed at the kid. "Ridiculous. Look at that. He can't be more than sixteen. If he were mine, I'd kill him."

Evan agreed, "No doubt. Rayne and I are really considering if we want children after everything we see on the streets."

Mitch grunted as they took the stairs. "I know I don't want none."

Evan lifted his brow as they stepped into the dawning morning. "You and Beautiful were careful, weren't you?"

Mitch stopped, froze in his tracks. Evan turned his head slowly, emphasized every word. "Tell me; you didn't go out in the rain without a coat?"

Almost in shock Mitch replied, "It started raining so fast."

He wanted to kick himself. He always, *always* used protection. "God, I hope I didn't get her pregnant."

"I hope for your sake you didn't. Big John will kill you," Evan added.

Chapter 107 – Counter the Reality

Deacon walked home from the police station. The streets were getting busy with the morning traffic, preparing for another day of hustle and bustle. The brakes on a large garbage truck screeched. A worker jumped off, grabbed the can, hooked it onto the lifting device in order to dispose the contents.

Deacon stood nearby and watched. Finally, he heard a shout from the worker, wearing a colorful bandana on his head. "You want something?"

Deacon leapt to attention, noticed he had been staring and replied, "Thanks for your service."

The dude released the lever, let the can down. Baffled, his eyes darted left, then right. "My service?" Deacon smiled, causing the man to step back. "You crazy or something, pal?"

"I appreciate what you do. You keep our community clean. Imagine what this place would look like if you didn't."

The guy didn't quite buy Deacon's sincere thanks. Without replying, he hopped onto the truck, gave it a loud slap and it trekked towards the next residence. Shaking his head, Deacon thought, "New Yorkers are so skeptical." Moving on, he bumped into a man. "Ollie?"

Ollie smirked at Deacon. "Must you talk to everyone? I was standing on your stoop. You didn't see me. You were talking to him." He pointed at the sanitation worker several feet away.

"I was thanking him."

Ollie stood, slanted his head. Deacon truly was a different kind of human. He had never in all his life thanked a sanitation worker.

Deacon said, "I was just about to call you."

Ollie's appearance perked up. "You got the letter from Marcel?"

Deacon laid a hand on Ollie's back, started guiding him toward his house. "Let's talk inside."

They climbed the concrete stairs and headed into the old dusty house. Mitch was never the cleaning type and since the situation with Desiree arose, Deacon hadn't cared to do it either. He pointed to the fading sofa, offered Ollie a seat. "I've got to check on someone, I'll be right back."

He started his exit down the short narrow hallway toward Nicodemus' room and received a pleasant surprise. "You're up!"

Not only was he up, he was dressed. He hunched, unable to stand completely erect. Most importantly, he was on his feet. Deacon wanted to help him into the living room, but was swatted away. "Don't need help. And wipe that big grin off your face."

Deacon *couldn't* wipe it off if he tried. Just eight weeks ago, he found the man dying on the cold streets of New York. Thankfully, after having a large portion of his intestines removed, he was recovering. Even on the thin side, he looked great. His complexion wasn't as ashen, the light blue shirt hung from his boney shoulders, as did the jeans from his frail hips. He looked incredible. "Nico, I think you're going to make it."

"Sure am." Pushing Deacon aside, he reported, "I'm going to make myself some eggs."

The hall was too narrow for them to walk side by side. Deacon stayed behind, positioned himself in case Nico needed some help. "Can you eat eggs?"

"I'm gonna eat 'em today."

Deacon admired his determination, he offered, "I can make you breakfast. Sorry; I've been out so much. The nurse come by?"

"Yeah, *he* came." He stopped to take a breath and ask, "Why you get me a male nurse? That ain't no fun."

Deacon's grin widened. "How do you like your eggs?"

Nico's steps picked up. "I like to make them myself. Is that okay with you?"

Deacon lifted his hands in surrender, although Nico couldn't see him from behind. "You have free reign. Go on. Make me some, too."

Nico turned into the living room, saw Ollie sitting on the couch. "You want some eggs?"

Ollie frowned at the skeleton of a man. Deacon made the introductions, "Nico, Ollie."

"I don't need to know his name to find out if he's hungry." He lifted his chin, asked once more, "You want some scrambled eggs?"

Concerned if he'd said no, he'd offend the stranger, he replied, "Hook me up."

"Great. Ollie, I'm just going to help Nico get settled." Deacon continued to take baby steps behind Nico.

Nico replied, "You don't need to help me start nothin'."

"Yeah, and you don't need to be bending."

It took several minutes for Deacon to help the frail man get settled in the kitchen before he returned and sat with Ollie.

"Who's that?" Ollie asked.

"He used to be homeless and sick. Now he's healing and sheltered."

Confounded, Ollie made a face. "You brought a complete stranger in your house? You're not normal, Deacon."

It wasn't the first time he heard that; it surely wouldn't be the last. "You don't know what he looked like before. He would have died. I got him to the hospital just in time."

Ollie thought for a minute. "What about his medical bills?"

"I got some of the money from the organization I work with. I haven't figured out how to pay all the bills. I'm sure God knows."

Ollie turned his head toward the kitchen. "Well, it's obvious that he can't work."

"Why?" Deacon tilted his head. "You have a job for him?"

"Maybe, I'm doing some painting at the church. Giving some of the rooms and offices a facelift. Long, long project. I can hire an assistant."

Deacon held his hands together, lifted them to his chin.

"What you thinking?" Ollie asked.

"I can help and earn some wages."

"Work, for him?" Ollie thumbed his finger towards the kitchen.

"Why not? And since it's a long project, when he's stronger, I'll hand the job over to him. He needs to work."

Ollie remained silent for a few seconds before confessing; "I see why she chose you over me."

"Desiree and I chose each other a long time ago. Neither one of us ever decided to let go."

"I couldn't get close to her. You were in the way. She's happy now."

"I wish she was." Deacon explained the current situation. Ollie's heart dropped as he listened, but he knew Mitch. "Your brother is going to do everything he can to get her back."

"I know that he will. William wanted you to know. He wants you to pray for her. We don't want the details to leak to the media. Desiree told me you have a praying family. I'm asking you to have them pray for Desiree and Tiona." He added, "And pray for me."

His eyes watered. "Please pray for me. My heart is getting full of contempt for Raymond. I think about what Marcel did to your wife. Have you gotten to the place of forgiveness, Ollie?"

A pause, a sigh and a confession followed, "Not yet. I'm not there yet. I'm trying. I know I can't afford to hate him."

Deacon closed his eyes for a moment. When he opened them, he said, "We can't afford that. If Raymond hurts Desiree, it could destroy me."

"It could. It won't. Losing Sassy, I had Olivia to live for. My wife would want me to give our child all the love and support we didn't have growing up. Desiree would want you to go on, taking care of strangers, showing them they are loved and wanted." He lifted his chin toward the kitchen. "That man is alive today, because you obeyed God. He knows the world is not a horrible place. That God cares about him. Don't let evil take away from God's good."

Gazing into the distance, the men sat silently until Ollie decided, "You're a different kind of human, but you are human. At first I saw you as the kind of Christian that didn't accept reality. You accept it, but you also counter it. You know we can make things better on this earth. That's what you do."

Ollie stuck out his right hand, and Deacon took it. "Right here, right now, we declare; Desiree and Tiona are blessed and coming out of this situation alive and well."

They shook hands and Deacon agreed, "Amen."

Chapter 108 – A Taste of Your Own Medicine

Lacy Reid rushed indoors set her soaking umbrella and raincoat aside. In the foyer, she heard noises and wondered if she had left the radio on. She entered the family room; saw her 54-year-old mother with her 27-year-old boyfriend, Enrique.

Her mother hadn't heard Lacy's swishy tennis shoes walk in. Gracelle was occupied with Enrique's hand massaging her expensive breasts.

Lacy cleared her throat, afraid for what was coming next when her mother's hand slipped inside his pants. "Mom!"

Gracelle's head perked up and turned. "Baby, we're back." She jumped up and floated over to embrace her daughter. Lacy held up her hand, stepped back. "Don't."

Enrique stood as well, greeted her. "Hi, Lacy." Even with only saying those two words, his Latin accent rang strong.

"How did you get in here?" Lacy asked, her eyes, cutting back and forth over their faces. They looked bright eyed, bushy tailed, and hormonally hungry.

"Your father's nurse let us in." Gracelle walked around to the coffee table. Lacy noted all the bags. "I have gifts for everyone." Her mother started looking in the bags, talking nonstop as she reported, "Lacy, Hawaii is incredible. We didn't want to leave. You and the children have to go."

"I can't leave Dad right now."

Gracelle pulled out a green colorful ring, walked over, and put it around Lacy's neck. "I didn't say now." She perched a minute, and exploded, "That looks so good on you. Oh, Ollie would love Hawaii, too, especially since he's so artistic. There's so much beauty." Lacy shook her head. Her mother had no concept of what had transpired in her life. She turned and started walking away.

Her mother ran over, skirting across the hardwood floors in four-inch heels. "Lacy, what's wrong? Is it your father?"

She just stood as heat radiated from her eyes.

"Lacy," her mother prompted, "what is the problem?"

"You should know that by now."

Gracelle squinted, studied her daughter's tight face. She hated that she had cut all of her pretty long hair off. She turned, brushed her hand at Enrique. "Go on into the den. Have a drink."

Like a good little boy, he smiled, nodded, and stepped out of the room.

Hooking an arm around her daughter's waist, she led her over to the sofa. "Things are not good between you and Ollie?"

When Lacy said nothing, Gracelle nudged her with her shoulder. Her mother smelled of sex and marijuana.

"It's only...," Lacy checked her watch, "nine twenty in the morning. You've already been smoking."

Gracelle flicked her wrists. Enrique and I are still on our vacation. "You should loosen up." Her mother reached over, lifted her designer red bag, and pulled out a skinny white handmade cigarette. "Here." She handed it to her. Lacy didn't accept it. Gracelle waved it. "You need this joint. Life is too short for you to be angry and upset all the time. I thought when you and Ollie got together you were going to live a little."

"Mom, you are so disconnected. Ollie raped me. I've filed charges against him. It's all over the news!"

The easy glossy look in her mother's eyes dissipated. "You did what!"

"I've filed charges. It's going to trial."

"You were going over to the man's house at least twice a week to sleep with him. There's no way he raped you. The way you described being with him, maybe you raped him."

Lacy rolled her eyes. Her mother asked, "What happened? Did he end it? You know you're not...," she paused, put it nicely, "you're not experienced in casual relationships. Some men just can't commit and you move on."

The water splashed down her cheeks faster then the rain that sluiced down the tall windows. "How dare you accuse me of acting like a rejected teenager! The last time we were together, it was rape. *I* was going to end it. He reacted like a madman. I said no! He went crazy. The world needs to know it."

Gracelle didn't reply, not right away. One thing that Lacy was really good at was lying. As a child, she'd lie to get what she wanted from her father – play the parents against one another. And as her father's baby girl and only child, it was easy to convince him. Gracelle often felt like the odd ball peeping in. Especially, since she believed she wasn't cut out for marriage.

Years ago, she admitted she couldn't commit to Lacy's father. Her spirit wanted to experience more. She left her family – the powerful man and the spoiled little girl. That little girl married a man very much like her father. Marcel was aggressive, arrogant, and rich. He gave Lacy everything she wanted. Unlike her father, he was not a faithful husband. Lacy never did very well with not getting her way.

Regretfully, her mother replied, "I should have tried harder to love your father – to stay and raise you. You needed me."

Lacy coughed up a laugh through her tears. "It's too late for confessions. And once again, you were gone while I've had to stay and deal with this, the kids and dad, alone."

Gracelle touched her shoulder. "What do you need?"

Through the big brown pools, Lacy stared at her mother. "The trial is going to start in a couple of weeks. Will you be with me?"

Gracelle nodded. "Are you sure…you want to go through this?"

"I don't want to walk into that courtroom alone. He's got his family and he's…." She began to sob as she dropped her head onto her mother's breast.

"He's what?"

"He's already, already involved with another woman." Lacy thought of Zoe, how they had walked closely, hand in hand. "He left me for that white woman," she thought. "Maybe she'd enjoy dating him behind a jail cell."

Gracelle reached up and embraced her daughter. She didn't believe it. Couldn't. She thought about the letter in her purse that Lacy had asked her to mail to Marcel. With her travels to Hawaii and Enrique keeping her busy, she had failed to mail or read it.

"Listen, baby," she patted her back, "you have my support. I have some errands to run. I'll be back. I can spend some time here with you and the kids. Stay a few days."

Lacy nodded. "Thanks, Mom."

Gracelle leaned in to kiss Lacy's cheek and she flinched. The subtle gesture was noticeable. Her daughter was using her.

She stood, called, "Enrique! Sweetie! We better get going."

Lacy eased up. "I need to check on Dad. I'll prepare a room for you." Lacy lifted her arms, pulled her mother in for a calculated embrace. "Thanks again. The past few weeks have been really challenging. I've felt so alone."

Gracelle pulled back to be eye level. "You're not alone, Lacy. I'm sorry you're going through this."

She turned at the sound of Enrique's shoes crossing the threshold. "Ready, Mama?"

"Yeah." She held up the joint, said to Lacy, "Smoke this."

"Mom, I don't do drugs."

"It's for medicinal purposes. You've been under a lot of stress. Relax." She pushed it into her hand.

Lacy accepted the token, nodded, and watched her mother rush out as she called over her shoulder, "I'll be back around six tonight."

Lacy smiled. Just this once, she decided she'd follow her mother's advice. She headed for the kitchen, lit up the medicine, and took a long, long puff.

Things were working out, perfectly. She had the physical evidence, the warrant was issued, the arrest was made, the trial was impending, and she had her mother's support. In just a little while, she would send a message to all men: You can't treat Lacy Reid like she didn't matter. And Ollie would be the first to know it.

Chapter 109 – Heart Fixer

Deacon had to keep his promise – not for Marcel or Ollie, but for his own sanity.

Marcel picked up the phone and said, "I didn't sleep these last two nights. You said there was a chance for me to see my kids, have a relationship with them. I expected you days ago."

Deacon let out a tired breath, apologized, "I need to talk to you Marcel." Marcel saw Deacon vulnerable. It did something for him…to him. He wanted to help Deacon – help the only person that came to see him in prison. "What is it?"

"I want you to know who I am."

Marcel waited a few seconds and replied, "I wondered if you were a reporter or a writer, pretending that you care about me, trying to get a story. No one cares."

"I came because I care. I wanted to build a relationship with you. Show you kindness. Have I done that?"

"You have. Tell me why."

"Marcel, do you believe in the divine plan of life?"

Deacon watched confusion wash over his face, he provided, "The divine plan to me is that there are very few coincidences in life. We connect, meet people for a reason. I told you about my best friend. Years ago, I fell in love with his fiancée. Because of my betrayal and guilt, I ran away. I came home a few months ago. It was time I faced what I did, tell the woman I loved her. But unbeknownst to me, she was already involved with another man. Ironically, my brother introduced them. Marcel, my brother is Detective Mitch Stephens, a homicide detective. He worked on the Sapphire Sparrow case."

A spark came into Marcel's eyes. Deacon saw he followed the dotted lines and went on, "During the investigation, Ollie and Mitch became good friends. The woman Ollie dated is my fiancée now." Marcel grinned. "You stole his woman."

"They ended their relationship. Ollie started seeing someone else…"Deacon halted, prepared and lowered the boom, "…he started seeing your wife."

Marcel touched his chest. "My Lacy? No, that's impossible. She left and she hasn't been back since…my arrest."

"She came back. Her father is very sick. She came home for him. She sought out Ollie. They had a brief affair."

"Wait," Marcel lifted his hand. "Hold up…I saw on the news, Ollie's been charged with rape. Don't tell me its Lacy?"

Deacon finished, "Lacy has falsely accused Ollie."

Marcel sat silently, his eyes clouded with anger and then filled with water. "He hates me. He did this to get back at me."

Deacon said quietly, "The charges are false. Lacy's angry because Ollie decided to end what they had. He wants to go on with his life, focus on his daughter. Your wife and children are hurting, Marcel. They need you."

If there was a letter, Deacon saw Marcel didn't have it. He had no knowledge of Ollie's relationship with Lacy.

Thinking for a moment, Marcel declared, "Those charges are not false. Ollie's going to end up with me." Thankful, he added, "There is justice in this world after all."

"What about your children?" Deacon asked.

At a complete lost, he answered, "How can I help them?"

"Accept responsibility for what you've done."

Marcel frowned. "I told you, when we first met, you would not convert me."

"And I told you that you would not convert me. Marcel, your only hope for a good future with your kids, is faith. I promise you, you build that, and you will see a change. You have a few years in this place. If I were you, I'd begin preparing to be the father your son and daughter deserve. All this hate and resentment that you've built in your heart will only destroy. You know that. Sapphire is dead because of it." Deacon began to rise and Marcel panicked, "Wait...is this it? No more visits from you?"

"I'll be back, Marcel. Think about what I've said. Pray."

"For what?"

"A change of heart, Marcel. That's the first thing you need fixed."

Chapter 110 – Hands Please

Evan and Mitch sat outside of the Bronx housing development where Raymond's accomplice resided.

Mitch didn't offer much conversation. Evan decided, "No need worrying about it. It'll be a few weeks before you know if Beautiful is pregnant. Maybe she's on birth control. I mean, she and Big John have been married for years and they never had kids." Mitch thought about his irresponsible actions. "Birth control never came up."

Evan swatted him on the shoulder. "Get your focus back. The reason why you missed Desiree's mark was because you weren't on your post."

Mitch's eyes wandered. He saw a young girl pushing a stroller. "You're right. Maybe since she doesn't want kids, she's on the pill or something. If she is pregnant, I can't see Beautiful being anyone's mother. She probably won't have it."

"You sound like abortion is a form of birth control."

Mitch's eyes landed on the building. "It's a form of something. You don't want a baby, you get rid of it. Easy as one, two, three."

Shaking his head, Evan replied, "I can't believe we are actually related. You think it will be easy for Beautiful to terminate a pregnancy? She might want it, just because it's yours."

"Mine?" Mitch lifted his voice and his brows.

"You're such an idiot. Beautiful thinks you're some sort of super cop. She's fascinated by you. I don't know…some kind of fantasy. She has it bad for you."

Mitch turned his head, pitched his voice even higher. "How you know?"

"Sisters…man. Beautiful talks to Rayne. She loves Big John, but she's infatuated by you."

"Well, what do you know?" Mitch smiled and looked back at the housing complex. He repeated, slowly, "What do you know." He patted Evan's arm. "Him."

Mitch pointed. "That dude spent a lot of time with Tiona's mother. I think he's one of the mother's faithful customers."

Evan gave the guy a quick study, noticed the expensive Timberlands, sagging jeans, plain white shirt, and black baseball cap. "He deals?"

"I think so. Tiona's mother doesn't just sell sex. She's got too much evening traffic in and out of her place. I don't care how good she is, she can't service that many people."

They looked on as the buzzer beeped and the man received clearance. A few seconds later, a car pulled up in front of the building.

There were two men in the front seat. "Look who's sitting in the back?" Mitch noted.

"I see her." Evan's voice lowered with speculation.

They observed as Tiona's mother exited the car and walked up the three short steps. She rang the bell and was buzzed into the building.

"This don't feel right," Mitch decided as he ran the plates. Evan called in the activity. Within minutes, silent police cars rushed in, surrounding the area.

Evan and Mitch leapt from the car, weapons drawn, shouting at the driver and passenger in the car. "POLICE, HANDS UP, NOW!"

Chapter 111 – Exposing Evil

Thompson and Fields were standing on the steps of Raymond's sister's house when their communicator went off. They listened and learned Raymond's accomplice was in custody along with Tiona's mother.

Interesting, they perched their lips. Fields realized, "I guess that explains why Tiona's mother wasn't home when we arrived earlier." She shoved her hands in the bright orange spring jacket she wore, rocked on her heals. "Thoughts?"

Thompson pulled out a stick of gum, unwrapped it slowly and stuck it in her mouth. "Who knows." She chewed. "The whole thing could be a set-up to get Desiree."

"You never offer me gum," Fields determined with a frown. Thompson retrieved a thick band from her jacket pocket, pulled her blond shoulder length dreads back with it. Raising her brows, she remarked, "You're really something. You are comfortable hitting on strange men, *any* man! But you want your partner of nine years to offer you a stick of gum? Just ask."

Thompson shrugged her shoulders, rang the doorbell again. The television blared. In a minute, she'd resort to pounding on the door.

"It's polite to offer," Fields said, ran her hand over her spiked hair. "And so is hitting on a man. They love it." She pointed at herself. "I'm an attractive woman, with a badge and I'm hitting on them." Feeling powerful, she placed her hands on her thin waist. "I'm telling you, it's a compliment to them."

Annoyed, Thompson began shuffling her feet. "It's free tail. That's what they love."

Fields disagreed, "Men don't like women telling them what to do. They say they can handle a strong woman, one that makes more money than them. They can't. It's hard being a cop and dating in this town. So…I create a little game. Let them think they've tamed me somehow. It's fun. You should try it."

Thompson leaned over the railing, hoping to see through the broken blinds of the window. Without looking at her partner, she said, "Taken."

"Taken? What? You and Calvin? You've been dating for four years. He's not marrying you. And you wanna know why?" Fields arched a brow, waiting.

Thompson rang the doorbell again, refusing to answer. Fields replied, "You're too strong. Soften up. Let him spank your fat booty from time to time."

She twirled her head, narrowed her eyes. "My booty isn't fat. It's muscle. And what? A spanking is gonna get me hitched?"

Fields showed off her bright smile. "Alright, let him spank the muscle. It'll be fun for Calvin." Revved up, she started, "Last week, I met this guy – cute little basketball player. We went back to his place and he had this…."

Thompson lifted her hand. "Shut up and start banging on this door."

She did and it opened up. The woman who answered was only 35 years old, but the tiredness upon her made her look to be in her 50s. She had a large blue wrap on her head, no make-up, huge golden hoops in her ears, and a tiny gold button in her left nostril. Her lips were darkened from years of smoking. She studied the two women who were studying her. "You're back."

"Lorraine, can we come in?"

She answered by stepping back and letting them walk in. Trained to do so, their eyes swept the untidy place. They noticed two bassinets in the living area. "I was trying to get them to sleep," Lorraine supplied.

Thompson looked up. "With the TV screaming like that?"

Lorraine looked down at the sleeping babies. "They asleep, ain't they?"

Fields walked up, cooed at the bundles covered in pink sleepers. "These your grandbabies?"

"Yeah, I'm keeping them while my girls finish school." Lorraine fell into the sinking sofa, picked up a pack of cigarettes, and held them out. Thompson shook her head no and Fields turned to her partner and gloated as she replied, "That's polite of *you* to offer, but I don't want to smoke around the babies."

Lorraine lit up, took a puff. "Humph, it's because of these damn babies that I smoke. I've been having babies since I was fifteen. Had all girls too, I wish these two," she waved the cigarette smoke back and forth in front of the bassinets and finished, "were boys. The girls bring the babies home. The boys keep running and making more babies."

She took a long drag and looked up. "Y'all sit down. You're making me nervous."

Thompson remembered the last time she sat on that sofa, she couldn't get up. "Mind if we pull up a couple of your kitchen chairs?"

Lorraine nodded as smoke seeped through her purple lips. They sat the chairs near the edge of the dirty brown sofa. At one point, they were certain it was white. "You heard from Raymond?" Thompson began.

"Look, I told you before, if he called, I'll tell you. He ain't tried to reach me. And my youngest Nyasia is torn up over it."

Point noted. Raymond bonded with his niece, but he had kidnapped Tiona. Fields asked, "Why do you think he's so close with Nyasia?"

Quick to rebuke any ill thinking, she replied, "He'd never lay a hand on her or any of my girls. Growing up, Raymond had a real close friend. When Ny was born, Ray said she looked like his friend. So I named her Nyasia. That was his friend's name. Plus, after having four girls already, I couldn't think of no more damn names."

"Why do you think your brother is doing this?" Fields asked.

"Y'all came back to ask the same questions. I told you before, I don't know."

Thompson's patience jumped out and all over Raymond's sister. "We need answers. And I think you have them. There's a little girl that's been missing for seven days now. Your brother took her from school, where he was hired to protect her."

"Should that mean something to me?" Lorraine retorted.

The finger came up. Fields knew when Thompson's finger began pointing she was ready to push hard, real hard. It was time. "You listen. You should care. What if it were one of your girls, or grandchildren? Imagine what your brother might be doing to this little girl. Your brother took an oath to protect."

Lorraine's small eyes turned into slits. "Ray will never hurt a child. I know him. And don't you dare come in my space, talking about protection. Who protected Ray and me years ago?"

Thompson was about to ask, but Fields gave her a hold-off look. Lorraine would tell it. The words were bursting at her heart. They listened. "Our parents were monsters. Complete crazy monsters. Right after I was born my father was injured at work. It must have been bad, because he couldn't work. It made him mean. Or I should say meaner. When I was ten years old, my mother met a man. He was real nice. Fine too. Ray looks like him." She paused, thinking back.

"Go on," Thompson directed.

"Mama wanted to leave my dad, but he cried and cried – gave her permission to be with another man. That's when I understood Dad couldn't have sex. The man that Mama hooked up with was a police officer. She got pregnant with Ray. Mama was so happy at that time. The man wanted to marry Mama, he begged her. I mean down on his knees begged her. She wouldn't leave my father.

"I remember one day Ray's father drove us out of the state, took us shopping to get ready for the baby. Mama wasn't showing then. But when she started to show, Dad couldn't live with it. He tried to kill himself – cut his wrists. We found him lying in his blood. The guilt drove Mama over the edge. And when she fell, she went insane. I didn't know her anymore. She pushed Ray's father away, me away, and cried until her heart dried up. And then, she was just plain evil and hateful – just like dad. It was like living with two demons.

"When Ray was born, Dad hated him. She never left Dad alone with Ray. She moved into another room in the house with her baby. She still worked, but expected me to take care of the house and cook – and watch Ray. If I ain't do something right, Dad would beat me like I was a grown man. Mama never said a word. Mama hated me, and I thought she loved Ray. She showered him with gifts. They spent a lot of time in their room. I got curious. I got jealous, peeped in one day."

Lorraine's eyes watered and lips trembled. She closed her eyes and shook her head. Fields reached over, patted her hand. "Tell us, please."

She opened her eyes, let the tears have free course down her cheeks. "Mama made him do things to her. He was crying, saying, 'Mama, please, I don't want to do it.' She'd smack him around, fought him, until he touched her."

Lorraine wailed, threw her hands over her face. Thompson and Fields gave her a minute, sat and looked at each other. "And I watched him with Mama. Ray was like an animal, trying to find his way, struggling to please Mama. Mama cursed, beat, and encouraged him. It was sick. So sick. I stepped back, eased the door shut and my father was standing there, looking down at me.

"I felt completely lost. Dad looked at me. He had water in his eyes, too. He never said a word. I understood that he accepted what Mama did. His eyes let me know that I better not ever tell. Ray was only five years old when I left home. I left him with those sick people. I went to find Ray's father, but his neighbors said he moved to New York. I didn't protect Ray. I never told anyone."

Even with the loud voices coming from the television, Lorraine's story silenced the room. Fields swallowed the tears, cleared her throat. "You're helping Raymond. We understand now. Where are your parents?"

Lorraine lifted her head; her face was drenched and covered from emotional exhaustion. "You ever heard the saying, evil never dies? My parents are still married, living in New Orleans." She took a deep cleansing breath. "I never told Ray that I knew what Mama did."

Thompson declared, "That's why evil never dies. You protect it in silence, and that's what it feeds on. It's going to stop today. The evil that your parents created in Raymond is still living in him. Exposing the truth will destroy it."

"Are you going to kill my brother? Do you know where he is?"

"We know. We don't want to kill him. We want to help him," Thompson provided.

Lorraine nodded as fresh tears fell. "It's not his fault...the way he is. In some ways, he's still that abused baby boy. Raymond's a good person. He really is."

Thompson nodded. Although she knew Tiona and Desiree didn't feel that way at the moment. "Thank you. We'll let you know when we have him."

Outside, Fields spoke first as they got into their vehicle. "I've been doing this job twelve years, and you think you've heard it all."

She buckled her seatbelt, sighed and stared at Lorraine's house.

Thompson fired the ignition. "Raymond's fixated on Desiree. He thinks she's his mother. Or at least, he sees her that way. She checked her watch. Let's get back to the station, interview the accomplice. Time is running out."

Fields agreed.

Thompson had a thought. "You still think a woman should degrade herself, let a man... as you say...spank her from time to time, because he has a problem accepting a woman in authority?"

"Hey." Fields turned her head. "That's not what I meant. Raymond's story is totally sick."

"So is your theory. Manipulation is a dangerous game, especially if you don't know who you're playing with. If you've got to do that for a man to feel powerful, you're not helping him or yourself for that matter."

Fields rolled her eyes, ordered, "Give me a stick of gum."

Thompson smiled and stuck her hand into her jacket pocket, pulled out the pack of gum.

"Here. See, wasn't that easy? No games."

Chapter 112 – Fight or Die

Desiree couldn't see Tiona, nor could she free her. The best she could do was rest her hands on the child's shoulders, sing for her – for them. She sang a song of deliverance and hope: God knows, he sees and he cares…. She had to hang onto her faith. God had a plan and he'd see them through.

When the door opened, and light seeped through, she felt a release, even with him standing there. "You've got a pretty voice – so sweet and soft. Let's see what we can do about that."

Raymond walked over. They listened as his hard boots scraped against the soiled floor. He took Desiree's arm, yanked her away from Tiona's shoulders. "It's time for your punishment."

Tiona protested and struggled against the restraints, cutting the metal deeper into her wrists. "Please, please don't take her away. Please."

"It's okay," Desiree soothed.

"No." The girl began to bounce in the chair. "He's going to hurt you. He's going to make you cry, like he did my mother."

Raymond stood in the doorway, laughed. "Your mother is a whore, Tiona. That's what every whore gets. Right, Principal Davenport?"

Desiree held her head down. He squeezed her arm tighter. "Right, Principal Davenport?" he repeated, spitting into her neck.

"Right, Officer Bonner."

He dragged her into an open dimly lit room. Just a large flashlight powered the room. He had covered the windows in heavy black cloth and she couldn't assess the time of day. A small table held his gun, drugs, and a syringe. She knew he was high and now she saw his choice of drug -- cocaine. What she didn't know was what was in the syringe. She pointed at it. "Is that what you gave me?"

"You liked it. Slept good. You didn't care about the rats crawling over you."

"Thanks for the rest. I haven't slept soundly since I got your note."

She saw the flicker of surprise in his eyes. The shadows under his eyes puffed up. "You'll get more. I got plans for you."

"I know you do. But, didn't I keep up my end of the deal? I'm here. That means you let Tiona go."

He grinned. "About that….see…she's insurance for me. In case you won't do everything I tell you."

Pointing at the table, she indicated, "You've got a gun and you are stronger than me. What can I do?"

Instantly, one of his hands grasped her throat, his arm extended and lifted her off her feet. Desiree brought her hands up, desperately trying to pry his away. It only made him increase the pressure. Her eyes bulged, and legs violently kicked. "I'm in charge here. You got that?"

As he brought her down on her bare feet, he removed his grip and she buckled, gasping for air.

"I said I'm in charge."

His boot came up, kicked a powerful blow into her chest. She flew across the room, landed on her bottom, and her head banged into the wall. Disoriented, she rolled, attempting to get up. Raymond snatched up the firearm, removed the safety. "Stay on your knees."

Literally trembling with rage, he used his free hand, unbuckled his belt.

From the next room, she heard Tiona scream, "STOP!"

Time to fight or die, she prayed.

"Lord, give me strength." And he did.

Chapter 113 – Tricks of the Trade

Thompson strode into the station, Fields at her side. Both cops' eyes were focused and determined. They stopped in front of the investigation room, met Evan and Mitch. "Give it up," Thompson ordered.

Mitch reported, "As instructed, we sat outside, parallel to the accomplice's residence. His name is Brian Lee, aka Busy. He's got a record of stealing everything and anything. No charges of armed robbery yet. It's probably coming. An electronics store 8.5 miles from the building where Desiree and Tiona are being held was robbed a few weeks back. Busy's prints were all over the electronic store. He's not too bright. We can get him on that."

Thompson stated, "I guess he is busy. Yeah, we'll hit him with it. For now, we need to know what his business is with Raymond Bonner. Go on."

Mitch picked up, "While there, we observed Quincy Marx, also known as Q-Money. He approached and gained access. I've seen Quincy enter the residence of Tiona's mother, Wanda Washington. He has a record of dealing."

"Drugs?" Fields chimed in.

All heads angled toward her. "No," Thompson replied, "cupcakes."

She frowned. "It could have been weapons," she sent back, sharply.

Thompson ignored her, turned back to Mitch, nodded. He continued, "That sent up a red flag. We continued to observe. Two minutes later, a black sedan rolls up, three occupants. Wanda Washington sat in the rear. She exited the car, approached, and entered the said building. We called it in, secured the area, took everyone into custody."

Testing, Thompson asked, "Has anyone been interviewed?"

"Your order was direct. We've been waiting for you."

"Good work." She pointed at him. "You can interview with me. Fields?"

Her partner slapped her mouth shut, concealed her distaste. Thompson was partnering with Mitch for the interview. "This is different," Fields commented.

"No, it isn't. You and Agent Ross take Wanda Washington. Find out why she was, where she was. Do it fast. We have a way into the building. We're taking it within the hour." Fields and Evan backed away, followed the order.

She laid a hand onto the doorknob of the interview room, and Mitch followed her lead.

Busy was sitting there, hands folded onto the table, looking like an astute student. Thompson sat down. She had a theory and not a lot of time to play, so she surmised. "You're holding stolen goods in the vacant building where Raymond is keeping the woman and child."

"I want my lawyer. I told this fool that." He pointed to Mitch.

Thompson looked over his dark skin and thick hair. She couldn't help it.

"Your dreads would look and smell better, if you washed them." She pointed to her head. "See mine, had 'em five years now. What, you too busy stealing electronics to practice good hygiene?"

He sucked his teeth. "I ain't stole nothing.'"

Thompson glanced at Mitch, smiled. She heard he was a solid cop, sharp, smart. She hoped he could roll with her without too much prompting.

"Come on, Busy," Mitch stepped in, "you know once we search the building, we're going to find the loot with your prints on it. That's why you agreed to help Raymond. You need him out to get the goods. I bet you got paying customers ready and waiting to take them off your hands. We want the woman and the girl. You want the loot. Cooperate."

Busy's fat cheeks puffed out air. "If I help y'all, I get my stuff?"

Mitch made his deep voice as gentle as possible. "We'll see what we can do. What can you do for us? What's your connection with Q-Money and Wanda Washington?"

"Who?"

It appeared to Mitch that Wanda had another name, too? Now, what was it? He turned to Thompson. She said, "Trixie."

Busy replied, "Oh, Trix and Q-Money they real tight. I know 'em from around the way. I hit 'em up, told them I could help get the girl back."

The guy was so done. Mitch played it out. "Great, we're all on the same page." Mitch asked, "What's the plan?"

Busy offered, "If you let us out of here, we got this. I know where they are and how to get into the building?"

"How?" Thompson leapt on it.

Mitch sent a subtle calm-down stare, turned to Busy for the answer.

"First floor, back door. It's not wired. He's holdin' 'em on the third floor."

"Thanks Busy. You've been very cooperative. So you and Q-Money were going in, take care of things and return the girl to her mother?"

He nodded. "Just bein' a good citizen. That's how I do."

Eyes cold, Thompson scooted her chair back, laid her palms flat on the table. "You're helping a very sick man, hurt innocent people.

That's *how* you do, Brian." She used his legal name then looked at Mitch. "Let's go."

"Wait!" Busy stood up and Mitch barked, "Sit down."

Busy didn't obey but stepped into Mitch's personal space. "You said you'd see what you could do for me."

Mitch looked down into his pathetic eyes. "I am. I see me doing nothin' for you. That's my brother's fiancée you drove into that hellhole. You disgraced her -- watched her take off her clothes."

It unleashed before he could pull it back. Mitch's fist balled up, barreled into Busy's jaw. Like rubber, the guy's head turned and snapped around. The blow shot spit and blood onto the table.

Thompson didn't flinch, said to Busy, "You really shouldn't have gotten in the detective's face."

"You're both dead," Busy threatened, clutching his jaw.

Thompson shrugged at Mitch. "If I had a nickel for every death threat, I'd be rich." As they headed for the door, Mitch agreed, "Tell me about it."

Outside, Thompson ordered a uniformed officer to book him with kidnapping.

Mitch and Thompson took brief steps down the hall, toward the adjacent interview room. As they approached, Evan and Fields walked out. Antsy, Thompson placed her hands on her hips, shuffled. Fields knew the signs, she talked fast, "They were planning to do our job, go in after the girl."

"We got that from Brian. What else?"

"The mother doesn't trust us. Said it's one of us that got her baby. She's crying – wants to go home."

Moving from foot to foot, Thompson recited, "Yeah, and people in hell want ice water. They ain't getting any."

Fields' eyes soften. Thompson hated when she did that. She looked like a red kitten with her crazy hair and sensitive face. "Don't, Tessa."

Using her cute kitten face, Fields pushed, "The woman is exhausted. She's been through a lot. Let her go. We can send a uniform with her."

Thompson recoiled, "Like we have the resources."

"Come on. It'll be over soon."

Thompson lifted her watch and decided, "We gotta move. Let her go. Keep Quincy. I'm sure we can charge him with something."

Fields smiled and Thompson warned, "If Trixie turns a trick, it's on you. Alright," she turned to the team, "suit up, vests on. I gotta go report to the LT. I'll be back with our plan...." she checked her watch again, "in twenty."

Before she jogged off, Mitch asked. "Are we going through the back door?"

Jogging backward, she shouted, "Hell no! Raymond's had plenty of time to wire the back door by now. He probably didn't earlier because Brian had to exit."

Chapter 114– Breath and Life

Desiree did as commanded, stayed on her hands and knees, watched Raymond slowly approach. In one hand, he aimed the gun at her; using the other he unbuckled his belt. He stepped before her, gave another order and following through, she unzipped his pants, pulled them down to his ankles.

She knew what she had to do in order to save Tiona's life. He pressed the gun into her right temple, warned, "One wrong move, Principal Davenport, you die and so does Tiona."

She closed her eyes, did her best to control the trembling of her body. She wasn't afraid to die, but she couldn't let a little girl die in a dark hole. Not today, not ever. She leaned in, opened her mouth and used the only weapon she had – her teeth. They sank down into his flesh and clamped with a force that broke the skin.

Simultaneously, her hand reached out and deflected the firing gun, sending a bullet through the covered window.

Pain, intense and increasing, debilitated him; regardless, she failed to free him. She kept the gun angled away and her teeth shut solid over his wilting flesh. And finally, she tasted blood, as he yelped and groaned.

This was war. She had to move quickly, when she heard him cry, she released his flesh. Raymond's knees crashed to the floor. With her bare foot, she stomped his wrist several times until he released the gun. She took possession of his weapon.

The enemy was temporarily down. She had his gun. Searching for a safe exit, she ran to the door. With her eyes, she traced the wires that ran down and connected to the explosives. Unsafe, she ran, went to another door in the dark apartment. That door, rigged also, rendered no option. She entered the room where Raymond continued to hold his middle, weeping, and swearing.

He would get up, come for her. Afraid to put the gun down, she searched his table for a phone. Looking over the cocaine, the syringe, and several beer bottles, she shouted, "Raymond, where's the phone?"

He moaned, "You're not getting out."

If God had anything to say about it, they were getting out, right now. She saw it, a dark green jacket hanging over the chair. Using one hand, she searched the numerous pockets, found a cell phone. "Thank God."

It had only one cell bar remaining, but she prayed it would be enough to call for help. She dialed 911, cradled the phone into her neck, keeping the gun aimed at Raymond while she identified herself.

He was rising, slowly. "Help please. He's getting up."

The operator patched the call within nanoseconds and Desiree heard the voice of Detective Thompson. "We're coming in now, Desiree. Stay away from the windows."

She nodded nervously, looked at the window behind Raymond. Tiona was screaming and crying in the adjacent room. On his feet now, he took a step.

Tears began to swim in her eyes and the cold sweat dripped down her back. Her voice trembling, she reported, "He's on his feet, he's coming for me. I've got his gun, he's coming for me."

"Injure him, shoot him, Desiree," Thompson ordered. The last bar on the cell phone died. Desiree lifted her head, let the useless phone fall from her shoulder. "Raymond, please don't come closer."

He didn't speak, but continued to limp forward. She focused, squeezed the trigger, begged once more, "Please, stop."

Another step and she fired a bullet into his arm. He staggered back, shouted in pain.

She peered over his shoulder, looked at the window. Thompson said they were coming. But no one had yet. She only heard an aircraft overhead. Its thundering presence shook the building, blocked out her shuddering breath, Tiona's crying, and Raymond's cursing. He started for her again. His face was monstrous. His eyes were red and evil. He begged, "Mama, look at what you did to me. I'm not a man because of you."

Desiree squinted, pleaded, "Raymond, stay where you are, please."

"Stop telling me what to do. You always tell me what to do. You made her go away. You made her stop loving me. I'm going to hurt you."

She didn't know where it came from, but he lifted a switchblade. "Let's see if you like this."

This time, he lunged and she fired several shots. The switchblade fell to the floor, but he stood, staggered as blood seeped from his lips. When he crashed to the floor, she jumped and screamed. The windows shattered. A SWAT team came swinging in.

There were two men in the room with her, and a third man had entered the adjacent room with Tiona. Quick, they moved fast. One went to her, took the gun.

"Are you injured?" he asked. She replied, "I killed him."

The officer didn't respond, only asked, "Other than you, him and the girl, anyone else in the house?"

She froze. "Desiree!" he shouted her name.

"No. No." She looked at the other officer on his knee, feeling for Raymond's pulse. "Is he alive?"

"Yes."

The officer, tending to her, directed, "My partner will get you out." He turned and went to work on disarming the bomb.

There was so much buzz, she heard communicators and saw lights flashing. An officer appeared out of the room where Tiona sat. He called Desiree, "Come with me." Noticing her bare feet, he cautioned, "Be careful. There's broken glass everywhere."

She left as one officer went to work on the bomb, the other stayed with Raymond. Desiree entered the room; saw Tiona was freed from the chair, finally. At the bare window, there was a fire ladder. They were going out through the window. He explained, "I'll take the girl first."

Desiree nodded. Tiona didn't run to the window, but to Desiree. She wrapped her little arms around her waist. "Thank you. You said they were coming. You said they were."

Hugging her back, Desiree said, "And you believed. Thank you. Go on, your mother is waiting."

The officer helped Tiona out of the window and onto the fire ladder. The girl looked back into Desiree's eyes before she escaped into the night. Desiree nodded and waved. "Go home, baby. Go home."

The officer assured her he'd be back for her in a minute. She stood there in the doorway, heard Raymond mumble behind her. He wasn't dead. Thank God. As promised, a minute later, the officer returned, eased back inside. She asked, "Is she safe?"

"Yes." He started toward her; his boots crunched the broken glass on the floor. Looking at her feet again, he decided, "Stay where you are. I'll carry you over to the window."

She was never more ready to go home. Nor did she give any regard to her fear of heights. She looked at her exit, begged, "Please, I want to get out of here."

He rushed over and she noticed he was not very big or brute. She had no worries that he could not support her weight. She believed that God had sent him and she trusted him. She wrapped her arm around his neck and he began to lift her, but halted when an alarm sounded. They looked back, saw the front door rush open and heard a voice yell, "Tiona! Tiona baby, it's Mommy! Tiona?"

Time slowed as Desiree saw Wanda Washington standing in the doorway and the officer near the explosives. The dire look in his eyes told all. He waved his hands, shouted at his partner in the doorway, "Run, get out of here. NOW!" The officer took Desiree's hand. No time to think of the broken glass on the floor, they ran for their lives. Impact sent them flying out of the window. Her face and body banged into the ladder with the officer upon her back.

His body worked as a shield, protecting her from the debris and the flames that lapped, licked, and landed against him – but not the smoke. It billowed around them, flooded their lungs. He kept her head tucked down, held his breath, and turned his neck to assess the damage. Beyond the smoke and fire he couldn't see and spoke in her ear, "Hold your breath and start moving down. Fast Desiree! Fast!" He moved off her back, exposing her to the elements. The dancing flames attached to the flimsy shirt she wore. His hands slapped the flames away.

"Come on," he barked. Shock started to set in, if they didn't stay focused, she'd faint and they'd both fall.

On the ground, Thompson paced and stared up into the black smoke. She saw the explosion and two bodies rush out of the window. But they never fell. She hoped to God they were on the ladder and on their way down.

A firefighter ordered, "Detective, you can't stay here." He grabbed her arm, dragging her away. Her eyes in the sky, Thompson fought him off.

"Wait! Wait! Look!" Her heart began to pump again, she shouted into her communicator, "She's alive! She's alive! She's making her way down!" As soon as Desiree and the SWAT officer's feet touched the ground, rushing firefighters snatched them up, away from the smoke, flames and debris that continued to fall and shatter.

Desiree found herself resting on a stretcher. Dazed, she looked into their eyes, felt a tightening in her chest. The air stopped circulating in her lungs, causing her brain to shut down. Just a second before her eyes closed, she saw him. She saw his smiling face.

Deacon fought, pushed back against the uniformed officer that wouldn't let him near Desiree. The paramedics moved swiftly, placing an oxygen mask on her face, checking her vitals. The female attending to her, shouted, "She's fading. Get her in." The stretcher lifted into the back of the ambulance and the doors started to close.

Mitch pushed his way in, told the officer, "He's her fiancé. Let him ride." Deacon rushed in, sat beside her. The ambulance began to move as the paramedic worked on her.

Compressing her chest, the paramedic shouted, "Come on! Desiree. Come on! Breathe! Breathe!"

Deacon's eyes filled with water, he prayed, "Come on, God. Not now. Come on, baby. Breathe, baby!"

Chapter 115 – Not Another Minute without You

She opened her eyes, looked into her father's. "Hey, baby." He smiled at her.

"Dad." She didn't recognize her scratchy voice. Her throat hurt. She turned her head, looked around the room, felt the oxygen monitor on her finger, heard the machine tracking her vitals. "I'm alive," she realized."

William Davenport held in the joyful tears. "You got out in the nick of time. The impact and smoke alone should have killed you." It should have, but it didn't. "Thank God," he thought.

"Deacon?" She remembered his smiling face.

He's outside. "When they said you were coming out of it, he let me come in first. I'll go get him."

"Dad...tell me?" Fragments of the night's events floated into focus. "The officer, the officer that got me out...how is he?"

He nodded, explained, "Officer Victor took the brunt of it. Third degree burns covered his back and legs. He swallowed more smoke than you did and he's got a concussion. He's been in and out of consciousness. The doctors are optimistic. He's young, strong. He's going to make it."

"Um." She figured she knew the answer but had to ask it anyway.

"Dad, the other two officers, Raymond and Tiona's mom?" He squinted, wondered, "Tiona's mom?"

He didn't know. The police hadn't disclosed what set the bomb off. Maybe, they didn't know. "Tiona's mother came in. She opened the door and the bomb went off."

Understanding, he provided, "No one other than you and Officer Victor survived the explosion."

She could not wrap her brain around it. Four people died tonight – two officers, Raymond, and a mother -- and for what? She took a breath as a tear fell out of her eye. The salty tear stung her raw skin. Her hand touched her left eye; found it swollen shut as was the left side of her face. "How badly am I hurt?" she inquired.

He went down the list. "Your left side must have impacted with the ladder. It's pretty banged up. You dislocated your left shoulder. Your arm is broken."

She looked down, saw it had been wrapped. "You have surgery at sunrise. It's a pretty bad break, but it will heal. The left side of your face is bruised and swollen. You had some burning in the center of your back." Lying on her back, she realized, "I feel nothing. They must have me on some pretty good drugs."

He nodded. "You'll need more soon."

She asked, "Is that all?"

"You have bite marks on your legs and cuts on the bottom of your feet. You're going to make it."

She was going to make it – and so was….

"Dad, Tiona?" she strained, raising her voice. He answered quickly, "She was on the ground and away from the building when it exploded. She's fine."

"But…does she know about her mother?"

William closed his eyes and opened them with a sigh. "I'm afraid not." Her father kissed her right cheek and walked out as Deacon walked in.

The beautiful smile on his face brought forth fresh tears. She saw his eyes dancing with joy. He asked, "Do your lips hurt?" She whispered, "No."

"Good." He kissed her softly. With her right hand she reached up, caressed his face. He took her hand, held it. "How do you feel?"

"Better now." He stood over her, smiling. She realized what she must look like. "Is my face horrendous?"

Quite the opposite, he said, "Beautiful. I can't take my eyes off of you." She closed her eye. "You're pretty beautiful yourself. I love you, Deacon."

"Good, because I set a date for our wedding."

She opened her eye. "I thought we already had one."

Shaking his head, he expressed, "I've lived fourteen years without you. Tonight, I thought I lost you forever. Please…," his voice trembled, "…don't make me wait two more months to marry you."

"I don't want to wait any longer either, Deacon. When?"

Deacon brushed his lips against hers and answered, "Tonight."

"I'm in a hospital."

"You could be in the morgue. I promise you, Desiree I'll cherish and care for you all the days of your life. Let me start tonight. I love you." Tears drifted in his eyes. Before she agreed, she needed to ask him a question. "Deacon, Tiona lost her mother."

Frowning, he wondered, "How?"

"She triggered the bomb. She was in the building when it went off. Tiona doesn't have anyone. If they let me, and if she wants me to take her, I will." Desiree waited, searched his eyes. "What do you think?"

"My desire, you've been through so much. Should you make this decision tonight?"

"You just made one…for us to get married."

He sighed. "I made this decision a long time ago. I always wanted you and I will always want you."

Deacon looked into her determined face and saw it – the love, concern, and compassion. "Are you sure?" he asked.

"I know what it's like to lose your mother at any age. I lost mine only two years ago." Her throat hurt, but she struggled through it. "I will be a good mother."

She would. Deacon remembered never having a mother in his life. Agreeing, his face transformed into a bright grin. "Okay, Mommy, I guess that makes me the daddy."

"Really?" she lifted her hoarse voice.

"Really."

She reached up, stroked his face. Taking her hand, he brought her palm to his mouth, kissed it. "Before the baby comes, we better get married," he joked. "I'll get everyone." Her right eye widened a bit. "Everyone?"

He smiled, telling her, "Everyone wants to see you, your sisters, Ollie and his family. Zoe, Karyn, your school secretary, Jack, your vice-principal and the mayor."

"What?"

"Baby, you're a hero."

She turned her head back and forth; thinking about the lives lost and began to cry. "I'm not. Really, I'm not."

Giving her hand a squeeze, he countered, "You are. You almost died to save Tiona. I call you a hero." He looked down into her watery face. "Are you ready to be mine?"

"I look awful."

He disagreed, shook his head. "You look awesome. Your sisters want to come in and fuss over you." Squeezing her hand again, he said, "The mayor is going to perform the ceremony."

"You've been busy," she noted.

His face turned serious as he remembered her lying in the ambulance a few hours ago -- unconscious -- not breathing. "You, too, baby. I'll be back."

With her swollen face, she attempted a smile.

"I'll be here."

Chapter 116 – The Most Beautiful Girl in the World

Fuss, did they ever. They worked with her hair, cutting off the damaged ends, styling, and covering the left side of her swollen bruised face. Her only make-up was lip-gloss. Strict doctor's orders had her in a hospital gown, serving as her wedding gown.

Doing all they could, tearful eyed, they stepped back, admired their sister. Melody, the peacemaker, spoke first, "You're a beautiful bride."

The smoke inhalation temporarily damaged Desiree's larynx, she whispered, "Don't lie to me."

Beautiful replied, "You really are. We thought we lost you. A block away, we stood down on the ground, watched that building blow to bits." She reached, took Desiree's hand. "We're able to touch you. You're here."

Sparkle, Rayne, and Melody followed, all reaching and touching arms and legs, connecting with parts of their sister, realizing they could be planning her funeral instead of a bedside wedding.

Rayne asked, "Do you want to marry Deacon? Like this? Tonight?"

Desiree closed her one good eye. She never imagined marrying the man of her dreams in such a broken state. Broken or whole, marrying Deacon was her dream come true. She opened her eye. "I wanted to marry him yesterday, and the day before that, and the day before that."

They laughed as Rayne offered, "I'll get your man and round up everyone."

The small room filled with family and friends. Desiree spouted tears as Sterling's wheelchair entered.

"Oh my God," she whispered.

He smiled. "I don't care if it is three in the morning. I wouldn't miss this for the world."

More folks filled the room. Her heart warmed at seeing Ollie and his family step in. Desiree saw everyone except the love of her life.

"Where's Deacon?" Heads turned, but no one knew where he was. The door opened again and Desiree gasped anticipating Deacon. Zoe walked in alone and smiled.

"Where is he," she thought. Had he changed his mind? Tears streamed down her cheeks and the room panicked, thinking she was in pain.

The door opened for the last time and, finally, Deacon entered. He had the mayor at his side as he held a large bouquet of red and white roses. He weaved through the crowd thanking everyone for joining them and took his place at Desiree's bedside.

"These are for you."

With fresh tears trailing down her face and using the little voice she had, she questioned, "Where did you get flowers at this hour?"

Smiling, Deacon placed the flowers in her good hand, leaned in for a gentle kiss. He answered, "Thanks to you, I know the mayor."

The mayor and Mitch stood at his side. Desiree's father and sisters stood on the opposite side of the bed.

Mayor Jamison began, "There is no greater love than a man that should lay down his life for a friend. Desiree, you have demonstrated that love. Thank you for what you have done for a little girl. In this early morning hour, you and Deacon have chosen to declare and pledge your love as husband and wife. I see you understand that love is not superficial, but exposing – accepting all the joy and disappointments that life has to offer. I must tell you that this is the most precious and sacred of wedding ceremonies that I have ever officiated."

Looking to Ollie's uncle, she requested, "Pastor Rose, will you pray before we begin?"

"My pleasure." He folded his hands in front of him, lowered his shoulders and head and prayed: "Let us bow our heads in prayer -- our precious and Heavenly Father, we thank you for life and love. We thank you for the miracle of marriage where you allow two to become one flesh. You spared our precious Desiree, allowed her this moment and miracle. Let your hand be upon this marriage. It is beginning with challenges as you heal Desiree's body, mind, and spirit. Father, we pray for the fallen this morning, the families who have lost a father, a son, a husband, a brother, a mother. Help us to be a comfort to them, help us to meet their needs and use us to show your love and compassion. Bless this room of witnesses, family and friends. Bless this union as long as they both shall live. Bless the children that they shall bring forth. In the name of the Lord Jesus Christ. Amen."

Chapter 117 – And What Did I Get?

Ollie ascertained Deacon and Desiree's wedding the most beautiful he had ever witnessed. Although at one time he had purchased a ring for Desiree, she wasn't designed for him. Some people had a seasonal position in his life, and some a lifetime. When Zoe stepped into the hospital room, he saw the woman he wanted forever. Their eyes met, but she turned away. Had he lost his chance?

After the ceremony, Desiree's pain level began rising. The nurses efficiently cleared the room, all except her new husband.

Zoe was first to congratulate the newlyweds and then quietly eased away. Ollie excused himself through the crowd, found her heading quickly for the elevator.

He caught up, touched her elbow. "Zoe, hi."

She boxed her arms over the black t-shirt and matching leather jacket. "Hi, Ollie."

Her face was tight. She offered him no lead in. Clearing his throat, he asked, "How've you been?"

She pursed her lips, replied, "Been great. You?"

"I've been better, been worse, too."

She ignored his cute crooked smile. "What?"

"Snippy," he thought and let go of the smile. "I just wanted to say hello. You still do work for me, don't you?"

"You don't pay me a salary. My salary gets re-invested into the foundation. You've said hello." She turned.

"Wait. Zoe, please. Can we go somewhere? I need to talk to you."

"Why? So you can tell me that you really didn't want to end what we barely got started? That you were afraid because we're so different? You thought things wouldn't work out? And now, that you've had a chance to think about it, you're not afraid anymore and you want to start over?"

Ollie's head pulled back, his eyes enlarged. She was royally upset with him. No need to fumble through it, he admitted, "You're right. Is it too late? I need you."

She pointed her finger in his chest. "You need a backbone."

He blinked, failing to see some of the wedding guests gathering in the hall and gaining an ear full as Zoe went on, "That's right, I said it."

She threw up her hands. "Be a man. Not a mouse. When you called me that night, I had a rough day, dealing with your attorney's pompous attitude about me, a white woman, dating you, a black man. Then I had to listen to my mother render me mentally incompetent because the man I love is facing trial for rape. And what kind of support did I get from you…," she imitated his raspy voice, "…well, if you want out, get out now."

His eyes further widened with her rising voice.

"I didn't want out! Do you know the meaning of bravery, Ollie?"

He started to open his mouth, but she answered for him, "It's what Desiree did for Tiona. Afraid, and yet, she went into an unknown dangerous situation with one goal in mind."

Pointing her finger at him, she confessed, "That was me. I was willing with all the negatives around us, to go through the fire with you, regardless of the unknown."

Amazing, she was simply amazing, and he, an idiot.

"Zoe," he pleaded, "I want to show you what's in my heart for you."

She sighed, looked into that incredibly inviting face of his. She lowered her voice. The onlookers moved as a unit, leaning in for her answer, "I don't know, Ollie. I need a man, someone strong. I don't know," she repeated and turned, leaving her long brown ponytail swinging in his face.

Ollie looked to his left and saw the men staring at him. Mitch commented, "Man, she told you." Ollie admitted, "She had every right to." Pastor Rose laughed, then advised; "Now that's a real woman. Son, you better go after her."

Ollie shook his head, watching Zoe step onto the elevator, wondering just how he would do that.

Chapter 118 – Trials Come to Make Me Strong

Ollie sat in the courtroom with his attorneys as they focused and dutifully recorded notes while listening to the opening statement of the prosecution. He hated the courtroom, it was so confining. No windows made him feel like the walls were closing in on him. Desiring an escape and a glimpse of her, he looked back for her. He didn't see her, and so he forced his attention on the fiery darts coming from the opposing attorney.

The man was sharp. Ollie gauged him to be in his late 50s; firmly fit, noticeably tanned, and sadly, experienced. Cain Keystone had been in the business of frying big fish for quite some time. Lacy had gone for the best prosecution in the state.

Cain studied the jury one by one and continued, "This is an emotional case. We will provide you with the facts. What led up to Oliver Sparrow violently pinning Lacy Reid down, using his hands and teeth to bruise her and break her skin? You'll see the evidence. Learn she's not a woman scorned but a victim of one man's rage. You'll learn what drives a man like Oliver Sparrow from a respected citizen of our community to a criminal of our time. This case is very emotional, yet I implore you, set the emotions aside, listen to the facts, view the evidence, and remove a man like this from our society." He pointed at Ollie in the courtroom.

"He's not a man you would want dating your daughters and sisters. His reasoning and understanding of right and wrong, good and evil, has been warped. And it is your job to take him off our streets. You'll hear his testimony. He'll tell you things got a little rough, but that's how Lacy wanted it. That she asked for it. Then you'll see the photos, the bruising, and you'll know, no reasonable woman would ask for that." He lowered his voice, bringing the jurors closer.

"The evidence speaks for itself. This case is not about what you feel; it's about the facts. You've been selected because the system believes *you* will not get caught up in the emotions. Lacy Reid trusts you to do your civic duty. She has faith in you."

He held up his long skinny finger, drove home his last point, "Listen to all the evidence, there you will find the truth."

Judge Parker turned his stern eyes, landed them on Kendall, "Defense, your opening statement."

Kendall Carter scooted her chair back, crossed the room wearing a designer black suit. She purposely wanted to look feminine. She went with a skirt, showing off her average-looking legs. She wore diamond studs on her lobes. Ollie noted that she put gel in her short hair to make it appear wavy and fun. She wanted the jury to see, like Lacy, she was an attractive woman. Yet unlike Lacy, she stood by Ollie and trusted him.

Simply the message she'd work to portray, Ollie was not a savage or enslaved prisoner of rage. No, just someone with poor judgment about the woman he let in his bed.

She began, "Ladies and gentlemen of the jury, I am so honored to have the opportunity to speak with you. If I had only heard Mr. Keystone's statement earlier, I'd be running through the streets now, locking my doors for fear of the man he has described. Thankfully, the man he speaks of, does not exist. Now…"

She lifted her finger, "I must agree with Mr. Keystone on several very important points. One, this is a very emotional case. And we're going to have to take you back to another trial – one that involved the murder of Mr. Sparrow's wife. And that murder was committed by Lacy Reid's husband, who is serving prison time."

Kendall, paused, walked slowly across the jury box. Finally she picked up, "How emotional is that for a wife? To learn that her husband had a two-year affair with a married woman and then held the gun that took her life. Mr. Keystone said no reasonable woman would ask to have pain inflicted upon her. But…."

Kendall turned, folded her hands in front of her and looked Lacy in the eye. The jury followed her gaze. "We're not looking at a reasonable woman."

She turned to face the jury again. "Ladies and gentlemen, there are photos of bruising against Mrs. Reid's skin. And guess what? There are photos of scratches and bruises on the body of Mr. Sparrow. The case is not one sided. And after hearing all evidence, you will see the relationship between Mrs. Reid and Mr. Sparrow was very much so mutual.

"Two hurt individuals, dealing with the lost of their spouses. Of course in different ways….Mrs. Sparrow is deceased and Mr. Reid lives in a prison cell. There has been no crime here – only poor judgment of my client. Who, in fact, is the victim here, falsely accused by an unreasonable, hurt, emotionally unstable wife? Listen as Mr. Keystone has already instructed you. Listen to Mrs. Reid's voice, her words, and you will hear the truth. Thank you."

In the very back of the courtroom, Zoe pushed her glasses up on her nose, studied the jurors, read their faces. Kendall made a good impact for starters, but the battle had just begun. When court adjourned, she slipped out, went to church, sat, and prayed for hours.

Chapter 119 – All Men, Say I!

Ollie shifted in his seat in the conference room of Kendall's law firm. Then, sighing, he finally got up, began pacing, causing Kendall to stop talking and ask, "Is this defense building interfering with your day?" She lifted her brows.

Lily rested her pencil, shifted in her seat. She understood Ollie was too creative for confinement. He despised closed-in spaces. First, he had to wear the suit throughout the trial – definitely not his choice of dress. Lily observed he had tossed the jacket, snatched off the tie, loosened the first two buttons of his shirt, and rolled up the sleeves. With his hands clenched in his pockets, he addressed Kendall, "You're not talking to me. You're talking to each other. Do I even need to be here?"

"Lily reminded him. We need you here…to clarify some things. And…don't forget Deacon is coming by. Hopefully with the letter we need."

Kendall popped in sarcastically, "A letter that I don't believe exists."

Lily retorted, "Let's just wait and see."

"While you're waiting, I'm building this case. How about less fairytales and more work."

Lily shifted again and Ollie stated, "Don't talk to her like that. She's been working non-stop." He compassionately asked his cousin, "You feeling okay?"

Tiredness had set in, but she replied, "Yes, I'm fine."

He looked at her expanding belly. "Go home," he ordered, "I don't want anything happening to you or the baby."

"You're so protective of her," Kendall remarked. "You sure you're not kissing cousins?"

Enough, Ollie strode up to her, banged his hand on the table and shouted, "What is your PROBLEM?"

Kendall eased her chair back, got on her feet. "You're my problem."

"If it wasn't for me, you wouldn't have this case. I'm paying you a ton of money."

"And I have a wimp for a client."

Ollie opened his mouth, turned his head and then looked back into the blazing eyes of his attorney. "What?"

With the palms of her hands, she pushed Ollie in the chest, forced him two paces back. His arm flew out in question. "What are you doing?"

"Where's your backbone? You're so love struck. I saw you looking back for your little white girlfriend. You need to focus in the courtroom. The jury is going to think you're not taking this seriously."

Disappointed, he said, "She wasn't there."

Kendall nearly spat fire. "She was. Way in the back, but she was. You could be on your way to prison and you've not shown any anger toward Lacy. What's the matter with you?" she shouted.

Lily defended her cousin, "That's not like him. Ollie is not going to get upset. And he's in love."

Kendall rolled her eyes, threw up her hands. "I'm working my behind off here. This is my neck that's on the line -- my reputation. The least you can do is act like you appreciate it. And if you want that white chick, than you better go after her. I don't want you rubbernecking while I'm questioning witnesses."

She stepped into his personal space; he felt her warm breath on his neck. "You better start acting like when I move in that courtroom, your life depends on it – eyes on me. You got that?"

He stared her down, but didn't answer. The phone rang and Lily answered, "Lily Carraway."

She lifted up her hand, quieted Kendall before she started ranting again. "Guys, it's Deacon." She put the phone back to her ear, listened. Ollie saw the disappointment cover her face. She thanked him and hung up.

"Deacon's not coming. Marcel doesn't have a letter. He didn't even know Lacy and you were involved."

Kendall shouted, "See!" She directed at Lily, "Back to work."

Before Lily could reply, Ollie informed them both, "Lily is going home." He picked up the phone, called her a car, lifted her briefcase and packed her things. "We'll wait for your car outside. Kendall, I'll be back in a minute."

Outside, he leaned against the building, clenched his jaw.

She took a breath. "The fresh air is nice. We've been cooped up all day."

"Thank you, for everything, Lily."

She rubbed his arm; then gripped it. "She's right you know. If you want Zoe, go after her. Having her in your life will help you focus."

"I can't. I want to, but I can't. What if we lose?"

Somewhat offended, Lily joked, "We don't lose. I'm good. So is Kendall."

"And so is Cain Keystone. You're all good. I know this isn't about the facts, or right or wrong. It's about perspective...how the jury sees me. What they think of me. You don't think I know what Kendall and Cain are doing?"

Lily explained, "They're performing. Trying to win the jury over, it's the way the system works. We need you involved. I know Kendall's tough, but she's right."

The black shiny car pulled up to the curb. Ollie walked her over, saw her safely in and handed over the briefcase. Before closing the door, he held it for a moment. "I'm getting tired of women telling me to man up."

She smiled. "Then do it. See you tomorrow."

He returned the smile.

"Night, Cookie," he called her by her childhood name.

Chapter 120 – I, Olivier Sparrow

Ollie put on another suit later that evening. This one was formal and, surprisingly, he was thankful to be wearing it.

His mother had come to New York to support him. Standing in the bathroom doorway, she boxed her arms against her chest. "Spiffy. I hope you're going to see Zoe."

"I'm going to try," he commented, straightening his tie in the mirror. "You don't mind watching Olivia?"

Flo replied, "My precious one and only granddaughter? Please." She flicked her wrist. "We're going to have so much fun."

Ollie admired his mother. She looked great, really great. They both had a very light complexion, but where his face was slim, hers was full. He had the look of his father, the hazel eyes and fuller lips. His mother's eyes were dark brown. They sparkled as she looked at her son. Her thin pink lips smiled.

After he splashed on some aftershave, he asked, "Does Roosta like your short silver hair cut?" speaking of his stepfather. She ran her hand over her head. "We both like it. You know he wanted to be here for you."

"It's alright, Mama." He walked up to her. "You have a family, if you need to...."

"Shush. I'm here to see you through this thing. And you...," she gave his bow-tie a tug, "...you need a solid woman like Zoe in your life. I met her a couple of years ago in Florida. She was a social worker then and I knew she was a special person. When she told me she was moving to New York, I hoped you two would hit it off."

He smirked at her wishful thinking.

Flo pointed out, "Don't get me wrong, I liked Desiree, but Zoe I knew."

He nodded his understanding as she went on, "Son, do not allow society to dictate whom you love. As human beings, we are beyond that. God didn't make one kind of flower. He's a diverse God." She kissed his cheek. "Go pick your flower."

******

He found his flower at a fundraiser, sitting in an elegant dining room. She wore a stunning green ball gown. The color reminded him of their first kiss.

At her table, she sat with her family. Watching from a distance, he wondered what he might say. Would he barge in and interrupt their evening? He didn't want to put too much thought into it and weaved quickly through the tables.

"Good evening."

Zoe froze, stopped buttering her roll at hearing his distinctive voice. She slowly lifted her eyes. Her reply came out stunned, "Good evening."

Marsha Cartwright stiffened and Zoe immediately started to diffuse the situation. "Mother, this is…."

Ollie offered his hand, "Sparrow, Oliver Sparrow. Mrs. Cartwright, it's a pleasure to meet you." Reluctantly, she shook his hand and he curtly nodded, turned to the other guests. "Aimee, Shaw, a pleasure to see you again."

"Likewise," Shaw returned. Aimee smiled and took a sip of her wine.

Ollie explained, "I saw Zoe from across the room. Zoe, may I have this dance?" His mischievous eyes flashed over the astonishment on her face.

Marsha ordered, "Zoe, don't you move. I've warned you." To Ollie she said, "No one is dancing now."

Ollie looked around, surveyed the room. "Clearly," he commented without glancing at her mother. He rested his eyes on Zoe. "Perhaps we can have our dance elsewhere, Dr. Landry."

Flabbergasted, her mother spat at Zoe, "You are not going to leave in the middle of a family dinner. How rude!"

Ollie spoke swiftly, "If rudeness is present tonight, please accept it as my own, and not Zoe's, although I would be very disappointed not to enjoy the pleasure of her company this evening."

Zoe's mouth completely dropped. "Who was this man? And why hadn't he come to rescue her sooner?" she wondered.

Ollie gracefully extended his hand and Zoe placed her own in his. She stood, her eyes completely fixated on Ollie's. "Mother, you will not miss me terribly."

As if her mother no longer existed. Ollie admitted softly, "You *are* a beautiful flower."

Zoe smiled. "And you must be the bee that has come to sting me." She leaned in and Ollie kissed her gently.

Marsha jumped up. "For crying out loud."

Zoe couldn't take her eyes off of Ollie. She barely heard her mother threaten, "If you leave with this man, I promise you I'll begin legal proceedings against you." She turned to her son-in-law. "Isn't that right, Shaw?"

Aimee pursed her lips, glared at her husband. "What is she talking about?"

Ollie, laced his fingers with Zoe's, guided her away from the madness.

In the lobby, she asked, "How did you know where to find me?"

"I just followed my heart." She lifted her brows. He added, "And the directions from your assistant."

Zoe shook her head, swaying the massive curls over her bare shoulders. "I should give Chelsea a raise."

"Definitely. Zoe, I love you."

She nodded, wrapped her arms around his waist. "I know."

Ollie recalled, "At the hospital you told me that you'd go through the fire with me and love me forever."

"I will."

He took her face in his hands. "My precious Zoe, I can't go through it without you. I need you."

Zoe looked over her shoulder and saw arguing at the table where her family sat. "I need you, too, Ollie."

He looked over with her and smiled. "I started quite a ruckus."

"Yep." She laughed. "You promised me a dance."

And right then and there, in the midst of his unknown future and her family chaos, Ollie wrapped her in his arms and danced with the flower he'd chosen.

Chapter 121 – The Verdict

Day in and day out, as promised, Zoe accompanied Ollie. She sat in the courtroom with his family and watched the gladiator attorneys battle.

Kendall, Ollie's gladiator, was undisputedly more brutal than the prosecution. She pulled out all sordid details, leaving little open for interpretation. She entertained the jury and attacked Lacy when she took the stand.

Painful to witness, Zoe blinked, refocused, and pushed up the glasses she wore in the courtroom. She never neglected an opportunity to absorb every solitary expression crossing the jurors' faces.

Kendall questioned, "Isn't it true, after only your first meeting with Mr. Sparrow, you asked him if you could sleep at his home?"

"Yes. It was…."

"And then you waited for him to fall asleep, removed all of your clothing, and climbed into bed with him?"

"Yes, I was…."

"And isn't it true after your first sexual encounter with him, he regretted it and told you that he was apprehensive about continuing to work with you on your book?"

"Yes, Ollie was also…."

"Just yes or no Mrs. Reid, please." Kendall smiled pleasantly at Lacy. Zoe could see the contempt building in Lacy's eyes. She hoped the jurors did also.

"Is that understood, Mrs. Reid…yes or no?"

The prosecution jumped to his feet. Lifting his hand, he shouted, "Your honor! The defense is clearly upsetting my client."

"The judge looked at Lacy, pursed his lips and offered instruction, "Mrs. Reid, please answer the questions yes or no. Mr. Keystone, please have your seat. Ms. Carter, proceed with questioning."

"Thank you, your honor. Now, Mrs. Reid, isn't it true, that your father is very ill. That he's unable to do anything for himself and is recovering at home from a stroke?"

"Yes, but what does that have to do with Ollie raping me!"

Lacy began to muster up tears. Her attorney rose again. "Your honor," he pleaded, "my client is clearly distraught."

Judge Parker folded his hands and replied, "Mrs. Reid, your testimony is required to continue. Can you go on?"

Lacy dabbed at her eyes with a withered tissue, and whimpered, "Yes, yes. I can continue. It's just my father and I are so very close. He's so sick. He's the only reason I returned to the states."

The judge nodded. "Ms. Carter, continue." He added sternly, "Mr. Keystone, your seat."

Once again, Kendall thanked the judge and walked closely to the witness box and rested her hand on it. "Mrs. Reid, I am sorry to hear about your father's condition. I'm sure it hasn't been easy. You're a single mom with two young children and caring for your ill father."

"No, no," Lacy whined, "It's been awful. We have a nurse, but I care for him as well."

"That's admirable, Mrs. Reid. I can see why you so desperately wanted to continue the sexual relationship with Mr. Sparrow. So much so that you left your babies, ages five and two at home with your father's nurse, simply for sex with Mr. Sparrow during the week."

Cain leaped to his feet, his nostrils flaring. "Objection! Speculation!"

Kendall whipped her small head around, replied calmly, "Fact, your honor. May I continue?"

"Overruled, Mr. Keystone."

"Thank you. Isn't it a fact Mrs. Reid that you left your children with your father's nurse at least twice a week to have sex with Mr. Sparrow?"

"No. I needed his help with my book."

Kendall nodded. "Yes, yes, the tell-all manuscript. So glad you brought that up. So were you giving Mr. Sparrow sex in exchange for information, so you might write a best seller?"

"Objection!" Cain rose.

"Overruled. Mrs. Reid, answer the question."

"No, I needed to know the truth and I knew Marcel wouldn't tell me."

"Yes, Marcel Reid, your husband...he had an affair with Mr. Sparrow's wife, then he shot and killed her." The jury began to wince, buzz and shift in their seats. Kendall didn't let up.

"From what we've learned...a yearlong affair. Mrs. Reid, you confirmed that your husband had purchased a condo for his lover, gave her a bank account, jewels, and clothing. She was in fact your husband's mistress. You confirmed that with your personal banker before you ever had your first conversation with Mr. Sparrow. In fact, you just sold the condo for a very nice profit. Isn't that true Mrs. Reid?"

Lacy snapped, "Yes! I confirmed it. And I had to sell it! I need the money. My husband is in jail and I have very little financial support."

Kendall lowered her voice, "You knew the truth about your husband's affair. What more than sex did you want from Mr. Sparrow."

"I was falling in love with Ollie. I thought he...."

Kendall wouldn't let her finish, she admitted, "Yes, I can see that you developed some feelings for Mr. Sparrow."

Kendall softened her eyes and her voice as she looked at perspiration on Lacy's forehead. "Yes," she repeated. "Mr. Sparrow has the reputation of being a kind, gentle man. We've heard from a number of character witnesses. And here you are, a single mother, caring for her sick father. You have a lot on your shoulders. You come into contact with someone who's willing to listen to your heart. Someone you trust with your body. Of course, you fell for someone so considerate."

Kendall paused. Saw the tears building in Lacy's eyes. "Yes, I see you thought what you felt was love. How did Mr. Sparrow react when you told him you wanted to share more than his bed – that you desired more from him?"

"I knew we couldn't have a future based on our spouses' past. It wasn't him. I ended our relationship."

Kendall blinked. She wasn't expecting the questioning to take this turn. And she should have. If she didn't redirect, it would count against them. Quickly, she replied, "Is that how it really happened, Mrs. Reid? Tell the jury the truth. Mr. Sparrow ended your relationship and because you believed you were falling in love with him, you wanted to punish him and you falsely accused him of rape. Isn't that what happened here?"

Lacy shouted, "He raped me! He didn't want me to leave. He started going crazy, saying, Sassy left, and Desiree left, and he wasn't going to let me go. He went crazy, and raped me." She sobbed.

Ollie jumped up. "She's lying. She's lying."

Lacy continued, "He hurt me. Oh, God, he raped me...."

The courtroom buzzed with chatter. Lily tugged on Ollie's hand. "Sit down."

The judge started banging his gavel. "Order! Order!"

They took a break after closing arguments and the entire family went back to Kendall's office. Kendall began fussing and cussing when she hit the conference room floor. No one in the room took a seat.

Ollie walked over to Kendall and rested his hand on her shoulder. "You did your best. Lacy's not who I thought she was."

"Kendall bit her lip and thought for a second. Yeah," she admitted. "That little wench got me."

Lily asked, "Do you think we'll have a decision today?"

Kendall let out a breath, folded her arms across her chest. "I'm afraid if they come back with a quick decision, it's not going to be good for Ollie." She turned to Zoe, asked, "Your take. I know you're good at reading people."

Zoe lifted her brows and boxed in her lips while she thought. The family seemed to beg her for positive perspective with their eyes. She had no choice but to tell them what she saw. "They believe her more. They feel sorry for her. My guess is, they'll rule in her favor."

Ollie let out a breath. He turned to his sister and brother-in-law. "You both sure you can handle Olivia? You got the twins."

Vaughn walked over, embraced Ollie, with tears clogging her throat, she said, "Stop it. Stop it. It's not over yet."

Ollie lifted his arms, letting her cry on his shoulder. When she let up, he turned to Kendall, "How long do you think I'll get? How much time?"

"You heard your sister. Let's not throw in the towel yet."

He barked, "How long Kendall?"

She lifted her eyebrow, "Five to Seven, if you're lucky."

Pastor Rose, spoke up, "We don't live by luck." He grabbed Ollie's hand. "We live by faith. Let's pray."

The family joined hands. Pastor Rose led, "Father, in this final hour, we need the truth to ring free. We know how the jurors feel. But please, let the truth prevail. In the name of the Father, Son, and the Holy Spirit, we believe that it will. Amen!" He started clapping his hands loudly, requested; "Let this family offer up praise and thanksgiving right now."

Their voices filled the room, some clapped, and some lifted their hands. Kendall was out of her element. She stood in the midst, breathed a prayer of her own, "God, if you've got an ace, pull it now."

After several minutes of audible praise, the phone rang. Lily answered, and reported, "We have a verdict."

The family filed outside; on the sidewalk the media flashed cameras and microphones in their faces. Their security pushed through the crowd, shielded the family and escorted them to the limo that waited at the curb.

With the downtown traffic it took 30 minutes before they were at the courthouse. More cameras and media awaited them. Again, they avoided the crowd as Kendall and Lily led them. Zoe and Ollie followed, with the family pushing behind. They filed into the courtroom.

Before Ollie took his seat at the defendant's table, he took Zoe's face between his hands. "I love you. No matter what happens, I want you to be happy. Zoe, I never expected you to wait for me."

She shushed him. "Sweetheart, if the fire includes five to seven, I'm in it. I know what I saw on the face of the jurors, but your uncle is right; Christians live by faith, not sight. Take your place, and tonight we celebrate." She gave him a sweet kiss and a bright smile.

Ollie looked at her. Why had he found her now? Why couldn't it have been Zoe before he met Desiree? He wouldn't have ever given Lacy a second thought. After giving her hand a final squeeze and a glance at his family, he took the hot seat.

Lacy sat with her attorney, dressed in a summer white suit, even though it was only May. She looked innocent and pure and Ollie wanted to strangle her.

The jurors were led back in; the bailiff called for all to rise, as the judge appeared. He turned to the jury. "Foreman, have your reached a unanimous verdict?"

"We have your honor."

"Bailiff, please secure the verdict."

The foreman released the small folded sheet of paper and handed it to the bailiff. Once received, the judge opened it, read it, folded it and returned it to the bailiff. Zoe couldn't read his expression as he ordered, "Will the defendant please rise."

He did, along with Kendall and Lily.

"Foreman, please read the verdict."

The foreman stood, looked directly at Ollie, and declared, "We the jury, find the defendant Oliver Samuel Sparrow, guilty."

The blow hit the room like a burst of wild wind. Flo screamed. And Ollie's eyes flooded. "We will reconvene for sentencing in twenty-four hours. Bailiff, please remove the prisoner from the courtroom."

The entire time, Vaughn kept her eyes on Lacy. She was very good at reading women. And when the verdict was read, Lacy smirked and Vaughn saw it.

"Liar! You dirty little liar!" Vaughn struggled against her husband trying to get at Lacy. He would not let her get through the aisle and over his long legs. "Sweetie," he gripped her, "calm down."

"Kyle, she was smirking. She was laughing. She lied!"

Vaughn shook and screamed. Her husband pulled her out of the courtroom. Outside, he held her close as she cried into his chest. "She lied."

"If she lied, it will come out. It will."

Ice cold, all the life drained from Zoe's body, she trembled as she watched the man she loved be handcuffed and escorted out. She couldn't move and she couldn't speak. If it were not for Vaughn's outburst, she would have sat there until the sentencing.

Chapter 122 – The Ace

Lacy didn't know what was happening to her mind. It seemed that the more she held up the charade, she became more and more indomitable. She sat at her kitchen island, sipping on a glass of white wine, tapping away at her keyboard. She had done it. She had convinced 12 strangers that she had been violated. And she had proven she was a force to be reckoned with. She reveled in her victory, lifted her glass, and toasted herself.

Her mother walked in. "Marcel Jr. wants you to read him a bedtime story."

She looked up at her mother. "Sure, I'm almost done here."

Her mother leaned over, rested her forearms against the counter. "So, how's it feel?"

"Great. I'm almost done with the book."

"Wow, what an accomplishment. You managed to write a novel and put an innocent man in jail. I always knew you were ambitious."

Lacy squinted, smiled, and then took another sip. "What are you talking about?"

Gracelle reached into her bra, pulled out the letter. "This."

Lacy rolled her eyes. "And what's that?"

"The letter you wrote your husband, telling him how much you enjoyed having sex with Ollie. How he was the first man to make you feel alive. How he touched you in a place Marcel never could."

Rolling her shoulders, she said, "So?"

"So, there's more. You say in the letter you and Ollie were going to live together. He was going to be a father to Marcel's kids."

"That's where Ollie drew the line. Isn't it, Lacy? Ollie couldn't do it. Could he?"

"Ollie had no right to use and toss me away like toxic waste."

"Well," Gracelle tilted her head, "I guess you showed him."

"Yeah, let's not forget his little woman."

Gracelle nodded slowly. "Let's not. And let's also remember the family you devastated. You broke his mother's heart in that courtroom today. And what about his baby girl? Your husband took her mother, and you took her father. Really, Lacy...," she shook her head. "Did the man deserve that? He made a mistake, getting involved with you. He was hurting and you used him. And like the spoiled brat that you are, when he told you no, you lied and manipulated until he was behind bars."

Trembling with disgust as she looked into her daughter's eyes, she asked, "I'll ask again, how does that feel?"

The fiend that rested on her shoulders boosted her. She sprang out of her chair. "It's feels great. I won! I won! He had no right. I lied, but

Ollie got exactly what he deserved. And how dare you!" She curled her lips at her mother. "Mother of all whores, you're one to judge. You left me and Daddy for your lovers."

Gracelle agreed, "I did. Looking at what you've become, I know that's a mistake I'll always regret. I have remorse for my mistakes."

Lacy spat, "I have none. Now, if you'll excuse me, I'm going to check on my children." She forged ahead; however, Lily and Kendall appeared in her kitchen doorway. Lacy stumbled back. "What's going on?"

"You're being charge for filing false rape charges," Kendall answered.

"Like hell I am. Get out of my house."

The two detectives that initially arrested Ollie followed in behind Lily and Kendall. They started towards Lacy as she pleaded, "This is a set-up. They're lying."

Kendall lifted a wire and a listening device. "Your mother was wired. We heard it all, Lacy. Great confession. Thank you."

Lacy started raising her voice, the female officer, spoke softly in her ear, "Your children are in this house. For their sake, don't make a scene."

She wouldn't, expecting her attorney would get her out of this. She lifted her shoulders and walked calmly with the officer out of the kitchen and into the family room.

Disbelief ended her steps. Her father sat, clutching the end of the sofa. "Daddy, you're up?" she whispered.

The effects of the stroke still controlled his speech, he stuttered, "Dddd, don't…lll…lie, ba, ba, baby." Lacy's eyes watered as she lowered her head and let the officer remove her from the premises.

******

On their victorious stroll out of the house, Kendall asked Lily, "What made you so sure there was a letter?"

Lily declared, "The Holy Spirit told me there was more and I was determined to find it. A woman scorned and one that loves to write, I was certain there was written proof. Lacy got cocky and driven. In that state, she couldn't cover all her bases. It seemed natural she'd have something documented, somewhere. Furthermore, when Vaughn told me that Lacy smirked in that courtroom today, I tried Gracelle. Zoe had been watching the jurors in the courtroom, but I asked Vaughn to keep her eye on Lacy and Gracelle. She read the remorse in Gracelle's eyes. She knew her daughter was setting up an innocent man."

They crossed the threshold, headed toward the sidewalk. Kendall looked up at night approaching. "You're good, Lily. And you're

398

right. I was cocky and driven, too. That's why Lacy caught me off guard on the stand today. I didn't care about the innocent man either."

Lily placed her hand on Kendall's shoulder and replied, "God's good. He allowed the truth to prevail, regardless of our faults."

Kendall let Lily's words simmer a moment, she asked, "Tell me more about this good God? I might need him for my next case."

Lily smiled and shook her head. "Oh, Kendall, I think I like you. How about dessert to celebrate?" She patted her belly. "The baby wants sweets."

"I'll buy, if you hook me up with this God."

Laughing, Lily replied, "I'll put a call in."

Chapter 123 – Plans to Prosper You

Some things never change and some things do. Ollie stepped inside the school building and stood at the security table. A new security guard protected the students and staff. She was female, young, smiling, and yet professional.

"Ollie Sparrow to see Principal Stephens."

The guard checked the list, scanned a visitor's card, instructed him to sign in, used a wand over his person, ensured he had no concealed weapons, called the office to announce his arrival, and finally, she cleared him.

Ollie held the visitor card, flipped it over in his hand and shook his head. Public school had become a guarded prison for children.

In the administrative office, Karyn sat at her desk and lifted her head with a bright flirtatious smile. She had in no way changed. "Hi handsome, I hear you've changed sides. What? The sistas ain't good enough for ya?" She licked her bright red lips.

Ollie gave his crooked smile. "All kind of sistas exists in the world."

She grinned. "Uh-huh, there are sistas and then there are sisters. You got a *sister*."

She tilted her head, gave him a long delicious glance. "Remember, if you want a little brown sugar for your fine vanilla dip, you know where to find me."

Desiree snapped, "Yeah, your brown sugar is going to be on the unemployment line, if you don't stop harassing my visitors." Frowning, she stepped aside from the doorway of her office. "Ollie, come in, please."

Karyn's smile turned upside down. She whispered, "The woman can hear a pin drop on a crowded concrete playground." Ollie grinned. "That's why she's the principal."

He walked toward Desiree, kissed her cheek.

"Principal Stephens."

"Hey, Ollie."

Once inside, he sat in a visitor's chair and she sat next to him. She looked cool in a white sleeveless blouse and navy trousers. Several weeks since she escaped the explosion, her arm was still set in a cast. Still, she looked great and he told her so. "Married life and motherhood agrees with you." She smiled, overjoyed at being Mrs. Deacon Stephens. "Thanks. I hear you popped the question and the lady said, "Yes."

Ollie smiled too, checked his watch. "In just seven months, five days and eight hours, Dr. Zoe Landry will be Dr. Zoe Sparrow."

"She will also be mother to the precious little Olivia."

"Yes, Liv adores her."

"She's a sweetheart. Oh…" Desiree got up, pulled a bag out of her closet and gave it to Ollie. It was a pretty pink and yellow sundress. "Tiona picked it out. She had to get it for Olivia."

Ollie held it up. "It's cute, thank you." He put the dress back in the bag, rested it on the floor and disclosed, "I have a proposition for you."

Desiree leaned back. "Okay."

"After the truth came out about me being falsely charged, all of my sponsors who pulled out have since returned. Some of them have invested additional funds. In addition, we've added a group of new sponsors."

"In other words, money is pouring in," Desiree noted.

"Big time. My future wife sees this as an opportunity to expand."

Desiree agreed, "I can see it. I stopped by the foundation a couple of days ago. I think you can bring on more students, hire more staff."

Ollie opened his hands. "Zoe and I are thinking bigger…a Christian School of the Performing Arts."

He looked at her eyes as they brightened. "Sounds amazing. I like the idea."

"Really? We'd like you in on this."

"In…as what?" She furrowed her arched brows. Ollie noticed she no longer wore her hair in a sexy flip over her left eye. It now curled loosely, hung back, and touched her shoulders. He noticed a side streak of gray in it. Before he told her of all his plans, he said, "Desiree, you're different."

She smiled, understanding completely. "We both are, Ollie. And I wouldn't change a thing." He nodded. "Neither would I. We're better now."   She reached out and he took her hand. She requested, "Tell me about your school."

Giving her hand a squeeze, he said, "Zoe and Lily believe you would be perfect as academic director. That's if, you'd be willing to leave the public schools and work for a smaller private organization."

Desiree looked around her office, pondering. She loved what she did; however, public school politics hindered her. This would be an opportunity to work in a faith-based environment. She felt a leap in her spirit. "I like it," she repeated, "I'll need to talk it over with Deacon."

Ollie perked up. "Yeah, the Deacon, we can use him, too. Zoe tells me he's a musical genius."

Desiree smirked. "What, did *he* tell you that, or Zoe?"

"Nah, Zoe did. She visited your church."

It fit, the idea, the people, and the lives they could touch. It fit like a glove for her and Deacon – music, ministry, education, and children. "You want me and Deacon?" She rolled it around in her mind.

Ollie answered, "Only if he can settle. As a missionary, I don't know if he can."

"He wants to do more local work, especially with us having a daughter now. He wants to be home." She nodded. Ollie let out a breath.

"Nervous?" she asked.

"This is much bigger than starting up the foundation or opening the gallery. A few years ago, I never saw any of this coming."

Desiree thought about her life, her past. She had to let go, forgive herself for what happened with Sterling years ago. And forget the guilt and the shame. When she did, God used her in an incredible way. She saved a life.

"God is trusting us with bigger assignments. Have you forgiven Marcel and Lacy?" Ollie thought a second. "I have. When God forgives, he forgets, throws it away. I had to do that. I'm free and moving forward."

"Freedom is amazing." She smiled.

So…" He released her hand. "…Will you consider it?"

"Today is the last day of school. I'll have some time to think and pray about it. When do you need an answer?"

Not really certain, he shrugged. "A few weeks."

"Alright. Thank you for considering us. We appreciate it."

"My pleasure." He stood. "I've got some running around to do."

Desiree recalled, "Zoe's birthday party is tomorrow, in the mountains. Sorry we can't make it."

"Your husband is taking you away for a couple of weeks. Don't be sorry. Your honeymoon, right?"

"We're excited, but I hate leaving Tiona." She frowned.

"You know your sister will fuss over her. Mitch told me that Beautiful's still in town?" Ollie lifted his brow.

Desiree lowered her voice. "She's pregnant."

"Mitch told me that, too."

Desiree shook her head. "She can't go home to her husband and he has no idea she's pregnant. What a mess." Desiree stood, prepared to walk Ollie out.

He commented, "We know about creating messes, don't we?"

"Hmm," she nodded. "And we know who to go to for help."

He smiled and stared into her eyes. "Thank God."

Desiree lifted her good arm and laid a hand on his handsome face. "Be happy, Ollie. Zoe is wonderful."

"She is. We are so blessed, and so are you. Enjoy your honeymoon."

Leaning in, she kissed his cheek. "Tell Zoe happy birthday for us."

Chapter 124 – Trusting the Plan

The scent of fragrant flowers opened Zoe's eyes. She lifted up on her elbows; looked on her left, saw the exotic purple and white arrangement and the card. She blinked the remaining sleep from her eyes and read the note.

"Good morning, beautiful. Happy birthday! I have a wonderful day planned for you. After your morning run, I'll pick you up at ten. Completely in love with you, Ollie."

Throwing back the white duvet, Zoe stretched and slipped out of bed. It was 7 in the morning. She had a few hours to get ready. After she showered, she put on her running gear, bounced downstairs, and jogged into the kitchen.

Chelsea looked up from her cereal bowl and the morning television show. "Happy birthday," she sang.

"Thank you." Zoe poured a cup of hot tea, picked up a bran muffin. "Thank you for delivering Ollie's flowers."

Chelsea wrinkled her nose. "Those were delivered by the flower fairy. I have no idea what you're talking about."

Zoe took a sip of tea, bit into her muffin. "Uh-huh. Well, flower fairy; you did a great job of sneaking in. You didn't wake me."

"Hey, I was a former pickpocket. I got skills." Chelsea grinned, looked back into her bowl.

Zoe commented, "You really should have a healthy breakfast. That sugary stuff is bad for ya."

Looking up, Chelsea said, "I love you, too. You better get running and back here. You know Ollie's never late."

Zoe grinned, thinking about her surprise day. She lifted her hair, wrapped a black elastic band around it. "Spill it. Where am I going?"

Without looking up, Chelsea said, "Where we take you. Now hit the pavement."

Exhilarated, Zoe abandoned the rest of her breakfast, stood and started jogging in place. On her way out, she ran over, wrapped her arms around Chelsea, and planted a loud smack on her cheek. "I love you, too. I'm not going to run long. I still have a few things to pack."

She put her earplugs in, and did as she was told, hit the pavement. Like she promised, she didn't run long. As a matter of fact, summer was in the air, she was in love and she wanted to walk a little. It took a minute before she recognized the person on her left. She was clearly walking with her, but why?

"What do you want?"

She gestured toward the bench to their left. "Sit and talk."

"I have nothing to say to you."

"You will, in seven months."

Zoe closed her eyes, shook her head. When she opened them she said, "Why seven?"

"Because that's when I'll be having your fiancé's baby."

The blood drained from her flushed happy cheeks.

Lacy had her attention. "Shall we sit?"

She had to sit; her legs were folding. Could she actually believe this person? "You're a liar. The world knows that."

"I lied. But why would I lie about this. Paternity is so easy to prove these days."

Right, why would she lie? It wasn't like Ollie would just take her word for it. "How much?" Lacy cocked her head. Zoe demanded, "How much? It's clear what you want. Otherwise, you'd be talking to him, not me."

"Alright. Let's cut to the chase. I'm broke. I spent all my money on attorneys. The first one put Ollie away. The second cleared my name. I used up almost all of my father's savings on his medical expenses. I need help."

"Of course, you do, how convenient to be pregnant."

"I may have lied before. The truth is he got me pregnant."

The women sat on the park bench. Zoe glanced at the morning commuters passing through Central Park, then up at the crystal blue sky. "Name your price."

"Seven million and I go away, forever."

Appalled, Zoe shifted her head. "You cannot be serious!"

"You have it. I know your family."

Zoe turned, wondered into Lacy's eyes. Her small demure face looked tired, despondent. Could she really make a deal with the devil? It was a gamble. The stakes were high. "I'm out of town a few days. I'll get back to you."

"When?" Lacy leapt on her last remark.

"When I get back to you. Do not contact me. I know how to reach you."

"Okay." Lacy got up, walked away, leaving Zoe on the park bench. She thought for two hours before she heard her cell ring.

"Zoe, where are you?" She popped up, started jogging home. "I'm on my way," she breathed into the phone. She rushed inside and found Ollie and Olivia waiting for her. Chelsea came barreling into the room. Ollie didn't have to ask, because Chelsea was all over her.

"What happened? You know we have to go!"

She was pale, distant as she stared into space. "I ran into someone. I'm sorry. I lost track of time. Give me a minute. I just need a minute to get a few more things packed." She scrambled out of the room, leaving Chelsea and Ollie staring at each other. He asked, "Can you keep an eye on Liv. I'll be right back."

"Sure. Liv, you wanna watch cartoons?" She took the little girl by the hand.

Ollie rushed up the stairs, taking them two by two, pushed her bedroom door open. "Talk to me." She wasn't packing, but sitting on the bed, shaking. He sat next to her. "Zoe, who did you run into?" She looked up and into his eyes. "Lacy. She's pregnant."

He didn't hear her correctly. "Repeat."

"Lacy is carrying your child. She's due in seven months."

"Impossible. I almost always wore protection."

"Almost is not always." She paused before providing, "For seven million dollars she said she'd go away forever."

"She's lying. She wants money."

"Why would she lie?" Zoe looked hopelessly at Ollie.

"Because that's what liars do." He reached out, took her hand. "She may be having a baby, but it ain't mine."

"Ollie, what if she's telling the truth this time? What about us, our future? I know this is selfish, and I don't care! I don't want Lacy in our lives." Agreeing, he nodded, "Neither do I. You're not giving her seven million dollars. It's extortion. I'll charge her with it."

She looked at him, long and hard, and the tears fell.

"Baby, please don't cry. I'll make this right." Almost hopeless, she lifted her hands, let them fall. "How?" she asked. He pulled and held her close to him. He didn't know how, but he knew he loved Zoe. He would not allow anything to come between them.

"I'm not going to lose you, Zoe. We're going to be happy together. I'll deal with Lacy, later. Today is your birthday. And nothing or no one is going to spoil this day for you. This news is a shock to us, but not to God. He has a plan for you and I. This is asking a lot of you, please trust God with me."

She pulled away from his protective embrace and stared into his eyes for a long time. His heart pounded wildly in his chest, waiting for her reply. And finally, releasing all doubt, Zoe wrapped her arms around the man she loved and trusted her God. "I love you, Ollie."

"And with all my heart, I love you, Zoe."

Dear Precious Reader,

Thank you for reading, *Forgetting Betrayal...*

Many say that I'll forgive, but I'll never forget. If anyone has wronged you, or you've wronged someone else, you may believe that you'll never forget. Can you truly move on, grow in grace, trust and love while remembering the past? If remembering is limiting you, you need to decide what you should remember.

Try remembering the life lessons from the experience, but forgive and forget the offense and the offender. I know this is difficult. You'll need the help of the Father, counseling, love, and support. It requires commitment and work. But it can be done!

For me, my mother physically abused me as a child during the time in her life when she was an alcoholic. When she became a recovering alcoholic, she wanted to reconcile our relationship. I remember the abuse, but *also* what I learned from it. I've learned what holding onto the past can do. It can cause a loving mother to drink, and abuse her children for years. I chose to forgive and forget and give my mother a chance at reconciliation. I now confess, before my mother passed away in 2001, she had become my best friend.

Please note, forgetting doesn't warrant reconciliation. Some relationships are not healthy to reconcile. In other words, forgive, forget, and close the chapter, if the relationship will be a detriment to you. Ask the Father and seek counseling about those relationships.

Choosing to <u>*not forget*</u> is the same as holding the offender in un-forgiveness. Remember what you've learned from the experience. First and foremost, you came out of it. You're still here, created with purpose and promise. You're probably stronger because of your past and you most certainly should be wiser. And remember, our heavenly father forgives and forgets; he casts our offenses into the depths of the sea and remembers them no more. Hebrews 8:12.

Now what will Ollie and Zoe do after learning of this impending news? You'll have to read my next book to find out.

Love, Grace and Peace,

Brook Lynn Dorcent